UnSuited

UNSUITED

AN AUGLAND NOVEL

ERIN CARROUGHER

UnSuited

© 2024, 2025 EECR, LLC

ISBN 979-8-99943-601-6 paperback
ISBN 979-8-99943-603-0 ebook
Library of Congress Control Number:
2022935954

Editorial and Book Packaging:
Inspira Literary Solutions
Gig Harbor, Washington
www.inspiralit.com

Cover Illustration by:
Lisa Guyaz
lisa@plumegraphicdesign.com

Printed in the U.S.A.

Gary, Glenn
&
Lisa
Love and miss you all

ACKNOWLEDGMENTS

Every time I hold the *Augland* series, I'm reminded of the day I decided to write a novel. I started this journey not realizing the countless hours of writing, editing, re-editing, workshops, and meetings it would take. It truly took a team to get to where I am now, holding the second *Augland* book in my hand.

To my Mom and Dad, there are no words to express the gratitude I have for your support, love, and guidance. You both truly are my number-one fans. Dad, the countless hours you've spent helping *Augland* become a reality is appreciated more than you'll ever know.

To my husband Joe, you've been so incredibly patient, loving, and understanding. I couldn't ask for a better half.

To Kerry, my editor, and the entire staff at Inspira Literary Solutions, you all are amazing and have believed in *Augland* since my first draft.

To the Carrougher clan, Reikow fam, and all my friends, I love all of you so much and could not have done this without your love and support.

All of us here at Augland 54 welcome you and your loved ones to the Pacific Northwest's most extravagant Augland park! Choose the life of your dreams from one of our seven parks, fitted with the most up-to-date technology and customized to your needs and the specifications of your Suit.

Augland 54 -
An Augland
Park Artificial
Existence
Center

WELCOME T(

BECAUSE YOU DESERVE 1

Augland 54 will soon be the first Augland to present Land of Legends, an interactive park like you l
Our Battle of the British Isles simulation is what you've been waiting for. At Augland 54 you ca

Let our Atlantis Park take you to the depths of your underwater fantasy or, if the city is more your scene, live in the sky-high towers on Hollywood Boulevard. Walk amongst nature's most beautiful creatures at Predator's Biome or spend your days lounging at our Maya Bay luxury resorts. Stroll the past at Victoria or party in outer space in Venus where every variation of person is celebrated.

TO AUGLAND

VE TO LIVE A GREAT LIFE

you have never experienced before! Have you ever wanted to be a king? Be in the midst of battle?
ou can live your dreams as the person of your dreams! Because you deserve to live a great life.

Part I

CHAPTER 1

Ashton

It was the little pleasures that helped piece Ashton back together after Sheva's death. Oyster shells on the shores, the crunching sound of her damp boots against rocky ground, the salty mist, and of course, the silence. It all meant one thing, she was far away from Augland 54. Its towering walls and glass dome were hidden behind the mountains, out of sight and a thirteen-hour hike away. That, most of all, helped.

It had been six months since the Colony had fled from its island refuge, known before Auglands and the war as Bainbridge Island. Wolfe, once Ashton's teacher, life saver, and love interest, had found them a new location far away from the domed, dystopian theme park that was Augland 54. Currently, the one hundred and sixty-three members of the Colony made their home on the shores of Hood Canal.

The canal's fjord of water ran long and deep, nestled along a mountain range that was rich in shellfish, salmon, and crab. Colony elders who knew the old history had told her it was a part of the Puget Sound, which had been named by England's Captain George Vancouver in the 1800s after his shipmate, Peter Puget. In later years, Hood Canal housed a nuclear submarine base, but that had been abandoned after the war. Ashton liked hearing the history of the world she had only grown to know in the past few months.

Ashton felt like her real self in the silence. For the first time in her life, she was free to choose. She had the choice to do what she wanted and when. She was not a worker, waiter, prisoner, or an escapee. In the tree-filled hills by the shore, she didn't have to talk to anyone or explain herself. She was finally just Ashton.

3

Only, she wasn't even sure who that was. And that made the silence lonely.

She had Hunter, but he split his time between NeuroEnergy, the utility company that supplied Augland with fusion energy, and the Colony. He now served as an emissary between the two. Every time he returned to the Colony, he sought her out, but she kept him and Versal, now his girlfriend, at arm's length. She was grateful to Hunter, but his relationship with her had changed too many times for Ashton to trust him completely. They'd gone from being rivals in the Augland park, to partners in escape, to friends, only to learn he was a NeuroEnergy spy the entire time.

The long summer months had faded into fall and now winter with no word from Augland 54. While Ashton breathed in the fresh, foggy air of Hood Canal, Wolfe was still inside the park, trying to change things from the inside—negotiating the complexities of corporate politics with sights on assuming the role of CEO of Augland. That was, if his father and the Executives ever gave him control. She wanted news of his progress, but even more, Ashton wanted to see Wolfe, though she wasn't sure he'd recognize her. Since ridding herself of the red wig, her brown, frizzy hair had grown back to below her ears, unrulier than ever.

The season brought changes, but no matter how much her hair grew and her body changed as she hiked the coastal hills, one thing would never change; the stone necklace around her neck. Every time she felt its weight, she missed Sheva. While Ashton's escape from Augland 54 felt like it was only yesterday, she could feel her distinct memories starting to slip away. Sheva's smile was disappearing, and Ashton could hardly hold onto the smell of her, a mix of motor oil and sage. It made Ashton feel both guilty and relieved, the pain of her memories too overwhelming.

Ashton's shovel hit home. *Jackpot.* A family of clams squirted and spat as her shovel dug past them. Rico would be happy with this morning's catch. She tossed the shovel to the side and reached her hands deep into the rough sand, pulling apart the land until the small shells exposed themselves. Her hands turned red in the cold water, and the tiny rocks exfoliated her skin. She pulled up one clam, then another, and placed them in her rusted bucket; the rich, salty water of Hood Canal corroded everything.

Ashton's clamming hole was close to her beachfront house and although, dilapidated, still commanded a gorgeous view. The early morning tide was low, the perfect time to dig clams. The canal ran wide and deep, spanning miles left and right. She had woken up before dawn while the fog stood still across the glass-like water.

4

The damaged dock was still usable and led out toward the deep canal with a breathtaking view of the Olympic Mountains when the sky was clear. Most Colony members had taken apartments in the abandoned rooms of a once-popular resort on the southern shores of the Canal. Wolfe had chosen it for its seclusion first and beauty second. The Colony now called this place home.

Ashton had decided to live offsite but nearby, as she wanted her own space. From her private house, she could watch the gentle waves lap onto the rocky beach. They weren't big waves like the ones at Maya Bay in Augland. These were subtle, as if singing a soft lullaby. *Swoosh, sheee, swoosh, sheee.*

When Rico inevitably asked how early she had gotten up, Ashton would lie. She hadn't slept well for months. Even with the threats of Augland far behind her, the nightmares kept Ashton awake. If it wasn't a dream about Sheva it was another about Wolfe.

Ashton hadn't made many friends since joining the Colony. Only a few people were receptive to her silence. One of those was Rico, the Colony cook. He was distant and grumpy, which meshed well with Ashton's need for space. She hated the passive aggressive reminders that it was her fault the Colony had to move, and even worse were the questions about Sheva. Rico didn't ask questions. He did, however, often obnoxiously, tell Ashton to get some rest.

He had a point: she looked bad—disheveled at best and haggard on her worst days. But he was one to talk. He had large bags under his eyes, messy brown hair, and a long, unkempt beard. His back snaked from left to right and contorted to the arched curve of the degenerative disease that hunched him forward and made him appear incredibly uncomfortable and stiff. He walked with a shuffled, unsteady gait, aided by his cane. Ashton had never asked about his disease; he'd only ever mentioned it once and they never spoke about it again. They didn't have the sort of relationship that allowed for details. Rico was a grump, but he didn't ask questions or try to cheer her up. Like her, he liked the silence.

Ashton stood and groaned as her back stiffened. She had filled her bucket with clams and would leave the rest. There was no need to hoard. Unlike the self-indulgent residents of Augland, the people of the Colony only took what was needed to survive. Rico had taught her that. He had taken her on as his sous chef, a challenge to them both as Ashton had never cooked a day in her life before leaving Augland.

"This morning's catch!"

Ashton plunked the bucket down on the resort's kitchen counter, spilling salt water across the rust-soaked, stainless-steel countertop. The best part of the Colony living in the resort was the large commercial kitchen, capable of preparing large quantities of food at a time.

Rico looked up from cutting vegetables and grunted. Ashton smirked. She immersed her red hands in the sink to warm them up.

"You didn't get them too small, did you? I told you we need the larger ones for chowder," Rico said in his deep voice, shaking his knife at her.

"All big ones," Ashton said, beaming. She was proud of her findings today. It had taken her all morning, but she knew she had done well.

"Atta girl," he said, smiling, as he went back to chopping. "You want to make sure that you get the meat, as much as you can. Leave out all the guts."

Ashton already knew that. This wasn't her first-time clamming. But she nodded. She knew Rico's gruff manners were his way of communicating. It was the most affection he could muster.

"Don't just stand there wasting water; get them cleaned and gutted," he snapped at her. Ashton nodded again and reluctantly pulled her hands out of the warm, running water.

The clams had grown comfortable in their bucket. Their necks were out, wiggling around and admiring their galvanized surroundings. They seemed content no matter where they were. Ashton envied them. She liked her new life at the Colony, but it felt foreign and out of place, like she was red in a sea of blue.

"Go get some fresh milk, too. I don't think Martha has been milked today."

Martha was a gift the Colony had received years ago from Augland 54, back when there had been a treaty between the Park and the Colony to leave each other alone.

How thoughtful. As if a cow could compensate for what Augland had planned to do next—break the treaty and take innocent children in the dead of night. And there was nothing the Colony could do about it.

Before she escaped from Augland, Ashton hadn't even known about the Colony, or the stolen children. Ashton had grown up in the Augland Center, spoon-fed on the propaganda of the Artificial Existence Center, the parent company of Augland.

Because you deserve to live a great life . . . Ashton repeated Augland's motto, which had been embedded in her brain—a motto directed to the wealthy elites who lived their life virtually, in Suits. But Ashton had been told that her life as a Suit-less worker had been a great life, protected from the post-war destruction of the uninhabitable world outside of Augland's walls.

But now Ashton knew the truth. She lived in a thriving Colony, outside of Augland's dome. And she knew about Augland's growing desperation, thanks to Cahya, the Colony's leader. Since her escape from Augland's prison, she had relied on Cahya and her Colony for survival. Cahya, and the Colony members, had welcomed Ashton as if she were their own.

On top of everything else, Augland had stolen from her again: the working men and women of Augland were becoming infertile. The Suits, of course, were fine—their human bodies were safely in pods in some warehouse—but the Suit-less workers in the parks were slowly being poisoned by the radiation of the Suits and their energy source.

Ashton hadn't even thought about having children but knowing the choice had been stripped from her had left her bitterly torn between sadness and anger. Maybe she wanted to have kids someday. *Maybe even with Wolfe.*

The sobering reality of infertility left her with emptiness. She was finally free to imagine a future unharmed by Augland, and still it had stolen from her. It was senseless, cruel, and irresponsible of Augland, and Ashton hated Augland even more for its disregard of human beings.

It had just been another loss to grieve until NeuroEnergy, the company outside of Augland, had told Hunter they were working on a cure. Hunter had relayed to Ashton that biologic engineers at NeuroEnergy had developed germ cell regeneration techniques by producing meiosis from somatic cells given to them by donors. Uterine support could be developed to allow pregnancy once cells were fused and implanted. The scientists said it would help mitigate the damage done by radiation from the Suits. It was completely experimental, but knowing that NeuroEnergy was trying meant this was one less thing in her future she had to worry about.

In the meantime, fewer children meant fewer workers, and Augland was getting more and more desperate. It now made sense to Ashton: why the AEC kept the Colony alive, why they stole children from innocent people, and why Augland used expendable workers as morbid entertainment for Suits in the Land of Legends, which had been her last stop before her escape. She bitterly realized the truth: if the workers within the walls could not create more workers, they were only good for entertainment. Artificial intelligence existed, but Suits preferred human interaction. It made their lives seem more believable, which is why workers like Ashton existed in the first place. Augland's goal was always for an optimal Suit experience no matter what the consequences might be. Besides, real workers were cheaper than maintaining robots, and robots were more efficient at daily maintenance tasks outside the view of customers.

Ashton had learned so much in her time away from Augland 54.

"Which one?" Ashton snapped back. "Clams or cows?"

Rico gave her an eye and she dropped her bucket. She knew that look and wouldn't push any further. But if she was going to go on another errand, she would go see if Jagatha wanted to join her. Like Hunter and Versal, Jagatha had adjusted well to life outside of Augland. When Ashton had first found Jagatha, the Augland cages had broken her otherwise energized seven-year-old spirit. Her captivity behind her, she had blossomed again around kids her age and was thoroughly enjoying her newfound freedom.

Ashton glanced at her gray, leather-bound watch, the one Wolfe had given her while in the cages of Augland, to aid in her escape. It was oversized for her small wrist, but she refused to take it off; just like her necklace, it was her connection to the two people she missed most.

Six forty-five a.m.—Jagatha wouldn't be in school yet. Perfect.

Jagatha lived on the top floor of the four-story repurposed resort with the other kids who didn't have parents. There were nine parentless children in Jagatha's class, the six through nine age group. They lived with two house parents in a penthouse suite with four rooms that took up most of the fourth floor of the north wing of the resort.

Jagatha had never known a family—Ashton was her family now. Most people in Augland never knew their mother or father. The Augland Center took them at birth and raised them, training and brainwashing them from infancy. That was all Jagatha and Ashton had ever known.

Ashton knocked on the penthouse door and the bright, brown-eyed girl with jet-black hair answered.

"Ashton!" she squealed and wrapped her tiny arms around Ashton.

"Hey, Bug." Ashton wasn't sure where she'd come up with "bug." It was either because Jagatha's oversized eyes didn't fit her body or because she constantly bugged Ashton to hang out.

"I've got to milk Martha, want to come?" Jagatha's eyes grew big in excitement. Ashton laughed. "All right, let the house parents know I'll have you back in time for class." As quickly as Jagatha disappeared, she was back again, pulling Ashton down the stairs.

Jagatha was vibrant and full of life, and she loved Ashton, for some unknown reason. Ashton had rescued Jagatha from the cages of Augland, but she was terrible with kids. Still, Jagatha had grown attached to her, and for that reason, Ashton had assumed responsibility and, after a time, affection for her.

Ashton watched as she bounced up and down toward the Colony farm. She half smiled, finding happiness in Jagatha's joy. Ashton hoped that someday she would have a daughter like her—that was, if NeuroEnergy spoke the truth of their ability to cure her. She doubted the company's good will, but if it allowed her the freedom of her body again, she needed, for her own sanity, to believe it was true. If not, at least she had Jagatha. They were family, born of Augland, and she would watch over the young one like Sheva had done to her.

The pastures weren't much to look at and did not have nearly as much space as the ones in Victorian Park in Augland, but the cows seemed happy enough. When the two girls arrived at the pasture, which had once been the resort's golf course, Ashton put her hand on Martha's black face.

"Shhh, shhh," Ashton murmured, soothing the cow as she led her to the former pro shop and practice facility, which had been converted into the barn. It took some time to get all the milk they needed, and Jagatha talked the whole time. Ashton didn't mind; she didn't have anything to say, and she loved hearing Jagatha fill the silence.

"Martha milk, as requested," Ashton said, slamming down the large bucket harder than she expected, spilling a little onto the steel counter. Rico sighed.

"How about a tea? Then we need to get started on the butter and bread."

Ashton poured two mugs full of the freshly brewed brown water, steam pouring out into the cold, damp room of the kitchen. Rico eased himself onto a stool beside Ashton. As she sat warming her hands on the mug, Ashton's eyes wandered. It wasn't like either of them to sit for too long, and she became anxious waiting for her next direction.

"So, how have things been?" Rico asked. Ashton shot him a quick glance. She wondered why he wanted to talk all of a sudden. The last six months had been blissful silence, something she had appreciated.

"Fine."

Everything was fine. She had her routine and ended each day in silence as the sun set below the trailing mountains beyond the canal. Did she not seem fine? What was "fine" anyway? Had Cahya set him up to this?

Ashton hadn't seen much of Cahya since the Colony's relocation. In fact, Cahya hadn't spoken directly to her since Ashton had delivered Wolfe's coordinates for their new home. Ashton sensed the older woman's reservations and found herself constantly over-analyzing the reason for Cahya's distance.

If Ashton's own guilt over their necessary relocation wasn't enough to drive her to seclusion, there was also the overwhelming sense of the others gossiping about her escape attempt which had forced the Colony's retreat. They had their own world on Bainbridge before Ashton had escaped Augland and put the Colony in jeopardy. Rico insisted no one blamed her, but Ashton wasn't so sure.

The abandoned resort Wolfe had picked was perfect to help the Colony stay safe. A fallen sign they had found indicated the area had once been called "Union." The log-style, main buildings expanded into a "V" with a large, grassy courtyard stretched out between the two sides, creating a perfect secluded area between the tall structures. The front of the resort, opposite the courtyard, had been blocked off, shielding them from the only road through the long canal. A dock jutted out into the water of the canal and was home to a few dilapidated fishing boats that would help in any needed escape. There weren't enough boats for everyone, though. That was something Cahya hoped to change.

Rico sighed and dropped the emotional fishing expedition he had planned.

"You're doing well," Rico said, pulling Ashton away from her thoughts. "I mean; you seem to be doing well. At least you aren't burning butter anymore." Rico gave a half smile.

"Well, I have a good teacher." Ashton smiled back. Rico let out a hearty laugh.

"Don't be trying to butter me u—" Rico started.

He was interrupted by a siren. It grew louder, ringing lower, then high: the ambush siren. Ashton jumped up, her response automatic.

Cahya ran meticulous drills and ran them often. After their move to Hood Canal, Wolfe had warned Cahya of Augland's desperation to keep the Augland parks sufficiently filled with workers through stealing children from rebel colonies. The Colony had people dedicated to protecting the twelve infants, others to lock down the resort, and others to fight. Each Colony member was equipped with a weapon, a photon gun—thanks to NeuroEnergy.

The siren would go off and all of the children under five would be taken to the safety cabin, while the older children would lock themselves in the nearest room and hide while the adults protected the resort entrances. They had been practicing since they arrived. But Ashton knew practicing and rehearsing were very different from the real thing. Nothing could prepare them sufficiently to face the Augland guards.

Rico and Ashton sprinted toward the kitchen exit and out onto the patio overlooking the partially enclosed courtyard that stretched out between the two wings, now enveloped in fog. Colony members darted left and right, targeting the resort doors, just like they had practiced. Cahya's security team yelled directions.

Ashton and Rico stood guard on the patio steps outside the kitchen door, overlooking the water near the center of the V. At first, she heard nothing but the sound of the piercing siren rising low and then high, but as the moments passed, she heard a slight hum in the distance. Ashton perceived the dark rumble of engines echoing through the trees—Augland trucks! The rumbling grew loud before the screech of halted tires pierced the air.

Suddenly, a parade of black guards descended into the resort's exposed center. Rico quickly disappeared back through the kitchen doors to grab his photon gun meant for this precise reason. Because this wasn't a drill. It was a raid.

CHAPTER 2

Ashton

An Augland army descended, dressed all in black from their shiny black jackets down to their thick, black rubber boots, sweeping in like a dark tidal wave. Just like the Augland guards who had chased Ashton through the parks when she made her escape, these were real men and women, not Suits. Augland preserved the almost indestructible Suits for their customers—again and again, showing their disregard for Suit-less lives.

Ashton stood at her assigned spot outside the patio doors that led into the kitchen. Out of the corner of her eye, Ashton saw Darla, one of the grade school teachers, holding and shoving young children into the safety cabin, chosen for its underground pantry that could be used as a bunker. The siren had rung too late; the scouts hadn't given them enough time to hide. Ashton saw the door close and hoped the children were safe and the quickly approaching guards had not seen them.

Ashton froze. *Jagatha.* She could only hope the young girl had locked herself in a room and was hiding out of sight.

The Augland guards were getting closer, and they knew what they were doing. They had not approached the resort from the back, which had once been the main entrance. This entrance had long been barricaded and booby-trapped. But the soldiers had not even tried that entrance, instead coming straight around to infiltrate the courtyard between the buildings. Ashton's mind raced; they clearly had insider knowledge.

As Ashton stared across the open field there were no children to be seen, but the manic search for them had begun. The Augland men flipped over chairs and art supplies from that day's school session. They would tear apart the grounds, and anyone who stood in their way.

Ashton wanted to stay frozen, and the shouting made her want to put her hands over her ears to shut out the noise. But her instincts kicked in and she sprinted down the patio staircase and toward the grass. Rico stayed behind to protect the patio door.

She targeted one soldier, running full speed toward him, ready to pounce to protect her new home and its most vulnerable residents. Her muscles burned, and as she came closer, she tensed her body to wrestle him to the ground. She was out of practice since her time playing her role as Freya, the Viking warrior; six months out of practice.

She made contact, but his outstretched arm clotheslined her neck as she barreled into him. Ashton fell hard on her back on the damp grass, gasping. She couldn't get the air back into her lungs quickly enough. Small raindrops hit her face.

Augland's army seemed unfazed, sprinting past her. She saw the flash of metal as the Augland men raised their photon guns toward anyone standing in their way. The bright lights of the electron photon bullets lit up the area.

Ashton watched the scene unfolding around her. The siren still pierced the air, along with screams and frantic demands from Colony leaders for them to hold their ground and protect the entrances to the resort. Ashton's job was to protect the patio entrance to the kitchen, the door she had just run away from. She had left Rico all alone but armed. Ashton couldn't seem to move. The cries rattled around in her head as she gasped at reality. While they had tried to prepare for this moment, it wasn't enough. Her heart was beating too fast. She was frozen on the ground, rain now pouring down.

Flashes of Land of Legends shot through her mind. She shifted from reality to memory. This felt too much like their enactment of the battlefield between the Saxons and Vikings. The screams triggered memories she thought she had tucked away for good. Ashton felt far away and present at the same time.

She lifted her head, trying to will herself to get up, to move. That was when she saw him, standing in the fog across the green grass, just yards away from the resort entrance. Her eyes widened, and her face became numb. It couldn't be. This nightmare suddenly took an unexpected turn.

13

Ashton could only stare as she scanned him up and down to make sure her eyes, or mind, weren't playing tricks on her. It had been long days and nights dreaming of their first encounter and it wasn't this. Ashton struggled to breathe as she stood up, now center stage on the courtyard battlefield. He was real; this was real. And he was not here to rescue her; he was part of the attack.

Wolfe.

CHAPTER 3

Ashton

Wolfe looked the same: rigid features, half-combed hair, light scruffy beard, icy blue eyes. He stood straighter though, almost taller than he had before. He wore a shirt and tie, neatly pressed, and the same dark, shiny jacket as the rest of the soldiers.

He seemed distant and unfazed, gloating in his authority. The Augland men surrounded him, like a shield. It wasn't like Wolfe to blend in and stay behind the scenes. He was a leader, not someone who cowered and watched. Then again, he let things like this happen in Land of Legends.

Still breathless on the ground, Ashton shook her head to force away the memory. She slowly rose to her feet, standing frozen in the middle of the courtyard, rain-soaked chaos swirling around her like a hurricane. She tried to meet his eyes, but Wolfe didn't even look in her direction. Ashton wanted to scream at him, make him look her way. She had to look into his eyes, let him know she was here. He would stop this if he saw her. Right?

None of this made sense. Why hadn't he warned them of the attack?

Wolfe had sworn to Cahya; he had promised Ashton that he would return to Augland and fulfill their mission. He would try to keep the Colony location hidden and stop the raids. But here he was, leading the attack. He had led the Colony here to protect them from Augland, only to turn around and take from the very people he had sworn to protect. He had betrayed them.

Drenched, Ashton's clothes clung to her as she stood on the puddled ground and shivered. It wasn't the cold or heaviness of her damp clothing that weighed her down most; it was shock.

Ashton had thought of Wolfe so many times these past long months, especially when she sat on her dock looking out toward the deep water, watching the sunsets as she sipped her night tea. She pictured him, strong and stoic. She didn't imagine him in Augland, though; she thought of him here, with her, sitting in peaceful camaraderie as they watched the sun go below the mountain range. She envisioned them together in tender moments that would melt away the cold, not like this. Perhaps she had only created a fantasy in her own mind, this false perception of the man she thought she knew.

As she watched, frozen in time, Wolfe stalked along the sidewalk from the resort toward the water, circling like a predator closing in around its prey. He walked right past Ashton, seemingly oblivious to her and to the pandemonium around him. *Is he actually enjoying this?* Ashton thought incredulously. When he thought no one was looking, he smiled, but quickly replaced it with a stern look as he surveyed the chaos around him.

Shay, a young woman slightly older than Ashton's eighteen years, ran past her dressed in a heavy trench coat. Shay looked weird and bulky as she darted toward the trees west of the resort. Ashton realized Shay was holding a baby, no older than a year, swallowed in her coat in hopes of deterring the Augland soldiers around her from noticing the small, squirming child. They must have found the bunker! Ashton snapped into the moment, her undivided attention now on the situation in front of her.

Casting one last look back at Wolfe approaching the resort, Ashton broke into a run. Before she could catch up to Shay and the baby, a guard grabbed Shay's oversized jacket and the baby screamed. The small cry was lost in the noise.

Colony members ran all around Ashton, trying to defend the Colony as they had practiced so many times. For the most part, the Augland soldiers didn't pay any attention to their meager efforts. Augland's weapons were more high-tech and stronger than the collection of rifles and photon guns of the Colony. The Augland guards were organized, almost rhythmic as they divided and conquered.

Ashton's mind pulled her in every direction. Rico and their post, whom she had deserted. Shay on the ground a few yards away from Ashton, holding her chest, still wrapped in the ripped trench coat, the child taken. Ashton saw Shay's white shirt turn a light shade of pink, then darken to red. Ashton moved. Standing wouldn't help. She was needed. Shay needed her.

Bending down, Ashton put her hand to Shay's wound.

"Shh, Shay; it will be all right."

She applied pressure to stop the bleeding. Ashton's mind flashed back to memories of her final moment with Sheva. The blood pooled and Sheva's last breath pounded in her ears. Ashton shook her head, bringing herself back to the present. Thinking quickly, she grabbed Shay's red-soaked shirt and ripped it hard, tearing the fragile cloth into a long strip. Ashton swiftly wrapped from Shay's armpit to her neck, tying the two ends together to put pressure on the inch-long gaping hole below her collarbone.

"Press hard; you need to put pressure on it."

Ashton stood up and looked for the next person in need. She didn't need to look far. A man covered his eye as blood trickled down his face. His screams in broken octaves. Ashton had seen him before but didn't remember his name. His face reddened as he screamed louder in pain and anger. Just beyond him, a soldier was struggling with an old man; somewhere else a child screamed.

Ashton's mind went quiet. She heard her breath as she inhaled, tuning out the noise around her. Disorder met stillness as the guards returned to their trucks. The chaos and calm blended like oil and water.

As quickly as they had come, they were gone. The last rumble of the trucks faded into the distance and the Colony was left in the aftermath of the raid.

Cahya assessed the damage. Bodies lay motionless on the ground of the secluded courtyard while others were already on stretchers, headed to the medical suite inside the resort. The siren had come too late, giving the Colony no time to mount a defense. But the cleanup: this was something the Colony knew how to do.

Inside the resort it was just as bad. Tables were overturned, drawers thrown open with their contents spilled across the floor, and doors hanging off their hinges. Muddy footprints led in and out of the resort entrance.

Ashton watched Cahya point toward the courtyard, directing help to those with medical needs and ordering others to check on the children and see how many had been taken.

Just beyond the resort's front doors, Augland had left behind a gift to the Colony. In the front parking lot sat pallets of clothes, canned food, and water jugs, wrapped in plastic like a present for the Colony to open. It was a sick substitute for the children they had just stolen, and even worse, Ashton knew it was a gift the Colony depended on. It was nearly impossible to survive with the constant relocation and lack of resources. The technology maintenance required for both Augland and NeuroEnergy exceeded productions and resources within the Pacific Northwest. There wasn't enough for everyone. Most everything had become overgrown, which meant that animals and insects were able to multiply with ease and destroy any edible food.

Ashton was angry, her fist balling as the rain pelted against her reddening face. She felt the fire again, something she had tucked away once out of Augland 54, but with every passing moment she could feel the force of her bitterness surface.

A hand gripped her shoulder and Ashton recoiled. Turning to see Rico beside her, Ashton sighed with relief. He squeezed hard; it was meant to be comforting but Ashton winced.

"It was silly to think things would change, Ashton. This is the world we live in."

"How can you say that? They just attacked us! And took people!"

"Not people, children. This time they seem to have taken some of the older ones as well." Rico wasn't surprised and he didn't hide it. People had just died! Children taken!

"We can't let them take them, Rico. They're children!" Ashton's voice broke. She wanted to scream. It was different now; these were children she knew, had grown to love, and had watched grow these past few months.

"There isn't anything we can do about it. We knew this day would come. We did what we could."

Ashton was furious. Rico was a man she had grown to appreciate, even respect. And now all she could do was stand in the aftermath and seethe. She was angry, but she knew she wasn't angry at Rico. He had simply chosen to accept and move on.

Ashton walked away before she said something she would regret. She walked toward the doors of the resort. Only yesterday, children had romped here, laughing and giggling as they played crabs and sea monsters in the courtyard. It was a game Jagatha had made up. She would play the crab, making her hands like pincers, clawing at the sea monsters.

"Three children!"

A Colony woman ran past Ashton and toward Cahya who stood only a few yards away. Ashton turned toward them.

"Only three?" Cahya asked.

"No," the woman spat, "only three left . . ."

Ashton's heart stopped.

Jagatha!

Ashton's legs moved fast as she darted past Cahya, back toward the center of the courtyard. Her eyes went wide as she scanned the area. The silence was deafening. Jagatha was never quiet.

"Jagatha!" Ashton screamed.

Her brain sent waves down her body, and she bolted back into the resort and up the staircase to the suites. Her muscles burned as she skipped two steps at a time.

"Jagatha!" she yelled again, but there was no response.

Ashton swung the suite door open to find the house parents crying in the main entrance. The room looked as if a tornado had swept through it. Ashton saw muddy footprints on the carpet. The two house parents looked up at Ashton, but she ignored them.

"Jagatha! J-Bug, where are you?" Ashton's voice cracked as she spoke the nickname. She knew what she would find before she even reached Jagatha's room. The Colony had done what they could. They had prepared as much as they could for this moment, but it hadn't been enough.

Ashton pushed Jagatha's door, now hanging by one hinge. She stepped back toward the wall as she saw Jagatha's bed, disheveled and out of place. Sinking down against the hard wall, Ashton shriveled, bringing her knees toward her face. Blackness closed in around her.

Everyone Ashton loved disappeared. Why would Jagatha be any different? Jagatha had experienced a fleeting taste of true life, a real life outside Augland's walls. But now she was on her way back to Augland's prison. Ashton knew Jagatha wouldn't be given a position in a park like Predator's Biome or Maya Bay. They would send her somewhere she wouldn't be exposed to other workers. Where she couldn't spread the truth about Augland. Somewhere like Land of Legends.

A cold draft hit Ashton, coming from the window near Jagatha's bed. Ashton reached for a blanket from Jagatha's tiny bed and pulled it around her. She held back tears. It wasn't just Jagatha. It was Wolfe too.

The sound of footsteps and heavy breathing interrupted her thoughts. Ashton looked up to see Hunter in the doorway, hair wet and face smeared with dirt. Like Ashton, Hunter had grown fond of Jagatha and her captivating smile.

Ashton sobbed, bringing the blanket up to her face. Hunter stood still, paralyzed. Ashton saw his chest hiccup with silent tears. She didn't have the strength to comfort him.

They hadn't seen much of each other recently. He and Versal sometimes came to have dinner with Ashton. Hunter was always talkative and discussed his negotiations with NeuroEnergy and his hunting expeditions. Hunter and Versal had seemed to adjust to life outside Augland much more quickly than Ashton had. But no matter what, Hunter and Ashton remained connected. They had been through so much together.

"They took her, then," he said, not looking at Ashton. Ashton didn't need to answer as they both stared at the bed.

"And you saw him?"

Ashton nodded. She was ready for Hunter to say something about not trusting Wolfe to begin with, but he held his tongue.

"You doing okay?" Hunter looked at Ashton, concerned.

Part of Ashton wanted to be okay, but it seemed impossible. So much loss: Sheva, Wolfe . . . and now Jagatha.

CHAPTER 4

Ashton

It took several days for the Colony to clean up what Augland had destroyed in a matter of hours. The crying didn't end. The screams of the children didn't fade. The rain didn't stop. The blood-soaked grass slowly faded to muddy brown in the rain.

Flashes of hiding children, Wolfe standing on the grass, and Jagatha's smile turning into fear circled Ashton's mind in an endless loop. As Ashton walked across the courtyard, she closed her eyes and made a promise: she would not let Augland get away with this again.

Before she knew it, Ashton found herself outside Hunter's cabin on the other side of the resort, near the rocky shores.

She pounded on the door.

"Hunter!"

It was still early morning and Hunter was probably asleep.

When he finally opened the door, his hair and now-grown-out beard was tousled, and he was pulling a woolen sweater over his head. His eyes were still half-asleep, contrasting with Ashton, who stood wide eyed on his doorstep.

"Ashton . . . what is it?"

"We need to go get her," Ashton announced. "We need to go get her now." Ashton tensed as hurt and anger stuttered her speech.

"We can't just walk back in there, Ash." Hunter shook his head.

"We can't just sit here! They'll be back, Hunter. Who will they take next? All the women? Men? When does this end? They've made us infertile, Hunter!" Ashton's tears had dried, and her deep blue eyes widened. "And there is no one on our side anymore. Wolfe . . ."

Hunter didn't say anything because he knew she was right. Wolfe had led Augland to their doorstep and now they weren't safe.

"So, what do we do?"

Ashton and Hunter walked toward Cahya's penthouse on the top floor of the east wing of the resort. Cahya sat outside on her balcony overlooking the courtyard and the sound beyond. The haze of early morning fog moved slowly across the water. During the day, Cahya had a direct view across the courtyard to the penthouse suite where the children lived in the opposite log structure.

Powlen, Cahya's personal guard, and several other Colony members stood around pointing at a 3D live model of hills, water, and roads with long lines going in various directions—a map of Hood Canal. Cahya used her finger to draw and zoom into specific locations until her eyes met with Ashton and Hunter through the map and she minimized it with one swipe of her hand. Powlen turned and frowned as he saw them. The fact that they were such recent refugees from Augland 54 to the Colony had always made them a bit suspect in his eyes.

"I wondered when I'd see you two."

Cahya was always calm, unfazed. Her braided hair tied up high and her eyes drooped and darkened from lack of sleep. Cahya had taken the defeat hard, but she stayed strong for her people. Her thin, tall, and strong frame was hunched over the table where she worked.

"I'm a little busy, so I'm hoping you two can be brief."

"What are we going to do, Cahya? How are we going to get them back?" Ashton blurted out, more passionately than expected.

"We . . . will do nothing." Cahya looked at Ashton with unwavering eye contact. Her relaxed attitude infuriated Ashton.

"How can you say that?"

"Ashton—"

Hunter put his hand on Ashton's shoulder, hoping to restrain her.

"No! I want to know why we repeatedly let Augland dictate everything around us. When will you stand up—"

Cahya straightened her towering frame.

"Everything I do is for the good of this Colony. Unlike some, I can't think with my emotions and sacrifice all for the good of a few. That is my burden and I have to decide what is best."

If Cahya was angry, she composed herself well. But she was firm.

"I—" Ashton started. She didn't understand how protecting the Colony meant letting their children be kidnapped. Cahya frowned. She gazed disapprovingly and took the words out of Ashton's mouth. Ashton shook with frustration.

"We will all miss the children. We will all miss Jagatha. My prayers are with her, with all of them."

Silence filled the room.

Hunter paced. His frustration matched Ashton's. Cahya presumed this had everything to do with Jagatha, but she was wrong. While the loss of Jagatha was a particularly driving force, Ashton knew the horrors within the Augland walls. Cahya had made her decision not really knowing the life she condemned those children to; it was a life she had never seen personally and did not know.

"Why didn't Wolfe warn us? I thought he was supposed to help us. Not—" Hunter asked what they had all been thinking, but stopped himself from admitting the obvious: Wolfe had turned on them.

"I haven't spoken to Wolfe in months . . ." Cahya shook her head. The silence around them thickened the air.

"I've been speaking with NeuroEnergy." Hunter sounded desperate. "We could go to them and ask for their help again. They've brought us generators, photon guns, and tons of technological resources. We can ask for their help."

Cahya slammed her hand on the table, spilling the light brown tea from her mug along its smooth surface. Powlen's attention heightened. Cahya put her hand up to stop any advancement.

"We've tried that, Hunter. We have tried every angle and we cannot put our people through that again. NeuroEnergy agrees. They have even more to lose than the Colony." She sighed. "I'll need some time now; we may look to relocate to another part of the Canal and if we do, I'd like to move fast."

So, the Colony will run again. This is how they deal with their problems. How many times would they start over?

Ashton stared down Cahya as she digested the words coming from her fearless leader. Her wonderful, kind-hearted, and misguided leader. They needed to fight, not cower away.

Ashton marched down the single-lane road that led to her waterfront home. Hunter trailed close behind her. She wasn't sure why he had followed her. She wanted to be alone. It was the reason she had selected a home that was a fifteen-minute walk away from everyone. If Hunter wasn't careful, she would lash out at him.

Hunter caught up to her and pulled her arm. Ashton spun and stared at him. His long, brown hair was pulled back in a ponytail, so different from the buzz cut he'd had in Augland.

"We can go to NeuroEnergy, you and me."

"Cahya just said—" Hunter rolled his eyes as Ashton spoke.

"Screw that. We go to NeuroEnergy; we convince them to help us. Where's the passion you had this morning?"

Hunter believed in NeuroEnergy, but Ashton had her reservations. Ashton didn't trust companies.

The Artificial Existence Center, AEC, that had created and still controlled the Augland parks, was corrupt. *Power always corrupts,* thought Ashton bitterly. Why would NeuroEnergy be any different? It too was controlled by the AEC, at least to some extent.

According to Hunter, NeuroEnergy's intentions were pure—they were simply concerned for the future of their business. While NeuroEnergy was also under the control of the AEC, they acted independently from the Augland parks. The parks needed NeuroEnergy's progressive power supply.

Augland had found ways to minimize its need for NeuroEnergy's power, using older methods such as hydroelectric and solar power, but those energy sources were not sufficient to run the Suits. If Augland could fuel the Suits, then NeuroEnergy would be obsolete. Augland did not fully trust NeuroEnergy and wanted either complete control over them or at least to replicate its energy production. NeuroEnergy assumed this, so while it did supply energy to the parks, it remained secretive about its true capabilities and methods.

The previous year, Hunter had been sent to the Pacific Northwest Augland park as a spy to provide NeuroEnergy with information about Augland's innovations and intentions. NeuroEnergy wanted proof that Augland was breaking the post-war contract and creating its own fusion-based energy.

Before the war, NeuroEnergy had been a rising utility star. The corporation had discovered new energy sources that transformed the way the world combined energy. It harnessed fusion for the first time and allowed the sun's energy to be replicated and stored in tiny metal polymer batteries. This method produced exponentially more power than any previous energy source—drilling, solar, or water—and it was compact and durable. Like the AEC's Suits, NeuroEnergy revolutionized the world.

The Artificial Existence Center partnered with NeuroEnergy, using its fusion energy to power the Suits and pods that allowed humans to virtually control the synthetic bio-androids. This greatly enhanced human life expectancy by decades— the human bodies inside the pods were in a reduced metabolic state, free of disease, illness, or even accidental death. The aging process slowed. While suspended inside energy plasma in the pods, the brain remained active, sending signals to transmitters controlling the android Suits. In turn, information from sensors in the Suits sent sensory signals back to the human in the pod. This allowed the human brain to control material technology without physical attachment.

The early use of Suits was directed at helping the aged or disabled with health limitations and the post humanistic movement. Both the government and people praised the ideology and adapted its advancements. When the AEC broke away from the health industry and began offering Suits to any individual with upfront money and a future co-investment commitment, NeuroEnergy began to suspect the AEC of plans to take over the American government. The AEC convinced the wealthy to put their money into lifelong memberships with them, free of taxes, and promised a life of dreams inside the Augland parks.

NeuroEnergy secretly began to investigate ways to weaponize its energy discoveries. The American government allied itself with NeuroEnergy out of concern about the AEC's growing power. However, the weapons were not ready when the war began, and the AEC had the upper hand in the conflict. The Suits and the artificial intelligence created by the AEC felt like an invincible combination. The government wasn't prepared to combat such a force, and it didn't take long for it to succumb to the corporate coup.

The war had only lasted two years. The overwhelming force of the battles destroyed most habited areas that technology had provided, and the residual radiation did the rest. Those still-intact areas were overtaken by the AEC and converted to Augland parks; everything else was left to wither away while the parks grew in size and power. Suit-less civilians had no choice but to seek refuge as workers within the Augland parks or live rudimentary lives in the resulting wilderness colonies. The AEC created a new world order maintained by their new authority.

When the war ended, the AEC controlled Washington, DC and the government. Laws were created in the boardroom instead of through constitutional legislation.

This meant limitless power for AEC executives and those willing to pay them, and dangerous inconsideration for those who were not: the Suit-less. NeuroEnergy had to continue to partner with the AEC to survive despite its misgivings and the recent wartime conflict.

Ashton studied Hunter as they sat around the newly built fire in her kitchen hearth. After her disappointing conversation with Cahya, Ashton had lost hope. If the Colony didn't believe there was hope for the children, why should Ashton? At this point, she was willing to try anything, even if that meant going to NeuroEnergy. If Hunter had a plan, Ashton would listen. She was out of ideas.

"What did you have in mind?"

Hunter beamed with excitement.

"We go to NeuroEnergy and talk to my old boss, Rye. He'll be able to help us get to the right people. We should go tomorrow."

Ashton nodded. Hunter beamed and began to rattle off the many things they needed to prepare for their trip. Ashton sat quietly as he paced around her. As soon as the plan was made, he disappeared. He had what he wanted: her commitment to go to NeuroEnergy with him.

Day turned to night and Ashton looked deep into the fire, never taking her sight from the pulsing lines of flame on the logs. The fire blazed its trail along the wood as it warmed her dinner for the night: canned beans. The heat sent tiny prickles along her cheek as the darkness surrounded her and stars sprinkled outside in the night sky. She felt hopeless in the dark.

Ashton's mind twisted in disappointment as she recounted her trust in Wolfe. The feeling of betrayal stung deeply. Niall, her brother-like friend from Maya Bay, used to tell her she was too trusting, too soft. Ashton was loyal, usually thinking of others before herself—even to a fault. While quiet most of the time, she had a fiery side. She hated seeing bad things happen to good people, and she thought Wolfe was the same. But she had been wrong. Wolfe was just like "them."

Before she knew it, she had been up all night and the light of day hovered above the mountains.

CHAPTER 5

Ashton

Ashton squinted as the bright light of day burned her eyes. A pounding sound pulsed through the air. She was still sitting on the floor, wrapped in a blanket. The fire from last night was gone, but warm embers remained.

Boom. Boom. Boom.

"Ashton! Wake up!"

She could hear Hunter calling from outside her locked door. Dragging her extra-large blanket with her, she opened her door. Her eyes were still halfway closed.

Hunter's eyebrows raised and he chuckled. Ashton grunted as he slid inside and pulled his backpack off his back. The irony of their switched situations from the day before was not lost on either of them.

"We should get going soon. It's at least an eight-hour trip. We can be there tonight."

Hunter strode past Ashton, grabbed the electric kettle and a mug, and began making tea. When he finished, he handed the mug to Ashton. It helped warm her as the cold, winter air of the Northwest shook her awake.

"C'mon, pull yourself together and let's go. Sleeping won't save those kids." Ashton closed her eyes. Hunter was too much this early in the morning.

"Give me five minutes," she groaned.

Ashton didn't have much clothing. She had a few items that Versal had made for her, which she almost never wore. It wasn't because they weren't beautiful garments, she just never did anything that warranted wearing something to impress. She spent most of her time outside and in the kitchen with Rico.

Her favorite gift from Versal was a dark-blue embroidered sweater that was a little big, especially with the weight she had lost after leaving Augland. She would leave it for when she returned. If she returned. Cahya seemed insistent on finding a new location.

Versal had embroidered clothing for Hunter to barter with at NeuroEnergy, in exchange for the extra supplies he used to keep his boat in pristine condition. Unlike Augland, the workers within the NeuroEnergy compounds were treated as employees. They didn't have customers in Suits to cater to day in and out. The people worked and lived within NeuroEnergy's walls, each contributing and taking—much like the Colony. Hunter had been one of them at some point. He still gloated a bit over his relationship with NeuroEnergy, even boasting about it to other Colony members. Ashton felt indifferent. NeuroEnergy had done nothing for her, or to her. Yet.

They walked along the abandoned road that wound along the shore. Trees swayed around them as the wind brushed by, chilling Ashton's face. Hunter's boat was at the end of the resort's dock, a floating wooden boat with dual motors. Its white paint peeled, and rusted nails shone a dirty orange in the sunshine peeking through the gray morning fog.

"Can't wait for you to see her in action." Hunter stalked a few feet in front of Ashton.

"Her?"

"*Freya*, my boat."

"You named her . . . *Freya?*" Ashton sounded defensive. Freya was the name of the warrior character Ashton had been forced to play; it was a name Ashton had discarded along with everything else from her days in Augland 54.

Ashton hadn't felt like her Viking warrior alter ego in a long time. She had lost Freya the moment she lost Sheva. Hunter didn't notice the discomfort the name brought her, the mixed emotions that bubbled as she recalled her last two months in Augland 54.

"Well, yeah, hoping she gets us the same luck you did getting us out of Augland. It doesn't look like much, but all the cabling and circuits are new."

Ashton and Hunter cut across the courtyard toward the end of the dock.

"Ashton, so good to see you! It's been too long." Versal's sweet voice echoed over the water. Her bright smile caught Ashton's attention.

"Good to see you too, Versal." It had been some time since Ashton had seen her, but Versal always seemed busy. She was a socialite and extremely popular in the Colony.

Versal swung a maroon-red scarf over Ashton's neck and tied it.

"It gets cold on the boat." Ashton stared down at the beautifully woven scarf, each stitch identical to the next. Ashton felt its instant relief from the cold.

"Thank you," Ashton smiled. Versal looked past her at Hunter, who had already begun packing his boat for the trip.

"Would you mind?" Versal pointed at some of the bags she had packed, full of homemade items like jam and bread and a few things Ashton knew were specifically for Hunter: his photon rifle, a large coat, and the items for him to barter.

"Of course." Ashton picked up two bags and walked alongside Versal as they carefully made their way along the uneven wooden dock.

"I'm so sorry about Jagatha; I know how close you two are." The mention of her name sent a sharp pain down Ashton's chest. "You've been more than just a friend to her; she looks up to you," Versal continued. Ashton fought back tears. Jagatha had expected Ashton to protect her, and Ashton had failed. Just like she had failed to save Sheva.

"Thanks. I know it hasn't been easy for you or Hunter either." Ashton knew the couple had become close to the young girl as well. Versal and Jagatha painted together. Ashton had hung one of Jagatha's paintings up in her home, a flower with bright red petals, a purple center, and a deep, olive-green stem.

Before long, *Freya* was packed and ready to go. Hunter busied himself turning on the electric motors and warming up the boat, which took only moments. The boat barely hummed; if the morning hadn't been so quiet, Ashton wouldn't have been able to tell it was running. *Freya* didn't look like anything special: paint peeling off the side, cloudy windows, and rusted hand railings, but Hunter beamed with excitement.

"See you both soon! Safe travels." Versal hugged Hunter across the water and said her goodbyes.

The boat creaked as Ashton climbed aboard. Ashton pulled herself up and felt the sliminess of the wood deck fence.

"So, what do you think?" Hunter turned to Ashton in excitement.

"It's . . . great." Ashton said. While it wasn't perfect, she could see the hard work that Hunter had put into his project. It wasn't pretty, but to get a boat in this condition running took true talent.

The boat moved gracefully across the gray early morning waters. Hunter sat with one knee driving; his back slouched against the chair.

Ashton stared off into the fog.

"We going to talk about Wolfe?"

Hunter didn't take his eyes off the horizon. Ashton had known the topic of Wolfe would come up. What she didn't know was how she was going to discuss it with Hunter. He had never trusted Wolfe or, by association, Ashton's decisions.

"Ashton?"

"There . . ." She cleared her throat. "There is nothing to talk about. You saw what I saw, Hunter. That's it." Ashton looked down. She wanted to look anywhere but at him. She didn't want him to see her hurt.

Ashton could feel Hunter search for words. Please don't ask. He didn't press any further. The gentle hum of the electric motor helped, but it was still too quiet as the question of Wolfe's betrayal lingered like the fog along the mountain range.

Ashton cleared her throat. "You never told me why NeuroEnergy sent you into Augland," she said, changing the subject.

Hunter half smiled.

"It's not like Augland at NeuroEnergy. I mean it's not great. It's still hard work, but we at least have freedom there. And they didn't send me to Augland 54; I volunteered."

"Why would you do that? Volunteer to leave?"

"Well, to be fair, I didn't know what to expect. I didn't realize I would be trapped, or, like, 'demoted' to a place like Land of Legends. I don't think NeuroEnergy even anticipated that."

Ashton thought he gave too much credit to NeuroEnergy. They had left him in Augland 54 to die. If it had been her, she would not have been so forgiving, but Hunter was blinded by his loyalty to the company.

Ashton didn't have the mental energy to start a fight with Hunter, so she didn't ask the daunting question: Can they be trusted? She let him tell her about his life at NeuroEnergy, the good times, his boss, and his friends. It helped the time pass.

". . . you'll like Rye. He was my boss and runs the Augland 54 technology operations division, two or three Augland parks in total, I think. He's been finding ways to get more intel from the AEC, and within the parks, for years. A little dry at times, but a character." Ashton nodded. Hunter laughed at some memory he replayed in his head.

"Why not go back, then? Just be there?" Ashton had wondered why he had stayed at the Colony.

Hunter paused; Ashton wasn't sure he even knew the answer.

"Versal, for one. And NeuroEnergy is repetitive. It's the same work every day. No change, no difference. The same people, same routine. It was boring to me. I guess that's why I went to Augland 54. I wanted something different. And I wanted to make a difference." Ashton could understand that; while at Maya Bay, she had felt similar. It was the same every day. The same beach. The same restaurant. The same awful Suit customers.

"I didn't want to go back to that. The Colony is freedom. I do this, then that, and then something else the next day. And then here I am today, with you, driving a boat up the canal."

Hunter smiled his flashy half grin. It soon turned to a frown.

"And . . . I don't know. There is this feeling working for the companies. Not as bad at NeuroEnergy, but definitely in Augland. The knowledge and fear of failure keeps you paralyzed. You become . . . lost, I guess. Sometimes you feel like you need to think like them, act like them. Just so you fit in with what they want."

Hunter's honesty felt warm.

"Why don't you get some sleep? It will be some time before we get to NeuroEnergy and we will have to hike. Besides, you look like crap and could probably use the extra rest." There he was, the too-honest Hunter Ashton knew. She smiled.

"Fine . . . jerk."

Hunter laughed. They were back to normal banter. Wrapping herself in the oversized crocheted scarf that Versal gave her, she headed down into the cabin of the boat. Ashton felt herself drifting away as the small waves cradled her to sleep.

Ashton was shaken awake by a sudden thud. She woke up, wide-eyed, as she remembered where she was and what she was doing.

"Get up!"

Hunter's enthusiasm was beginning to get on Ashton's nerves, and she threw her scarf over her head. Hunter's footsteps could be heard above, on the bow of the boat. She groaned. Reluctantly, she joined Hunter on deck.

The dock before them was like the small one outside of her Colony home: rickety, with loose, slimy boards that trailed out to a rocky shore and tall trees that walled up a towering hill.

After an hour of hiking, they made it to the top of the large hill just as the sun went down behind the trees. As they crested the hill, the NeuroEnergy compound came into view. It was an industrial park with block-like cement walls that spanned across Ashton's view. More walls. Inside were rows and rows of long buildings stacked side by side in perfect uniform.

"Cool, huh? NeuroEnergy's P.A. headquarters. It stands for Port something. That's what they used to call this town." Hunter exhaled. Ashton noticed that while he was excited, he also looked nervous.

"Looks . . . deserted." Ashton had thought it would be more like Augland 54, where there was constant movement. "So, this is where you worked?"

"Oh no, this place is for directors and executives. I was at the engineering center, working on broken-down fusion plants. Rye used to manage all the engineers there before his promotion to oversee Augland 54 operations. Honestly, I've only been here a couple times . . . but Rye will take care of us."

Hunter brushed off this new information as if it shouldn't be a surprise to Ashton.

Ashton shook her head. She knew he had kept this information from her for a reason. They were at NeuroEnergy's equivalent of the Executive suite. Just like in Augland, workers worked to *hopefully* someday earn their way into the Executive office, like her good friend Niall had always wanted at Maya Bay. Why would NeuroEnergy be any different?

Ashton looked at the large, cement buildings. They were plain, and cold, and colored an ashy gray that blended in with the cloud-filled Pacific Northwest sky. She didn't see Hunter's view of this world. At some point, this could become their divide.

CHAPTER 6

Ashton

Ashton and Hunter stood before a large, steel door, that like the walls of Augland, was meant to keep whatever was outside out and inside in. Hunter pushed several buttons on a small, glowing screen and they waited in front of the cold and uninviting metal barrier that divided NeuroEnergy from the overgrown ruins outside.

"Please. Swipe. Entrance. Card." A monotone voice droned at them from an unseen speaker. Hunter pulled out a clear, almost glass-like card and pressed it on the green lit screen.

"What's that for?"

"Security; you have to have your own identification card to get in. You'll be fine. I've already submitted your information as a guest of mine."

Ashton shivered in the cold as Hunter bragged about his prestigious and newly acquired access card. He had received it after becoming an emissary, and Ashton guessed it was their way of making him feel better after leaving him in Augland.

The steel door lifted, screeching as it slowly rose, and Ashton and Hunter entered NeuroEnergy. The first thing Ashton saw was the heavily armed NeuroEnergy security team. As their bags were searched and Hunter talked to the guards, Ashton looked around in shocked silence. The NeuroEnergy campus spanned for what could have been one or two miles in either direction with each building reaching only three to four stories high. Ashton had to remind herself that this wasn't Augland, but NeuroEnergy confused her. Why would a technology company look so dark, somber, and uninviting?

Hunter guided them down a main road to a large, cement compound. Their footsteps echoed as they walked. Everything was made of concrete or metal, uniform and blocky. There was no pomp and circumstance to the place; everything was dull and practical, utilitarian. With no customers to impress, NeuroEnergy was pure company.

Ashton shivered. NeuroEnergy had walls, but they did not form a dome overhead and Ashton could see the cloudy night sky above. Square buildings lined both sides of the road; each building had gray lettering indicating its function. Ashton found this helpful, as each building resembled the next and seemed impossible to tell apart without the signage.

At the end of the road, they reached a building that stood out from the others. In big, gray letters it read, "NeuroEnergy Northwest Headquarters."

Hunter guided her up the bare concrete staircase. Augland would have utilized every square inch. The walkway would have been made of decorative stone and draped in greens and flowers. But even without the gaudy extravagance, NeuroEnergy wreaked of division, executives still set apart from the common workers. It made Ashton uneasy.

When they reached the door, Hunter had to input his card to gain access. As the doors opened, two tall and well-muscled male guards stepped out. Ashton jumped in surprise.

"Don't worry, they are just searching us for any weapons," Hunter assured Ashton. The two men approached them and took out a stick-like wand and ran it up and down Ashton and Hunter. Ashton stood wide-eyed and frozen as it beeped loudly, then gave a green light. The men stepped away, saying nothing and allowed them to continue.

Hunter led them down a long hallway toward an elevator. If he hadn't seemed so sure, and there wasn't security guarding the entrance, Ashton would have assumed this place was abandoned. Where were the people? She listened intently for any sound, any movement, but nothing. Eerie.

"Where is everyone?" Her voice echoed.

"It's working hours. Besides, no one is on the first floor. You have to be given access to go up to any floor. It's for safety." Hunter reached again for his badge. In a walled city, it seemed suspicious to Ashton that the Executives needed this much protection, or separation.

The elevator doors creaked open.

"Name, code, and look up at the camera."

Hunter did as he was asked, staring toward the upper left corner of the elevator.

"Hunter, B12TX7." Ashton wondered if she should say something. Up to this point, Hunter had only needed a key card and nothing from her. She momentarily panicked and thought about sprinting through the elevator doors. *If it's this hard to get in, it's going to be just as hard to get out. This could be a trap.*

Ashton wanted to go back to the Colony, to her home, where she felt safe. The walls here felt too close to her, and as she prepared to move, Hunter grabbed her hand.

"It will be fine. Don't worry." He gave her a sweet glare as he intently looked at her. While she kept Hunter emotionally away, he still was able to recognize her fear. Ashton knew Hunter wouldn't intentionally put them in any danger and that brought her some comfort. He had come here and returned with no problems, but Ashton was paralyzed with the fear of being trapped again. The doors closed while Hunter held her hand tight.

The elevator slowly lifted, beeping once, and again before stopping and opening. Hunter dropped Ashton's hand and headed out.

Bright lights blinded Ashton as her eyes adjusted from the night to blaring illumination of the vast open space of the windowless second floor. She walked cautiously behind Hunter as he quickly walked past desk after desk. Behind each surface was a NeuroEnergy worker, not paying any attention to them.

Ashton couldn't help but stare. They all wore the same thin, framed glasses, and their hands danced around in midair as if swatting flies. She passed a man and saw that the glasses projected information only the eyes of the people who looked through their lenses could see. She slowed to get a better view as the NeuroEnergy worker moved data around in a chart. He flicked his hand, and the data was replaced with a virtual map containing red pinpoints. He turned to glare at her and she realized she had drawn close behind him, mesmerized by the images behind his glasses. Ashton quickly hurried away to catch up to Hunter.

Hunter stood next to a desk talking to a tall man with rolled-up sleeves and a plain vest. Ashton assumed he was important because his desk was surrounded with paper and thin, translucent pieces of glass. The room was littered with charts, graphs, and videos. None of the others had this advanced type of workstation. A worker approached him, almost timidly, before she nodded and skittered away.

The man pushed his data projection glasses toward his face as he glanced at Hunter and Ashton.

"Rye, man, how's it been?" Rye didn't answer. He continued concentrating midair at objects through his glasses.

35

"What are you doing here? Didn't see any meeting set."

Hunter recoiled, but quickly regained his composure. Ashton had presumed through his positive dialogue about NeuroEnergy that they would receive a warmer welcome.

"The Colony was raided by Augland. We came here because we need your and Georgina's help."

Ashton hadn't heard that second name before. Or maybe Hunter had spoken of her, but Ashton hadn't paid attention. She tended to do that when Hunter rambled on about NeuroEnergy.

Rye didn't seem to be listening, his eyes focused on the invisible projection in front of him. A young man came up to Rye, presenting him with something on a glass sheet. Rye touched the glass a few times and the man disappeared back to a desk.

Ashton stared at the coldness of the space around them. There were no bright colors or decorations of any kind. And it was so silent. It wasn't what she had pictured at all. She had thought NeuroEnergy would be like Augland—glamorous, perfect, refined. This seemed more structured, but madness at the same time. No one seemed to notice their presence; they were all too focused on whatever they saw through their glasses. Just like in Augland, she felt invisible and unimportant.

Rye sighed. "Hunter, we've been through this with Cahya—and you, for that matter. There isn't anything we can do."

"This attack was different." Hunter lowered his voice. "You think they won't come after you next?"

Rye pushed a button on his glasses and nodded his head to signal for Hunter and Ashton to follow him. He promptly guided them toward a small corner office encased floor to ceiling with glass walls.

Once the door shut behind them, Rye groaned as he sat down in his chair.

"Hunter, you are asking us to, what? Side with the Colony? Defend the Colony? Go against Augland and break the treaty that ended the war? Disrupt the entire post-war stability of this country?" Rye softened. "I know you are angry and upset at Augland; we are too. But until we get some proof that Augland is breaking the treaty they have with us, we can't do anything. You know this."

Rye motioned for Hunter and Ashton to have a seat before he continued.

"Georgina . . . and I . . . we are not going to take any action, including working with the Colony, until we know for certain that there are bigger plans. Augland, just by numbers, could come in and ruin all this work in a day. We can't risk being in the same position as the Colony, and we don't want to start another war that we know we won't win. We need Augland as much as Augland needs us. And until otherwise, end of story."

Hunter clenched his fists. "Call her. I need to hear it from Georgina." His demanding tone startled Ashton. He didn't seem to be in a position to make demands, and the desperation in his voice frightened her. Ashton didn't know who Georgina was, but she sounded important. Hunter and Rye stared at each other, neither willing to speak or look away first. Ashton presumed this was a continuation of an old argument.

Rye's eye contact broke as he became distracted by something in his glasses—something Hunter and Ashton couldn't see. He stood up quickly from his chair as the office door opened.

"Hunter, I heard you had decided to visit; to what do we owe the pleasure?"

A poised and attractive older woman strolled into the room. Her perfectly styled black-and white-hair came just below her shoulders. She wore all black on her tiny frame with a tiny emerald belt, brighter than anything Ashton had seen since Venus Park. If she hadn't noticed the wrinkles, at first glance Ashton would have assumed she was a Suit. No worker was that well-dressed.

"Georgina. Ma'am," Hunter said with an inflection in his voice as he turned toward the elegant woman. Ashton noticed a shift in the room. Georgina obviously held power.

Rye stood and Georgina took the seat behind the desk. As soon as she sat, Rye and Hunter began talking, bombarding the woman with a conversation she had not intended on having when she walked into Rye's office. Ashton felt out of place, in a world beyond her comprehension. As the discussions continued, no one paid any attention to her. The triangle of people shifted their gaze between each other as they spoke. She could walk away, and no one would notice.

As Hunter described the events of the previous week, Ashton watched through the glass walls of Rye's office as the workers behind the tables focused on the technology within their glasses. There were no uniforms, although gray seemed to be the preferred color choice, which matched the aesthetics of the ash-colored building. There was no one walking around, evaluating their every move. Ashton watched as two individuals turned to each other and laughed. She wondered if they knew about Augland's cruelty or if they were kept hidden from the truth like Hunter had been.

"Ashton."

She turned to see Hunter, Rye, and Georgina looking at her. Hunter looked embarrassed at Ashton's lack of attention to their conversation.

"Sorry," was all she could muster as blood rushed to her face.

"This is Georgina; she runs the Pacific Northwest NeuroEnergy territory."

"Hunter has told me so much about you."

"Same," Ashton lied.

"I want to say, sincerely, that I'm sorry for what you went through in Augland. I can't imagine the struggles you faced." She looked sincere, but Ashton had learned people weren't always what they seemed. She had been disappointed by too many people that had seemed kind and good.

"Hunter, I wish we could help, but our hands are tied here. Cahya knows this."

"There isn't anything you could do? Ashton and I are willing to do anything. We can't go on looking over our shoulders, waiting for Wolfe and his men to come back." Ashton's heart sank hearing Wolfe's name spoken aloud.

Georgina sighed, then paused. "Rye, call my assistant and schedule a meeting for the four of us tomorrow morning. I won't make promises, but I may have an option. I don't think you'll like it, though." She shifted her eyes between Hunter and Ashton.

"Thank you! We will be open to anything!" Hunter almost leaped out his skin. Ashton could already hear him saying, I told you so.

"Now, I do need to speak to Rye. Alone please. My assistant can find you a place to stay for the night."

Ashton and Hunter left the small glass office where they were greeted by a young girl who had likely been summoned by Georgina through her glasses while they had been talking.

"This way . . ."

The young girl led Ashton and Hunter back to the elevator and out of the head-quarters to a nearby building. The same gray seemed to be consistent everywhere, no matter where they went.

"Told you this would work. They could have an army or something."

Hunter paced back and forth in the large, dark room where Georgina's assistant had them stay until their meeting with Georgina the next day. While spacious, the room resembled the rest of NeuroEnergy: simple, dull, and cold. While much nicer, and clean, it reminded Ashton of her room back in Augland, before everything changed.

"She said we won't like it." Ashton sat on the carpeted ground of their shared room. Hunter had theorized every scenario Georgina might have planned. It was getting irritating. He had been guessing all night.

"Maybe they want to bring the Colony here!"

Ashton shook her head. If NeuroEnergy was concerned about becoming a target, that was a surefire way to become one. That wouldn't solve anything. Hunter had become too ingrained in his connections at NeuroEnergy that he missed the entire mission coming here: to see if NeuroEnergy would go against Augland to help them get the stolen children back. Ashton knew NeuroEnergy wouldn't put its neck on the line for them. Rye had confirmed it. If they wanted to, they would have done something already. It was exactly what Ashton had predicted. There was no hope, and it was only a matter of time before Hunter figured that out for himself.

Before their mid-morning meeting with Georgina and Rye, Hunter wanted to show Ashton around, especially the indoor market. As they walked out through their building's door, they joined the throng of NeuroEnergy workers on their way to work.

The entire market was indoors, but the ceiling was painted like the sky. As soon as the elevator doors opened, the sweet smell of homemade biscuits and buttered herbs filled the air. The room, the same size as the desk-filled room they had visited the night before, was busy with little stations of makeshift goods. Potted plants, baskets filled with fruits and vegetables, and homemade items littered the long, wide walkway. Signs pointed to whatever goods the shop sold—sweets, bread, tea, coffee, clothes. Ashton was in awe. She had expected the same dingy office atmosphere, but this was quaint and beautiful, full of life.

Hunter directed Ashton to a small booth where a waiter served her a biscuit and tea. This was a first for Ashton; never had she been to a restaurant where she was the one being served. Hunter left her there to go barter Versal's goods and Ashton sat uninterrupted and nearly alone as only a few other patrons sat nearby talking among themselves. It felt surreal, to be treated with such dignity.

After breakfast, Hunter returned, and they strolled through the indoor walkway that connected several buildings. There were gyms, grocery stores, technology stores, and dozens of pop-up stalls where people sold and traded homemade items. As they walked past them, she looked at the NeuroEnergy workers, all of whom were busy with their lives. Living. She studied each face, staring at their eyes behind their glasses. Warmth filled her as she saw these people free. When they weren't working, they did what they wanted, when they wanted.

The entire place closed at eight a.m. NeuroEnergy had strict schedules for free and work time, but at least they had some freedom.

CHAPTER 7

Ashton

Georgina sat behind a solid wood desk that was heavily grained with dark growth veins. In her enormous office, she looked smaller than the day before. Towering, curved screens and tall potted plants were positioned around the room. A light breeze surrounded them. Ashton had never seen so much technology juxtaposed with greenery and earth tones.

"Please excuse the formality, but we will need to do a quick security scan before we speak." Rye brought out a small wand that he brought up to Hunter and then Ashton, which emitted a bright, red light that danced from the top of their heads down to their feet. Only a second passed before the red light turned green and Rye nodded to Georgina.

"Just a precaution. It's looking for weapons or any listening devices. Take a seat."

Georgina didn't look up from the empty space in front of her, looking at something in her glasses that Hunter and Ashton couldn't see. Ashton only knew it was there because of a small glare from the lenses. Clicking sounds from her keyboard filled the silence while Hunter and Ashton sat in the two seats facing her desk. Hunter's knees pulsed up and down as he tried to control his anxiety.

Georgina sighed before taking off her glasses.

"We know that it has been hard for you both. You've had quite an . . . adventure, but you have to understand where we are as a company. We can't take risks that will put us in jeopardy with the AEC."

Hunter's shoulder slouched, showing his disappointment at the direction of this conversation.

"Hunter, you know well about our needs to find out more about Augland's energy initiatives. If we can prove that Augland, or even Augland 54, is making its own energy, we will have proof that the treaty has been broken. We have not been successful in our pursuit, as you know."

Ashton knew Georgina referred to Hunter's failed mission at Augland 54. As if on instinct, she wanted to defend him, tell Georgina that he had done all he could in Augland. It was their fault for not setting him up for success. It was a miracle Hunter had been able to make it out of Augland alive. Before she could say anything, Georgina continued.

"That being said, our team has recently stumbled upon a recycled bio-android Artificial Existence Being."

Stumbled upon? Ashton knew there was no way Georgina had managed to simply find an empty Suit.

"We have been studying how Augland uses our energy to facilitate the transfer of minds into the bodies," Georgina continued. "The neuron plasma and the AEC techno-chips within the Suit we acquired are fried, and we haven't been able to replicate it. But we've come close."

Georgina intently looked at them both. Ashton had interacted with Suits her whole life, but she realized she had no idea how they worked.

"We would be willing to have one of you go into the Suit and attempt to get information from within Augland . . . and to find the children stolen from the Colony."

Hunter's leg stopped moving. He and Ashton sat in shocked silence as they digested Georgina's suggestion. The dots started to connect in Ashton's head. NeuroEnergy wouldn't help them, not in the way that they needed help—manpower, support. NeuroEnergy would only help them if they could get something in return, and they had just found two willing volunteers. Ashton's mind clouded as she replayed what Georgina had just suggested.

"You want to put us inside one of those things and have us go back to Augland?" Ashton couldn't believe the words coming out of her mouth. "That's insane!"

"That is what we are willing to offer. Again, your ask is that we jeopardize our company and put the employees, and families of NeuroEnergy at risk to help rescue the stolen children. I can't do that. Not publicly." Ashton thought Georgina sounded like Cahya.

41

"How would we get into Augland?" Hunter asked. Ashton spun around to glare at him, stunned they both weren't walking out of this office and straight back to the Colony.

"We have a contact on the supply route who will let us ride on the boat that brings supplies to Maya Bay and has been known to transport visitors. As for the Suit, we can create an alias and a formal application for the Suit to vacation in Augland 54."

"You can't be serious, Hunter. We can't do this!" Ashton was heated. She turned back to Georgina and Rye, who was standing behind her.

"And you said the Suit was fried? What does that mean? How will we get out?"

They had spent so much time getting away from Augland, she couldn't believe Hunter would even entertain this idea. Even more so, to be put into a barely functioning Suit. Everything about this idea seemed wrong. Hunter ignored Ashton.

"How long would we have in Augland?"

"She just said they don't have the technology, Hunter, this is . . . this is . . ." Ashton was at a loss for words.

"Ten days. That is when the supply boat is scheduled to return."

"We'll do it."

Ashton felt like a ghost. The louder she protested the further away she drifted from the conversation.

Georgina's office overlooked the street leading up to the main building. Ashton looked out over the gray cement buildings. She resented Hunter. He had dragged her here to be subjected to yet another company's horrible ideas that could get them killed. He wasn't considering her or others. How would Versal react to this? Had he forgotten all the terrible things that had happened because of Suits?

Georgina grinned.

"I'll note again, as Ashton pointed out, we haven't perfected the technology. The interaction between host and body does not last long, at most five to seven days. You'll have to find a way back to the boat after that."

"Understood," Hunter affirmed without hesitation.

"This is crazy. You expect us to return to Augland for ten days in a Suit that only lasts five?" Ashton stood up and paced a few steps, trying to wrap her mind around all of this. Am I the only sane person in this room?

Georgina leaned over her desk, smiling at Hunter. Ashton saw right through it. She was just another self-interested leader who used people to her advantage.

"We need information this time, Hunter. Understand that we are giving you another chance, but it is your last. And, as before, if you get caught, we will deny all knowledge of this mission. We will not make any attempt to rescue you."

Hunter nodded and Georgina rose, walking around the desk and putting her hand on Hunter's shoulder. His faith in this half-baked plan astonished Ashton.

"Think about it first. There are risks and you both should be fully committed before taking this on. The boat comes by in two days, so if we are to do this, we will need to act fast."

Ashton felt stuck in the middle. It was funny, both Augland and NeuroEnergy had their reservations about the other. They both feared the other taking over: Augland trying to create energy and NeuroEnergy trying to replicate Suits. And they both used workers to get what they wanted.

Rye led Hunter and Ashton out of Georgina's office. Georgina wanted them to mull over the information she'd provided to them, which wasn't much. As they headed back to their room, Ashton couldn't shake the feeling that she was a ghost, floating along the paths of others as the walls closed in around her.

Ashton was furious.

"This isn't a good plan, Hunter."

Hunter sat on his bed and Ashton on the floor looking up at the light-gray ceiling.

"We should say no, go back home."

"We don't have another choice, Ash. If we want to get back into Augland with a chance of rescuing Jagatha, this is it. You know it, I know it, Georgina knows it."

That was all they said to each other.

Ashton felt trapped, like she was sinking through the cold cement walls around her, cold and stuck. She knew Hunter was right and that made her angrier. They weren't in a place to make demands or request something without payment in return. She should have seen this coming. Georgina needed someone to take the risks she wasn't willing to take herself.

All Ashton wanted was peace and happiness, but that seemed to always come at a price. Augland promised her nothing and had cost her the chance of having children. The Colony was freedom, but with the ever-looming fear of starvation and attack. NeuroEnergy provided shelter, food, and the technological capabilities in exchange for unceasing monotony of work in this dull, gray world. No matter what she chose, someone else had control over her life.

She had sworn she would never go back to Augland. Never be part of that life again. But she didn't have a choice—she was going to save Jagatha, save all the children if she could. But Georgina's plan was too small. How could one faulty Suit save all the children and end the system? What they needed was an army to go against Augland. They needed to make Augland return what they had taken.

She had come here for help, and instead was being asked to help NeuroEnergy in its corporate battle. This wasn't for the children or Ashton or Hunter. This was for the good of NeuroEnergy. Ashton was tired of both companies' propensity to exploit and use workers to further their own initiatives.

But Hunter was right about one thing; this was their only shot. If they said no, they would return to the Colony and the children would be lost within the Augland walls forever. They had no other option. NeuroEnergy was their last resort, and if there was a chance they could save Jagatha, they both would take it. Even if it meant going back into Augland for ten days with a faulty Suit that would last, at most, for seven.

Ashton hated every aspect of the scheme.

CHAPTER 8

Ashton

By afternoon, Ashton and Hunter had agreed to Georgina's plan and were taken to an underground bunker where they would spend the next two days preparing for their infiltration of Augland.

The bunker was a giant, underground cement box, broken into sections with the same glass walls that filled the offices above. The doors in and out of the bunker were heavily guarded. Ashton had assumed, correctly, that the presence of this Suit and their mission were both to be kept secret from the staff of NeuroEnergy.

In a corner of the bunker was a glass room with a large conference table. With a push of a button, the glass came alive with maps, tables, and drone photos of Augland 54, and more 3D maps covered the table. Rye had given both Hunter and Ashton a pair of the NeuroEnergy glasses to access the technology, but the constant stream of information made Ashton sick. She left Hunter, who had grown up with the glasses, to take over the logistics planning; she needed to become familiar with the Suit.

Testing in the Suit would not be possible. The doctor and NeuroEnergy scientist indicated they had one chip that, once activated, couldn't be turned off. That gave them one shot and allowed Ashton very little time during transit to become used to living in an android. At first, Hunter volunteered to be the one in the Suit, but given that she knew more about Augland and Wolfe, it was decided Ashton be the one in the Suit.

Ashton's experience with Suits came in handy as they prepared for her role, and Hunter's attention to detail helped streamline the plan. Hunter would be the Suit's personal worker, as workers that were dedicated to Suits had special privileges and didn't have the same restrictions as those who worked within the parks.

For two days, they came up with scenarios, places, and people she would need to see, and above all, how she would get close to Wolfe. Warren, Wolfe's father and the CEO, would be next to impossible to get close to. Rye had secured a high-profile identity, which would give her access to people in the Executive office.

On the other side of the bunker, Ashton stared at the Suit. Behind her, she heard Georgina's heels tapping against the concrete.

"She's beautiful, isn't she?" Ashton said nothing, but she didn't take her eyes off of it. She was mesmerized. The redheaded, long-haired Suit was slim and tall, with white rubber-like skin. It lay motionless on the table and Ashton felt like she was looking at a corpse, not an android.

Ashton didn't respond.

"I had the same reaction . . . I was a young girl when they first came out. It was an advancement no one thought possible. Alone, NeuroEnergy's power was incredible; combined with the AEC's artificial androids, it was magnificent."

Georgina looked like she was in her fifties; she would have been only a young child when the war ended.

"The people were blinded by it. The ideal life—living through a Suit, riskless, enjoyable. They were looking for any way out, no matter the consequence, especially with how the world was going—wars, food shortages, global warming, government corruption . . ."

Ashton turned toward Georgina. How could she blame the people for this? This was greed. This was corporate corruption. That is what caused this. If Georgina was attempting to gain her trust, it wouldn't work.

"Did you know about the radiation?"

Unlike Hunter, Ashton questioned the morale of NeuroEnergy's intentions. They had an entire division dedicated to Augland research; they must have had some idea.

"We tried to warn Augland, and they wouldn't listen—but that is why we decided to help create a solution. To help you all."

Georgina placed her hand on Ashton's shoulder, eyeing her closely. Ashton could also tell that Georgina sensed her distrust. Georgina had the same look in her eyes. She didn't know if she trusted Ashton either. That was okay with Ashton. Maybe Georgina shouldn't.

Augland had let the radiation of the Suits hurt the workers—the cause of Ashton's own infertility—and NeuroEnergy had known about it.

Ashton shifted and Georgina's hand dropped. She was tired of people pretending to have good intentions. Like Wolfe, Georgina was part of the system Ashton despised wholeheartedly.

The Suit was the only leverage Ashton and Hunter had, and the only shot NeuroEnergy had at infiltrating Augland. Georgina thought she had all the power here, but she didn't. She needed Ashton's knowledge and willingness. If Georgina wanted a true alliance, she would need to prove that Ashton could trust her.

A man dressed all in white joined Ashton and handed her a skintight bodysuit that exposed her arms and legs. It was time that they started prepping Ashton for her Suit.

Beside the table where the Suit lay was a smooth, white oval the length of Ashton. She had never seen a pod before; in Augland they were always stored away, out of sight. It hummed, and Ashton tried not to look, knowing her body would soon be encapsulated within its walls.

The man in the white coat didn't speak as he concentrated on placing tiny electro-chips in the center of small, white patches. Ashton watched him carefully.

"They are transmitters. They allow your brain to send movement directions to your android."

The transmitters covered her entire head through an elastic cap that came down to just above her eyes. A slight jolt of electricity made every muscle in Ashton's body tense. It took her by surprise, and she almost fell out of the chair. The doctor seemed unfazed by her sudden movement as he tested each transmitter. A little warning would have been nice.

Hunter entered the room with his eyes distracted by something in his glasses.

"Whoa!" was all he could say as he looked up to see what he could barely tell was Ashton through the various wires. "Good look on you."

Ashton chuckled and looked at Hunter's now-shaved face with darkened scruff around his mouth. "I could say the same. Nice 'stache."

"It's for my disguise." Hunter continued. "We have it all arranged. You have official credentials as Charlotte Maxwell from Augland 2."

Ashton tried to concentrate as Hunter kept talking and the transmitters sent shocks through her body, but she was getting used to the feeling.

Her cover was official. The Suit's father was Charles Maxwell, a prominent politician who had deep ties to Augland 2. Rye's many attempts to infiltrate Augland had involved impersonating different Suits across various parks. One of his employees had

47

been impersonating Charles through correspondence as a cover for about two years. It made the plan at least plausible.

Hunter flipped through several documents with a swiping movement of his fingers. In the moment of silence, Ashton took a deep breath, hoping to relieve her nerves. It worked for only a moment. Even with Hunter going with her, the thought of going back into Augland on her own felt terrifying.

"Are you sure about this?" Ashton whispered as the man turned away to grab another piece of technology. Hunter had been preoccupied, but he gave her his full attention as she questioned their mission.

He sighed. "Ash, we've been over this. I don't think we have any other options. Do you?"

It wasn't a question. He was being rational, and Ashton was letting her fear and doubts cloud her mind. She knew Hunter was right. She knew he would go in with her, so she wasn't alone. She also knew they may not make it out this time and, silently, they had both accepted that possibility.

They had talked about this countless times during the last two days, but as the minutes crept closer, Ashton became increasingly nervous. Hunter and Rye had every detail of the mission mapped out. They seemed too confident in a plan with so many unknowns.

Hunter and Rye simply expected her to get close to Wolfe and get information. Hunter had mentioned their closeness and his help getting her out of Augland, which made him a perfect target. This was the part of the plan that worried Ashton the most. What if he figured it out? What if she couldn't do it?

She wanted Hunter to promise her everything was going to be okay, to ease some of the tension she felt draped across her chest. She wanted to be strong, independent, and fearless, but deep down, she knew she wanted someone to take away the fear and tell her everything was going to be all right. Even if it wasn't.

Each time the electricity pulsed; Ashton gave a nod of recognition. Test after test. Ashton just sat there. Occasionally, she was asked to do something, say a word, or think of a sensation. She watched as a model of the Suit on a screen began mimicking her thoughts. As time went by, the requests grew more and more obscure. This went on for hours and Ashton was exhausted. Then, suddenly, as she was pretending to eat a strawberry, she tasted it in her mouth: red, juicy, and delicious.

Ashton gasped and the man laughed.

"The transmitters work both ways. You tell the Suit what to do, and the simulators inside the parks send sensations back to you."

The car ride to the boat took two hours. They sat in silence. Georgina followed in a car behind them. Hunter wanted to use his glasses up until the very last moment to review the plan documents and maps. Ashton could tell he was nervous too; he was just better at hiding it than she was.

"I'll try to stay with you as much as I can, but we will get separated." Hunter's fingers swiped through screen after screen, his knee rising and falling in a rapid motion.

Ashton stayed silent. She looked out the window and saw her reflection. Her head was covered by a cap littered with patches. She had been warned not to touch anything on the ride as it could interfere with the transmitter's ability to communicate to the Suit when she was in the pod. NeuroEnergy hadn't quite figured out why the connection between the transmitters on her head and the ones programmed in the Suit failed after five days.

She looked out of the car window, watching the trees as they quickly moved past her—dark, green, and high. The winding road divided the forest as they made their way through the hills. As she watched trees pass behind her reflection, she noticed the dark circles around her eyes. She had hardly slept the last two days, but once she settled into the pod, maybe for once in her life her body would be at rest.

"Wolfe has confirmed your arrival. Rye let me know that they've been in conversation with him since yesterday. Apparently, he's very excited to meet you."

Ashton let out a sigh. She didn't know what made her more nervous—that she would be around Wolfe again or that she was going back to a place she had so desperately tried to escape. Hunter paused and grabbed Ashton's hand.

"We can do this. You and me." He seemed so sure of this plan. Ashton smiled; it was him and her again. Just like it had been before.

Ashton tried to breathe. She had to constantly remind herself why she was doing this. This was for Jagatha. This was for the innocent people of the Colony. They all deserved to live a great life, a life outside the walls of Augland. To grow up and see beauty.

A massive red boat, with white trimming and spanning the canal water line, came into view, and Ashton's eyes darted toward the familiar vessel. She had seen these boats throughout the years, coming onto the shores of Maya Bay and unloading at the dock. There it was: their ride into Augland.

As she stepped out of the car, the cold air sent shivers down Ashton's spine as it breezed over her. Since the transmitters died so quickly, they wanted to wait until the last possible moment to submerge Ashton's body into the goo within the pearly white pod.

The supply boat was too large to come close to the shore, so Rye, Hunter, Ashton, Georgina, Ashton's Suit and the pod rode out to the boat on NeuroEnergy's charter yacht. They sat inside a beautiful gold and white room, on cushioned seats, as they waited to get close to the boat. Hunter and Ashton both shifted in their seats as Georgina sipped on her tea. It felt too nice. Too posh for her and Hunter to be sitting on their nice furniture. It was the first taste of Suit living that Ashton had ever experienced. She straightened her back like Georgina and mimicked her movements. This is how she would have to behave if she was going to convince anyone of her status.

"What you both are doing is quite brave." Georgina broke the silence. "I hope you know if you find out Augland is attempting to make its own energy, we will protect you from Augland. I want you to know you have my word." Ashton wanted to roll her eyes. Like they were protecting the Colony? Like they were protecting Ashton and Hunter by sending them back into Augland? Like there was anything at all NeuroEnergy would do if something went wrong inside the walls of Augland 54?

"Thank you, Georgina, I hope you know how thankful Ashton and I are for your help."

Help. Ashton was disgusted by Hunter's loyalty to Georgina. The woman who sat on snow-white cushions while the Colony felt hunger daily. This wasn't helping.

The motors slowed and the boat bobbed while its anchor fell to the deep sea floor. Georgina didn't move; instead, she sipped her tea again. After a few minutes, they heard loud footsteps above them and coming down the staircase.

"Captain Gerhart, welcome."

Georgina stood and shook the oil-stained hand of the rugged man in front of her. His black and white beard went down to his chest and moved when he walked.

"Georgina. These the stowaways?" Gerhart tilted his head toward Hunter and Ashton. His cigar-smoke-stained clothing filled Ashton's nostrils.

"Yes, and we appreciate your willingness here. I promise full discretion. No one will know what you have done."

"And payment."

Gerhart went right to the point.

"Half now and half when you return. Your men can grab the weapons from the top deck."

Weapons? That was the first Ashton had heard of any trade.

"No promises these two make it back. If they aren't there by next Monday at seven a.m., we leave, and I still get my other half."

"Understood."

That was it. A completed transaction. It was time to board the boat that would shuttle them through the towering glass walls of Augland 54 and onto the Maya Bay beach Ashton knew so well.

"Ashton, it's time." Georgina put her hand on Ashton's shoulder, and she rose. Taking a deep breath, she followed Georgina into the boat's secluded command center. There the shiny and smooth white pod lay open, half-filled with glowing goo. Ashton stared into it and saw her distorted reflection. She took a deep breath. The pod would need to be close to her while they transported into Augland, so she didn't lose the signal. Augland possessed the technology to extend the transmission to the pod outside its walls, but NeuroEnergy hadn't yet acquired this ability. Hunter had said that, once they were in Augland, the transmitters would work wherever she was in the parks as long as her pod and body were in the park.

"See you on the other side," Rye said with a forced cheerfulness as Ashton disrobed to her skin-tight body suit. Sheva's necklace and Wolfe's watch were the only other things she wore until the end. They suggested she take everything off and these were her most prized possessions. She slid off first Wolfe's watch and next Sheva's moonstone necklace, handing them over to Georgina. "I want these back," she said, letting them go into Georgina's palm. The other woman nodded. Ashton slid into the warm goo and lay down while Rye clicked buttons on the pod's control panel.

"All right, time to go under; hold your breath and count to five." Ashton did as she was told and completely submerged herself. It was quiet and the thick liquid surrounded her. Her heart beat rapidly as she tried to calm herself down. She began to panic. It wasn't working; she was going to drown. She was about to get up before they closed the lid, shutting her in. She wasn't strong enough. She wasn't ready.

Then, everything went black.

CHAPTER 9

Ashton

Ashton blinked. Everything around her seemed fuzzy, like she was in a fog. Slowly, the world around her became clear. Dark wood. A musty smell. Sea salt. Oranges, avocados—piles of them. Then pallets of wool, drapes of cloth piled high. It went on for what seemed like forever.

"Where . . ." Ashton began. But before she finished her sentence she remembered where she was—on the large red-and-white ship—and who she was—an elite Suit named Charlotte Maxwell.

Ashton tried to pull herself up.

"Whoa, slow down." Hunter took her arm as Ashton tried to steady herself. Her body felt heavy, almost weighted down. Her breathing began to quicken again as panic set it. Everything seemed . . . not normal. Her mind knew what she wanted; it spoke as a tiny voice in her head, but her body wasn't listening. She lifted her arm, only to lift from her elbow, and her hand fell. The muscles in her stomach tensed as she tried to remember how to pull herself up.

"It's muscle memory. Your Suit is learning how you speak to it. Just be patient." Hunter pulled at her arm to help her up, but he struggled with the weight of the Suit.

"This. doesn't . . . feel . . . right." Ashton could barely get the words out. Everything in her mind worked, but her body didn't understand her commands. Pictures of her environment flashed and stilled, giving her a flip book of the belly of the ship, slowly building momentum as her vision came together.

"You have to give it a second. Calm down and think clearly. What do you want to do?"

Ashton thought about it. She wanted to stand.

"I . . . want to . . . stand." Before she could finish her sentence, her legs moved, and her arms helped her rise. She swayed a little, but Hunter helped her keep her balance. Ashton laughed and heard a different voice come out of her—higher pitched, and soft. Hunter smiled.

"You did it!"

Ashton stared directly at Hunter, who now was eye level with her. Ashton was short and this was new territory for her.

"You're . . . shorter than I remember."

"All right, you're fine." Hunter laughed. "It will just take some getting used to, that's all. Keep working on telling your body what you want it to do and eventually it will seem normal."

Hunter was right; all it took was practicing over and over again for Ashton to start to understand how to control the Suit. Her lengthy limbs danced around as she moved. She looked down at her skin which was porcelain white. She brushed her hands through her red hair that came just below her shoulder and straightened out the wrinkles on her cream-colored pencil skirt and white, flowy blouse. While she still felt the difference, it was at least easier to cope with than she had originally thought. She actually enjoyed it.

"Okay, so who are you again?" Hunter quizzed Ashton as she practiced walking in circles. She stretched her muscles and felt the ease of movement.

"Charlotte Maxwell."

"And who is your father?"

"Charles Maxwell, the esteemed politician of Augland 2."

"And who am I?"

"Alonso, my trusty right-hand mustached worker who does everything for me," Ashton teased. Hunter laughed.

"And what do you need to do when you are there?"

"I need to get Wolfe to tell me Warren's plans to develop their own energy source." Rye had told them that Wolfe had been promoted to Head of Security, but that was all the information they had. Augland kept security tight, and information was hard to come by.

"We need proof. Something we can bring back to NeuroEnergy." Hunter pulled on Ashton's synthetic arm and put a bracelet around her wrist.

"A recording device." Ashton studied the dainty pearl encrusted bracelet. "You just need Wolfe to talk."

Georgina had mentioned that they had some sort of device to track Ashton. It was clever to disguise it as a bracelet.

"So, you'll go to the Center first?" Ashton quizzed Hunter in return.

"Yes, I hope they will be there. Then try the cages if I can get there." The Augland Center was only for young workers, most likely where the kids under five would be, but the older ones could have been sent to the cages. Ashton wouldn't be given a tour of either the Center or the cages. The Executives never exposed Suits to the inner workings of the parks.

A horn sounded off in the distance, interrupting Hunter.

"We're approaching Maya Bay. We need to get up to the visitor center now."

Ashton's heart leaped out of her chest.

"Am I presentable?"

"Yes, you look just like them." Ashton exhaled. She tried to feel like Freya again. That was what she needed now. The red hair felt familiar; Hunter was right, the irony that her Suit and her character both shared that similar physical trait was not lost on her. At the same time, it brought her shame. Why couldn't she feel this powerful as just Ashton? Why did she need to wear a mask?

As they made their way to the top deck of the supply boat, Ashton passed by her reflection in the window just as the dome of Augland 54 appeared in the distance. Her eyes glistened blue and her perfectly curled maroon-red hair flowed freely, just like Freya. Her smile was picture perfect with white, glistening teeth; her cheek bones prominent. She looked so different, but she could see herself in the eyes. The Suit was beautiful and that gave her confidence. Instantly, she straightened. *Show time.*

The sun glistened through the windows, and, for the first time, Ashton felt the Suit's temperature gauge and experienced the warmth. The sun beat down on her face and she closed her eyes as the rays of sun warmed her—another perk of the artificial atmosphere and the Suit's intelligence creating the perfect blend for Ashton's senses. It was not the same for Hunter, who could only feel the cool fifty-two degrees of the Pacific Northwest. The sea breeze smelled salty, but sweet. This was not the Maya Bay she remembered. This was paradise.

Ashton closed her eyes as the warm weather prickled at her skin. The sun shone down on the flawless beach and crystal-blue water. Upbeat music played in the distance, becoming louder as they grew closer to the shores near the resorts.

Hunter shivered as the breeze from the boat chilled him. He wore something similar to what he'd worn in Victorian: an all-black pantsuit with a white shirt and black tie. He kept his long hair slicked back in a ponytail. Ashton looked at him and she knew his disguise would work. He looked nothing like the Hunter Wolfe had known in Land of Legends.

"We've got this," Hunter muttered to Ashton as he quickly squeezed her hand in secret. They were both nervous. This could get them killed. This could be their end.

A charter boat danced above the waves as it met the vessel to escort Hunter and Ashton to shore, with Ashton's pod secured in a special storage compartment. When they arrived, workers would take it to the outer rim of Predator's Biome, where an enclosed area housed the pods, somewhere the workers and Suits called "the spa." She quickly glanced at the shiny white pod, knowing her body was submerged somewhere in there. It was both frightening and foreign to her.

Hunter helped her out of the boat as it rocked on the sandy shore of Maya Bay. They made it to solid ground and, as she turned, she saw the red-and-white boat depart. This was it. They were back in Augland, and it hadn't changed; it was the same prison she remembered. But she had to play her part. This time, she was a Suit, someone here to bathe in luxury and see workers as little more than an inconvenience.

Several workers were waiting on the shore with flowers and a tropical drink. They greeted Ashton as she approached. Ashton smiled sheepishly as the world became centered around her.

"Welcome! We are so thrilled to have you here, Charlotte," said a familiar voice. Ashton turned to see a man in a tux walking straight for her. For a moment she recoiled but caught herself. She wasn't Ashton; she was a Suit named Charlotte.

"My name is Wolfgang, CEO of Augland 54. It is a great pleasure to meet you."

Part II

CHAPTER 10

Wolfe
Six Months Earlier

W olfe pressed his back against the elevator wall as the metal box soared upward. He took a deep breath as the elevator began its ascent to the top of the Columbia Building on Hollywood Boulevard.

It had been a long day of drawn-out meetings that could have been five-minute conversations, and Wolfe's displeasure with corporate bureaucracy was bringing out his short temper. There were so many changes Wolfe wanted to make to reform the injustice and flat-out violence of Augland 54, but he was surrounded by the insignificant dilemmas of the Executives. It had only been a week, and he was exhausted. *Patience,* he thought. He needed to be careful and strategic.

Seven days had passed since Ashton's escape from the suffocating snarls of Augland 54 and Wolfe's promotion to Head of Security. Ashton was safe, and so was the Colony, but her escape and the relocation of the Colony made Wolfe's new position difficult. Four people had escaped, one more than he had anticipated, which garnered extra attention, given the young girl's age. *Jagatha.* Wolfe recounted her name. He had to crack down on security and punish the collaborators to gain Warren's trust so he would hand Wolfe more power. That had been the plan anyway, but Warren had his fingers interlaced in all of Wolfe's decisions, making it increasingly difficult for Wolfe to distance himself from his father's micromanagement.

Now, it was time for the second phase of Wolfe's plan—cast doubt on Warren's ability to run Augland 54 and convince the Executives of Wolfe's ability. Luckily, everything that had happened with Ashton and the Colony had begun to work for Wolfe. For the first time, workers had escaped and even destroyed a Suit, all under Warren's leadership. On top of that, the Colony had moved without Warren's knowledge, making his plans for the Colony that much harder to achieve.

Warren had reservations about Wolfe's involvement but would have trouble convincing the Executives without proof. Warren's beloved security man and interrogator, Brock, had been blamed for the escape.

Whispers were circling that despite the youthful appearance of Warren's Suit's, he was getting too old to lead. Warren continued to sweep these worries under the rug with promises of future plans; Land of Legends was only the beginning. But he was losing control and he knew it.

As the elevator rose, Wolfe went over the Executive board members in his head. They held all the power in Augland 54 and were the ones he needed to convince.

Wolfe knew Wintefred was a widow, old and bored with her mundane life, who appreciated male company. Her inherited title— Head of Development for Corporate Strategy—after her husband's passing had increased her sense of superiority as the only female Executive. She consistently upgraded her Suit to the latest trends, which made her, at times, unrecognizable. However, her nose in the air gave her away every time.

Lee was a follower. He never spoke his mind and preferred to blend in behind the scenes. His lengthy body with broad shoulders and curly locks gave him an approachable look, no doubt manufactured to look that way. If Executive titles were people, he was his title: Vice President of Customer Experience.

Reuben, Head of Operations, was Warren's right-hand man and long-time friend. Warren and Reuben fought like brothers, but Reuben always bent to Warren's will. For most of his life, Wolfe had looked to Reuben as an uncle. That was until he learned of his father's dictatorship and Reuben's acceptance of Warren's corruption. Wolfe hadn't directly spoken to Reuben in nearly five years.

Wolfe didn't know much about Sebastian, the Head of Supply Chain, because he separated himself from the Executive pack. He was much older and quieter than the rest.

As Head of Marketing, Boren was a talker, especially after a few whiskeys and cigars. He couldn't help but expose all the skeletons hidden in everyone else's closet. Boren would be Wolfe's first target. If he wanted any information to get around the office, it would need to come from someone like Boren.

Wolfe stepped off the elevator into the "Sky High" lounge, the most prominent club on Hollywood Boulevard, located on the top floor of the skyscraper once known as the Columbia Tower in downtown then-Seattle.

Piano notes rang in the distance, and the mimicked cigar smoke fogged the air. Men sat around the lounge smoking expensive-looking cigars. As the only Suit-less Executive in the room, Wolfe was the only one who could smoke a cigar—and the only one affected by the ashy smoke left in the air.

The clinking of glasses pulled Wolfe's attention to the long row of chairs in front of a glass case of liquor overlooking the city lights against the night sky. Boren was alone, just as Wolfe had hoped. He strutted down the stairs and over to the hunched man with broad shoulders and muscles that appeared about to rip through his neatly pressed shirt. Wolfe was not intimidated by the man's size; he knew the muscles were simply a Suit modification. However, just because the muscles were machine-made didn't make them any less strong.

Wolfe loosened his tie, breathing a sigh of relief. He missed the days, just weeks earlier, before his promotion to Head of Security, when he could wear what he wanted, but Executive culture was strictly business attire.

"Boren, what a pleasure to see you here."

"Wolfe!" Boren swayed as the liquor sensors in his Suit's brain considered the amount of alcohol in his system. Even drunkenness could be imitated for the Suits; of course, it never came with a hangover.

"Care if I join you?" Wolfe motioned to the seat beside Boren.

"Of course!"

Wolfe sat down.

"My apologies. I never congratulated you on your promotion to Head of Security. I never doubted you!" Boren swung his drink and spilled liquid onto the dark glossy wood of the bar.

"Hey . . . Hey!" Boren said, looking around for the bartender. "I need a round of drinks for my new colleague . . . and friend. The good stuff." Boren shook Wolfe's shoulder. Wolfe grinned at his very intoxicated coworker.

The bartender brought several rounds of drinks out to Boren and Wolfe. Wolfe smiled sympathetically at the haggard-looking worker, wondering how long his shift was, but Boren didn't seem to notice the worker at all. The worker was just part of the woodwork.

"I remember when you were just a boy," Boren slurred. "And your mother, oh, what is her name?" Wolfe tensed, tightening his grip on the glass.

"Anastasia."

"Right! Oh my, what a looker she was, even out of her Suit." He nudged Wolfe. "She was chasing you down the halls of the Executive offices. You must have been six or seven and butt naked!" Boren exhaled a hearty laugh. Wolfe smiled politely. He wanted to appease the man but needed to be seen as a fellow Executive, not a naked child running down the halls chased by his mother.

After Wolfe was born, Anastasia, his mother, had decided not to return to her Suit. This shocked everyone, especially Warren who was climbing the ranks to CEO. Rejecting a Suit was unheard of; you either had to be crazy or part of the antihumanism movement and neither was a good look for the spouse of the future CEO.

When he was young, Wolfe had always thought the reason his mother remained Suit-less was because she wanted the memories Wolfe had of her to be real, not a memory of a mechanical face. Anastasia had instilled in Wolfe the dangers of living in a false reality.

"Integrity is everything, and part of that is being honest with yourself," she used to repeat to Wolfe. She made him promise to never be in a Suit. She was a silent woman but powerful, and Wolfe trusted her judgment.

Anastasia's downfall was her honesty. She hated the political and corporate rules of Auglands and the AEC alike, but nevertheless recognized the importance of laws in a strong society. But in the posthuman society, she feared what Warren would do if her views were openly exposed. In public, she would smile silently, even while holding vicious secrets that could expose the deep darkness of Warren's colleagues.

Anastasia was day to Warren's night. Their differences had caused them to gravitate toward one another, but soon after Wolfe's birth had become their divide. Warren blamed Wolfe.

While Warren climbed the corporate ladder, Anastasia made her own allies. There was a secret small subset of high-ranking individuals who were concerned about the new posthuman society. They were concerned for human existence with such a technology-fueled lifestyle and the sociologic decay that could result from a dissociation of mind and body. In their own ways, they resisted the Suits and the AEC and some, like Anastasia, went so far as to reject a Suit altogether.

Warren was more concerned that she might hurt his career, so he tucked her away from others so they wouldn't know of her views. She complied rather than fought against him. Warren claimed it was because he still loved her and didn't want others to judge or get the wrong idea, but Wolfe knew that love didn't act like Warren did. He wanted to control her.

Warren had spouted his venom about Wolfe's mother to anyone who would listen, insinuating her deteriorating cognitive state. His father taught him, "Fists only leave a bruise for a few days. Words can change reality." Warren had stripped his wife of her pride, truth, and power. Wolfe didn't wonder why after having a child, she had hidden herself away from it all.

"I miss having kids around the office," Boren continued, jolting Wolfe from thoughts of his mother and back to Boren's conversation. "You know, Martha and I thought about adopting one of those Colony kids. Of course, Warren said no."

"Why?" Wolfe was only half-interested. Boren would soon be too inebriated to be any good to him, and he would need to figure out how he could leave.

"Well," Boren leaned in conspiratorially, "ever since he found out about the infertility . . ."

Wolfe snapped to attention. Maybe Boren would spill some useful information after all. Wolfe needed to tread carefully. The man was drunk, but if he realized he was sharing information Wolfe wasn't supposed to know, he might clam up.

"Yes, I was talking with Warren about that the other day," Wolfe ventured, hoping to fish out more information.

"Warren knows my wife and I can't have children, but wouldn't they be gorgeous?" The man motioned to his toned body and let out an obnoxious laugh at his joke. Wolfe shook his head; he had no idea what Boren's children would look like because Boren's real body was suspended somewhere in a pod.

Boren slurred, "Warren is hoarding them all for his new parks. He won't let me have just one." Boren slammed his drink down. Instantaneously, the bartender cleaned up the mess and refilled the man's cup.

Wolfe didn't care about this Suit's deranged desire to steal a child. Boren had mentioned the children stolen from the Colony, and Wolfe had to find out more. Maybe he would find out something valuable he could tell Cahya and Ashton. The thought of Ashton reminded Wolfe of the importance of his mission and his patience dissolved.

Wolfe ventured into dangerous territory, "You mentioned the Colony kids. Do you know why Warren is so hell-bent on stealing them?"

Boren whispered conspiratorially, "With this infertility, we are running out of workers. He's buying time until there's a cure."

Wolfe raised his eyebrows, encouraging the man to keep spilling his slurred words.

"Yeah, you know, they can't have children. The augmented bodies," he gestured to his muscled arms, "they omit something. I don't know how it works. But what can

63

you do? I guess Martha and I aren't meant to have children of our own."

Wolfe dismissed Boren's last comment. All Boren and his wife needed to do to have a child was to come out of their Suits, but they would never do that. After decades of being young and protected, they would never consider life outside a Suit.

"It's sad, of course, but we will manage."

Boren mistook Wolfe's silent astonishment as sympathy for Warren's refusal to let Boren steal a child for himself. But Wolfe's mind was reeling. How had he never heard of the infertility? If it affects those outside Suits, does that mean him? Ashton? If this were true, it made his father's insistence that Wolfe get a Suit make sense, as did Warren's plans to steal children from outside these walls and his disregard for the lives of the workers in Land of Legends.

Wolfe felt sick to his stomach. He needed to talk to Cahya. But right now, he still had a mission and would take any opportunity he could to cast doubt on Warren's leadership.

"I just don't think it's fair, Boren. You and Martha, you're both prestigious members of Augland 54. You've sacrificed a lot of time running and managing Augland business." Wolfe saw the wheels begin to turn as he planted anger in the Executive's mind. "The only thing that would make Martha happy is a baby, just one baby . . . It seems a bit, I don't know, unfair that Warren won't give you a child. That's just me, though."

Boren took a swig of his caramel liquid. "You know, you're right! I've sacrificed a lot for Augland 54, serving your father faithfully, getting him more prestige and power. And this is the thanks I get?"

"I'm sure he doesn't know how important it is to you." Wolfe was playing innocent.

"Oh, no, Warren knows! He knows this is the only thing we want. That . . ." Boren struggled to find the words.

Wolfe motioned for the bartender, who was standing dazed in front of the glassware. Wolfe had noticed his shifting eyes as they spoke about infertility and wondered if the worker had known. Workers had a knack for staying in the background while listening intently for information to spread among themselves. Any worker who had access to Executives had done so by keeping the secrets to themselves and being rewarded for their discretion, knowing full well the hand that fed them.

"Another one for my friend."

Boren gave a side glance to Wolfe and smiled. "Bet ya wished you would have listened to your father now."

Wolfe looked perplexed.

64

"Could have avoided this by getting into an android. Oh well, I'm sure they will find a way to help you have kids of your own someday."

It did not take long to get from the Columbia Tower bar to the front steps of the Executive offices. Wolfe stormed out of the elevator doors. His eyes were on the large oak doors that led to his parents' penthouse suite at the top of the Space Needle, just below the long-stemmed needle leading to the sphere above. The Executives had converted the second story of the circular building into six penthouses for each one of the board members and their families.

Wolfe pounded on his father's door, and the echo shook the otherwise silent hallway. Next, he rang the intercom, pushing it harder than needed. He wanted his father's attention, and he wanted it now. His fists balled as he waited and rocked in his uncomfortable leather oxfords.

To the right of the door to his father's apartment in the suite, Wolfe could see his mother's door. He hoped his pounding hadn't woken her.

"What?!" The sound of Warren's voice shouted through the intercom.

"I need to speak with you. Now."

Warren sighed before pushing a button to release the lock on the double oak doors. Wolfe didn't wait before pushing himself through. Warren stood in his vast living room, wrapped in a white silk robe. He poured himself a drink and sat in the middle of a giant leather sofa. He perceived his son was upset and was taking his time on purpose.

"Now, what is this about, Wolfgang?"

His father's patronizing gaze infuriated Wolfe further.

"The Suits cause infertility? When were you going to tell me?" Wolfe's rage didn't allow him to sit down. He wanted the high ground.

"Oh, calm down and stop being so dramatic."

"Dramatic?! Wow, you're delusional."

"It was your decision not to be in an android, and that was before we knew anything about the effects of their radiation on the human bodies around them. I didn't think the information would change your mind. You really are so stubborn sometimes."

"You didn't think to tell me?"

"I mean, you got what you wanted, right? To live a true life, a real one? Well. Welcome to the real world, Wolfgang."

Wolfe was at a loss for words, seething with anger at his father, who was twisting the narrative again to justify his actions.

"You're . . ." Wolfe began, unsure of what he would say next.

"I'm just as devastated as you, Wolfgang. To think I won't have an heir to be proud of someday, to take on the legacy I've worked my entire life to perfect."

The words stung. Even though Wolfe didn't want the legacy his father spoke of, his father's ruthless words cut deeply.

"Go to bed. No sense in wallowing in things we can't change." Warren turned, leaving Wolfe in the darkness of the cold living room.

As quickly as the heat had overtaken Wolfe, a cold washed over him. He would need to process this information later, alone, where he could think. He needed to compartmentalize this information and use it to protect those he cared about: the Colony, Ashton, and the children.

Land of Legends was dark and silent. A slight metallic smell filled the night. The clanking of metal still reverberated through the air, and blood clotted the grass. Wolfe felt a visceral unrest as he strolled through the battlegrounds. Before his promotion, Wolfe had suggested a new park to help rehabilitate workers needing discipline. Of course, Warren had molded his idea into something much more sinister: a park that killed workers for the amusement of the elite. Now his memories haunted him.

The trees swayed as a gust of wind made Wolfe shiver. He walked along the battlefield between the castle and the Viking camp. Not much had changed since the previous week. Wolfe hadn't been to a production since Ashton had destroyed a Suit right there in Land of Legends and escaped. Land of Legends had a new Freya now, and a new Queen of the Saxons; the show went on.

From what Jorgeon, Wolfe's assistant at Land of Legends, had said, they'd had a hard time convincing Suits to try out the park after the rumor spread that a worker had destroyed a Suit. Since the relaunch and a remarkable marketing effort, reviews of the Viking-Saxon re-enactment park had been successful. They'd had back-to-back productions all week.

Before long, Wolfe had reached the secluded rock behind the battlefield bordering the forest, the spot where he and Ashton had found their solace. It felt lonely now without her, but it was private.

Wolfe pulled out a thin piece of glass framed with a black line, his personal interconnect, and landed on the channel he had created to communicate with Cahya, one he knew no one would use. He had given it to Cahya on his last visit when he'd had to bring Ashton back to Augland 54 and into the depths of Augland's belly—the cages.

"Cahya." Wolfe waited.

". . . Wolfe?" The familiar voice of Cahya reported back. Wolfe sighed in relief.

"Did you make it okay?" he asked, knowing full well they had made it to the old resort on the shores of the Hood Canal.

"Yes, we are fine. It's late, Wolfe. What's happened?"

"Cahya, Warren . . ." Wolfe didn't know where to begin. He took a deep breath. "The Suits make women and men infertile. That is why Augland takes the children. The Suits make the workers, me, us, infertile. That is why they need Colony bodies." He added as an afterthought, "They aren't going to stop."

There was silence as Wolfe was sure Cahya was processing the news.

"So, they will come here for us?" Cahya's voice shook as she waited for Wolfe. She already knew the answer. "How long do we have?" It was a fair question and one that Wolfe didn't have an answer to just yet.

"I don't know, but Warren will find you, and his troops will come again. I'll try to give you a warning, but you have to prepare for the worst."

It pained Wolfe to give such directions. He knew that when Augland made their move—and they would—the Colony had no hope. Wolfe had finally connected the missing pieces he had been trying to piece together for so long. Warren didn't want to get rid of the Colony because he *needed* them to have children, away from the Suits, before taking them. The only thing Wolfe could do was to give the Colony some time to defend themselves.

There was no answer.

"Cahya, did you hear me?" he asked.

"Yes, yes, I did. Thank you, Wolfe." Cahya's voice was strong, but he could tell the news shook her.

He wanted to ask about Ashton but knew he shouldn't. This was bigger than just him and Ashton. Much bigger. Besides, knowing would be to bring up old feelings, feelings he wasn't prepared to think about.

"And, Wolfe . . ."

"Yeah?"

"She's fine."

Wolfe felt a sudden change in his stance, an instant relief.

"Thanks, Cahya. Take care."

CHAPTER 11

Wolfe
Four Months Earlier

Warren stood front and center of the Executive conference room, surrounded by a large oval table and leather-backed chairs. Daylight streamed through the sphere enclosing the Executive offices. Before the dome of Augland 54 was built, Seattle had been primarily gray and rainy, but under the dome, the city always had perfect weather.

Wolfe's problem remained; even disgruntled, the Executives feared Warren's impulsive behavior and power. These Suits ran the day-to-day operations of Augland 54, but none were directly affected by their operational choices. The Executives hardly even noticed the workers, who were part of the machinery of Augland as far as they were concerned.

So, the Executives let Warren's cruelty slide. Wolfe hadn't expected the cowardice these five powerful, but pitiful, Executives showed inside and out of the boardroom. It was no wonder Warren had gotten away with murder through the years. The corporate sheep turned a blind eye to the madness.

"I've come today with news—news I couldn't be happier about supporting," Warren boomed, standing while Wolfe and the board sat. Warren enjoyed feeling tall and invincible in his lofty and muscular Suit with a salt and pepper goatee.

"I've had this project under wraps for some time, and I can't divulge all the information now, but I'm happy to announce my support with our new Augland 54 customer service initiative."

Warren lifted his arms as if welcoming a new child into the world.

"We will begin to heighten our workers' capabilities to provide the best customer service experience. With this advancement, their every move will be tracked, recorded, and their ability to better serve our customers enhanced—all with the latest and greatest technology. We will be at the forefront of all that Augland has to offer, and it will start here, at Augland 54."

Warren pressed a button on a device he had been holding. Small pixels formed on the center of the marbled white oval table. The illustration formed into a 3D version of a young woman. Her eyes were icy blue, then shifted to a glowing white with a thin black line circling the iris.

"Countless surveys have suggested that workers are essential to the framework of Auglands. Customers want to feel the reality of the park, and that means having real people waiting on them. As you can see, here we have a typical worker, but what you don't know is her enhanced eyes can see customer ID numbers, their likes and dislikes, and their request sheet, if applicable."

The 3D artificial intelligence model rotated as Warren spoke. A glowing speck on the back of the model's head appeared and glowed brightly. "We have also implanted small chips that will give suggestive terminology for customers, aligning with their typical activity and desires . . ."

The chip pulsed as it glowed. The model spoke, "Would you like me to schedule a tennis match for this afternoon, Warren?"

Wolfe's eyes grew wide as he stared at the 3D model. His breath caught as she rotated around, reminding him of workers he knew and cared for. A flash of Ashton's face replaced the model. Her eyes turned gray, and her mind cleared of all resistance—her very existence stripped from her. Wolfe shivered. This had to be the most diabolical of everything Warren had ever come up with.

"This solves everything. We will no longer have worker disobedience or customer satisfaction issues because we have created the perfect workers. Real *and* enhanced." Wolfe looked around, reading the room. Each Executive was deep in thought as they hung on Warren's words, taking in the technology without understanding the ramifications.

"It will depress the need for our workers to sleep and eliminate any impulses they have for insubordination." Warren spoke like he had perfected a product malfunction.

Boren, who sat next to Wolfe, was leaning in, lapping up Warren's words. Lee slowly began to clap. The others followed.

"Well done, Warren." Wintefred beamed.

Wolfe's mouth gaped as he tried to compose himself. Warren was talking about implanting some sort of customer service chips into workers' minds and eyes. This was insanity.

Wolfe had to think quickly. If the Executives thought this was a good idea, it could help Warren's cause stay in power. The board was easily swayed, and Warren used it to his advantage.

Wolfe needed to expose a negative to Warren's plan. He knew what most Executives cared about. Pulling at their fabricated heartstrings for the poor workers that would need to endure this new technology would not work. Executives cared about power and being served—*they deserve to live a great life*—and increasingly, it seemed that the workers deserved nothing.

"Has the AEC approved this budget? You know the reason why we hadn't incorporated AI before was the cost. Workers, as they are, are much cheaper."

Sebastian, an older Executive, spoke up. He rarely said anything and was past his prime, although his Suit left him perpetually in his thirties. While Wolfe had gotten used to old men looking young, an air of "I know more because I've seen more" hung over the older Executives. Sebastian should have retired but refused to leave.

The room went quiet as Warren's smile soon faded.

"Preliminary testing, yes. Once they see it in action, they will no doubt approve. Just like Land of Legends."

"And what does this cost us? What supplies must we trade to get the material needed for this new technology?" Sebastian's questions weren't out of line. He oversaw the supply chain and procurement for everything in Augland.

Warren's fists tightened and he took in a deep breath to help control his clear annoyance with Sebastian's line of questioning. "Not nearly as much as you would assume, dear friend. The small cost of resources is essential. We've already begun testing and have had outstanding results."

"You mean to say you've already started? Without the Executive vote?" Wolfe blurted before thinking about what he was saying and to whom he was saying it.

The five Executives began to whisper among themselves. Boren moved closer to Wolfe and leaned back in his chair. Wolfe instantly rolled his chair a few inches away, thinking of the radiation emitted from the Suits that caused the infertility. What am I doing? I've been around Suits my whole life; a few inches won't make any difference.

Warren gazed narrowly at his son. Wolfe was stepping into territory his father would lecture him about later.

"Testing is just to prove viability, nothing more. I, of course, wouldn't dream of executing anything this big without the support of this room."

Warren was a master of manipulation, and Wolfe saw right through it.

"And what do these results look like?" Wolfe asked. He knew he was pushing his boundaries, but he couldn't help it. "Customer surveys have always indicated that they prefer real humans, not the bionic androids."

It was true; the surveys had, in fact, demonstrated what Wolfe said. Suits preferred to live in the real world, but not with unreal things, which is why they transferred all bionic androids to engineer and manufacturing stations.

"We—we initially had some hiccups, but those are being worked out. We currently have three successful implants. And you can hardly tell the difference . . ."

"And how many workers did we lose?" Boren was being bold, but Wolfe presumed that his conversation from the Sky High bar still rattled in his mind. Warren had told him he couldn't have his own child, but he was willing to test new technology on them.

"Some could not handle it, but we learned from the mistakes made." Warren's eyes shifted from one Executive member to the next as he tried to control the room. "I think we are missing the bigger picture here. We are innovators. Augland 54 will go down in history as the first Augland to become technology-forward with the highest-ranking customer satisfaction. We could be an elite park. We may lose a little along the way, but the investments we make in this room today will give us our bright future."

Wolfe had to give it to Warren: his father had a way of taking the most heinous theory and turning it into a plausible idea. Wolfe stared around the room. Wintefred seemed to admire Warren's drive. Lee played with his stylus, deep in thought. Boren and Sebastian scowled. Rueben, Warren's right-hand man and Head of Operations, gave an obligatory approving nod in support.

"So, you're throwing away more workers . . ." Wolfe used Boren's disagreement to his advantage. He needed more disagreement from the others.

"Not throwing away, and I've said this before, we can always get more workers."

"You are being frivolous with our resources." Boren was playing with fire, but Wolfe had lit the flame.

For the next three hours, the Executives argued among themselves. Boren, Wolfe, and Sebastian against Warren, Wintefred, Lee, and Rueben.

"All right, all right! I think that is all we will get accomplished today. We need to break from this and revisit it later." Warren smiled. "Boren, how about we go for a round of golf? And Lee and Sebastian, I recall that Maya Bay's luau is tonight. It would be great for us to get out and have some fun."

The tension in the room quickly subsided as Warren's ability to alleviate the conflict dissipated any frustration. Wolfe's smile faded. Warren was diverting. Wolfe had seen this time and time again from Warren. He had perfected his manipulation craft over the years, and all the Executives consistently and predictably fell into his trap.

Warren's eyes shifted until they rested on Wolfe. Wolfe knew his father well enough to see the open threat he was making as if spelled in capital letters on the boardroom table. Warren's bright eyes mocked Wolfe as he relished the failure of Wolfe's feeble attempt to gain allies. Distrust built its impenetrable walls between them. Warren would keep his eyes on Wolfe at every turn.

With a sinking feeling, Wolfe knew his scheme would be much harder to complete than he initially thought. It would take so much more than just discontent within the Executive office. It would take a miracle to replace Warren as CEO.

CHAPTER 12

Ashton

SATURDAY 9:37 a.m.

Ashton was becoming more comfortable as Charlotte. Her biosynthetic feet sank deep into the warm, white sand. She had returned to Maya Bay, but it was a different Maya Bay than the one she had known as a worker. This time, the world was programmed for her. She could not only see the artificial sun but also feel it on her synthetic skin. The façades of the resorts and restaurants stretched out in front of her, and the gentle lapping waves behind. Walking was effortless, and the euphoric feeling of this tropical heaven was intoxicating. From this side, it was paradise.

But Ashton had lived behind the scenes: emerging from the gray train behind the resorts to enter The Hook restaurant from the back to work long, grueling hours. She had never felt the false sun. The bitter reality of the Pacific Northwest weather was still real for those without a Suit. Ashton remembered when her manager at The Hook, Marius, had made her do beach duty in the damp cold when she showed up to work late with a purple bruise covering half her face. The Augland guards had done that to her when they took Sheva. She couldn't think about that now. *Stay focused,* she internally reprimanded herself.

As she took another step under the artificial sun in her tall, gorgeous body, Ashton remembered how her back had ached after combing the beach for trash carelessly discarded by Suits. She had been so cold her body had convulsed. It could be that cold today, but she would never know.

The wind blew as the sound of crashing waves disrupted her memories. Ashton needed to stay in the present. She was Charlotte, a Suit used to paradise.

Hunter and Ashton walked up the sloped sand, away from the boat that had dropped them off at Augland's door. Workers greeted them, surrounding Ashton and relegating Hunter to the back. They handed Ashton a multi-colored blended beverage and flower-encrusted necklace that engulfed her with the scent of sweet gardenias and hibiscus flowers. If Ashton was honest, it was all very overwhelming.

"Charlotte." Ashton heard her new name and turned to see Wolfe among the beautiful chaos surrounding her. His smile was bright and his stoic features prominent as he strode past the Maya Bay workers and headed directly for Ashton—or Charlotte.

Wolfe reached out his arm to shake her hand. Ashton's heart stopped, and she didn't know how to react for a moment. It had been so long since she had seen him up close. The last time she had seen him, he had strutted across the Colony grounds with his Augland army, but even then, she hadn't looked him in the eyes. He looked exactly how she remembered him in her dreams: tall, with short, mahogany-brown hair on the sides and longer hair on top of his head. He had a short beard, just enough to surround his face with a dark shadow.

Hunter nudged Ashton, bringing her attention back to the illusion of Maya Bay. "I'm sorry?" was all she could muster.

"Hello, Ms. Charlotte. My name is Wolfgang; I'm CEO of Augland 54. I wanted to ensure you received a proper welcome to our parks."

Ashton's mind went numb as she processed Wolfe's words. His outstretched hand awaited hers. Her mind reeled, and her ears thundered as she processed. She had found out from Georgina that Wolfe had been promoted to Head of Security, but the news of his promotion to CEO was new. *Why am I even here? If he is CEO, he can change things now as we planned.*

But, if what Wolfe said was true, he should have ended the tyranny. He would have sent word to Cahya that they did not need to fear the wrath of Augland 54. Everything should have stopped: taking children, worker prisons, and the power struggles between Augland and NeuroEnergy. But she had seen Wolfe just days ago, apparently as CEO, march into the Colony and steal children.

Ashton's heart sank as the evil entanglement of betrayal wrapped around her, tightening its grip as her false reality of Wolfe crumbled. Could he have been this evil all along? Had his relationship with the Colony been fake? His relationship with her? If NeuroEnergy had no idea Wolfe was CEO, what else had they missed while prepping for this mission?

Wolfe dropped his hand in the awkward moment. Hunter nudged her again.

"Oh, um, I'm—I'm Charlotte."

Wolfe laughed. He had already said her name.

"Well, Charlotte, I'd love to show you around if that suits you." Ashton studied him. She couldn't take her eyes off him. He was there, standing right there in front of her as the CEO of Augland 54.

"Sure. I mean, yes, of course." She needed to pull herself together. She was Charlotte Maxwell from Augland 2 and used to fraternizing with Executives.

"Alonso, I'll be traveling with Wolfgang. Please ensure my bags and pod are attended to."

"Yes, no problem, Ms. Charlotte."

After all the years she'd spent around Suits, Ashton knew how to mimic their posh speaking. She wasn't sure it had come out as eloquently as she hoped, but it should work.

"Shall we?" Wolfe reached out his arm. To be leaving Hunter so soon did not feel smart, but this was her chance. Wolfe meeting them at Maya Bay was unexpected, but it brought them exactly where they needed to be: in proximity to the CEO.

Ashton was sure her anxiety was making her hands sweat, but as she nervously intertwined her fingers, they were dry. It seemed the perks of being a Suit were endless.

She accepted Wolfe's arm, and his thumb grazed the hand of her Suit. She wanted to feel a surge of electricity, a warmth that felt normal, but one thing Suit technology couldn't replicate was human touch.

Wolfe guided her toward the center of the beautiful Maya Bay Resorts. The largest and most elegant of the four resorts sat on the far left, cradled between the sandy beach and a rocky cliff that separated it from the rest of the bay.

They stepped off the beach onto the resort's paved walkway. Palm trees lined the outer edges of a pool, creating a small oasis reminiscent of a tropical jungle, except this jungle had tassel-lined umbrellas and lush-pillowed pool chairs. Suits danced along the pool's edges as the makeshift sun beat down on them, laughing as they sipped on their flower-topped pineapple drinks.

"You look radiant."

Ashton caught Wolfe staring at her and blushed. She wondered if the transmitters could sense that and would make her Suit turn red for Wolfe to see. Wolfe sounded different, but then again, she wasn't a worker. This could be how he spoke to upper-class customers.

Ashton cleared her throat.

"I didn't expect the CEO to greet me when I arrived."

"Well, only when we have someone of your stature do I make the time to give a warm welcome. I'm sure your father would insist I take good care of you." Wolfe smiled. Charlotte returned his charming smile. While it broke Ashton's heart to see Wolfe flirting, she would make sure Charlotte played his game.

"Where are you taking me?"

Ashton also didn't want Wolfe asking too many questions about Charles, her "father." While she and Hunter had obtained some information, she feared missing important details that would give her ruse away, especially since they had missed Wolfe becoming CEO.

"Well, I thought I'd give you a tour of the Executive offices, then to wherever you'd like to stay. We've got several options: the Chateau Sandcastle in Atlantis, the Maya Bay Resorts, or the bungalows at Predator's Biome." He gestured extravagantly. "And tomorrow, I'd love to show you our latest attraction: Land of Legends. It's been a great hit with prominent figures of Augland 54."

Wolfe spoke fast, barely pausing for Ashton to say anything. Not that she minded; she wouldn't even know what to talk about.

Ashton and Wolfe walked along the winding sidewalk and through the Maya Bay resort. While she paid close attention to Wolfe's words, she couldn't help but marvel at the scenery. This was the first time she had experienced Maya Bay's resorts. Ashton had seen it from afar while she was a waiter at The Hook, but would never have been able to stroll through the grounds like she was now.

When Ashton was a worker, life at The Hook had been consistent; the last time she remembered things being normal. She went to work every day and spent time with Niall, whom she had known most of her life. They'd met in Victorian when they were children. He was only a few years older than Ashton but had helped mentor her. Over the years, he became like a brother: comforting her in times of need, making her laugh, and making the Augland workdays more bearable.

Then Sheva was abducted that day on the train, and everything changed. And now she was back at Maya Bay—this time, as a Suit.

The resort around her was immaculate—long marble pillars wrapped with foliage and bright, beautiful flowers that contrasted nicely against the white and gold.

Inside was even grander, wide-open spaces with chandeliers that dangled with crystals. Ashton took it all in, and excitement raced through her. She felt important, and it was intoxicating. Everyone looked at her while she walked with Wolfe. She didn't look much different than any of them, but she was arm-in-arm with the CEO.

Ashton and Wolfe were alone in one of the small gondolas Augland 54 utilized to transport Suits between the parks. The intricately designed floating boxes provided a sweeping view of the beach below.

She saw the outline of Atlantis Park below the water, where tiny figures raced down below the water's edge like fish. Then she saw The Hook, where she'd worked for three years. She could only assume Niall was still working there if Wolfe had done what he had promised and protected him from affiliation with her.

While she had seen the Suit's gondolas, Ashton had never been on one. It was strictly for Suit transit. Workers used the old train system.

Ashton studied her surroundings as she stared out the circular windows. The gondola rose above the Bay resorts and took them up at an incredible speed.

Wolfe touched the shoulder of Ashton's Suit, Charlotte.

"Do you have a beach park in Augland 2?"

"Mm-hmm . . ." *Don't give too much away.* "Yours is much more . . . expansive." Ashton tried to sound impressed. Wolfe beamed with pride.

"We take a lot of pride in our parks, and we are discussing even more expansion," he gloated.

The gondola took them higher and higher, and Ashton became uncomfortable. She had never been this high before. She forgot she was indestructible; even if they fell and her Suit smashed to the ground, her body was safe in her pod.

"Oh . . ." Ashton couldn't help but panic.

"Charlotte, is everything okay?" Wolfe took her hand.

That didn't help.

"High, I mean, this is much higher than I expected." Ashton tried to breathe, but her hands started to tremble.

The gondola entered a small window-like slit that brought them into the next park. Each park was enclosed by walls lined with screens that projected the aesthetics of each location. The hole looked dark, but Ashton knew they would soon disappear into the next park.

She glanced back before the darkness engulfed her.

"Where are we?" Ashton asked as she saw a sunset in the distance and towering city structures, beautiful and uniform, come into view. She had only heard of Hollywood Boulevard. Versal was from the city, and she often told stories of her time as a worker there.

"It's beautiful . . ."

"The city? Yes, Seattle was a beautiful place. Most of the structures were here before Augland 54. Hollywood Boulevard was the very first park created after the war, and almost every building was refurbished to mimic the historic skyscrapers."

Before the war, Augland 54 had only encompassed Maya Bay and spanned a few miles along what used to be Harbor Island, an industrial island near the greater Seattle area. They'd repurposed the solar initiatives of the factory island. After the war, and much destruction of the original buildings, expansion had been inevitable, and the downtown area of Seattle and Bellevue had soon been overtaken by the Augland park.

Wolfe leaned toward Ashton. She held her breath, not wanting to smell his musty scent that had grown so comforting during their talks on the rock all those months ago. But as he leaned across, giving an aerial tour of the city, Ashton didn't smell anything. Nothing about this man she was supposed to know was familiar.

Ashton's paranoia made her shy away from him, but Wolfe seemed amused by her coyness.

"We are close. Right there, the long skinny building with what looks like a saucer, that's the Executive building."

"Will Warren be there?" Ashton asked. Wolfe's eyes glistened, and he turned from her.

"No, Warren has retired. He's living out his days in Victorian. He will sometimes make an appearance. I mean, he still plays a vital role in helping me run Augland 54."

Ashton wanted to press further and understand how and when Wolfe had become CEO, but she didn't want to draw suspicion.

An elevator took them up the needle-like structure. Wolfe talked the whole time, discussing the small details of the park and what made them different from the other Auglands.

As the elevator doors opened, Wolfe ushered Ashton into the main lobby of the Executive suites. Everything was white and black, blotched with specks of gold. Colorful exotic flowers adorned the room in elegant bouquets. Ashton felt like royalty as she stepped into what she could only define as perfection.

Wolfe waved at the receptionist as they walked past toward a row of windows that overlooked Augland 54. They were higher than the screen-lined walls separating the parks, and Ashton saw the park's magnitude for the first time. From the streets of each park, the tall walls made the park look isolated and expansive—an endless paradise.

Rolling hills of swaying grass met a cement stone castle; Land of Legends was now in plain view. It looked peaceful now, but Ashton had seen so much bloodshed, loss, and betrayal there. A shudder ran up her spine—a visible reaction of her Suit to her emotion of revulsion.

She took a step back instinctively. Her mind felt numb, frozen in fear that she would end up there again if this all failed.

"It's amazing, isn't it?" Wolfe stepped up beside her. "I'm not sure if you are up for partaking in a little adventure, but it is a lot of fun. Very realistic." He had seen her staring at Land of Legends. *It's realistic because it's real. Real for everyone but the Suits.*

Ashton wanted to spin around to face Wolfe and scream at him. How was Land of Legends still happening? Why hadn't he stopped it? But she couldn't say anything that would give herself away.

Wolfe continued his tour, next showing Ashton the Executive suites. The loop of the tour eventually landed them on the outdoor, glass-enclosed patio above Hollywood Boulevard. In the distance, through the dome of Augland that separated the park from reality, Ashton saw Mount Rainer.

The more Ashton gave her undivided attention to Wolfe, the more he divulged. Her eyes glossed over as she attempted to keep her attention on his self-centric conversation. His flirtation didn't go unnoticed. It was exhausting. The pull to keep her attention so centered drained her. She had never known Wolfe to talk so much about himself.

There were moments when Ashton thought she saw him and swore it was the Wolfe she knew, but they were quickly replaced with this new and flirtatious version of him. Ashton couldn't identify exactly what it was about him that was so different, but she could feel the memories of the man she knew slipping away.

"If you like that, you should see our plans for the future of Augland 54. It will be like nothing you've ever seen."

"Like what?" Ashton was growing impatient for him to open up to her, give her anything she could use to help rescue the children and stop the violence of Augland 54. To get all she needed within a day would be a miracle, but not impossible.

"Oh, wouldn't you like to know?" Wolfe flirted. "Top secret, I'm afraid."

"I would." Ashton flashed a bright smile, hoping it came across well with her fictitious character.

Wolfe smiled back. "Well, my apologies, Charlotte, but I have business to attend to. We should get you to your home away from home while you are here. Where would you like to stay?"

Ashton hadn't thought about that. She had been fixated on Wolfe's strange demeanor. He acted as if he was trying to impress her, but that wasn't the Wolfe she remembered. She had never had the option to live anywhere she wanted. She didn't have to stay in Hollywood Boulevard, so why not enjoy at least living somewhere she could only dream of?

"Atlantis."

Why not? She had always looked out at the outline of the underwater world when she worked in Maya Bay. This might be her only chance to experience the fantasy of Atlantis.

Wolfe offered to have someone escort her, but she dismissed the idea, saying she was open to the adventure of finding Atlantis herself. He only smiled and told Ashton he would be in touch the following day and guided her toward the exit.

CHAPTER 13

Ashton
SATURDAY 6:49 p.m.

Ashton spent the rest of the day at Maya Bay. She would not see Wolfe again until tomorrow, and for the first time in her life, she treated herself to an afternoon of pampering. Workers provided a bathing suit while her things had been sent to her room in Atlantis.

Ashton sat on a secluded beach chair, drink in hand. She wanted a moment of solitude away from the Suits at the resort. She could be herself in the stillness and felt the world's chaos become quiet.

She replayed the day's events, and her mind relived the moment she saw Wolfe and heard the words, "I'm the CEO of Augland 54."

Ashton's memory brought her back to the sentimental moments she and Wolfe had shared. When they first met, he was rigid and cold. But, as she soon learned, there was a side to him that was kind and empathetic. They'd shared a kiss at the rock, their rock, in Land of Legends.

Then, when they walked from the Colony to Augland, after her escape, he confessed he cared for her, that they were more than just "friends," and Ashton had admitted the same. He had promised to save her in the Augland cages, and he had done just that.

Their brief interlude had been shattered by the urgency of the moment. Wolfe would go back into Augland to do his best to save the Colony's future and disrupt his father's cruel plans for the workers. Ashton would go to the Colony and make a life in Hood Canal until they could be reunited. Or so she had thought.

During their time apart, Ashton had thought of him daily, pretending their lives were different. He sat beside her at Hood Canal, by the fire eating one of Rico's famous dinners.

She frowned and dug her synthetic feet into the sand. As she looked across the water, the sun began its descent below the water's edge.

Ashton stepped closer to the small, rippled waves of Maya Bay. There were easier ways to get to Atlantis, but Ashton decided to walk out into the Puget Sound water. She had witnessed plenty of Suits who used this way to Atlantis, stepping into the water and diving deep into the deep blue, and she wanted to try it herself. Suits did not need to breathe and could swim underwater for extended periods. There were also glass tunnels leading to the air-pressurized park, allowing more accessible entrance to the underwater aquarium. Workers were transported by an underwater shuttle directly connected to the train.

Ashton stepped forward, noticing the heavenly feeling of the warm water against her biofabricated skin, the sand exfoliating her feet. With each step she took, excitement swirled around her. Living as Charlotte wasn't so bad. She couldn't help but think about how life would be different if she had a Suit. If she could stay in Charlotte, she could live in this paradise forever, maybe even be with Wolfe. Ashton wanted just a moment where she didn't have to feel guilty for wanting an easy life.

Before long, she was neck deep in the water. Her body felt light as her android body bobbed in the waves. Taking in a deep breath, she dove below, opening her eyes and feeling the slight pressure of the water that surrounded her. It felt real. She had to convince her lungs to breathe, overcoming her body's instinctive knowledge that this was not normal. She exhaled and noticed she could inhale water as if it were air.

Ashton smiled and glided along the sea floor toward the dimly-lit underworld filled with Grecian ruins and sunken barnacle-lined ships. She was light as air. Her synthetic body swayed with the tide, and her feet barely touched the rocky sand beneath her.

The deeper Ashton swam, the more distance she felt from reality. Long stems of swaying, lime-green seaweed towered above her; vine-like branches of coral shaded the bright sun from above the surface as she walked along the seabed. A narrow sand pathway helped guide her as she "hiked" the jungle of the sea.

In the distance, she saw the towering colonnades of Atlantis, but she took her time as she admired the vibrant coral, treacherous-looking sea urchins, holed rock, and misty turquoise water. Underwater lights illuminated the entire sea floor. With each step she took, more life around her emerged. The wavering fins of tiny wildlife clustered together and moving with the tide's push and pull. The marbled light reflected the waves onto the darkening seabed. Even eerie crevices and caves lined with eroded, sunken pre-war artifacts were overgrown with nature's touch. It was beautiful, majestic, and silent. Ashton had missed silence.

The Suits were designed for underwater parks. In it, sights and sounds were amplified. Motion seemed effortless. The sensors even interpreted tastes and smells to enhance the underwater experience.

The deeper Ashton went, the less light trickled down from above. Augland had done well to create a soothing, well-lit ambience as she swam along the sandy walkway through towering greenery and gigantic glowing seashells. Living sea creatures swam around her as if she weren't an oddity. Ashton smiled at the small fish as her red hair swayed in the motion of the waves.

It was bittersweet to come to the end of her journey to Atlantis, but the giant bubble engulfing the underwater city was just as enticing, and Ashton swam through a sliding glass door to enter it. As soon as it closed, the air pressurized around her. The salty water of the Puget Sound quickly drained and dried.

At first glance, it looked like a city of the gods long forgotten underwater. Spotted rocks chiseled perfectly into columns held up a stack of stone. Rows of bowed entrances echoed in perfect pattern down the long, outside sidewalk. Suits sat and danced on patios, and the delicious aroma of bread and fish filled the air.

As Ashton walked along the walkway, it felt historical and modern at the same time. To her right, there was a boat-filled moat—below her, an underwater river. Above her, she could see through the dome to the dark seawater, full of swarming sea creatures.

She walked for miles along the seemingly endless city. In the center of the town, she arrived at a castle much like the one from Land of Legends, but this one was made of sand, or at least something resembling the granular material one would find on a beach. Stepping inside, her feet fairly glided across dark-green marble floors of the castle's luxurious interior.

"Ms. Charlotte?"

"Uh . . . yes." Ashton hadn't expected anyone to greet her personally.

"I've been sent to take care of you during your stay here. May I show you to your room?" Apparently, Wolfe had arranged for her to have a suite here, at the Sand Chateau Resort and Spa.

The young worker walked with Ashton, and they made their way to the top of the castle to a vast room overlooking the ocean floor.

"My name is Helen. If you need anything, please interconnect and I'll be happy to assist you."

As quickly as Helen had appeared, she disappeared, and Ashton was left in a large, exquisitely beautiful room. She slowly walked around the four corners of the ivory-white open space, allowing the silence to encompass her before finally sitting at the edge of a plush bed. She smiled, taking in a deep breath, and feeling the weight of the mission and the moments leading up to this evening melt away. After days of Hunter and Georgina, and her recent interaction with Wolfe, she welcomed the quiet.

That night, Ashton bathed in a luxurious tub and finally burrowed into the fluffy bed. She didn't feel awkward or out of place like she had while working at the parks, nor did she feel cast out and siloed like she did at the Colony. There was something so enjoyable about being Charlotte, and not herself. At least as Charlotte she could pretend to be anyone, enjoy anything, be happy and outgoing, like Versal. Who knew? Maybe Ashton would find out more about herself by becoming someone completely different.

She felt more than saw the light seeping through from the water's surface and slowly opened her eyes—calm, peace, serenity. Nothing could touch her, harm her. She slept better than she ever had and breathed in the sweet, salty air as morning woke her. It made sense to Ashton now.

No wonder the Suits don't care or even worry about life outside. Why would anyone do anything to ruin this illusion? At the thought, an instant wave of shame rippled through Ashton. She snapped out of her tranquility. She was here to rescue the stolen children. She wouldn't forget her mission, no matter how easy life in a Suit was. She didn't have many days to enjoy it, anyway. The more days passed, the more in danger the children were.

SUNDAY 8:29 a.m.

As Ashton exited the hotel and walked along the sea floor, she thought of her next move. Wolfe had seemed flirtatious toward her, which she could potentially use to her advantage. If she reacted, maybe even became too forward, he might lower his guard. She tried to forget the hurt she'd felt at his flirtation. Deep down, she still hoped Wolfe had feelings for her. If he did, he wasn't showing it.

"Good morning, Ms. Charlotte. I hope you slept well." Helen's soft, chipper demeanor greeted Ashton.

"Good morning, Helen," Ashton said kindly as she approached her desk. "I'd like to schedule a breakfast meeting. Something not too fancy." Ashton wanted to meet Wolfe somewhere she knew he could feel more himself. If she could take him away from the corporate world, maybe she could bring out the real him—a more relaxed version.

"Of course! We have wonderful dining experiences down here. Titan's is a very nice place with an amazing seafood omelet . . ."

Ashton knew Helen most likely didn't know what an omelet tasted like; Ashton hadn't known until Rico had made her one at the Colony's kitchen. Workers only were fed an Augland-approved diet that consisted mostly of nutrition bars and shakes—enough food to stay alive.

The only restaurant Ashton knew was the one in Maya Bay where she had worked. A thought struck her; maybe she could see Niall again. She knew it was a bad idea, but her heart won the argument. She wanted confirmation he was still alive. Wolfe had broken every promise he had made to her; she hoped he had kept this one, to save her friends.

"There's a restaurant, I believe, called The Hook, on the shore of Maya Bay. I'd like to go there. Would you ask if Wolfe, I mean Wolfgang, the CEO, could join me?"

Ashton still felt awkward calling him by his full name and new title. Helen didn't react or seem surprised by her request to meet with the CEO of Augland.

"Of course, Ms. Charlotte. I'd be happy to inquire about a meeting. Would you like me to request a reservation?"

Ashton nodded.

Helen ushered her to a waiting area for her transport to the surface. The entrance was grand and spiraled up to give a view of the water. Ashton took time to admire the beauty of the emerald- and pearl-studded room around her, filled with Suits of all shapes and colors, chatting and laughing. Ashton couldn't help but smile as others gave a small wave, acknowledging her. Being a customer came with its own notoriety; as a worker, she had been invisible.

"Ms. Charlotte?" Ashton didn't pay attention. "Excuse me, Ms. Charlotte?" It took Ashton a moment to remember who she was supposed to be.

"Yes?" She turned to see Helen.

"Wolfgang has confirmed his availability, and your transport is here to take you to shore."

Here we go.

CHAPTER 14

Ashton

SUNDAY 10:14 a.m.

shton stood only steps away from the front entrance of The Hook. Around the side, she saw the same stairs she had walked down to do beach duty when Marius, her old boss, was upset with her. Again, she had a sinking feeling this was a bad idea. There were too many distracting memories.

She raised her black maxi dress, kicked off her sandals, and pressed her bare feet onto the wooden steps to the patio. She felt the warm breeze tickle her skin, and breathed in the sweet, salty air. The waves on the shore crashed only yards in front of her. The synthetic sun peeked up along the horizon, warming her. She knew it was fake, but its beauty and familiarity brought her peace. She remembered standing in this spot looking out at the same sun before all the drama in the last year had happened—so many things had changed.

Only four days ago, she had been happy in her home on Hood Canal, building her fire and making tea. If she were there right now, she would be doing prep work for the Colony's breakfast and whatever Rico had planned for dinner.

"Someone is an early riser."

Wolfe's voice shook Ashton out of her reverie. He stood tall in front of her. He wore a button-up shirt without a tie, tan shorts, and sandals. Ashton smiled as he took his seat across from her.

"I trust you slept well, Charlotte."

"I did. Thank you . . . and thank you for taking the time to have breakfast with me. You do know how to make a girl feel welcome."

Wolfe smiled back.

"Good morning,"

Ashton recognized that deep voice. She sighed in relief at the sound of her long-time friend, Niall. He was safe. Perhaps Wolfe had kept all his promises and was simply a better actor than she had guessed.

Ashton prepared a neutral expression. She knew Niall could not recognize her in her red-haired Suit, but she needed to address him as simply a worker, not a friend.

Plastering a smile on her face, she turned. Niall stood straight, his bright smile gone, and his dark skin dull. Her smile faded. He wore an eye patch over his left eye, and an outline of a darkened scar that looked like lightning disappeared underneath the black fabric.

"What happened to your face?!"

Ashton rose out of her seat, forgetting who she was pretending to be. She wanted to put her hands over his wound and embrace her friend, her confident and light-hearted brother, her protector.

Niall recoiled. He quickly gave an embarrassed smile and stepped back out of her reach, startled by her reaction.

"I'm fine, ma'am. I'm sorry for my disturbance."

Ashton was at a loss for words. The upbeat, handsome young man she remembered had been scarred by something . . . or someone. Ashton couldn't look away.

"He's fine, Charlotte."

Wolfe was reaching out to her, motioning for her to sit down, a worried expression on his face. Ashton's heart sickened as she realized he was more worried about her strange behavior than about Niall's scarred face.

Ashton noticed she was causing a scene, something that would make Wolfe concerned. He would be able to tell something was wrong.

"If you'd like, we could get another waiter."

Wolfe snapped his fingers, and Marius came over to them.

"Yes, sir."

Marius stood only inches from Ashton with his mousy voice and oversized glasses.

This was a mistake. Why had she thought it would be a good idea to come to a place she was so familiar with, so connected to? The last person she wanted to see was the man who had started all of this: Marius. He was the one who had sent her to be "rehabilitated" in Land of Legends. He looked the same.

"I'll take a coffee and the eggs Benedict."

Marius nodded and looked at Ashton. She wanted to slap him, show him how much she disliked him. She had so much anger inside her, but she could not blow her cover or give any more indication that she was not a typical Suit than she already had.

"I'll do the same."

As quickly as Marius appeared, he left, and Ashton breathed a sigh of relief. Shaking off the abrupt and awkward scene, Ashton asked Wolfe to tell her more about himself. She wanted information and needed him to be comfortable opening up to her.

"Not much to know . . . I grew up in the Executive offices." Wolfe paused and relaxed as he leaned back in his chair. "As soon as I could work, I asked my father to make me a security manager. From there, I was promoted to run Land of Legends, which I can't wait to show you, Charlotte. After that success, I became Head of Security. Warren recently retired, and I was voted in as CEO. Youngest CEO of an Augland, I might add."

Wolfe's narrative confused Ashton. She had asked him about himself, and he'd only given his resume of work. When they had sat together on the rock at Land of Legends, just six months earlier, Wolfe had been much more open about his distaste for the corporate world.

Was he acting, playing the part of Executive? Afraid to show who he really was? Ashton needed him to open up more and give her a glimpse behind his façade, as he had done at Land of Legends.

She remembered the rock in Land of Legends; it had been their sanctuary, a moment in time when they'd both dropped the strings of the Augland puppet show that controlled them and everything else. For that moment, the world had been real—unaltered and unscripted. Wolfe had taught her how to fight, protect herself, and be her true self in the character she played—Freya. She wanted so deeply to see that man who had shown compassion and empathy.

"Any hobbies?" Ashton dug deeper. She needed to gain his trust or connect with him on some level.

Wolfe looked away, concentrating. "I—" he began. "I don't really have hobbies. I'm married to my work. I care a lot about the success of Augland 54."

He was reserved, not giving away any information.

"What do you mean? Isn't it already successful?" She made the question sound flirty, playing to his ego.

Wolfe's eyes grew with a spark of excitement. "Well, yes, but I don't want it to be an average Augland. I want it to be a premier park. Somewhere . . ." He stopped and raised his glass toward Ashton. "I don't want to bore you with the details. What about you? Tell me about yourself."

She should have guessed he would turn things around on her. He was being reserved, and it had something to do with her ties to Augland 2. He didn't want to divulge information. It might not have been the right play to have her be someone of notoriety from a different Augland.

"Nothing special. I mean, I like nature. . .it's quiet and calming."

"Oh, goodness!" Wolfe recoiled and laughed. "I hate the silence. It creeps me out."

Ashton was surprised, but she chuckled along with him, trying to keep the conversation playful. Their mutual love of silence was how they'd connected back in Land of Legends.

"I like action and order. I don't think this Augland would be as good as it is without the constant need to improve, which means I'm always on the move."

That was new to Ashton. Something she and Wolfe had had in common was their need to get away from the world around them. The rock was their refuge in Land of Legends. A place they could let down their guard.

Ashton wasn't getting anywhere with Wolfe. She studied him. If this was going to work, she needed to stop thinking about who she thought Wolfe was. The plan she had worked through with Hunter was flawed; it bet that she would be able to understand Wolfe and elicit information because she knew him. It didn't account for this stranger.

"What about Augland 2? What's it like?" Wolfe relaxed back in his chair as Marius approached with their meals.

"Not as grand as Augland 54. I'm not sure I'll ever want to leave."

Ashton had been around Suits and managers long enough to know that sometimes you needed to make them feel important. "I'm impressed with what I see. Atlantis is so beautiful. You've really gone above and beyond with the architecture."

Wolfe grinned wide.

"Never leave, huh?"

"I mean, why would I? If everything is so much nicer here, I have no reason to go back."

"No special someone back home?" Wolfe was teasing her, but at least it was a reaction. "What about your father? Won't he be upset?"

Wolfe leaned in close, intently looking at her. She had gained his interest and now needed to keep it.

"No." Ashton painted a flirtatious smile on her face. Finally, she had a sliver of hope.

She ate her food slowly, listening to Wolfe's every word—laughing when she needed to laugh, giving a sympathetic look when he said something sad about his privileged life. She had an entire life of experience pretending, so much of it here in this very restaurant.

Ashton was worn down by the end of their meal, and after story after story of Wolfe's time in the Executive Office. Behind her laughter and attentive behavior, she was broken and ashamed. With each moment that passed, she saw her version of Wolfe slip away. He was clearly not the man she thought she had fallen in love with—the one so different from all the other Executives—the one who cared and was going to change Augland 54 and free the workers.

Wolfe was no different than any other Suit, even though he technically wasn't in one. If he was different from the Suits, his acting was impressive. Had he been playing her all along? Using her to get closer to Cahya, closer to extinguishing the Colony for his own political game? Ashton didn't want to believe it, but it seemed so obvious with each passing moment. Never again would she so blindly believe or be so naïve to the selfishness of this world.

She wanted to crawl out of her fake skin and run away, but she stayed, keeping a fictitious smile painted across her face while looking betrayal in its ugly face.

Long after their plates were cleared and they had drunk their fill of coffee, Wolfe looked at his watch and stated he had to leave. They both stood up, and he took her fake arm with the dainty pearl bracelet and kissed her hand. Smiling, Ashton pretended to be flattered. Inside, she was devastated.

"I'd like to see you again tonight; there's an amazing event for some of the more prestigious members of this Augland. I'd love to introduce you to them."

Ashton shied away but nodded excitedly. Wolfe beamed and left her on the crowded patio. It was still strange to see the view of the water and sky she had seen a thousand times, but never through the advanced senses of a Suit. The sun was warm and yellow in the sky, the water a vivid Caribbean blue. But Ashton knew behind the filter the sky was gray and the water cold.

As soon as Wolfe disappeared, Ashton slouched down in her wooden chair. She sighed as she let the façade fade. A tear rolled down her face as she turned away and looked toward the horizon. She choked back sobs. Her mind felt numb.

"You okay, ma'am?" Niall's voice, almost a whisper, sounded from behind her. She shut her eyes hard. Niall was safe, but they had done something to him, and she wasn't sure she could look at him again without falling apart.

"Yes. I'm fine," she lied, wiping away her tears.

He didn't pry anymore and left her alone. The warmth prickled with heat as she shut her fake eyes. She needed to pull herself together. Instead of wallowing, she thought of Hunter and hoped his luck had been better than hers.

SUNDAY 5:21 p.m.

Ashton was ready at four o'clock that afternoon, wearing the nicest dress Georgina had packed for her. It sparkled black and shone with glittering rhinestones as she moved.

Wolfe had asked that he meet her at a restaurant in Predator's Biome at five p.m. for drinks before the main event. Predator's Biome was located at the opposite end of Augland from Atlantis, and it took almost an hour to get there by gondola.

Green leaves surrounded her small table, which overlooked an expansive jungle and a glittering waterfall in the distance. Birds chirped, and wild animal cries echoed around the cliffside restaurant.

Wolfe was late. Ashton had sat at the table for over twenty minutes when a small monkey approached, looking at her with wide eyes. He was small, with a dark brown coat and a lengthy tail. Delighted, Ashton put her hand out as the creature studied her.

"It's all right, little guy," she said with a smile. He was curious and looked above and below her hand. His small and furry face drew close to her outstretched palm.

"See, I won't hurt you." He came close. The monkey was about to let Ashton pet it when Wolfe approached.

"You, my dear, look radiant." His loud voice broke the tranquil moment. The small monkey darted into the dense trees that trailed down along the cliffside. Ashton's smile faded, but before she looked up at Wolfe, she quickly resumed her character, plastering a welcoming smile on her face.

"Well, thank you." Ashton turned and put her hands down the rhinestone-encrusted dress. She did feel confident. "This place is beautiful."

"Not as beautiful as you."

Ashton pretended to be flattered. She felt uncomfortable with his constant attention to her appearance.

91

"Apologies for my tardiness; I wish we could have had time to linger here and talk, but we don't want to be late for the main event."

"Where are we going?" Ashton asked.

"Don't worry; it will be fun." Wolfe grabbed Ashton's hand, interlaced his fingers with hers, and guided her toward the exit. Ashton looked down at their intertwined hands. She wanted so badly for this to be different, to feel different.

CHAPTER 15

Wolfe
Two Months Earlier

Wolfe shoved his chair back, tipping it over. The sound reverberated off the fishbowl windows. The five other Executives stared at him as he walked around the conference table and out the door.

The board was discussing the next invasion of the Colony, and Wolfe couldn't hold in his emotions any longer. He'd thought he would have made more progress before Warren decided to attack the Colony again. He had promised Cahya he would keep them safe.

Wolfe was gaining trust among some of the Executives—specifically Boren, Sebastian, and Lee. He knew this outburst would be viewed as childish and unprofessional. But as he slammed the Executive conference room door, he didn't care.

The every-two-day board meetings had grown intense. While Warren was skilled at diversion, he could not make every Executive happy. Repeatedly, they bent to his will. He had too much power over them, to the benefit of the majority. Wolfe wasn't sure what his father had over them. It must be something powerful because he won the argument every time.

Wolfe sat at his white desk in his large office, staring unseeingly out its floor-to-ceiling windows. It was an identical office to his father's, but the aesthetics were very different. Warren cared for fragile and expensive art sculptures and paintings. Wolfe had rejected his father's minimalist tech decor and antiques from before the war. He had an entire shelf of real paper books, which were hard to come by now that everyone had a personal screen. While Warren let the artificial sun pour in, Wolfe typically kept his shades down, hiding the Augland world from his view. It reminded him of the prison he was in—just like the workers.

Wolfe tried hard to think of every possible scenario, anything more he could do to help turn the others against his father and, at the very least, stop this next attack on the Colony.

Nothing he'd tried so far had worked. He'd attempted befriending Wintefred, but she was too close to Warren. He tried with Lee, good old Lee, one of the nicest guys, but he didn't have a backbone. It would take a miracle to get him on Wolfe's side. Lee didn't want to trouble anyone and had obtained his position out of pure luck and devotion to Warren.

Wolfe knew he wouldn't get to Reuben, who would have been the most influential as Warren's right-hand man. Warren and Reuben had grown up together; Reuben's father had been friends with Wolfe's grandfather, the previous CEO—generations of loyalty.

Bzzz. Bzzz. Wolfe's interconnect rumbled, and a message appeared on the screen, a summons to his father's office.

When Wolfe arrived, Warren stood looking out his floor-to-ceiling windows at the sparkling night sky and city lights; there was no light pollution when the sky was fake. Warren's hands were crossed, which was not a good sign for Wolfe.

"Take a seat."

Wolfe did as he was told and waited patiently for his father to speak.

"When you were a boy, you came into the office. You were playing around with Roger, or . . ."

"Rufus," Wolfe corrected, thinking of the small black cat with bright golden eyes that had been his pet as a child. His mother had given it to Wolfe for his seventh birthday, a baby from a litter of jaguars in Predator's Biome.

"Yes, Rufus, your pet. You were playing around, and you knocked over my antique sculpture. You know, the one with the two dancing people. It didn't shatter, only a small crack on the woman's arm, so you thought it would be okay. And I got mad at you, didn't I?"

"Yes."

"Do you know why I was so angry?" Wolfe didn't know where Warren was going with this story, but he knew why his father was mad. Wolfe shook his head.

"Because when there is one crack, that small crack becomes bigger and bigger over time. Every time you look at it, all you see is that imperfection. It is forever changed." Warren paused. "Wolfgang, I'm telling this to you because you are attempting to chip away at my perfection, my Augland."

Warren emphasized the possessiveness he felt over Augland 54. In his mind, Warren had built Augland 54 into what it was today. In a way, he was right, depending on how one defined "perfect."

"I took away your pet because there are always consequences. Act recklessly when there are things worth so much, things get taken away . . . I'm hoping I am making myself crystal clear. You're a smart boy."

Wolfe understood. Warren had not simply taken Rufus away. He had ordered the jaguar to be put down and made Wolfe watch.

"I do, sir," Wolfe said in a whisper, defeat creeping up his throat. Warren had seen what Wolfe was trying to do in the boardroom and was warning Wolfe that there would be consequences. And what Warren wanted, Warren got.

"Good. And I hope this is the end of this, then. You stay out of my things, or I will take away something you hold dear . . . do I make myself clear?"

Wolfe paused and hung his head. The defeat made his ears ring. His father knew what he had been planning. He didn't say it, but he knew. He had a knack for getting his point across without being completely specific.

"Good, that will be all."

Warren turned around. It was Wolfe's cue to leave.

"Wolfgang," his father glanced to his side, "I teach you these lessons to make you stronger. That's my job as a father. As a man."

Walking down the long corridor of the Executive suite, Wolfe's mind reeled. It had been glaringly obvious that his father had known, and he should have been more careful. Wolfe's heart pounded and the world seemed to spin around him. His steps slowed. Wolfe concentrated hard on his father's words.

Wolfe felt the emotion and loneliness of the past six months weigh down on him. He wanted to feel cared for, understood. He felt unsure. His feet moved, without his thinking, toward the far side of the sphere-shaped building, toward the penthouse apartments where his father and mother lived. He passed his father's deep oak doors to one painted white, with a flowery ring hanging in its center. His father's apartment was dark and cold, his mother's bright and cheery.

Wolfe knocked softly. His mother didn't care for technology and rarely used the intercom to greet guests. She was tender, understanding, and intuitive. He hoped she would be the comfort he needed. He had kept her in the dark these past six months, but he knew she could help him see this through. He could not tell her everything, but he could trust her discretion.

A small woman with graying mahogany hair opened the door slightly and looked at Wolfe before swinging it all the way open.

"Wolfe, you know you never need to knock," Anastasia said, a hint of her Russian accent breaking through. Her father and mother had both immigrated to the West Coast after the war and had set roots in Augland 13.

She embraced Wolfe, squeezing him tightly, her frail arms barely reaching around him. Wolfe pressed his face into her shoulder.

"What's wrong?" she asked concernedly.

Wolfe inhaled deeply, smelling her strong fragrance of orange blossoms. She always smelled sweet.

"I'll put tea on for us."

Anastasia lived in a smaller version of Warren's penthouse and, while connected by a door to Warren's quarters, they had lived separately for some time.

She had once been a prominent figure of Augland 13, as her father had been a wealthy man. She'd met Warren while traveling with her father to different Auglands, and they'd quickly fallen in love. Unfortunately, the feelings hadn't lasted long.

Wolfe had never understood his parents' relationship. He barely remembered them together when he was growing up. Even more so, Wolfe didn't understand how Anastasia could seemingly ignore the world around her, especially considering how much power she held.

The room was bright with white walls and hand-painted artwork. Anastasia was creative and had crafted most of the decorations herself. While the decor sometimes clashed aesthetically, his mother's apartment felt homier than any other place Wolfe could think of. More like the Colony—less like Augland.

He sat down at a small table and chairs in her kitchen while she poured hot water into two mugs. She sat down next to Wolfe and slid a mug of tea across the table.

"Why the visit so late? Don't get me wrong, you can always come here." She reached up and stroked Wolfe's overgrown facial hair.

"I—I don't know where to begin."

His mother sat patiently, sipping her tea as she waited for him to continue.

"Father, he. . ." Wolfe sighed and looked down into his tea. "We don't agree completely on Augland. And I don't think we ever will."

Anastasia straightened and her eyes narrowed.

"What has he done now?"

Wolfe envied his mother's ability to detach herself from their reality. She didn't insert herself into the company politics, nor did she ever ask Warren about any business. She was blissfully, completely, in the dark. But she wasn't naïve, and she knew what her husband was capable of.

"He's gone mad. He wants to do so many horrible things to the workers. He treats them like they're disposable, and I can't stop him. He's too powerful. None of the Executives will even question him. I thought . . . I thought I'd have a chance to change things if I made it to the boardroom, but I feel less in control now than I did before."

The words poured out of Wolfe's mouth more quickly than he had anticipated. It felt good to release his frustration.

"And . . . and I fear that we are going in a direction we can't come back from. A horrible world. A sick world."

Anastasia grabbed Wolfe's hand and squeezed it hard. Wolfe had confided in his mother several times before about Warren's torturous reign. She had never disagreed, most often wanting to stay a neutral party between her son and her husband. Wolfe thought it was because she didn't want to give up her peaceful life. Warren had a hold on her he didn't understand.

"Oh, honey, your father . . . your father." She stuttered, at a loss for words. "He's a passionate man, but I do know that his passion can blind him."

"He won't change. I've tried. I just came from his office where he threatened to take me out of the Executive office if I kept disagreeing with him. I don't know what to do."

"You, Wolfe, will always follow good. But you live in a world of expectations. You know this." Wolfe nodded.

Anastasia didn't understand and Wolfe couldn't explain it, but when he looked into her eyes, she read him. She knew his thoughts, his feelings. Instead of saying anything or trying to persuade him to act differently, she pulled him into an embrace. It was what he had wanted, but it left him just as lost as he had been before.

Wolfe struggled to sleep that night, feeling the weight of Augland on his shoulders. During times like these, he needed an escape. Opening a dusty, plastic-encased CD player, he opened the vintage music player. From what Wolfe knew, he was the only person who still enjoyed antiques like these from the previous world. He blew hard at the old technology and carefully pushed the disc inside a small slit. The room flooded with smooth guitar and a husky voice that paired beautifully with the vibration of the guitar strings. Wolfe closed his eyes and let the music surround him.

It was at that moment Wolfe had a realization. He had been playing this game with his father hoping good would prevail, but that was not a strategic move. The stakes were too high to be patient. He needed to play the game the way his father would—not by attempting to befriend, but by power and manipulation—fight fire with fire. That would be the only way his plan could be salvaged. That meant he needed to become what he despised: a man like his father.

The music stopped and the disc scratched: all the songs had played. Wolfe's eyes turned dark as he turned off his emotions. It was time to redefine who he was.

CHAPTER 16

Wolfe
One Month Earlier

Wolfe woke up early. He showered, combed his hair back, and shaved so he didn't look so disheveled. He pulled on his sports coat and tightened his tie, which fell in line cooperatively with his pressed shirt. Looking into the mirror, he barely recognized himself. For the past five months, he had tried to blend in, but he never quite looked like the other Executives. This morning, however, Wolfe felt confident as he looked at the tailored version of himself—black jacket, maroon tie, and white shirt, perfectly fitted to his athletic build.

Wolfe walked down the long corridor that led to the Executive conference room. He took his typical chair in the farthest corner from the entrance. The other Executives slowly trickled in, giving Wolfe a once-over and commenting on his new, more sophisticated look. His beard and hair were perfectly groomed, a change from his usual scruff.

When Reuben arrived, he glared at Wolfe as he took a seat, uncharacteristic of his typical superior attitude. Wolfe looked away multiple times, but in his peripherals could see Reuben was not taking his eyes off him. He was studying Wolfe.

Five years had taken its toll on Reuben and Wolfe's relationship, and Wolfe wasn't sure who the man was anymore. His mother spoke highly of him, but Wolfe wasn't as easily fooled. In his reality, he saw Reuben as a pawn in Warren's game. He had felt Reuben's eyes on him at every turn throughout the years, spying on him in the shadows to expose him to Warren. Even if his mother couldn't see it, Wolfe wasn't blind to it.

Warren entered and quickly dove into the business of the day, from operations to supply chain restraints coming from eastern ship routes, and, finally, the budget. Wolfe paid close attention, nodding in agreement as he stayed silent, Warren's threat of consequences looming in his mind. His stomach turned as he bent to the will of his father. Every time he agreed, he felt overwhelming shame. His father relished it and gave an approving smile with each surrender.

"If there is nothing else—" Warren began to wrap up the meeting.

Reuben interrupted, "I want to bring up the customer service initiative again, Warren. I hope you don't mind." Reuben's dark complexion and piercing, speckled, brown-and-green eyes stayed on Wolfe as he spoke, then shifted to Warren.

"Of course, what would you like to bring up?" Warren hid his surprise at being interrupted with a placating smile.

"The bylaws state that before any corporate funds are spent on development, it must be voted on by the boardroom. I believe we may have skipped that step when you decided to start this project of yours . . . and I believe developing new technology requires corporate funds."

Warren was speechless. He kept his face passive, but Wolfe knew his father well enough to see the flick of anger behind his eyes.

"Reuben, you know it was never my intention to go behind the board's back on this. I was merely trying to see if it was viable. We've been over this."

"Yes, you've said that. But the bylaws are something we are all governed by to ensure we don't fall into a . . . dictatorship. You aren't the only one making decisions here. We have Augland and AEC stakeholders to answer to."

Wolfe didn't move. He kept his eyes locked with Reuben, a man who had never said a word against his father publicly, a man whom Warren trusted completely.

The room was silent. No one moved; no one said a word. Warren narrowed his gaze at Reuben. He took a deep, patronizing breath and gave a small chuckle.

"I think this is a conversation you and I should have in private, Reuben."

"Not this time, Warren." Warren twitched in frustration, but if there were any doubt of Reuben's seriousness, it disappeared as he stared intently at Warren. "We can't move forward, not without a vote," Reuben demanded. "Let's vote on it now."

Warren clicked his stylus on his interconnect, a paper-thin, translucent sheet that mimicked a traditional pen and paper. He was buying time, no doubt thinking of a way to avoid a vote. The customer service initiative was his dream, and Warren would not let it fail.

Wolfe held his breath. Neither he nor Warren had seen this coming.

"All right, Reuben. Fair enough. We'll take a vote. Those in favor of continuing to invest in the future of an elite Augland 54, using corporate funds to create technology that enhances our worker's customer service capabilities, say 'Aye.' Those who oppose, say 'Nay.'" Warren paused for a moment. "Aye," he started and looked at Wintefred.

"Aye," she said, too quickly.

Boren paused as he stared across the room. He thought hard, considering the pros and cons. He didn't look up. "Nay," he finally said.

There was a pause while Sebastian thought. He had been vocal about his distrust of the misuse of resources.

"Nay."

"Aye," Lee said, without hesitation. He never went against Warren.

"Nay," Reuben said passively. Warren scoffed, biting his tongue.

Warren looked at his son. Wolfe had the power to side with his father and tie the vote. It would prove to Warren that Wolfe was on his side.

Wolfe looked at Reuben, who was sitting back in his chair, staring him down. He wondered about Reuben's intentions. Was he really going against the man he had spent a lifetime with? Generations of support and comradery? Had he finally had enough of Warren after all these years? Or was this a trap to show Wolfe's hand? Was Warren in on this test? Or did Reuben have another reason to go against Warren?

There was silence as Wolfe pondered what he should do. There was no right answer. If Wolfe voted with his father, he would lose any chance of changing things for workers. If he went against Warren, he could lose his position altogether.

"Nay," Wolfe said, looking at his father, who closed his eyes in disappointment. Wolfe could not let his father bully him. Maybe this is what they had in common.

Reuben remained unfazed, indifferent to his motion's success.

"The nays have it." He stood up, signaling the meeting was over. "We must stop the customer service initiative immediately. We also need to talk about repercussions for going against our code and bylaws Warren, but I think this is enough for tonight."

If Warren was surprised, he didn't show it. Instead, he slowly rose, coming face to face with Reuben, and walked out of the boardroom—alone.

Wolfe looked around in disbelief. This was a turn of events he hadn't expected. Maybe Wolfe could use this to his advantage.

CHAPTER 17

Ashton
SUNDAY 5:44 p.m.

Wolfe had been late to the restaurant and had arrived without time for them to even grab a drink, much less have dinner. He was in a hurry, and Ashton had no choice but to follow as he pulled her down the steps of the cliffside restaurant and into the depths of the jungle park.

With each step, the chatter of the restaurant was drowned by the howls and whistles of wildlife. Wolfe guided her down a winding pathway overhung with greenery. As he walked, he kept looking back, smiling at her as they went deeper into the foliage. His bright smile beamed as the shades of the sun seeped through the cracks of the swaying trees.

Ashton admired the lush greenery and breathed in the humid air as she walked through the dense jungle of Predator's Biome. As Charlotte, she was afforded the luxury of strolling through the parks without working at them. It reminded her of the tall, green trees and steep hillside near her home in Hood Canal. It was calming, yet brought an ache to her heart at the same time.

Wolfe hurried her along, interrupting her moment of serenity. The thought of home and Wolfe snapped Ashton out of her trance. She remembered why she was here. It wasn't to admire the world she had tried so hard to leave behind. She was here for the children, Hunter, and the entire Colony. *Stop forgetting that. What is wrong with you?*

"Where are we going?"

Wolfe smiled encouragingly as he tugged her hand.

"You're going to love it."

She breathed in deeply as the wildlife whistled and the smell of fragrant flowers, no doubt synthesized, swirled around her. Above her, a gigantic black cat lay on a thick branch, peering down at them. Before Ashton could wonder how the big animals were kept away from the guests, she saw a glimmer of an electric fence, almost invisible. She thought of the monkey that had almost touched her hand and wondered how it had been lucky enough to escape.

"Augland 54's finest will be there," Wolfe was saying. In the background, Ashton could hear chattering voices growing in the distance, cutting through the jungle.

Her introverted nature cowered at the thought of being around so many others, especially the Augland elite. She tried to think of a way out of it, but she was exactly where she needed to be, next to Wolfe and people who potentially knew where the children were being held.

The jungle opened and before them was a large, curled tree whose branches had twisted themselves into a natural awning. Beyond the lavish, candlelit archway, Ashton saw dozens of Suits drinking and laughing. The event was nestled in a vast, rock-paved opening cut into the wall of the thick jungle. The manmade space was lined with tables and chairs and in the center was a band, all workers, playing soft music. The whole scene looked like a woodland fairytale. Lanterns and chandeliers were suspended from the branches, illuminating long, elaborate tables filled with mounds of fruits and cheeses.

At the entrance stood two security guards dressed in black. Ashton knew all too well that this was only a dreamland if you were a Suit. Wolfe waved at the security guards as they passed and Ashton tensed, sure they could see through her ruse. But they did not.

As soon as they entered, Ashton felt the soothing effects of the transmitters in her brain. Her fear of entering the lion's den was dulled by whatever the Suit's signals were pumping into her body back in her pod. It was frightening how much the technology had control over her, but Ashton welcomed the feeling. This could be fun. She had fooled Wolfe so far, what could possibly go wrong?

Wolfe pulled Ashton close to him and ushered her toward a group of Suits sprawled on lush carpets and bed-like chairs. Leaves dangled from overarching trees swaying in the artificial wind. In the distance, a stream of water trickled. The sun hovered over the trees, flooding the party with soft, golden light.

"Reuben!" Wolfe remarked cheerfully as he pulled Ashton next to a tall man with ebony black hair and a woman in a tight, cheetah-print dress, obviously his companion.

"Wolfgang. And who might you be?" The man reached out to shake Wolfe's hand and glanced toward Ashton's Suit.

"This is Charlotte Maxwell, Charles Maxwell's daughter, who has come to visit us from Augland 2," Wolfe answered for Ashton. "Charlotte's been enjoying her stay. She even said she may never want to leave."

Reuben raised his eyebrows in a coy smile. "Is that so?"

"Yes, and Charlotte, my dear, this is Reuben. He's been my—a family—friend and Executive in Augland 54 for years. A great and loyal friend." Wolfe pounded Reuben's shoulder and emphasized "loyal."

Ashton saw through the over-exaggerated friendliness and sensed an awkwardness, even a dislike, between the men.

Reuben gave a slight chuckle.

"Quite a handful you have in this young man," he said, giving a lighthearted laugh, eyeing Ashton. It was clearly an inside joke she was not privy to. She gave a fake smile, wishing she had a drink in her hand. But at least she didn't feel so out of place; everyone here was playing a part, just like her, and that gave her an unexpected confidence.

While the men talked for her and over her, Ashton nodded at a worker who came by with a glass of clear, bubbly liquid. She picked it up eagerly and took a gulp, almost spitting it out. She had never tasted sparkling wine before. She gulped, then felt her body shiver as she acclimated to the semi-sweet taste of the bubbly champagne, and a warm calming sensation washed over her.

Ashton shadowed Wolfe as he made his rounds around the banquet hall. What a life these people lived, to be surrounded by such beauty and ease. And here Ashton was, an ex-worker, enjoying the life to which she had never been entitled.

The evening was magical—the dresses, the champagne, the fairy lights—but Wolfe's gloating pleasure grounded her. It was awkward, following him around like a show toy and smiling at his aggrandizement.

"What do you think?" Wolfe came close to her, swaying a little with the effects of the alcohol.

"It's so . . . extravagant. I've never seen anything like it." Ashton was becoming annoyed. She was running out of synonyms for "great."

Taking another big gulp of her drink, she swayed to the beautiful music and took her time, admiring all that privilege lent to her. It was only day two; she had plenty more days to get information, she decided. Nothing more would happen tonight; she might as well have fun.

Wolfe pulled Ashton from the crowded dance floor and guided her to the front of the gala near the waterfall. His CEO title gave him prime assigned seating and Ashton saw Charlotte's name highlighted next to Wolfe's.

"Wolfgang!"

Before they could sit, a large, muscular man approached, sloshing a glass of brown liquid.

"Boren, glad you made it!"

"I'd like you to meet someone." Boren turned to a Suit holding a small, blonde baby in her arms.

Ashton froze. Her happiness disappeared in an instant as shock tensed her body. She recognized the curly-haired, wide-eyed infant. Memories of the Colony raid flashed through her mind; Shay running across the field, screaming as an Augland guard pulled this same blonde-haired baby out of her arms.

Ashton couldn't breathe. It felt like her dress was tightening around her ribs. Her knees shook at the shock of seeing the child, who was obviously trying to claw away from her new adoptive parents.

"Meet Cassandra, the newest addition to our family. We can't thank you enough, Wolfgang. While I had originally hoped for a boy, the little rat has grown on me."

Boren stuck his finger into the little girl's cheek. She screamed, her face reddening as she shied away from a world she didn't recognize. Boren recoiled and stepped back.

"Ah, well, she's still getting used to this life, I'm afraid."

"No thanks needed, Boren. I couldn't think of anyone better who deserved a family. And what a cute one at that."

Ashton couldn't take her eyes off the girl. How could they talk about a child this way, as if she were an object one could just buy whenever they wanted? Ashton didn't know the parents or the child by name, but she had seen them at the Colony. A happy young family. She could imagine the girl's parents trying to console one other, their baby ripped from their lives.

Ashton's anger boiled. This was Augland, grotesque and violent, and at its roots, being celebrated as a wonder by the elite. How could she have even enjoyed herself for a moment? She tightened her grip on her champagne flute, and the glass shattered. Chatter stopped. The party went still. Most eyes turned to look at her.

"Charlotte!"

Wolfe was astonished as shards of glass rained to the ground beneath her. Ashton finally took her eyes off the child and stared at the shattered glass. Her fingers were filled with fragments, but there was no blood, she felt no pain. Everything here was fake.

Ashton started breathing heavily and took a step back as faint memories burrowed into her vision. Wolfe was staring at her, evaluating her outburst. She was sure he was putting the pieces together, but she couldn't calm down. She wanted to scream. To grab the Colony child and run. To save the poor child from a life full of lies.

Ashton backed away slowly as the world around her darkened. How had she dined and laughed with people who thought it was okay to steal innocent children?

She wanted to climb out of her skin. She didn't want transmitters flooding her system. For a moment she had thought she could fit in, even be one of them, but she could not. She could not turn herself away from the horror the Suits around her were willing to accept.

She couldn't figure out what to do, how to salvage the situation and continue the mission. But as she looked into Wolfe's eyes, she knew he knew something was wrong. She had failed Hunter.

Ashton turned and ran. The Suits stood still as she barreled through the dance floor toward the tall, tangled tree archway.

Run. It was the only thing she knew how to do. Her heels clinked against the paved walkway as she ran past the guards and down the same pathway Wolfe had led her down just hours before.

Wolfe was running after her. She turned and saw him wave a hand at the guards, telling them to stand down. He was gaining speed. Ashton couldn't run any faster. She was still awkward in her Suit, and the heels didn't help.

Wolfe had chased her before when she had run from Land of Legends, but this time Ashton knew she couldn't outrun him. She stopped, her heart beating out of her chest, and let Wolfe catch up to her. She was out of breath, but she shouldn't have been winded in a Suit. She tried to focus her eyes but couldn't blink away the black spots clouding her vision.

"What has gotten into you?" Wolfe yelled. He was suspicious, angry, and embarrassed.

Ashton wanted to answer, to scream, but she couldn't seem to catch her breath. She felt like she was underwater. The world was turning dark, and the greenery of the trees spun. Now was not the time for an anxiety attack! She needed to pull herself together.

She tried to still her vision, but when she opened her eyes, the world was still black. Ashton screamed. She felt something slimy touching her body. She blinked. She was in the jungle, Wolfe staring at her.

The world was spinning again. Wolfe held out his arm and she caught it as she lost her footing. Ashton tried to focus on Wolfe, but the world went black again. Her Suit buckled at the knees, and she saw the flash of Wolfe's face.

"Wolfe, what's happening?" Ashton said as she panicked and gripped his arm. She saw his eyes shift as he watched her fall. She had caught him off guard and he grew suspicious.

"What did you call me?"

That was the last thing Ashton heard as Charlotte collapsed to the ground.

Ashton opened her eyes in darkness. Something was wrong. She was floating in some kind of goo. She flailed her arms, trying to stand up, but she was trapped in a small compartment.

The pod. She was in the pod.

What was happening? Had Hunter already come for her? A second ago, she had been Charlotte. Her Suit must have failed. She remembered collapsing into Wolfe's arms. Ashton continued to panic, the reality of the situation becoming more dire. How had the Suit failed so quickly? She had only had two days in it. Had it failed? If so, it had not even lasted half as long as Georgina had predicted. Did NeuroEnergy set her up?

There was no time to think about that. She needed to get out of this claustro-phobic, coffin-like pod. With her empty Suit laying in Wolfe's arms, someone would come looking for her, and they wouldn't find Charlotte.

Ashton put her hands against the hard exterior of the pod and tried to push, but she couldn't get any traction in the goo.

Click.

Somewhere outside the pod, a latch opened. The top half of the pod began to rise. The bright white light made Ashton squint. She tried to push her body far away from the opening light, unsure of what was about to happen. A woman dressed all in white greeted her, her dark skin enhancing her icy blue eyes rimmed by a thin line of black. Ashton gawked at the sudden change in eye color that then shifted back to a deep hazel color.

107

Ashton had been prepared to either pretend to be Charlotte or fight as Ashton, but instead, she began to sob. Her anxiety felt like a monster clawing its way out of her body.

"Please relax, Ms. Charlotte. The emotions can feel intense at first when emerging from the pod." She handed Ashton a glass of dark green juice. "Please drink this."

The woman shoved the glass into her hand, Ashton was shaking as she stood in the pod's goo, still covered in wires. She did as she was asked and gulped down the thick green substance. Instantly, her mind felt a numbing sensation and her anxiety slowly dissipated.

"What is this?" Ashton said as she took a deep breath.

"Medicine, to help with the loss of connectivity. It's a mood stabilizer."

While Ashton was in the Suit, the transmitters in her brain were flooded with euphoria. No wonder she had been so distracted by Augland and Wolfe. She felt foolish now for getting so distracted from the mission.

Ashton shook her head, trying to shake away the numbing sensation. She wanted to go back to the feeling of anxiety. There she felt safe and clearheaded. She needed to think objectively to figure out what to do. Should she keep up the ruse, or run? But she couldn't get a grasp on her thoughts as the medicine overcame her senses.

Out of her brain fog, she heard the woman say, "I'm sorry, Ms. Charlotte, but it seems you are not in our system."

The worker's dark eyes glanced at Ashton. The woman looked down at the glass square she held. It turned red. Ashton's employee ID and face began flashing on the screen.

This was bad.

CHAPTER 18

Wolfe
One Month Earlier

One by one, the Executives followed Warren out of the boardroom. The vote Reuben had incited against the new customer service initiative—against Warren—had sent a wave of unease across the board. As each member left in silence, Wolfe and Reuben remained seated.

Wolfe eyed Reuben cautiously. The spacious, white boardroom seemed to close in on him and his father's closest friend. Something was going on and Wolfe needed to know what.

Reuben sat across from Wolfe at the other end of the table, stoic and inscrutable, as always. Wolfe could not read him.

If this had been a test, Wolfe had failed. His vote against his father solidified his position against Warren. On the other hand, Warren's surprise at Reuben's betrayal seemed genuine. Did Reuben have a scheme of his own?

"Are you going to ask or just continue to stare at me?"

Reuben played his chess piece and waited for Wolfe to make his move.

"Why?" It wasn't a strategic question, but Wolfe needed to understand what was going on.

"I've got my reasons." Reuben gave him a sly smile and twirled his pen between his fingers. "I've given you your chance. It's what you wanted, right? To take the CEO position from your father?"

Wolfe was speechless. Had he been so obvious that even Reuben knew his intentions? Had the others seen through him as well?

Reuben sighed.

"When you become CEO, I will be your right hand. That cannot change. And don't worry about the others; they are easily swayed. I mean, good effort, but it's gifts and bribes that win hearts, not good intentions."

Reuben mocked Wolfe's naivety and it stung. Wolfe prided himself on being aware and ahead of the game, but Reuben had seen right through him.

His mind spun as he tried to grasp this twist of new events. Reuben was implying he would start the vote for repercussions against Warren at the next board meeting. He had not said it in as many words, but everyone knew that was the direction things were going. Had Reuben seen the turning of the tide and decided to back Wolfe instead of Warren? He would not be surprised if Reuben's lifelong loyalty to his father was just loyalty to power. But if Reuben was backing him, did that mean he had a chance at becoming CEO? He didn't want Reuben by his side, but if it meant becoming CEO, and having the power to change things, it might be worth it.

Reuben stood and collected his interconnect from the boardroom table. "I didn't do this for you, whatever is going through your mind about me going against your father. While I don't agree with everything that man does, and everyone knows we haven't seen eye to eye on some things, he is more suited for this position than you will ever be in this lifetime, which is why you need me. I did this for Ana, and you'll do me the favor of letting her know that. She will know what this means."

This was another curveball Wolfe had not seen coming. His mother, Anastasia, had played a role in this? His mother and Reuben? Wolfe had always thought his mother stayed away from the political games. Was this another trick?

Wolfe made his way down the long corridor to his mother's penthouse suite, visiting her for the second time in a week. He knocked softly on the door.

"Come in!" rang the sweet voice of his mother. She was too trusting of the political prowlers that lived around the corner, but it was something he loved about her.

"I thought I'd see you."

She sat at her dining room table in white coveralls covered in drips of green and white paint. Next to her was a giant canvas. She was painting a lamb, the beautiful young animal lying in the middle of a green pasture.

"What did you do . . . ?" Wolfe whispered as he entered her apartment and wrapped his arms around his mother from behind, cradling her back and forth.

She sighed heavily, pushing her face against Wolfe's cheek.

"Pushed things along for you. Just a little motherly nudge. Reuben's a good man. He watched you grow up and cares for you . . . and Augland."

Wolfe knew she was downplaying her involvement. She had something on Reuben, maybe a political influence. There was no way he would go against a lifelong loyalty for nothing.

Wolfe sometimes forgot where his mother had come from. She was a prestigious, well-thought-of, and highly sought-after woman when Warren married her. She had played the political game that helped propel Warren to power.

However, after Wolfe was born, her perspective and attitude changed. She had turned away from posthumanism, the foundation of Augland's mission statement, which believed technology advancements enhanced human existence. Over the years, her concerns became deeper. She harbored some ideological skepticism of furthering society into this posthuman world. She had once told Wolfe the reason she did not go back into a Suit after giving birth to him was that she was tired—tired of the games, lies, and unrealistic reality.

Wolfe could understand that. He was tired of it too.

He didn't pry any further into his mother's involvement and Reuben's recent actions; he knew she would not tell him. She would not say what she had against Reuben or how she was able to persuade him to side with Wolfe. All he knew was that his mother was helping him achieve the impossible. He loved her for that. While she portrayed a meek, uninvolved Augland mother, deep down she had influence he had previously not appreciated. There were many things Wolfe had yet to learn.

Wolfe was eager to attend the next meeting two days later and was the first person in the boardroom. He had not seen his father since the last board meeting. Warren had stayed away and Wolfe had not tried to see him.

Wolfe had filled his time managing the security detail of Augland, overseeing recent security updates on the outer walls, and creating a new program that would allow security men to rise within the Executive ranks. Joao, his right-hand man, had brought up the concept to him. While it was technically possible for workers to climb the corporate ladder, in reality, it was nearly impossible—the Executives saw to that. Wolfe had worked with the security detail for years and it was the least he could do to help another person below him succeed. He made Joao the new Director of Security, overseeing his previous obligations.

While Wolfe enjoyed the distance, it did concern him that he had not been brought to Warren's office for a reprimand or to be forced to publicly retract his vote. Either Warren knew Wolfe had the upper hand, or he and Reuben had a plan up their sleeve. Wolfe didn't know what was going on, but he trusted his mother and would take every advantage he could to become CEO and have a chance to save the workers of Augland.

The Executives soon assembled, the atmosphere tense as everyone waited to see what the day's agenda would be. Finally, Warren arrived, wearing his typical black suit and multi-colored tie, with slicked-back hair and his signature salt-and-pepper goatee manicured perfectly. His eyes narrowed as he glanced around the room.

Wolfe sat at the end of the table, with Lee on his left and Boren on his right. Warren stood at the other end of the table, Wintefred and Sebastian on his left and Reuben on his right. Warren looked each Executive in the eyes, and Wolfe followed his gaze. Boren looked down at his hands—

Wintefred somber, Lee fixated on Warren, Sebastian grinning, and Reuben clenched.

"I've made a decision. Given recent discussions with this board, it pains me to say I'm not what Augland 54 needs anymore. Under my leadership, Augland 54 has become prosperous. I don't need to remind you that we were not a prominent Augland when my father ran this company." Warren didn't look in Wolfe's direction. "That being said, my actions are inexcusable, and I take full responsibility. As Reuben so astutely pointed out in our last meeting, I've gone behind the backs of those who have trusted me. I've grown old—and tired, I might add, of the constant need to turn something that is already great into perfection. I think it is time for a change, something different. And so, with great enthusiasm, and as my last act as CEO, I cast my vote for the new CEO of Augland 54 to my son, Wolfgang, a man I trust will go forward with honor and integrity."

Surprise hit Wolfe like a punch in the gut. The silence in the air was deafening as Warren's words reverberated around the room. Wolfe had expected to fight his father every step of the way to CEO, but here Warren was, giving his blessing.

Conversation broke out around the room and Warren cleared his throat to regain attention. He smiled; a grin was painted across his face as if he were happy to pass down his legacy. Wolfe knew better.

"All in favor of appointing Wolfgang as new CEO of Augland 54, say 'Aye.'"

Boren nodded his head yes before belting out, "Aye." It didn't take long before others smiled and followed. Lee spoke up next, then Wintefred, and finally Reuben. The ayes rang around the room like a symphony and Wolfe felt an overwhelming sense of pride. It had worked. The years of preparing for this day had come down to these few seconds.

It was over. An overwhelming relief washed over Wolfe as the world around him brightened. All the suffering, the carnage, the inconceivable hurt. It was now time for a new dawn, and it would be something Wolfe would be proud of, something that would make life for the Colony easier, and finally, it would make Ashton proud. He held in his excitement to remain professional around the elite of Augland.

Everyone turned to look at Wolfe and he realized they were waiting for him to speak. As Warren sat, Wolfe stood.

"I—I don't know what to say, only that I won't let you down. This is a true honor."

He should have said he could not hope to fill his father's shoes, but Wolfe no longer needed to lie. A new dawn approached.

There was a knock on the door to Wolfe's office. He had retreated there after the Executives had all congratulated him on his promotion. They had all gone out for drinks to blow off the steam of the past few days, but Wolfe had excused himself early. He needed a moment to regain his composure.

Before he could respond to the knock, his father opened the door and came in with two glasses and an expensive bottle of whiskey. Suits didn't need real whiskey, but Warren had always wanted to consume the real thing, not a programmed version of the expensive liquor. Warren smiled, but Wolfe felt the hair on his arms stand on end. Despite Warren's far-reaching grin, Wolfe knew his father's anger had not dissipated that quickly. But Wolfe would not be afraid of his father anymore. He was now CEO. Wolfe had the power.

"I believe congrats are in order."

Warren stalked in and looked around Wolfe's office as if for the first time, the usual judgment in his eyes as he made his way to the chair in front of Wolfe's desk. He sat. Wolfe remained where he was, standing behind the desk.

"Please sit, we are celebrating!" Warren poured a glass of liquor, passed the glass to Wolfe, and then poured his own.

Warren took a deep breath. Perhaps this was a genuine visit; an admirable acceptance of defeat. Wolfe sat down and grabbed the drink.

113

"To the new CEO of Augland 54."

They clinked glasses and took sips.

"Why?" It was the same question he had asked Reuben. His father had a reason for everything, and Wolfe wanted to know the angle his father was playing.

A half-smile crept up the right side of Warren's face. "I did it for me," he said through gritted teeth. Wolfe tried to keep the confusion off his face.

"You have repeatedly disappointed me. Over and over again. I give you a chance and you find a way to screw it up. Every time. And I truly blame your mother for that. She was passive with you, too nurturing. She gave you more . . . feelings. And you clearly don't get that from me. Or your grandfather."

His father's words stung deeply. Wolfe struggled to keep his face passive and his anger under control. He did not want to let his father talk about his mother that way, but he needed to see where Warren was going.

Wolfe took another sip of the whiskey and sighed. "I don't really care what you think anymore." He finally had the upper hand. "No matter your angle or plan, you lost the CEO chair because you're selfish and greedy. And the board agreed."

Warren laughed, and Wolfe frowned, confused by his father's smugness.

"You think those buffoons would have agreed if I hadn't been the one to cast a vote? They do what I want. Always." His eyes narrowed in on his son. Wolfe was missing some clear piece to his father's puzzle.

"Let me paint the picture for you. Because you clearly have no idea what just happened. I allowed you to become CEO of Augland 54. Your mother got to Reuben; I saw right through that one. Reuben's too soft. He's like you sometimes, always babbling about workers and rights . . . *sustainability*," Warren mocked. "Clever to involve Ana. I'll have words with her about putting herself into my affairs. Everyone knows your poor mother is sick; her time out of her android has affected her mind's stability. She may need to be locked away."

Wolfe stood up, furious at his father's threat.

"You won't touch her!" Wolfe narrowed his eyes, breathing quickly. For the first time, they were both letting their true emotions out. "Might have to lock you away too, old man. It will take years to rebuild the destruction you've done."

"You've got me there, son. Looks like you'll win after all. I might as well raise my white flag." Warren raised his glass and swished his drink in the air, mimicking a waving flag.

Wolfe's patience with his father's patronization was gone. He almost inhaled the last of his drink. "I think you'd better go," Wolfe whispered, slamming the glass on his desk.

There was a long pause. His father stayed still; his grin still plastered on his face. Suddenly, Wolfe started to feel strange. The office around him began to blur out of focus.

"What . . ." was all Wolfe could say as he tried to focus on his father's face. Warren only stared at his drink, continuing to swirl it around as Wolfe put his hands on his desk to steady himself.

He realized what was happening. One drink would not have gotten him drunk. An overwhelming pressure to shut his eyes clouded Wolfe's senses.

"What did . . . you do?" he accused his father, struggling to get the words out of his mouth. Warren looked at him, the grin still on his face.

"I told you. You touch something important to me, you lose something you love."

Wolfe swayed. Then . . . black.

CHAPTER 19

Ashton
SUNDAY 8:08 p.m.

Ashton stood, calf deep in the light-blue goo of the pod that glowed beneath her. The room was blinding white. Rows of pods stretched as far as she could see, looking like neatly stacked eggs. The walls of the room were white, the ceiling and floor were white, and the woman in front of her was dressed all in white. The only color in the room was the woman's deep-brown skin and Ashton's red face still flashing on the screen.

Ashton stood, frozen, time seeming to slow down as she waited for the woman in front of her to make a move. Maybe this worker had heard of Ashton, or at least realized that the girl in the goo was in trouble. With one click of her button, this woman could turn Ashton in and alert all security that there was a breach.

The woman stood unnaturally still in her all-white uniform. Ashton looked from the flashing screen into her eyes, but something weird was happening. Suddenly, the woman's expression went blank and the dark brown of her iris shifted, lightening. . .and then turned pure white as they focused in on Ashton. Her eyes glowed bright white around her black pupils, thinly outlined and shifting back and forth as the woman focused robotically on something Ashton couldn't see.

What was happening? Ashton had thought this woman was a worker, human, but she couldn't be with those eyes. She had looked so real, so lifelike! She had every imperfection of a worker: gnawed-down fingernails from anxiety, a sprinkling of gray

116

hairs on her head that revealed her age, even wrinkles around her eyes. This was no Suit, but *it* wasn't natural either.

The realization of what stood in front of her stopped Ashton from running. Augland had manipulated this worker, who had surely once been human, and turned her into some kind of machine, entangled with technology. A product. It made Ashton's stomach turn.

Suddenly, she thought of Niall and the scar across his eye that disappeared under a black eye patch. Could the two be related? Could what Augland had done to this poor woman have been attempted on her best friend at Maya Bay? Had he been experimented on?

"You don't seem to be in our system, Charlotte. Is there another name I should check?" Ashton knew the woman had all the information she needed; Ashton obviously wasn't who she said she was. She was not a Suit, she was not an elite, she was a worker. Ashton screamed inside, searching for any possible excuse, anyway she could get out of this. *Should I deny it? Demand they check again?* But that wouldn't help. The screen blaring red lettering with her worker identification and face couldn't be more obvious.

The woman's eyes shifted once again from sparkling hazel to a stoic white, outlined by black.

"Please—" Ashton attempted to plead.

"I believe we may have a security breach in Branch Seven of the pod accommodations." The woman brought her interconnect to her mouth, and with no emotion, turned Ashton in.

Ashton was speechless. There was no getting out of this now. She could not reason with technology, not when her narrative was controlled by Augland. How could this woman have had her own body so cruelly altered by Augland—and still turn her in?

It didn't matter now; Ashton had to run. Her cover was blown, and she was in an area of Augland 54 she had never visited before. White walls rose high above her as the interconnect echoed in the large room. Her pod rested in a row of pearly, dome-like clams, shutting in their human occupants between their shells. Ashton stood outside of them, in wide-open space, just waiting to be plucked by Augland's predators.

During their time in the small underground office of NeuroEnergy, Hunter and Ashton had mapped out a specific day and time when Hunter would come to retrieve her pod and hide it in Maya Bay until their boat arrived. He would even show up early in case the Suit failed sooner than they had planned. Ashton thought they had at least seven days. They'd banked on five just to be safe. While she entertained Wolfe

117

to try and extract information, Hunter would escort her pod and would come to get it when her "vacation" ended, and it was time to board the ship back home. It would be the only way to keep her cover and escape out of Augland undetected. That was key. Undetected and discreet.

Now, Hunter would have no idea that Charlotte's Suit had failed three days before their planned agenda and that retrieval and escape were impossible. Ashton wondered if Georgina had known about the Suit and betrayed them, but there was no time to think about that now. Now, she had to move and would need to fight to survive. Again.

Ashton darted out of the goo and onto the sleek, white, marbled floor. She didn't know how to get out of this colorless maze, but she knew she couldn't wait for security, or Wolfe, to get her.

Her right foot hit the ground and slid on goo, her knee crashing into the solid marble floor. Ashton's hair and skin-tight suit still dripped with goo. The room was cold, sending shivers up her spine. She felt disoriented and disjointed.

She had trained her mind to move the artificial body of the Suit and respond to the sensations programmed into the pod, and now her own body felt foreign and clumsy. Her legs cramped from lack of movement and the tingling of her muscles slowed her response time. The combination made it exceedingly hard to function normally. She pulled her knee up from the ground and propelled herself forward. Her mind spelled out each command to her body: *Get up. Move your foot forward. Run.*

The augmented worker didn't chase Ashton, but instead brought up her interconnect and summoned again for security.

Ashton ran to the left, away from the semi-mechanical worker and, she hoped, toward an exit. She was running as fast as her unadjusted physique could go, but her body couldn't keep up with her racing mind and she stumbled again. There was nowhere to get away. The force of her forward trajectory through what felt like a never-ending room confused her. Finally, sighing with relief, she saw the shadow outline of a double door in the distance.

But just as she saw it, the door opened and a swarm of black security men spilled through. It looked like a nest of spiders cracking open and bursting into the white room. Ashton's heart pounded, and she could feel her looming entrapment. There was nothing but pods and the endless white corridor and the security team running toward them. Her only exit was closed. She put her hands up to her head in panic as the world around her spun. This was it.

Someone was yelling at her, but Ashton couldn't make out what they were saying. Her brain was fuzzy. She slumped down to her knees. She was tired. She was not sure if it was sadness, fear, defeat, or just the feeling of exhaustion, but she could not fight through the swirling, ravaging emotions.

The security guards reached her, and a woman grabbed her unresisting hand and twisted it behind her back, handcuffing her. The woman guard said something, but Ashton heard only muffled sounds as a tear escaped her eyes. She had failed, the mission had failed, and she was on her knees, numb with disappointment.

A man approached and through the fog Ashton heard a voice she recognized.

"Didn't think I'd see you again, Ashton."

It was Joao, Wolfe's Director of Security. Joao was Wolfe's employee, but from what Wolfe had mentioned, she knew they were brother-like friends.

Staring Joao in the eyes, Ashton made one thrashing attempt at freedom, but the cuffs tightened around her wrists. Her time in the pod had left her weak and out of breath.

Joao said nothing but threw a pair of black pants and a black T-shirt at her; the standard Augland worker attire. She was uncuffed only long enough to slip the clothes over the slick bathing suit she had worn in the pod.

SUNDAY 9:10 p.m.

"Where are we going?" Ashton asked Joao as he pushed her along, reminding her of the time he had taken her to the cages, the first time she had returned to Augland.

"Well, seeing as you have a habit of escaping, Wolfe wanted me to bring you straight to him. I think he'd like a quick word before taking you down to the cages."

Ashton's eyes shut. She was sure Wolfe would know the truth now, that Charlotte had been Ashton the whole time. But she could now look him in the eyes and show the betrayal she felt. Let him know that she had seen who he truly was and now despised him. If it had not been clear before, she knew now that Wolfe was just that, a wolf in sheep's clothing. Warren did not compare to the manipulation and lies that Wolfe was capable of, and she wanted him to see that she knew the truth.

Joao pushed Ashton down a long corridor. Out the windows, she could see the tropical landscape of Predator's Biome. They were inside the walls of Augland. Ashton and Hunter had memorized the detailed map of Augland they had received from Georgina. While Georgina may have lied about the Suit, the map was current and Ashton knew the layout of the parks, both the customer and worker-only sections.

Joao was taking her down the outer rim of Predator's Biome. It was where they kept all the pods and Suit-related technology workshops.

They finally exited the wall, where Joao led her into a gondola to take her to the Executive suites. Ashton sat next to Joao and looked down at the parks below her. She and Wolfe, when she was Charlotte, had taken this route just a day before. Then, it had been majestic and romantic. But now Ashton felt the unrelenting cold of reality penetrate her skin. She shivered. Without saying a word, Joao took off his black security jacket and wrapped it around her. It was a small gesture but appreciated.

"Don't do this . . ." Ashton whispered loud enough for Joao to hear. She now looked at the high-level workers who did the bidding of Augland as misguided rather than evil. She realized now they had been brainwashed to serve something so toxic.

"I can't help you."

Joao escorted her into the expanse of a lobby and then down a long hallway toward the Executive suites.

"You do his bidding, kill people—workers just like you—because they tell you to do it." She tensed as his grasp around her elbow tightened.

"I do my job. They feed me, clothe me, and give me shelter. Wolfe, he protects me and those I love. You think there are no consequences for biting the hand that feeds. Unlike you, I take care of the person who takes care of me."

"You're a joke." That is all she could think of saying, the words flowing from anger. She meant to hurt his ego.

They went past the large windows where Wolfe had showed Charlotte Land of Legends and down a long corridor Ashton had never been down. It was narrow, but wide enough for Joao and Ashton to walk side by side. The spotless white walls and marble floor mimicked the clean feeling of the pod room. Soon, the hallway became dark, barely lit by the dull light bulbs above them.

"You know they'll just kill me . . . and you're willing to let that happen."

Ashton wanted to hurt Joao with her words, but she desperately hoped they weren't true. She hoped the moment Wolfe saw her he would beg for her forgiveness and tell her this was all a lie.

Joao and Ashton remained silent until suddenly they stopped at a set of double-deep oak doors. He pressed the intercom on the right side of the doors, and with a soft click, they unlocked. Joao ushered her through first and closed the doors behind her. A strong, earthy scent of sage and sandalwood surrounded her. The room was lit only by the bright stars of the open windows. She was in Wolfe's home.

CHAPTER 20

Ashton
SUNDAY 10:13 p.m.

Wolfe's home was like nothing else in Augland. It had none of the modern technology and opulence Ashton had become used to as Charlotte. His apartment had deep-brown paneled walls lined with wooden bookshelves. In the center was a large desk with leather chairs. The room smelled like leather and wood and Ashton felt as though she had stepped into a modern log cabin. The cold, chic, and polished concrete beneath her bare feet gave Augland away.

"Sit." Joao sat her down in one of the leather chairs that faced an empty chair. Ashton was not sure how long they waited in silence before the door's lock made a clicking sound and Wolfe entered angrily. He still wore his suit and tie from the Jungle Gala, which contrasted with Ashton's all-black worker attire, Joao's oversized jacket, and her wet hair.

"Could you wait outside, Joao, we just need a moment. You can uncuff her; she can't hurt me." Joao stood straight, and Ashton noticed how similar he was to Wolfe. Joao was tall, although much thinner than Wolfe, with the same short hair and dark brown beard. They could be brothers. Joao nodded and did as he was asked.

As soon as Joao left, Ashton looked at Wolfe. Despite everything, she wanted him to drop his façade, tell her everything had been an act, and beg for her forgiveness. She wanted Wolfe to explain the Colony raid and his behavior to her as Charlotte; she wanted him to assure her it was all part of a bigger plan. Ashton studied Wolfe as the door shut, but he didn't shift or change his demeanor. For months she had waited for this, to see him face to face, to be reunited. But this was no longer the Wolfe she thought she had loved.

The Wolfe she knew was not this man. Until now, she had maintained hope that she could be wrong, but he was not the same Wolfe she had fallen in love with. He oozed conceitedness. She'd wanted to see him break his character once Joao left, but here he was, the same man she'd known when she was Charlotte.

"How could you?" Ashton spat.

"Could I do what?" Wolfe shook his head, mocking Ashton.

"You took those children from the Colony." Ashton was trying to keep tears from her eyes. She would not show Wolfe weakness. He had seen her soft side once, but she would never again let her guard down.

"Oh, that? It's a small price they pay for us allowing them to live outside these walls. Live off the resources of Augland without their own contribution. My father was right; it's only fair we get our payment." Ashton couldn't believe what she was hearing.

Her chest tightened. He didn't even care that he was breaking her heart. She stared stonily out the windows at the skyline of Augland, not making eye contact with Wolfe. She was not ready for him to feel her emotional daggers. She was still shivering under Joao's jacket, but now it was not from cold or fear; she shook with anger. Wolfe had been caught in his own lies and he had the audacity to be so casual with her.

Wolfe slowly walked past Ashton, behind her chair, where he stood facing his wall with a built-in bar. He grabbed two glasses and a bottle. The clinking was loud against the silence. Without a word, he sat them on the dense wood table and poured two glasses of amber liquid.

"Take one, please." Ashton inhaled deeply, sitting still in protest. She was happy to be defiant. She let him place the glass in front of her and watched as he sat down and took a big sip from his own glass. He smacked his lips with satisfaction.

"Ashton, right?" Wolfe said.

Ashton let her anger show on her face. Was he really stooping so low that he was pretending not to know her?

"That was quite a trick you played. Landing a Suit of your own, not something I would think the Colony took stock of."

Ashton finally glanced at Wolfe. He stared through her, his eyes fixated, reading her.

"No, not without help from NeuroEnergy. Georgina, I'm sure, had her vicious teeth sunk into this ploy. I mean, to send one of my ex-employees in to spy on me. Clever, and ruthless. But she obviously did not have the guts to do it herself." Wolfe laughed.

As much as Ashton wanted to disagree, she had come to the same conclusion. Georgina must have known the Suit was faulty and would never have taken the risk herself. She had used Ashton as a guinea pig. The Suit did not last as long as any of them had hoped. Two days was a pathetic attempt—and a waste, given her current situation.

"You've caused quite a bit of a problem for me and I'm getting tired of it. But the game you've played is done." Wolfe took a big breath in. "I thought the moment I heard you had come back I would just have you killed, and your body sent back to the Colony. But then I thought I could use you. Quite a bit in fact. While I tried hard not to allow your escape out of Augland to make its way around the office, it did. There has been a need for quite a bit of rehabilitation for workers because of you."

Wolfe stood up; his drink finished. He thrust his hands deep into his tuxedo pockets as he slowly walked around the open living room.

"I'm not sure if you saw it, but we have a fantastic new customer service initiative. The worker who greeted you outside your pod. And that server at the restaurant you had such a reaction to—it makes sense now. I suspect you know him? He was one of our first attempts; unfortunately, it didn't work so well for him."

Ashton's eyes grew wide as she put pieces together. A flashback to Niall's scarred face and the glowing eyes of the worker who had called security on her. Wolfe was experimenting on workers. Augmenting them into machines.

Ashton's face turned red as anger boiled in her belly. Wolfe was a monster; she was sure of it now. She saw who he truly was. Finally, the man without a mask. Silence filled the air. Ashton's brow furrowed as she tried to figure out his next move. Wolfe obviously needed to fill the silence, to gloat.

"Love is hard; you know I was in love once. It was beautiful, too. It can be powerful and useful, if used correctly."

He was mocking her feelings for him.

"I don't love you." Ashton spat out the words. She would not let him manipulate her.

Wolfe just smirked. "Let me ask you, why did you come as Charlotte?"

"You stole from the Colony," she yelled. "Children, tiny innocent children. You stole them."

"Then why not go to them, why spend time with me? You could have gone undetected searching for them without getting close to me and exposing yourself."

123

Wolfe was intelligent, she would give him that. She wanted to scream at him. She knew Georgina needed information, but part of Ashton knew she had selfishly wanted to see Wolfe. But none of that mattered now. She would not give him the satisfaction of being right.

"I'm not going to get anything out of you and that's fair. I understand your reservations. But people can be easily persuaded."

Wolfe stood up and headed out of the room.

"Don't disappear on me now."

Ashton followed him with her eyes until he was out of sight. As soon as he was gone, she jumped from her chair and ran to the heavy oak doors. They were locked. She yanked hard, but they didn't budge. She glanced at the windows with a large patio looking across Augland. She was too high up. The Space Needle looked out over all of Augland and was far too high. She would never survive the jump.

She looked around, panicking. There had to be another way out. She darted across the living room, past the chairs, and up a set of wooden stairs that disappeared into the darkness. As she reached the top, she pressed hard at the door. It too was locked. She pounded on it and slid down to the floor, tears welling up in her eyes as the world began to enclose around her. Wolfe left, knowing she would try to escape, and that there would be no way out. She felt silly to have even tried.

"Ashton," Wolfe called up from the bottom of the stairs. "It's no use." He sounded irritated. She straightened and looked once more at the door. All thoughts of escape faded from her mind. There was no getting out, no leaving. There was no hope.

Ashton slowly made her way down the steps toward Wolfe. When she was within reach of him, he grabbed her and forced her down the remaining steps. He dragged her across the room and shoved her back into the leather chair. She breathed heavily as Wolfe sighed in frustration. Ashton's mind went numb again as Wolfe's action again broke her.

His intercom buzzed and Wolfe allowed whoever was outside the doors to enter. The floor-to-ceiling doors opened and Joao entered pulling something behind him—someone. Ashton saw the sway of long black locks first and then the big, golden-brown eyes. Her heart stopped.

"Jagatha . . ." she said under her breath. She was frozen in place.

"Ash!" Jagatha yelled as their eyes locked. Jagatha tried to run to Ashton, but Joao held her in place. Ashton did not have the same restriction and ran to her young friend, falling to the floor as she wrapped her arms around the small girl. Jagatha cried

124

as she tightened her grip around Ashton. Ashton pulled the girl just far enough away so she could see her face. Her tears mirrored Ashton's.

"Are you okay? You're okay, right, J-Bug?" Ashton tried to quiet the girl's sobbing.

Ashton's heart thumped wildly as if it would jump right out of her chest and onto the hard concrete floor. Wolfe and Joao just stood by, watching them.

Ashton knew this was not a happy reunion. Wolfe wanted something from her and knew how to get it. He was threatening her without words.

"What do you want?!" She refused to look at him and kept her eyes on Jagatha.

"How did you get the Suit?"

Ashton paused. It was easy to be defiant when she thought she had nothing to lose, but now she held something dear to her, someone, that meant more than anything.

"Georgina." Ashton closed her eyes, giving in to defeat.

"They built it?"

"No, found it. And worked on recreating the AEC's technology."

Wolfe came close to them now and patted Jagatha's long, black hair.

"And sent you to do what?" His voice was soft, as if he were not dangling a precious life in front of her. Ashton paused and then looked up at the man she had trusted and even envisioned a life with. He did not break eye contact.

"You know why," she said flatly. "You said yourself that NeuroEnergy only needs to find out what energy sources Augland is creating. If they find out you are breaking the treaty that ended the war, they have ammunition to take Augland 54 to DC."

"Is NeuroEnergy working with the Colony?" Wolfe's line of questioning confused Ashton. He had been in contact with Cahya and had more information about the Colony than she did. Did he need to Ashton to confirm it? Was it because Joao was here?

"No, not really. They provide some technology and some supplies, but I wouldn't call them 'helpful.'"

Wolfe stood, towering above Ashton and Jagatha, and took in a deep breath. Jagatha's cries had softened, but she still dug fiercely into Ashton.

"Thank you, Ashton. You've been immensely helpful."

Wolfe motioned for Joao to take Ashton. Joao did as he was told. He wrapped an arm around Ashton, who quickly went into defense mode. She let go of Jagatha to dig her elbow deep into his side. Joao winced in pain before turning Ashton around and wrapping her in a bear-like grip, rendering her defenseless and facing Wolfe. Ashton's anger boiled until she saw Wolfe grab Jagatha, and she began to panic as he dragged the child away from her. Jagatha never took her eyes off Ashton and reached for her frantically, screaming. Ashton used all her strength, but she couldn't escape Joao's grasp.

"Wolfe, Wolfe what are you doing? I told you what you wanted; now, just let her go," Ashton begged.

Wolfe's anger made his eyes wide. This was a different anger, a crazed anger, something Ashton had never seen before.

"You made this happen! I gave you an opportunity to tell me and you refused. It was not so hard to admit what we all already knew!" He was a lunatic.

"Who are you?!" Ashton screamed. It was as if he had become a whole new person, with no evidence of the man she had known. Wolfe did not answer. Instead, he turned and dragged Jagatha with him out the glass door onto his patio. The sliding glass doors opened without effort and the wind howled as it slammed glass against glass without shattering. Jagatha's hair whirled around as she reached out for Ashton, desperate with fear.

Ashton shouted as she struggled to tear herself away from Joao. Every muscle in her body strained and her body movements became erratic. Ashton would do anything to get away from Joao and run to Jagatha.

The world was silent, except for Jagatha's screams; they bounced in Ashton's mind, never losing momentum. Ashton knew what would happen before it did. She hoped her mind was only going to such a dark place to then rewind and pull back to reality. But this was real.

Jagatha continued to flail as Wolfe dragged the terrified youngster up to her feet and brought her up over the glass railing. Everything was happening in slow motion. Jagatha's eyes were wide with terror and her screams deafening. She clawed at Wolfe as fear consumed her tiny body. It was the primal instinct of survival.

"Wolfe, please!!" Ashton screamed, tears rolling down her face. "I'll do anything! Say anything, anything—just don't hurt her!" She wasn't beneath begging or negotiating. In that moment, she would have traded positions with Jagatha. She would give up anything—or everything.

Wolfe turned to look at Ashton.

"Yes, you will."

His eyes were black and emotionless. A true villain. Ashton's breath escaped her. He wouldn't. He couldn't. This was a scare tactic to get her to cooperate and it was working. But then . . . he let go.

Time slowed down. Jagatha reached out and her eyes shifted to Ashton in a split second. Her big, gold, beautiful eyes begged in that split second for Ashton to save her and then . . . she disappeared beneath the ledge. Her scream lessened as the distance grew.

Ashton's heart shattered. A pain she had yet to even fathom radiated through her. It took her breath, and her mind went numb.

A deep, guttural sound escaped Ashton, animalistic, as she cried out. Anguish and rage vibrated into an intense, heart-shattering ache that pierced Ashton's soul like being submerged into freezing water.

Ashton sobbed as she lost all ability to move, to breathe. She closed her eyes and collapsed into Joao's arms. He held her, lessening his forceful grip, embracing her to his chest. Ashton felt his heart beating, matching her own. She tried again to breathe, but it was as if her throat had been strung so tight it could not take oxygen—that, or her mind failed to tell her body to receive oxygen. She was breaking down. She thought of Sheva, and all the other pain she had witnessed, and it felt like she had been pushed off the ledge herself. Ashton held her chest as Joao let her fall, gently holding her as she collapsed.

"You can leave." Wolfe motioned to Joao without emotion.

Joao tensed and paused, but as the moment passed, he respected Wolfe's command. Before leaving, he whispered in Ashton's ear.

"I'm so sorry." He squeezed her shoulder. It meant nothing to her. She knew it was unlikely he could have stopped Wolfe, but he could have tried—and for that, she would never forgive Joao. Joao turned and left Ashton alone with someone she was now convinced she hated more than life itself.

"She was an innocent child! She had nothing to do with this!" Ashton screamed, feeling her heart harden to protect herself from the overwhelming pain. "Who are you? Who have you become? You told me you wanted none of this, that it was Warren. I trusted you! You're a . . . a liar!"

She had much more venom to spew, but her body was fueled by too many emotions. Wolfe turned to her.

"It's like you don't even know me. Betrayal of someone you hold close to you is so . . . hurtful, isn't it? It's funny, I guess you and I have that in common."

Ashton sobbed uncontrollably and barely paid attention to Wolfe's confusing words; Wolfe had gone mad. This was a different person entirely from the one she had fallen in love with. She felt foolish. She felt maddened. Then, she couldn't feel anymore. She shut down and put away any semblance of her sanity. She was hollow.

Wolfe poured himself another drink and then handed her one too.

"Drink." He did not ask as he shoved the glass into her hand. Ashton rose, only to show no fear. Taking the drink, she poured the burning liquor down her throat. She winced as the sharp liquid sent shivers down her spine. Ashton swayed as the liquid slithered through her bloodstream, and she felt faint. Something was happening to her body.

She looked at Wolfe and realized he had put something in her drink. He had poisoned her. Ashton didn't even care as she felt her body swaying. Now that Jagatha was dead, not much mattered anymore.

"I wish you understood the irony. It would make this moment so much sweeter."

Ashton swayed. Then . . . black.

CHAPTER 21

Wolfe
Three Weeks Earlier

Wolfe lay still on the bed, wrapping around his fingers the shoelace he had taken from his father's leather shoes. It was out of sheer boredom that he created activities and fiddle toys from various items in the closet that had converted into a prison. The last moment Wolfe remembered—the moment he played over and over in his mind—was drinking with his father in his office after he had been named CEO. He had sipped the bourbon, not knowing his father had laced it with a sedative and felt a shadow world creep into his mind. He had woken up here, in his father's closet.

The closet was a gloomy upstairs room that connected to Wolfe's living quarters, a measure his father had ensured when Wolfe was a teenager first living on his own. The room was filled with rows of high-end shoes, sport coats, white shirts, and ties. Wolfe slept on the floor. He prided himself on his strength, but the last few days he had felt lost and vulnerable. The solitude messed with his mind. He had not seen the light of day in several weeks.

The realization of what his father had done had come slowly and over time. At first, Wolfe was confused by his imprisonment, sure that one of the Executives would notice their newly appointed CEO was missing. But the days went by and nothing happened. He expected Joao to come to his rescue. His years and years of commitment and loyalty, along with Wolfe's sacrifices for Joao, had made them inseparable the last few years. But no one appeared, and hours came and went. After days, Wolfe realized no one was coming for him.

On top of everything, Wolfe was sure his father laced his scarce food with sedatives. At times, he refused to eat, yearning for thought clarity, but the overwhelming drive to nourish brought him to consume the daily rations. The weight of seclusion and fatigue pulled his mind and body out of reality. He still tried to keep active, doing push-ups and sit-ups to stay in shape. He scratched his face as his beard grew well past his typical five o'clock shadow.

Wolfe paced back and forth in the narrow room between the door and the wool mattress his father had placed on the floor in the dark room. The lack of windows made it impossible for him to tell time, and he felt his thoughts too loudly as the darkness enclosed around him. There were moments he talked to himself, replaying different things he would say to his father when he finally returned. Sometimes he reasoned with his father, and other times he lashed out in imaginary fights. But mostly, Wolfe dwelled on all the horrific scenarios of what could or would be happening in his absence.

Minutes, hours, days after he had been shut away, the door to the closet opened. For a moment, the intense light blinded Wolfe and all he saw was the outline of a figure, Warren. But as his eyes came into focus, it wasn't Warren. In the doorway, in front of Wolfe, was Wolfe himself.

I've gone insane.

Wolfe panicked as his brain tried to understand what was in front of him. He watched as his own mouth let out a wicked laugh. He stared into his own bright-blue eyes. He could never seem to fully gain consciousness and clarity. And now he had gone insane.

Wolfe watched as his body came into the room. With a raise of an eyebrow, his mirror image did a spin, showing off every angle. Suddenly, Wolfe understood. He was looking at a replica of himself. It seemed almost identical, except this new version of himself had a hardened look that suggested an evil intent that Wolfe had never possessed. It was a look he had seen in Warren his whole life.

What stood before Wolfe was a complete reproduction of himself. Wolfe finally let out an exhale, his shock wearing off to anger. Out of all the things his father could have done, this had to be the craziest plan of all of them. To create a Suit that looked just like Wolfe.

"Have you gone completely psychotic?!" Wolfe could simply not believe the lengths Warren would go to keep power—to create a Suit that more than resembled Wolfe, to *become* Wolfe.

Warren didn't say anything, only dressed and fixed his shirt and tie as he prepared for whatever he had planned. Wolfe vaguely remembered his father pulling each button and the twist and turns of the tie as his hands—Wolfe's own hands—tightened around the knot. Wolfe remembered as he unsteadily rose from the mattress pad and wobbled to his father, clenching his fists. Whatever Warren was putting in his food made Wolfe weak. Before he reached his father, the older man walked out of the closet without a look behind him. Wolfe watched his father leave and collapsed onto the mattress with despair as he imagined what Warren was doing in his name.

Their next encounter didn't go much differently. Wolfe put his hands up to his face to shield the blinding light as his father entered the dark room. Once he realized who it was, he jumped into action, targeting his father with all his strength. Before he could think about what he was doing, he was going after his father in a feeble attempt to release his anger. Warren, in his Wolfe Suit, caught his hands and with ease pushed him back, catching Wolfe off guard.

"You know you can't hurt me; I don't know why you would even try," Warren said roughly, twisting Wolfe's arm behind his back and slamming him into the dresser drawer, knocking the wind out of him. Wolfe struggled to free his arm, but he had gone weak in the past few weeks from lack of food and movement. He could not compete with his Suit self.

"You made a Suit of me!" Wolfe shouted. "You can't even let go of your ego to see if I could run things."

"My ego?! All you had to do was wait until my job here was done. I could have set you up for success and our future generations. But no, no, you had to go and ruin things. I didn't do this, Wolfgang. You did."

Warren let him go and Wolfe turned to face his father. They were eye to eye now that Warren was in Wolfe's body.

"So, what happens next? Huh? You run things like me? Keep me holed up in this room? For how long? You think no one will know? You think no one will tell the difference?"

Warren put his hands deep in his black slacks and smiled. "It's worked so far. The latest version of the Artificial Existence Being is quite remarkable. Such detail. Anyway, I'm running things as you, yes, and my ideas are becoming reality. People were wary of me after Reuben's little stunt, but they are eager to follow you. After all, you were always the moral one, so I can convince them to do anything. And when I'm done, I'll work hard to ruin everything for you like you tried to do to me."

Wolfe was speechless as he listened to his father's plan. He didn't want to believe it was working, but no one had come to rescue him, so it must be. His father had somehow fooled everyone into thinking he was Wolfe, and now Wolfe was trapped in this endless prison.

Warren continued, "I'll complete the customer service initiative; I'll make my idea of customer service a reality, and if it fails, it's on you. Then, I'll attack your precious Colony. Become even more heartless and ruthless, even for Augland. Eventually, I'll make the board hate you so much they'll be begging me to come out of retirement to run Augland 54 once again."

Warren's anger gave him away. Even through a mask, Warren's twisted mind exposed him. It was a disguise he couldn't hide. Wolfe shook his head in frustration, dumbfounded by what lengths his father would go to.

"Now, if you don't mind, I'm late and have evening plans." Warren stormed out, not waiting for his son's response.

Another week went by. The room spun as Wolfe tried to keep his gaze on anything to steady his vertigo. The color-coded shirts, the perfectly tailored jackets. The dark wood trim contrasted against the navy-blue wall. There were moments he forgot what was happening and others when the unknown of what his father was doing in his name tortured him with anxiety.

When he had energy, Wolfe chipped away at the lock on the door with a clothes hanger, spiking the metal hood and digging it into the steel pillar that stuck into the wall. He even tried using the hefty dresser that housed Warren's many golf clothes as a battering ram, but it didn't make a dent in the door. Warren had made escape impossible.

Warren visited at least every other day. He must have been lonely . . . that, or he wanted someone to know the truth. Warren told Wolfe everything, each detail of the customer success initiative. Even during these times, Wolfe nodded in and out of consciousness. He realized Warren's ego wanted to tell someone what he was doing. It must have killed Warren to know that Wolfe was receiving credit for all of it.

Warren described the experimental nature of the customer service initiative in gory detail. How they were trying to figure out how to successfully integrate robotic appendages onto worker bodies, how robotic arms were stronger and more accurate, and how they had eyes that were able to scan the Suits and receive detailed information to aid in their service.

To add to Wolfe's misery, Warren related how they had started the experiments on the friends of Ashton who Wolfe had sworn to protect. Warren didn't care about the names of the participants. It only mattered what worked and what didn't. Most of the time, Wolfe was left to guess who had been his father's victim. Niall had lost an eye. But Wolfe hoped that Bez was safe: he had worked out a new location for her after Ashton's escape, and she was under the protection of Joao. He hadn't had time to find one for Niall, though, and instantly regretted not fulfilling his promise to take care of him.

Then, Warren told Wolfe about the Colony raid. Wolfe cried out as his father recounted the many Colony children taken and the members who had died. Wolfe could only imagine the betrayal they felt, seeing his hands lead a reign of terror over their small community. His heart broke when he thought of Ashton. Had she seen Warren in Wolfe's Suit and thought it was him? He could only imagine the betrayal she must feel.

Warren reveled in Wolfe's agony. He left, chuckling, as Wolfe collapsed in tears on the worn mattress. Wolfe didn't know how long he stayed like that in the dark, imagining the look of hurt and anger on Ashton's face and the devastation to her heart.

SUNDAY 11:02 p.m.

Wolfe was sound asleep when he was shaken awake by his father. It still caught Wolfe off guard every time he saw his own face appear before him.

"Come, I have something to show you." Wolfe rubbed his eyes, the constant sedatives weighing heavy on his mind. Wolfe's fight was gone. Whatever his father wanted him to see would just make Wolfe another witness to injustice he was useless to fight.

Wolfe stood at the door frame for a moment, eyeing his surroundings carefully. As much as he wanted to leave the small closet, he didn't want to walk into a trap.

"You'll want to see this," Warren murmured.

CHAPTER 22

Wolfe
SUNDAY 11:27 p.m.

The air was thick as Wolfe walked down the wooden stairs into his living room. He was weak from lack of exercise, food, and many weeks locked away in a dark room. But it was more than that; he had a sickening feeling the reason his father had finally released him was not cause for celebration.

Wolfe slowly made his way to the bottom of the stairs, where his father stood pouring himself a typical glass of whiskey. It was quiet except for the humming of the wind against the windows of his own patio doors overlooking Augland 54. It was evening, and the sun hovered just below the windowsill.

Warren had not changed the room much; the dark leather chairs sat exactly where Wolfe had left them. Even if Warren had completely remodeled his son's living room, no one would have noticed. Wolfe was sure the Executives were not inspecting Wolfe's living quarters to make sure he wasn't a Suit in disguise. The idea still seemed impossible, even to Wolfe, who stood before the exact replica of himself.

His eyes shifted away from his father, and he noticed a foot sticking out from behind one of the leather arm chairs. It was motionless. He stepped forward instinctively to get a better view. A small body lay on the ground, a head of curly brown hair covering her face. Wolfe recognized her at once.

It couldn't be. Ashton?

Wolfe lunged toward her, scraping her curly locks out of her face, and pulling her into his embrace. She did not move, but she was breathing. She was alive. Wolfe's mind whirled. How was she here? Why wasn't she safe at the Colony? Had his father captured Ashton specifically to torture him? It would be suicide for Ashton to come back on her own. Still, here she was, and Wolfe wanted nothing more than to grab her and run away. This was not safe for either of them.

"What did you do to her?" Wolfe shouted at his father.

He looked at every feature of Ashton's face and body, each freckle that blended in with her light skin, her long lashes that looked less prominent when they were not shaping her big, ocean-blue eyes. Her chestnut-brown curls looked wet, coated in a thick, semi-dry liquid. She was dressed in all black—black skin-tight pants and a light, black shirt that cut off at the shoulders. She wore a large jacket that could only be from a Security team member. She didn't seem hurt.

"Oh, don't worry. She's just asleep." Warren sounded annoyed.

Wolfe slowly let Ashton slip from his arms, gently placing her head on the ground as he rose, not taking his eyes off her. His mind seared with disgust at what his father had become and what he had resorted to. Wolfe's fists balled as he rose to face his father. He knew his body was weak, but his mind felt stronger than ever.

Wolfe hated the man in front of him, and he hated himself. He had failed, but more than that, he had not done enough to stop his father. Ashton had been right; he should have done more when he had the chance. To think they had more time had been naïve. There were times he could have stopped his father and he had not. Now, Wolfe had no power at all.

"I hope your time alone has given you some time to think about your actions." Wolfe knew Warren referred to him overstepping his father and becoming the new named CEO. "It was foolish and an ungrateful move on your part." Warren took a sip. "For now, my plans are unfolding a little sooner than expected. I will do what I said: I will tarnish your good name, and face, as you did mine. While you think I'm a monster now, I'm still your father and this was a valuable lesson. Sometimes, lessons are hard to learn."

Wolfe put his hands in the slacks he had stolen from his father's wardrobe, along with an oversized, white, button-up shirt. They hung loosely on his frame.

"Kidnapping me and taking my identity was a valuable lesson to learn?" Wolfe spat the words at his father. "You are right, though; my time alone has given me time to think about my actions."

His living room was spacious with two sofa chairs and a leather couch, but a rectangular coffee table was the only thing that stood between him and his father.

"But not in the way you think . . ." Wolfe was ready to fire words that would tear through his father. He wanted to make his father understand what he thought about him. How he no longer considered Warren his father. How for years, he had wanted Warren out of his life and out of Augland.

"Before you go down the road of telling me how you'll never forgive me or some silliness like that, I have a proposition for you, one I think you will want to hear before you try to distance yourself from me. While you may be thinking you don't have anything else to lose, I beg to differ."

Once again, his father was right. He held the trump card. Wolfe's blood boiled as he brought his gaze back to his father. His ears burned red.

"Well!" Wolfe grew impatient. Warren took a deep breath, enjoying the moment of suspense.

"You've missed so much during your time away. So much has happened. Your little friend," he motioned to Ashton's motionless form, "returned to us. She came back pretending to be a prestigious member of Augland 2. Charlotte Maxwell, the daughter of Charles Maxwell, and she came in a Suit." Warren paused while Wolfe digested what he had just heard.

"I don't know exactly how she did it, but she had help from NeuroEnergy and the Colony. She tried to get close to me—well, to you—and we had a nice little relationship."

Wolfe knew his father was taunting him, but he had no idea how much of what his father was saying was the truth. He felt sick to his stomach when he realized that Ashton had sought him out, only to find Warren in disguise. Wolfe's stomach dropped. He ached for the betrayal he could only imagine Ashton felt.

Warren continued, enjoying watching Wolfe process all he was saying. "During our annual Jungle Gala to raise money, her Suit malfunctioned. Hence where we are today. Your dear girl lying on my living room floor."

Wolfe closed his eyes. Why would Ashton come back to this place?

Warren was done taunting Wolfe. He sat down in a leather armchair, swirling his glass in his hand.

"At the next board meeting, you will denounce your CEO title and offer a new vote to reinstate me."

"And why would I do that, or more so, why wouldn't you just do it for me since you've mastered that already?"

136

"My dear boy, I can't be in two places at once. So, you'll do it, as you. As the real you."

"I don't really look myself if you couldn't tell. Lack of movement and eating has not done much for my physique."

"It's not enough that anyone would pay much mind. Besides, you know we have advancements that will fix you right up. I'm sure if questions come up, you'll think of something. You've been sick. Feeling under the weather. Stuff like that."

Wolfe shivered with anger.

"And if I refuse?"

Warren shoved Ashton's head with his foot.

"I'll tell the board that you let her into Augland. That you have been working with the Colony and NeuroEnergy this whole time. I'll suggest you be cast to live among the workers. And . . . I'll kill her."

Warren pointed to Ashton's motionless body. Wolfe didn't look. He knew this tactic: giving an ultimatum with one offer much better than the other. Wolfe had used this same tactic himself at times when pursuing escaped workers.

"Look, I don't mean to be so callous about this, she really is a charming girl, but you need to understand what is at stake. I've done what I've done for the good of Augland. If we don't have structure, rules, and consequences, a company of our size just won't function. It may have been a mistake to mix our family in company affairs, and I know that now. I take ownership of that mistake. Do this for me, and I will let you and your friend here live out your days outside these walls." Warren waved his hand, indicating somewhere far away. "Come back for holidays, visits, whatever. I'll tell the board she manipulated you. And I'll run Augland the way we've done for decades."

Wolfe thought for a moment. He wanted to believe his father's ultimatum. Warren looked almost sincere, his brow high with an empathetic smile. But Wolfe couldn't trust his father when he looked so eerily content.

"You'd allow Ashton and me to leave? Unharmed?" Wolfe questioned.

"Absolutely. I don't want to take away your happiness, Wolfgang. You're still my son. I allowed your mother to live outside a Suit, to have a close relationship with Reuben behind my back. I would allow anyone who didn't see this as their career path in life to venture off on their own. I'm not the monster you think I am you just haven't had the same life experiences as me. You don't know what you don't know. I can't blame you for that."

Wolfe shook his head. His father motioned for him to take a seat on the opposite sofa chair, but Wolfe didn't want to leave where he stood, standing between his father and the woman he loved.

Wolfe considered his options. He thought of every scenario. He could say no, keep the CEO position, and somehow outmaneuver his father. But could he do that to Ashton? Could he risk her life for only a sliver of opportunity? Wolfe sat down next to his father. Warren put his hand on Wolfe's shoulder.

"A hard decision, I know. Augland or a girl."

Warren insincerely attempted to console his son. This wasn't a legitimate decision; this was a clear attempt to manipulate Wolfe. But Warren was right. Considering the alternatives, Wolfe had no choice but to trust his father would keep his promises.

Wolfe let out a sigh of defeat, momentarily easing the strangling sensation that wrapped around his chest. He wanted to cry, scream, and strangle his father all at once. They had played a game of chess and his father had won. He had outmaneuvered Wolfe at every turn. For every play that Wolfe had, his father had always been two steps ahead. It was only when Wolfe played Warren's game that he had a chance.

"Okay, I'll denounce my CEO position," Wolfe sighed. "I'll tell them I allowed Ashton into Augland. I'll give you credit for my demise." Wolfe had failed to implement change for the workers, but he wasn't going to allow his father to cast aside any more chess pieces. He just wanted to take Ashton and get out of Augland.

Warren smiled as he patted his son's knee.

"You've made the right decision. And remember, this is our secret. No one will know."

Wolfe wasn't convinced he had made the right choice. Hopefully, he had protected an innocent life. Too many people had already lost their lives to his plan.

CHAPTER 23

Ashton

MONDAY 12:12 a.m.

Ashton's eyes slowly opened to the ground bobbing beneath her. She had been flung over the shoulder of a figure dressed in all black. As her eyes adjusted, she saw dark blobs that focused into shoes walking on white, spotless ground. Her head pounded to the beat of her heart as the blood pooled around her head, which bounced upside down against the man's back. She blinked repeatedly to jolt her body and mind into focus.

The last thing she remembered was Wolfe as he sat across from her after dropping Jagatha off his balcony on the needle structure. Jagatha's tiny body and terrified face flashed across Ashton's mind and all her emotions came crashing back.

Ashton began to thrash, pounding her hands against the man's back. The man stopped and dropped her to the ground. She looked up, stunned, and Joao's face came into focus.

"All right, calm down." Joao put his hands up in defense as Ashton scurried to the wall, which only put her a few feet away from Joao in a small hallway.

"Where am I? What happened?" Ashton resisted Joao's outreached hand. She had thought she was dead when she realized her drink had been drugged by Wolfe. She wasn't sure this was better.

"I just need you to calm down. I don't want to take you unwillingly."

"Take me where?!" Ashton's mind raced. She wanted to demand answers as she felt all control of her slip out of her hands. She looked around; the tall glass on the opposite side of the hallway overlooked the glorious beauty of Predator's Biome. Ashton realized she must be inside of the Augland wall, on the outskirts of the Biome.

Joao just sighed in frustration. "Ashton, please, don't make this hard." Joao's eyes seemed kind to Ashton, but her distrust in Augland superseded any sympathy she had for parties related to Wolfe or the parks.

"Then just tell me where we are going!" she screamed, still swatting and kicking him, sliding farther away on the ground as he inched closer to her.

"Wolfe directed me to put you in Apparel . . . you know, where they make the clothes." Ashton had heard of other divisions of Augland besides customer service, but nothing specific to clothing. Joao must have sensed her confusion as he continued. "It's where they make the clothing for workers in different parks. The normal black attire, or stuff for Venus, Victorian . . . even clothes for other Auglands."

Ashton was confused. Why send her to Apparel? Why hadn't Wolfe just sent her to the cages until she withered away to nothing and then tossed her out to the world outside of the walls? Why hadn't he just killed her like he killed Jagatha?

Ashton closed her eyes and began to cry. The overwhelming sense to rid herself of the pain she felt deep inside consumed her mind and her tears burned as they slid down her face.

"Don't cry. Please." Joao sounded both annoyed and sympathetic. Ashton wasn't sure which one it was until he came to embrace her, bending down to where she was on the floor. "I'm sorry about your friend. I didn't know he was going to do that. I want you to know that I personally . . . took care of her body. She will get a proper burial. I can promise you that."

Joao thought he was soothing her concerns, but Ashton just sobbed harder. He patted her back as she sobbed into his shoulder. While she disliked Joao and how he was able to stand beside Wolfe while he committed such evil, she needed comfort. She hadn't had time to process her heartbreak over Wolfe, over Jagatha, over the stolen children, over the failed plan. But she couldn't deny that his efforts for a young girl he didn't know and his compassion for her were helping. Somewhat.

Ashton hadn't thought Augland could take anything more from her than they already had. Sheva's death was tragic. Sheva had lived her entire life in Augland and had become like a mother to Ashton. When she died, it had hurt. But, as Hunter had pointed out to her after her death, Sheva lived a full life. But Jagatha was different. Jagatha was a child, innocent. She was pure, and the world had been so cruel to her.

Eventually, Ashton had no tears left. Her eyes were swollen, and her body felt heavy. She could feel the walls around her building as the hurt reached a whole new dimension. Wolfe had betrayed her. Jagatha was gone. Niall had been hurt and there was no word about the others she cared about: Bez, the young woman from the brothel in Victorian who had helped her escape Augland, and Hunter, who was somewhere in Augland in danger of being imprisoned—or worse, killed.

"I know this is hard for you." Joao paused and Ashton heard grief in his voice. "He really is a good guy; he's been off the last few weeks but he's under so much pressure. Wolfe has always cared for you, for you all, so much." Joao's soft brown eyes met hers and she pushed him away angrily.

"That is not a man in there. That is a monster. A murderer." She wasn't going to sugarcoat anything for Joao, a man who had dedicated his life to Wolfe. He was willing to turn his eyes away from the bad and see only the good, but Ashton wouldn't be so naïve. Not anymore. She had been burned by the manipulation of others too many times.

"We'd best be going, Joao; wouldn't want to keep your precious Executives waiting. Please take me to my next prison so I can be forced to serve your most precious Suits."

It felt poetic: Ashton had known the gift of freedom, and so the labor in Augland's confinement filled her with stubbornness and hatred. But Joao had never known anything different. He hadn't seen freedom, known its vibrance and calmness. Ashton almost felt sorry for him. But the memory of Jagatha's body falling and Joao doing nothing would never allow her to feel anything for this man.

Joao rose and put his hand out for Ashton's, pulling her up so they could walk together. They walked beside each other along the perimeter of Augland, Joao not straying too far away from arm's length in case she decided to run. The hallway was long, with windows that looked out into Predator's Biome, the tall trees, and the jungle with overarching cliffs. She could see the wind pulling and swaying the pine trees in various directions. The windows flanked their entire walk along the perimeter of Augland. She was nowhere near the Executive Suites anymore, nowhere near Wolfe.

Joao spoke again. "For what's it worth—and I know that doesn't seem like much now, Ashton—I know Wolfe cared for you. I know because he told me when he helped you escape from the Augland cages with your friends. You don't understand the amount of stress he's under. How his father is. Just try and stay out of trouble in Apparel and you'll live longer. It's not like the parks down there."

Joao was trying to make Ashton feel better, but his words just angered her. He was letting Wolfe's actions go unchecked, and that infuriated her. She wanted to fight him, to take a swing and try to escape. But she felt weak and hopeless. She had already escaped once; she did not see the possibility of that happening again.

Ashton scoffed. "You think I care about living longer? You don't get it. This life isn't worth living, not when you can't be free."

"You're right; it won't be the same, but giving up is just surrendering. You'll make friends; you'll find a new way to live." Joao was kind. Strangely, Ashton found it increasingly hard to stay angry at him. She saw the good in him, although some of his choices were questionable.

She decided to remain quiet the rest of the way. Joao continued to talk occasionally, but he was met with silence as Ashton just looked out toward the arching cliffside rocks and tree line of Predator's Biome.

Joao and Ashton made it to a floor-to-ceiling elevator that blended in with the hallway walls. It took her a moment to even realize what they had stopped for. Joao pressed his thumb against a small, black circle, and the elevator outline illuminated green. His access had been granted and two doors opened. Joao put his hand behind her back, which Ashton figured meant he wanted her to enter first. It wasn't as if she could run; where would she go? The hallway ran along the perimeter of Augland's walls and went on for miles as it encased the seven parks of Augland.

Ashton took one last look over her shoulder at the daylight streaming through the windows and the green beyond. She was a liability and, because of that, would be put away for good. This might be the last time she saw the light of Augland's fake reality.

She felt the pressure of Joao's hand on her back and didn't fight it. She wouldn't fight him or the system anymore. She had nothing else to lose. Augland had her. Wolfe had broken her. The doors closed and the elevator slowly began to descend.

Ashton looked at her reflection in the metal doors. Her eyes were swollen from crying, her brown hair unruly and matted. She didn't recognize the woman she saw and looked away. She didn't want to look at this version of herself who had given up, who had shut down to feel nothing. Her ears hummed as her eyes glossed over with sadness.

The doors opened and darkness surrounded them. Joao again put his hand behind her and scooted Ashton forward. The darkness surrounded her until her movement triggered flickering lighting that clicked on down a long, drawn-out hallway with doors.

"This is Apparel?" It looked too dark and abandoned to be a worker division of Augland.

"We have one stop to make before we get there," Joao confessed.

"What for?"

"Don't worry, it's a precautionary measure. They are starting to do it for all workers, starting with Apparel." Ashton's heart began to race. A precautionary measure? For what?

The walls were bare; there was nothing in the hallway but closed, white doors. It was a ghost town, an abandoned office where Augland stowed away its accessories. Joao's footsteps echoed along the hallway as they went past each door. The lights flickered above them.

"Here." Joao stopped and put his hand on a door that had no marking. He must have known exactly where he was going because Ashton thought everything looked the same, a maze of door after door. Joao opened the door and Ashton peered in. There was a single chair in the center of the room. As he pushed her through the door, she saw an all-black machine in the corner. It had human features: a torso, head, and legs, but it also had several sets of mechanical arms. Ashton backed away. Something was wrong.

"Just take a seat. It only hurts a little."

"What is that?" Ashton pointed to the metal mannequin, unmoving in the corner of the room.

"It's a tattoo machine. We've got some androids for non-customer-facing things. This one is new, gives you a tattoo with microchips that provide Augland with extensive information about your health, feelings, and location." Joao motioned for her to sit on the chair centered in the small room.

"You're kidding me." Ashton looked at him in astonishment. "It's a tracker. They're tracking us now?"

Joao shrugged. "I don't make the decisions."

"You just fulfill the orders . . ." She was taking cheap shots. She could tell by Joao's demeanor that this wasn't what he wanted to do, but still, he had led her to this room.

Joao looked down instead of answering Ashton. She rolled her eyes and strutted to the chair, sitting down hard as a small act of resistance. She knew there was nothing for her to do; she couldn't run.

Joao pushed a button and the machine hummed to life, a round red circle illuminating its chest as the mechanical hands began to move. A long, needled hand approached the chair as another clamped Ashton's arms to the leather armrests of the chair.

"Just stay still; it's going to go on your wrist." Joao stood in front of Ashton as another hand of the machine gently took Ashton's right wrist into its synthetic hand. The arm with the needle drew closer.

Suddenly, Ashton resisted. She could not, would not, accept this.

"Let go of me!" she screamed, and tried to stand up—but Joao was quick and pushed her back into the chair.

"Ashton, please, this will only take a moment. It won't hurt, I promise." The once-gentle hand of the machine tightened its grip. Ashton's legs flailed, but she was trapped in the chair.

"Stop it! Stop!"

The pinch sent a sharp pain up Ashton's arm and her head whipped to the robotic finger that now drilled into her skin. It wasn't too painful, like a sharp nail dragging across her wrist. Her eyes went wide as black lines were painted across her skin. She was attentive and waited for the other shoe to drop. But nothing else happened.

Ashton examined her throbbing wrist as tiny specks of blood and swollen tissue outlined alternating thick, crystal-white lines with numbers. The mannequin hadn't left her side or let go of her arm, but it had finished mutilating her.

"Asset tag complete," the robot said in a monotone voice.

A what?

"Time to go." Joao pulled Ashton out of the chair and the hands of the machine retreated into place.

"What's an asset tag?" Ashton said as she let Joao guide her out of the small room back into the dimly lit hallway.

"It's a tag, like, uh . . . a tracking barcode. It allows you to be scanned and it relays information about you."

Ashton felt the blood rush from her face. She had been branded by Augland. She was no longer herself, no longer Ashton, but a piece of property.

CHAPTER 24

Ashton
MONDAY 12:45 a.m.

Joao and Ashton took the same elevator down, deeper into Augland. Ashton hadn't realized there were layers to Augland 54. The surface was only that; its depths knew much more. She knew that wherever the elevator was leading them, it was kept secret from both the Suits and the workers for a reason.

As they stood side by side in the capsule steel box, Ashton examined her new body art. The mannequin Suit had been careful; the lines were perfectly synchronized, all the same length but varying in thickness and space between each. The crystalized shade of white was barely noticeable unless the sun hit it and its brightness materialized. She had never seen anything like it. Below the lines there were numbers: JR105–RT1. The first part of the sequence she knew well. That was her worker ID number. But the three characters following the dash were new.

"What's 'RT1'?" Ashton asked, grazing her fingers above the raised ink.

"What?" Joao hadn't been paying attention.

"Just what does it stand for?" Ashton asked again.

"Oh, uh, Rogue Tier 1, I think—that or Renegade." Joao stared at his reflection in the elevator doors, making sure not to look over at Ashton. He shifted in discomfort. "It's the top tier for insubordination. So, they know to treat you with . . . care." Joao paused and finally glanced at Ashton as he said the last word.

"Care" was an interesting way to put it. This mark was so they didn't mistake her for an employee that hadn't run away, killed a Suit, broken out of the cages, and impersonated a Suit. She was creating quite the resumé. Ashton began to laugh, shaking her head as she thought about how far she had come from the days of mistaking carrot juice for orange when she worked in Maya Bay. She'd thought that had been an unthinkable act against a Suit. What a mistake.

The doors to the elevator opened. Ashton's senses were overwhelmed as the quiet of the elevator was replaced by the loud, continuous tapping of machinery. She squinted her eyes, trying to adjust to the high-beamed florescent lights that shone above row after row of workers hunched over machines. There were no whispers of people chatting, just the *tosh, tosh, tosh, tosh* of the machinery.

"Come on." Joao guided Ashton as he pushed her to the outer rim of the large room. She could tell it was a central area, with walkways leading out to random hallways.

"Where . . ." is all Ashton could muster as she stared, wide eyed, at the workers around her. One woman bled from her fingertips as she pulsed thread through fabric. Another, with one mechanical arm, was pulling fabric through a sewing machine. Another worker had an eye patch, like Niall's.

"We've got a new worker and are in the lobby of the main concourse of the sewing room." Joao announced over his interconnect. Ashton overheard a jumbled reply.

As they waited, Ashton looked around at her new normal. How could this ever feel normal? What *was* normal? It had been so long since she had been a worker of Augland 54. But "worker" had a different meaning to her now. She had been a worker in the Colony; she worked so others could eat, and so she could eat. Hunter hunted. Versal sewed. Jagatha blessed those around her with sunshine.

Ashton's eyes began to well with tears at the thought of her now-gone friend. She focused her attention on the redundancy of the workers' duties and her overwhelming sadness. The solemn faces before her concentrated so hard on their work, but there was little joy or life in them. These people worked too long and too hard for nothing beyond survival and sleep.

"Hello, Ashton, yes? I'm Forest, your manager." A young man with similar curly locks to her own approached them. Joao nudged her to attention. Ashton didn't have any energy for customer service or common decency.

"What is this place?" she more muttered than asked.

"As I'm sure Joao has already told you, this is Apparel. It is the factory that manufactures and distributes clothing to the many facets of Augland 54."

Forest spoke matter-of-factly. He was a young man who must have made his way into management early on. He most likely was proud of that accomplishment, not that he showed any emotion. He barely looked at her. Ashton felt sorry for him. She knew his hard work and loyalty to Augland would do him little good in this corporate world. They would find something to fault him with, something to shame him with, because he wasn't one of "them." He was a worker. He would always be a worker. Ashton looked from Forest to Joao and wished she could show them what Augland really thought of them.

"Sounds like captivity," Ashton remarked, not caring about the consequences of her comment.

The young man just chuckled awkwardly. "Perhaps, only with less chance of escape. There is only one entrance and exit through the elevator." He took her sarcastic truth as a joke.

It was clear that Forest knew who Ashton was, or at least that she was an RT1. She had been placed in Apparel so she could not escape again.

"If you'll follow me this way." Forest began walking, and Joao pulled Ashton's elbow after him. She went willingly; she had no motivation to do anything else. "Bezenine will get you started in laundry. You've come just before the shift ends, so we won't do too much this evening before bed at two a.m. and up again at six a.m. sharp. We have strict rules here; no tardiness is accepted. No downtime, except during designated breaks, which come twice during your shift."

Ashton wanted to laugh at the air of power the young man was putting on. How could she take him seriously? How could she take anyone here seriously? They had not seen the world for what it was. They had not seen freedom. Augland thought it could intimidate her with threats, but Ashton had nothing else to lose.

The three of them walked around the center sewing room and down a maze of long corridors until the scent of chlorine filled Ashton's nostrils. Forest guided them to a laundry section of the basement floor filled with workers piling clothes in and out of machines. Like clockwork, they transitioned the clothes from one side of the room to the other: one row took the damp, heavy clothes and came back with dry ones; then those clothes shifted to another row of workers for folding and ironing. It was a machine of workers rather than a working machine.

"Ah! Bezenine, I'd like you to meet our newest addition, Ashton."

A woman with a brown-haired bun answered. "I told you Forest, it's B or Be—" The woman turned around and stopped mid-sentence as she saw Ashton. Her eyes

147

went wide in recognition. Ashton instantly felt the numbness in her heart ease as she saw the face of a friend.

"Ashton, nice to meet you. Bez, was it?" Ashton smiled and stuck out her hand toward the woman who had helped her escape Augland. She wore the same loose bun in her thick, brown hair as she had at the brothel in Victorian.

"Yes, it's Bez. Ashton, it is great to have you here." She turned to Forest. "I'm fairly busy, you know, washing stuff," she said in her typical sarcastic manner. "Do you need Ashton for anything else? Or is she free to start working?"

"Of course. I don't see why she couldn't start now." Forest seemed somewhat nervous around Bez, as if trying not to show he was intimidated, and wanting to keep an authoritative demeanor.

Even if Ashton and Bez had given away their recognition of each other, it didn't seem like Joao or Forest had noticed. Ashton turned to Joao. "I guess this is goodbye, then. I wish I could say it's been a pleasure."

Joao looked regretful, almost sad. Ashton knew he thought he had been as friendly with her as he could, and he had, but her tolerance and forgiveness were too low to care about his feelings.

"I guess you're right; goodbye Ashton." He paused for a moment, as if he had something to say to her, but then his eyes shifted to Bez, and he blushed. "Bez," he said, nodding to her. For a moment Ashton saw a new sadness flash in his eyes, an unspoken and curious look she couldn't explain but quickly dismissed.

Joao and Forest turned and walked away, leaving Ashton with Bez. As soon as they left the room, the women turned to each other and embraced.

"You're either crazy or stupid. Or both."

Part III

CHAPTER 25

Ashton

MONDAY 1:03 a.m.

Bez could not pull Ashton away from eavesdropping workers and overbearing managers fast enough. She dragged Ashton to a small corner hidden from the ever-watchful eyes of the cameras. Bez looked around to make sure no managers were nearby. Joao had left, and Forest seemed too preoccupied with his interconnect to pay much attention to them.

"What are you doing here?" Bez whispered, grabbing Ashton by the shoulders so she could get a good look at her. Ashton pulled Bez into an embrace. She had been so worried about Bez and Niall, and after seeing what had happened to Niall, she was concerned something worse had happened to Bez. Wolfe had promised to protect her friends, but so far, he had broken every promise.

Bez pulled away, again making sure no one could see them.

"I—" Where could Ashton begin? She hadn't seen Bez since she had found shelter in the brothel in Victorian where Bez worked. Bez had risked her safety to help Ashton escape Augland. And Ashton had come back.

"I got out, Bez; I escaped. I made it to a Colony outside Augland," Ashton began, trying to find a way to sum up the last seven months without putting both their lives at risk.

"But Augland attacked . . . they came to the Colony and took all the children. So, Hunter, my friend who I escaped with, got NeuroEnergy to help us—they are looking for more information about Augland's re-creation of energy resources. So, I came back in a Suit; NeuroEnergy gave me one, to help get that information . . ."

Ashton realized her word vomit was creating more questions than it answered. She could tell Bez was trying hard to follow, but just seeing Ashton back in Augland had been a shock.

"I got caught, though, and Wolfe took my friend Jagatha and he . . ." Ashton struggled to even say the words, "killed her," she whispered violently.

"Wolfe? No, that isn't right." Bez shook her head. Ashton realized Bez knew Wolfe, but that wasn't the issue. Ashton had thought she'd known Wolfe too.

"Bez, listen to me. I saw him do it." Ashton was on the verge of tears. She was not willing to let another Wolfe supporter go without hearing the truth about him.

"It can't—"

"Hey!"

Bez was interrupted as a manager caught sight of them behind the steel beam they had hidden behind. She was now weaving her way through the rows of folding stations toward them.

When the woman reached them, Bez threw up her hands.

"Training this one on the difference between bleach and detergent. You'd think they'd test for some sort of competence before just letting anyone down here," Bez scoffed at Ashton. The manager gave a chuckle before directing her attention to another worker who had just dropped a pile of neatly pressed clothes on the ground.

"You're picking that up and re-pressing each and every one of those!" the woman screamed.

"We can't talk now. I'll find a way to contact you. There is a woman, Roan; she's got the black hair pulled back tight." Bez pointed to a worker who was placing bags of clothes in a large, metallic hole. She was an older woman, like Sheva, and moved slowly across the hard concrete ground. Her oversized dress was dripping off her tiny, frail body. "Let her know I told you to stick by her for the rest of the shift. I'll find you soon, and . . . don't get in trouble." Bez grinned with untamed excitement, shaking her head. "You got out, Ashton; the others aren't going to believe it. Now go." Bez pushed Ashton toward Roan before she could ask what Bez meant. What others? Believe what?

"You gonna need to be fast. Whites separate; they get bleach. Colors don't need it." Ashton tried to keep up as Roan spoke in fragmented English and pointed out the laundry machines.

152

She gave Ashton an apparel uniform to wear; a stark white dress that was two times too big. It hung low on her and past her knees. The uniform almost looked nice on Bez, who was much taller, but Ashton felt like a child playing dress-up. The dampness and frigid air of the underground open space drifted through the skirt and Ashton could feel the real cold of the underground basement.

Roan was skinny with midnight black hair, but she looked strong for her age. Her hip must have given out at some point because she walked with a makeshift wooden cane. Her speech suggested to Ashton that she hadn't gone through the Augland Center speech training, because she spoke with a heavy accent. She might have been a first-generation worker, one who like Sheva, had been born outside of the Augland walls.

"The colors—no, every time, they need be dyed if don't meet color code after dry."

Ashton took note as they ran past rows of circular steel boxes that rotated round and round. Each one alternated between colors and white, swirling around in a soapy, bubbling liquid. Each laundry box was big enough for Ashton to walk in and out of without ducking.

"This fabric . . ." Ashton scurried to catch up to Roan, who had picked up a shirt. "Made from beech tree, grown in Biome." Roan looked at Ashton to gauge her knowledge, but Ashton had never even wondered where her Augland clothes came from. "They don't make real thing anymore, silk gone, cotton gone. Leather sometimes, but for customers. Cheaper to grow local." Roan sounded annoyed, as if "back in my day" was about to spill out of her mouth.

"All synthetic now, nonwoven. Easier to make than spin but no keep wrinkle-free." Roan put down the shirt and kept walking. "Once dry, you send to folding station. 'Folders' there."

Roan pointed her trembling, loose hand to the workers who lined table after table, going through huge piles of dried clothes and sheets.

"That there is sewing. Big moving arms—don't get in the way! They don't stop moving. Many workers been sewn in something nasty by beasts . . . become part of garments." Large sewing arms reached down from the ceiling, moving thread and clothes at an impossible speed.

Finally, they came full circle to the area Ashton had first entered with Joao, with row after row of sewing machines and cutting tables.

"Each hour, you get people doing pickup and delivery. That happens at end of line. Management check to make sure we efficient, so quality n' quantity need to be good." Ashton tried to keep up with Roan. It was so much to take in, and the heavily accented and sometimes-broken English didn't help.

"Question?" Roan and Ashton had now come to the end of the line, walking from one end of the underground cellar to the end of the assembly line.

Ashton shook her head no. Roan had gone quickly, too quickly for Ashton to absorb much, but she wasn't about to ask the old woman to walk through it again.

Ashton spent the remaining hour of the shift following Roan like a shadow, working through the color station. She took worker clothes and costumes from dirty laundry to the gigantic washer. Like clockwork, they came in by the pallet every hour.

Ashton found it hard to concentrate, although the work was tedious and did not need much attention. Her world had changed so drastically in such a short of time. One moment, she was in an elegant suit named Charlotte, draped with rhinestones, and the next she was an apparel worker in a one-size-fits-all uniform.

Finally, it was two a.m.—the end of a long and torturous day. Ashton followed the hordes of overworked Augland workers silently marching out of the corners of Apparel toward the sleeping quarters. It wasn't a long walk down a short hall and into another underground bunker. With a pit in her stomach, she realized that the Apparel workers never went above ground and never breathed fresh air. No wonder they all looked so sallow and frail. Ashton might have missed her waterfront home at the Colony if she wasn't tired beyond belief.

The line of workers turned into a room lined with cubby holes stacked three high. Roan had told Ashton that each worker had their own sleeping quarters; Ashton had not realized it would be two boards pushed up against the wall with a blanket and pillow. Roan led Ashton to the farthest corner of the room, to a small, empty cubby.

"You'll be here. Good spot. Not so much noise." Roan spoke softly as other workers were already asleep, having knocked out as soon as their heads hit their pillows. Roan didn't wait for a reply and left Ashton to crawl into the tiny space.

Ashton was smaller than most, and it was still difficult for her to maneuver. There was a tiny light bulb illuminating her cubby, and she used the dim light to digest her surroundings. The hard floor was cold beneath her, and the snores of her roommates floated around her like a dissonant symphony. She curled up into a tiny ball, her light now the only one still lit, but she didn't want to turn it off. She didn't want to feel the darkness in a place that still felt so foreign.

"Light!" someone yelled, and Ashton reluctantly plunged herself into darkness.

154

She lay wide-eyed, even though her body screamed for sleep. She missed her bed, she missed her Colony, she missed her daydreams and day hikes up on the hills overlooking the canal. She missed Jagatha. The thought of her friend, now gone, brought uncontrollable tears to her eyes, and she held in the sounds of her sobs. She wanted nothing more than to wake up tomorrow in her home on Hood Canal before all of this had begun. Ashton shut her eyes and soon sleep took over. She dreamed of home.

"Up!" A loud shout shook Ashton awake. The morning light was not the soft, yellow sunshine of Hood Canal's beautiful sunrise that sat just along the mountain range, but the flickering of fluorescent lights.

She patted down her unruly dark hair as she slowly rose, still trying to remember where she was. Her back was stiff from sleeping on the hard wood and her eyes felt like sandpaper as she blinked the sleep from her gaze. Roan walked past her, only to stop in her tracks.

"Need be fast in morning. Management only asks once."

She left Ashton, not waiting for a response. Like they had the night before, the management staff—Suit-less workers who liked the power and privilege over other workers—led them back to the workrooms of Apparel. Ashton followed behind a woman until the laundry department came into view. Forest, the man she had first met when Joao dropped her off, stood nearby, a clipboard in hand, eyes avoiding direct eye contact and directing workers where they would be working.

"Ashton . . . Ashton." Forest took a long, hard look at his interconnect screen. It had a list of names and worker IDs. "Ah! You're still in training. You'll be with Pat; he is managing the apparel for Venus today. He's the first station on the left. At folding."

Forest glanced at her with a furrowed brow when she didn't move.

"Was I not clear?"

"Uh, no. I mean, yes, you were clear."

"Then go." Forest would not look at Ashton; he only shuffled away, whispering something under his breath.

Pat was fast, almost erratic, as he paced back and forth between laundry and folding stations. Roan, while not the most welcoming person, at least was pleasant to be around. Pat had instructed a worker to show Ashton how to fold laundry. It wasn't hard; none of it was. Ashton's job was to place the garments into a folding machine,

155

take the folded material, and situate it within an ironing machine that emitted hot steam to remove wrinkles from the dryer. Then repeat.

The piles of clothes were endless, and the line of workers worked in impressive unison. Before long, Ashton's face dripped with sweat from the steaming hot machinery.

Her curiosity became unavoidable as she folded, and she found herself peering over at the sewing area. The sewing station closest to her worked on bright and vibrant outfits. Neon-purple layered skirts, polka dot black-and-yellow crop tops, a painfully bright pink tutu, silky neon-yellow gloves that went from the fingers up to right below the shoulder, and a plastic purple-and-brown coat that dragged on the ground. The mannequins were draped with wild colors, both long and short skirts, and feathered, dressy tops.

A short distance away, more mannequins stood, but this time in long gowns with rich fabrics that looked heavy. They were layered in elegance with lace and the deep colors of Victorian.

But it wasn't only the outfits that caught Ashton's eye. As she focused her attention along the tiny hallway between the seated workers and their machines, she felt the tingling sensation of others watching her too, slowly lifting their eyes and turning to her, only to turn back to their work as soon as she looked in their direction. Pat didn't seem to notice; he was too busy speaking to every single detail that was needed by the workers. He took his job too seriously. He caught her distracted once and reprimanded her for not paying attention. For her "insubordination," an extra hour that evening while the others went to bed would be her punishment. Ashton sighed as the limited sleep she had already received seemed like enough punishment. Six in the morning was too early to start.

The hours in Apparel were worse than when she'd worked as a server at The Hook in Maya Bay. Even worse than Land of Legends. The repetitive nature of the work was mind-numbing. Pat eventually shifted Ashton from folding Venus's clothing to starting on the black worker uniforms.

"I'll need these back before you leave today. We've run behind and need to catch up." Ashton looked down at the high pile of clothes as Pat continued, "the machine that sorts is being worked on by android engineers, so they'll need to be hand separated by gender and size."

Ashton knew that if the boredom of consistency didn't, the lack of sleep would drive her mad.

CHAPTER 26

Wolfe

TUESDAY 7:26 a.m.

Wolfe straightened as he surveyed his office. After a month of being shut away in the small, dark closet, he was relieved to be in the familiarity of his home with its smooth chestnut desk and comfortably worn, black leather couch. His white walls were bare the way he liked them. He had a bookshelf that held his now-dusty CD player and other pre-Augland memorabilia.

A slight musk scent still hung over the room. Papers were strewn everywhere and several neckties still lay draped across the couch from when Wolfe had hastily prepared for his last board meeting as Head of Security. He had been in such a rush to look presentable that he'd ignored the mess, and while he felt guilty about it, he had expected a worker to clean up after him. Wolfe was not neat *per se*, but he had some standards and would have cleaned if he knew he was about to be away for such an unexpected length of time.

Warren, while impersonating Wolfe, had moved into his own office and residence as the "new" acting CEO, which had left Wolfe's office unoccupied. The curtains were drawn, exposing the gracious, elevated view that overlooked Augland, and the artificial sun glaring at him almost mockingly above the windowsill. Wolfe took a deep breath as he opened the door to his patio to let fresh air fill the stuffy office space.

It had been the early hours of the day before that he had been standing between his father and Ashton. The flashing images of her body lying across his floor burned in his mind. He could still feel her hair between his fingers. Wolfe sighed. While the fresh air felt good on his now-fallow skin, his chest tightened with anxiety. He had pictured his reunion with Ashton so many times, and finding her unconscious on the floor of his apartment was not one he'd envisioned.

He reminded himself that Ashton was safe while he still held the CEO title and his father awaited Wolfe's renouncement. Warren had promised to take care of Ashton: without that assurance, Wolfe would never have agreed to his terms. Wolfe would meet with the Executives soon, in two days, and renounce the title of CEO. Until then, he had been cast aside to wait and get himself together. He took a deep breath. The fresh air brought little comfort.

Wolfe paced the perimeter of his office, picking up random items, loosely folding clothes and putting them back into their original places. He needed to feel some sense of normalcy. As the last items were situated, he sat down at his desk, now stripped of his computer and interconnect. His father had trusted Wolfe would not try to escape while he had Ashton—not that he would not try undermining Warren's plan. It was a tactical move, something Wolfe would do too if he held someone prisoner. That, and line the room with cameras to watch that prisoner's every move, which he assumed his father had done. It was a new prison, but it was a familiar one. He sighed, frustrated with his lack of control and privacy.

There was a knock at the door and the intercom buzzed. Wolfe didn't look up; Warren would be the only one to visit him. But instead of his eerie double walking through the door, the father he recognized stepped in. Warren had transformed back into the Suit Wolfe knew—there was his typical black-and-white goatee, perfectly symmetrical bone structure, and striking blue eyes. Warren had rid himself of Wolfe's costume and replaced it with his own Suit. Wolfe let out a breath, knowing his father no longer wore his face.

"I'm liking our daily meetings—father-son bonding," Warren chuckled ominously as he entered. "Came to see how you were settling back in."

That was a lie and Wolfe knew it. His father was checking in, making sure he wasn't scheming some plan. Wolfe turned from his father, picked up a sweatshirt from the couch's arm, and began folding it.

"Good to be home?"

Wolfe took a deep breath, not knowing how to answer and not particularly interested in small talk.

"What will become of me once I renounce the CEO position?" Wolfe wasn't going to exchange pleasantries with his father.

Warren took a deep breath in, replying, "I would say you have endless possibilities. It's kind of exciting really. You could find a home. I've got a few friends in Augland 27; they've got a wonderful Alps-inspired park. Very secluded and has great skiing. Or go to an overwater bungalow at their Oasis park. I've been there, to 27, lovely Augland park."

"So, hide away. Outside of Augland 54."

"If you want to view it like that, then by all means. You can't come back to work here, not now at least. And you really don't have to work. Not with your name and status. I'd be willing to fund it." Warren took a deep, exaggerated breath as he ran his hands through his hair and back down to his face. "Besides, the board would not trust you, and to be frank, neither would I. And, after some time, I'll return Ashton to you. Once everything has blown over. You have my word on that."

Wolfe scoffed and shook his head. They were far beyond trusting each other at this point.

"Look, eventually things will blow over and you and your mother can gossip about all the horrible things you think I've done. You can come by for holidays and dedicated events. I'll eventually welcome you back as a member of the family and convince the board to do the same. But until then, I'll need you to disappear for some time. Either here or in another Augland."

Wolfe picked up a plate of food that had been delivered after his arrival and threw it. The shatter radiated from wall to wall. His anger boiled and the pure frustration of defeat made his hands tense. He could not look at Warren, unsure he could tame the beast that fueled his anger. He could lie to himself and say it was all directed at his father, but he knew he truly was angry with himself for letting things get to this point.

"Well, in a couple of days, I hope you'll stop feeling so sorry for yourself. Ideally before the board meeting. I'll leave you alone, but you do need to make yourself more presentable." Warren made a sour, pitying face at him, then casually strolled toward the exit before stopping just before the door. "I've ordered some workers to help put you back together. By the time we have the board meeting, you'll look as good as new." Warren smiled and turned away. "Oh, and let's keep the secret between us." He pointed to every corner of the room. Just as Wolfe had predicted, his office had been bugged to make sure he didn't tell anyone of his father's actions. "Don't want anyone else getting hurt," Warren discreetly threatened. He turned and walked out the door, shutting and locking Wolfe inside his new, familiar prison.

Wolfe's body tensed as he shifted his anger to something tangible. Placing his hands on the first thing he could, he flipped the coffee table over, the steel tabletop toppling next to his couch and knocking over the nearby lamp. He screamed, trying to expel the desperation and frustration from his body, uncaring if his father heard or saw his rebellion. This is how the workers must feel, all of them, he thought. Hopelessness and despair from a cruel world that shows little mercy to those who don't follow the rules. He would never presume he knew how hard their lives were, but in that moment, he connected in a way that bridled him.

A knock, the muted tones of the intercom code, and the click of the door unlocking interrupted his outburst. Wolfe was breathing hard, and his head was full of anger-fueled adrenaline. Three young women workers entered, followed by one male worker. Something clicked behind them, which Wolfe recognized as the sound of the door locking. He looked at them, bewildered. They must have heard the commotion. That should have stopped anyone from entering.

"Can I help you?" Wolfe asked with more annoyance than necessary. He felt a self-conscious pang of regret. After all, they were workers and innocent people that didn't need to be the target of his frustration.

"Good afternoon, Wolfgang. Please let us know where we can set up." Before Wolfe could say a word, three of the workers walked into his office and immediately began picking up what he had set out to destroy in his anger.

"Please, you don't have to—" he started, but the women workers ignored him. Wolfe felt ashamed of his outburst, especially of the need to have others clean up the result of his tantrum.

The man righted Wolfe's toppled office chair and motioned for him to sit down. "This shall do; please take a seat, sir."

The man gazed at Wolfe. His large dark eyes overshadowed every other feature of his face. He was a tall man, who couldn't have been much older than Wolfe. That wasn't what Wolfe paid attention to, though; the worker wore a half-aware and strange expression. His eyelids were pinned back, and his eyes stared unblinkingly at him like he was a shadow, invisible and distant. It made Wolfe look behind him. Something was off.

Wolfe did as he was told. A plastic blanket swung around the front of him and was pinned behind him just below his neck; it appeared he was about to get a haircut.

"We are here for your scheduled upgrade. While we typically work with Artificial Existence Beings, we are completely adept at working with human bodies as well."

Wolfe examined the man, who continued to lazily stare at him, awaiting his response with a tight grin that twitched slightly at the corners. The silence stretched between them as Wolfe processed the oddity of sending human workers into his office and temporary home. He could overpower them and make his way out the door. Force them to open it. It would be easy enough. Wolfe wanted to know what his father had planned that he hadn't figured out.

"This shall do; please remain seated, sir." The worker kept smiling.

"Yes, you said that."

The young man began to work on Wolfe's hair, which had grown shaggy over the past weeks. While the man worked on his unruly beard and hair, the women around him cleaned his apartment, taking out all the old clothing items and replacing them with various colored t-shirts and black pants. They swept up the half-eaten food from the plate he'd thrown. The room even smelled better. Within twenty minutes, his office was back in pristine condition and his face and hair were on their way to his typical five-o-clock shadow and stylish buzz cut. Wolfe's manic rage slowly dissipated as the hour went by, and he only tensed at the awkwardness of the people invading his room.

The man handed Wolfe a mirror and he stared at the man in the reflection, paralyzed by who he knew he was and the man he saw. His cheeks were sunken and the bags under his eyes had darkened. His typically bright, icy blue eyes were dulled into a foggy ash gray. Wolfe couldn't help but look away as he barely recognized the man who stared back at him.

"Looks fine." Wolfe handed back the mirror.

The women workers had dusted and cleaned the windows that looked out to the world of Augland. It was bright outside. His office had a direct view over Land of Legends—a constant reminder of his first mistake, thinking he could make a change for the workers. Instead, he'd scared them all senseless with certain death on the Viking-Saxon battlefield.

Wolfe thought of Ashton. Her sedated body still flashed in his mind, and the fear of losing her was unthinkable. Through the months, he had thought of her often, wondering where she was and how life at the Colony was treating her. He often thought of her half-moon ocean eyes as she smiled big and the freckles that spotted her nose. He loved the way she so easily blushed. Wolfe had decided when she left to live at the Colony that he would try and forget her, but that had proved to be more difficult than expected, especially with the boredom of seclusion in his father's closet. But now he dreaded what would happen when she found out he'd failed. How would she look at him? Differently? Disappointed? He knew he would be. He knew he was disappointed in himself.

"I believe that is all for us. A nurse will be in soon with your dinner and medication. If you would like, one of the girls can stay and help you shower and dress." The worker stood still as he waited for Wolfe to answer. Wolfe was repulsed by the suggestion; he was not like the Suits of Augland who needed such servitude.

"I believe that is all for us," the male worker repeated. "A nurse will be in soon with your dinner and medication. If you would like, one of the girls can stay and help you shower and dress."

"No, I heard you. No, no, I don't need any help with that." Wolfe dismissed him.

"Perfect, thank you, sir. Please let me know if you need anything else."

"No, I'm fine." Wolfe stood awkwardly while the workers packed their things and headed to the exit.

"Very well, sir, and of course, feel free to give a review of your experience today. We are always looking for ways to improve our service."

"Uh, sure," Wolfe said uncertainly, taken aback by the worker's odd script. Was this a new thing? A survey conducted by the workers?

Wolfe watched as they stepped toward the door, a door, he knew, that would be locked after they left. As soon as the door was unlocked—it must have been controlled remotely—Wolfe bolted to the door. Suddenly, one of the women pulled a blade from the male worker's barber kit and brought it up to her throat. Wolfe stopped in his tracks.

"If you try and leave, I'll be forced to cut." The woman spoke softly with a forced grin on her face, but her eyes welled with tears.

"What are you doing!" Wolfe yelled, putting his hands up and backing up slightly. She shook with fear, the blade close enough to her throat that it could draw blood.

"Please put that down!" Wolfe panicked and took a step forward. The worker moved the blade slightly, causing a small incision, all with a smile still plastered on her face. A small trickle of blood succumbed to gravity and streamed down her neck. Wolfe backed up wide-eyed. *Why is this woman willing to sacrifice herself?* he wondered.

The woman's sharp tool began to lower. The tension in the air surrounded them as Wolfe defused the attempt on the woman's life. His heart skipped a beat as a sudden rush of astonishment mixed with disappointment washed over him. This was what he'd feared. His father had continued the customer service initiative during Wolfe's captivity with success.

He looked at the woman's fear-filled eyes as he realized what exactly had happened to her. He remembered the 3D model his father had shown the Executives. His father had mentioned implanting chips into the frontal lobes of the workers to "support a better customer experience." The woman knew what she was doing would kill her, but she didn't have the ability to stop it.

The difference between hearing what Warren had planned versus seeing it first-hand shocked Wolfe. This was exactly what his father had wanted him to see. These workers were no longer themselves. They could no longer trust their own thoughts and exercise control over themselves. Augland had stripped that from them.

Once the woman trusted Wolfe was not going to go for the door, she slowly loosened her grip on the blade, allowing it to fall from her hand to the ground. Her hands shook vigorously.

"I'm sorry, let me grab that." She bent down to the floor and picked up the sharp tool. The woman had no facial reaction to the fact that she'd almost committed suicide moments earlier. Swiftly, she turned and shut the door behind her. Wolfe heard the click of the lock. Then, there was silence.

CHAPTER 27

Ashton

WEDNESDAY 8:52 a.m.

Pull clothes from pile; place in folding machine; take to steamer; place in stack to be picked up. Repeat.

Ashton could not handle the boredom of Apparel and found her eyes wandering often. Halfway through the morning, she locked eyes with a young boy with mocha skin and buzzed hair who was folding at a table to her right. He glanced at her and quickly looked away.

As the day wore on, he caught her eye again and again. Ashton made sure to smile at him every time he stole a glance. She guessed he was the same age as Jagatha and it made her think of her now-gone friend. He was barely strong enough to lift the heavy folding machine. He struggled. Throughout the morning, he had been berated by managers for not keeping up with the day's quota. Ashton's eyes welled with tears. The painful memory of Jagatha hurt deeply. The monotonous work did not even distract her and she was left with the breathtaking reality of Jagatha's death.

"Where's your red hair . . ." The young boy whispered so softly Ashton didn't hear him at first. She was too wrapped in her own misery to pay much attention.

"Huh?" Ashton asked, louder than she meant.

"No talking!" Pat yelled from across the room, narrowing his gaze at Ashton. She did as she was told, returning to her folding, but waiting for the boy to speak again.

"Shhh, don't talk loud," the young boy whispered as he reached for a vibrant red jacket and placed it in the folding machine.

"I thought you had red hair," the boy said again, and Ashton was sure she'd misheard him. Why was he asking about her hair? Was she supposed to know him from somewhere? Had he been in Land of Legends?

"What do you mean?" Ashton whispered back, confusion in her voice.

"Some . . . some . . . someone said you were the woman in red, you know, with the red hair," the boy said with a nervous stutter. "Who . . ." the boy paused as he looked around him. "Who . . . got out." He furrowed his brow in a way that reminded Ashton so painfully of Jagatha. "But you don't have red hair."

Ashton couldn't help but look at him with bewildered curiosity. How did he know? When she had destroyed a Suit in Land of Legends, which left her no choice but to run, she had been playing a character with red hair. The character, Freya, had worn a red wig, but no one except those forced into the deadly play at Land of Legends would know that. Except Bez, Ashton suddenly remembered. Ashton had been wearing the red wig when Bez had first helped her in Victorian during her escape.

"How . . ." Ashton was interrupted before she could finish her sentence and she jumped, startled by a raucous male voice.

"I swear. If you folded as good as you talked . . ." Pat didn't know how to finish his attempt at an insult. "Do I need to give you another hour? At this rate, you won't have any time to sleep." Pat hovered near the boy, who flushed with embarrassment.

"Hey, lay off the kid!"

Pat's attention whipped around to Ashton and the workers around her froze, watching. "Excuse me?"

"It's not his fault. I don't know why you're so tough on him. He was just asking me a question!"

Ashton watched as the towering figure of Pat walked toward her. He looked straight at her, then shifted his gaze to the tall pile of clothes that had been carefully folded and stacked for the workers to come and gather them. Pat walked over to the hours of work for the five workers that shared Ashton's table. He looked at the piled black worker clothes then back at Ashton, who eyed him cautiously.

"Mateo, come here."

The small boy's body came out from behind another worker, and he cautiously walked toward Pat.

"Push the pile over." Mateo's eyes looked up at Pat with confusion. "Go on, push it over, really mess it around."

"Oh c'mon." Ashton couldn't help but react. Pat just smiled.

"Go on, Mateo, push it over, really get in there." The pallet that Pat pointed to was nearly half a day's worth of folding. Mateo slowly put his hands up to the pallet and pushed the stack over. Black clothes spilled onto the hard concrete.

"Oh, you can do better than that, Mateo!" Pat then went to the pile on the ground and shoved the clothes around with his feet, making sure everything was beyond salvaging. He stepped back to a speechless group of workers, panting.

"There, see? Now, no one goes to bed until we've finished the entire day's quota and cleaned up this mess."

The workers around Ashton scowled, but Ashton just looked at Pat with a growing disdain. He reminded her of her old manager, Marius, in Maya Bay, who had the same mad power that leadership gave him.

THURSDAY 11:22 a.m.

Ashton was running on only four hours of sleep. Pat's harsh punishment had taught Ashton that management here was less forgiving than up on the main level of Augland parks. At first, taking hours of sleep had seemed like a harmless punishment—that was until Ashton's eyes stung with the need for sleep.

Pat shifted her to another folding station with new workers. The workers at her old station had probably rejoiced that her anger couldn't give them any more trouble.

Pull clothes from pile; place in folding machine; take to . . . Ashton felt her eyes closing. She fought to stay awake, but her mind shut off before she could scream for it to stay awake. The tension and anxiety of being constantly watched and overworked faded away as the blissfulness of rest took over.

CRACK! An instant pain swept across Ashton's shoulder. She opened her eyes to see Pat's face stewed in frustration.

"Get up!" Ashton blinked wide-eyed as the pain spread across her shoulder and down her back. How long had she been asleep? It couldn't have been long. She'd only shut her eyes for a second.

"You're going to be a troublemaker, aren't you?" Pat crossed his arms. Ashton noticed his stout posture and resting scowl. "Another hour tonight and if I catch you sleeping again, we will have to resort to further consequences."

Ashton was wide awake now. She put her hand on her shoulder and applied pressure, trying to relieve the pain, and checked to make sure she wasn't bleeding. She wasn't. Whatever Pat had hit her with wasn't sharp enough to cut the skin, but it didn't feel good. Ashton just nodded in some form of acknowledgment. She hoped it was sufficient for Pat to leave her alone and keep her far away from any further repercussions.

Apparel workers were given two breaks during the day. Both times, workers were expected to eat and use the restroom. When the afternoon break finally arrived, Ashton ran as quickly as she could toward the bathrooms. There was just one single-person bathroom and she wanted, needed, to get to it. She needed a moment to herself. This work was hard for everyone, and she didn't want anyone to see her tears after just four days.

Ashton made it to the bathroom and slammed the door behind her. She looked into the mirror and didn't recognize the woman who stared back at her. Her eyes were bloodshot and there were shadows of darkness around her now-pale blue eyes. They began to well with tears. Then, the door's knob jiggled and opened.

"I'm in here," Ashton yelled, frustrated that even this moment was being taken away from her. She sniffed back tears and quickly wiped them away. Bez entered, wide-eyed, and quickly shut the door behind her. She stood and stared for a moment.

"Your third full day and you're already falling apart?"

Ashton didn't blame Bez for not understanding. She didn't know how it felt to finally be free, and then captured again and forced into this. It was her own doing and her own fault. Ashton didn't answer and pressed hard against her face, wiping the remaining remnants of her tears.

"I'm sorry. I sometimes talk before thinking." She looked down. "But we don't have much time. I wanted to speak to you. It's gotten around that you are here, and the others are . . . well, excited; they think you can help them. Us." Bez was smiling vibrantly, almost beaming.

Ashton had to catch herself from laughing at the thought. "Help? I can't help. I'm stuck here too."

"No, I know you are, but you got out once . . . all these people want is hope! They will go against Augland if they know there is hope. A chance at life. You can give that to them! Tell them your story. Let them know about the world outside these walls. Show them they can fight and win. We didn't know it was possible but now . . .

167

now they will see! And they will join us." Bez spoke in a passionate fervor but quickly checked herself, lowering her voice. "The people here are tired, Ash; they want to know that if they fight, they fight for a reason."

"Fight? Augland? You've gone mad." Ashton was furious. They had so little time and Bez had come to talk nonsense. Ashton had known hope, and there was none in this dark place. "The more you fight them, the worse it gets. For everyone." Ashton shook her head, her gaze wide at Bez in disbelief.

"You can't think that way," Bez urged. "You can help us. We are all ready for a new beginning; we just need hope. Come on, Ashton, you can be that for them! We—we've already started. We've been getting ready for a rebellion. But we need to get the people on our side. They just need to hear it's possible."

Ashton knew Bez was high-spirited, but she had gone too far. Ashton's story wasn't inspiring. She had gotten out, but Augland had still won. They had still taken children from the Colony and Ashton had failed. The best thing any of them could do now was keep their heads down.

"I can't. I can't do what you ask, Bez. I don't know who you've been talking to, but you need to stop. If you go against Augland, you will lose."

Bez took a step back, her mouth slightly agape from astonishment.

"What has happened to you? You risked everything to escape. And everything to come back here. What for, then? What else for but because you wanted others to know what you know? The workers want this! They are just too scared of the unknown. You are the one who revolted against the machine. I heard the story: you killed a Suit. You ran and escaped. You did. They need to know that they have that strength, that they have that power. All I'm asking is that you be that light for them. They need the strength you had when you got out. That's all I'm asking for."

Ashton didn't know what to say. She wished so badly she could be the girl with the red hair that Bez needed, but she couldn't. How could she be the light of a rebellion when she was right back in Augland where she started?

Suddenly, they were interrupted by a knock on the door. Bez finally looked away from Ashton's eyes. "I've got to go, but please think about it. We need people to believe because the mass is the workers' power. Without a spark, time will keep going and we all will die down here eventually. For me, and for so many out in the parks, they'd rather die for a real chance at life."

Bez slowly opened the door and, just as quickly as she had appeared, she was gone. Ashton turned around and stared at herself once more in the mirror. Her head was throbbing. Bez had asked her to tell the workers they had a chance if they rallied against Augland. But Ashton didn't know if that was true. They could lose and Bez and Ashton would be the cause. She didn't think she could handle any more loss.

Ashton returned to work, slow and sluggish. The day had lasted forever and she still had so many hours of folding to go. She was plagued by drowsiness and her own self-pity. The conversation with Bez only tormented her further. She wanted so badly to feel better, to not feel the impending sadness of her loss, but the exhaustion and emptiness were all-consuming.

When Bez approached Ashton in the back room, Ashton had been taken off guard. She felt bad, but Bez was wrong. They didn't need hope; they needed a miracle—and Ashton wouldn't give them hope that would lead to their death. The last time she'd left Augland, Sheva had died, Byron and Pais had disappeared, and Niall had been disfigured. How could Bez ask something like this of her? Who knew what would happen to the workers if they tried to escape? There were too many of them to save, so, whom would they leave behind? Bez didn't think of these things and those were the very things that would haunt them eventually. The cost of rebellion was just too high.

"Ashton, I need you to come with me." Ashton jumped and snapped out of her folding trance. She had been so lost in her thoughts she hadn't heard anyone approach. Thinking Pat had caught her slacking, she began to grovel, but when she turned around, it was Joao who stood behind her.

With a sigh of relief, Ashton let out a breath. "Geez!" She shook her head. "Rather not." Sleep deprivation gave her anger very little filter as the words left her mouth abruptly.

"Just come, please. You'll be fine, I promise." Ashton was about to make some retort, but she was too exhausted. It wouldn't be worth getting one less hour of sleep that night.

"Since you asked so nicely," she said sarcastically and stood up to follow Joao to wherever he had planned to take her.

CHAPTER 28

Wolfe

THURSDAY 10:36 a.m.

Today wasn't going to be fun. Today was the day Wolfe would officially surrender. He was going to stand in the board room, in front of all the Executives, and renounce his CEO title. It was a loss he had thought long and hard about.

At first, Wolfe thought he would stand in front of the Executives, and instead of renouncing his CEO title, he would turn on his father. Tell how Warren had made a Suit that looked just Wolfe and had taken his identity. But that wouldn't work. No one would believe him, and Warren would say he was crazy. If Wolfe was in their situation, he might agree.

His next idea was to overpower his father when he came to escort Wolfe to the board room. But Wolfe's strength was still not up to par and his father was in a Suit. Anyway, he knew the moment his father was released he would be back in the same situation. Besides, if Wolfe didn't do what he was told, he would be subjecting Ashton to a life of servitude.

The only way he could prove to the Executives that his father had taken his face and name was to prove that the Suit existed, but there was no way to do that in a day, and definitely not while he was trapped in this room. The worst part of this was, either way, the workers would continue to suffer. At least in renouncing his title of CEO, he was saving Ashton. But he didn't know if she would ever forgive him for giving up. He wasn't sure he could forgive himself.

Wolfe looked around his room. It had been destroyed. Curtains had been ripped from their posts, tables overturned, and books thrown. He had torn apart his office more than once in the past few days, but it hadn't done any good. Workers would just come in and replace all that had been broken. And every time they came, Wolfe's anger grew. It was a vicious cycle. He couldn't handle his father's depravity in stooping to the customer service initiative, leaving these workers a fraction of themselves; he couldn't stand himself for giving up and letting it happen.

The sun barely hovered over the city's skyscrapers. It was late morning and Wolfe had barely slept. While the days hadn't been nearly as bad as those in his father's closet, and the drugs had finally worn off, he still felt the disquietude of captivity. His strength was returning, and he finally felt clear-headed. Nurses had come in to feed him and give him muscle enhancement treatments that, over the last day and a half, had transformed him back to his masculine shape. It wouldn't have been Wolfe's first choice of a way to regain his typical muscle mass, but he did trust its effectiveness. Many of the security men had taken it before joining his team, back when he was the Director of Security.

The door opened and Warren appeared. Wolfe didn't move or acknowledge his father.

"Beautiful morning, isn't it?" Warren cooed with false warmth. Wolfe didn't respond. "I wanted to check in and see how you are feeling. Make sure we are on the same page before the board meeting."

"Don't worry. Plans haven't changed." It pained Wolfe to succumb so easily. He wished he had a plan, anything, except doing this. "As long as you've kept your part of the bargain."

"If it's proof you want of that girl's well-being, I can arrange that." Wolfe nodded. He didn't trust his father. If he was about to give up on everything he and Ashton had worked so hard for, he needed to know that at least she was safe. Wolfe finally stared at his father, wondering why he would allow him to see Ashton, but if he had an opportunity to see her and hopefully explain what had happened, he would take it.

"I also need you to stop the customer service initiative. The workers don't deserve that kind of torture . . ." Wolfe knew he was pushing Warren's patience, but he was about to give up everything and wasn't going to go down without trying.

Warren pondered his request.

"I'm not sure you're in the position to be making demands. Besides, customer satisfaction scores have gone up among our residents, and we now have use for the bodies in the cages. It's recycling, and it's very prosperous. Even if I wanted to, I'm not sure I could convince the board."

"Wasn't it you who said they do what you want?" Wolfe spat back. Warren chuckled, coming closer and sitting on the corner of Wolfe's desk.

"*Touché.*" That was Warren's way of saying that Wolfe was right. The board did what he wanted and he didn't want to stop the customer service initiative. "Well, we've got a little over an hour before the meeting starts. Get ready; wear a nice jacket and pressed shirt. I'll come fetch you so we can walk together."

Wolfe closed his eyes and sighed, giving in to defeat.

A sense of *déjà vu* enveloped Wolfe as he stood, front and center, before the stark white board room. Exotic flowers sprawled across the center of the table, giving the blinding room a splash of color. The board members trickled in, babbling to each other, oblivious of what was about to happen. They nodded in acknowledgment as they passed Warren and Wolfe, and several stopped to welcome Warren back home. Reuben was the only one who didn't look their way, instead heading straight for his chair.

"Take your seats please," Warren said. The moment they heard Warren's voice, the others became silent and sat down. "Ladies and gentlemen, it is so great to see all of you after my time away. I can't tell you how much I've enjoyed retirement. Now, I know you are wondering why I am here—"

A knock at the door interrupted Warren's speech.

"Ah, Joao, right on time." Wolfe's longtime friend opened the door. He looked at Wolfe before looking behind him and ushering in a small frame with frazzled brown hair. Wolfe's heart dropped.

Ashton.

Her sunken eyes were surrounded by puffiness. Her entire body sagged. It broke Wolfe's heart. She appeared disheveled and likely hadn't showered in days. Her eyes swam with sadness as she looked . . . defeated. He wanted to run to her, hug her, and take her away from Augland. And there was so much to say. But Ashton didn't look at him; instead, she kept her furrowed gaze on the ground, her fingers tightly clasped in front of her.

Warren cleared his throat as he pointedly looked at Wolfe and then at Ashton.

"Today is a painful day. . . First, I'd like to introduce you all to someone. This is employee JR105, a worker from Land of Legends and the one that escaped through Augland seven months ago. Her insubordination, no doubt, will go down in history, identifying her as the worst worker in Augland 54." Snickers could be heard across the room. Wolfe sat there, demoralized by the contempt in his mind, fuming with anger at the injustice . . . but he had been given a chance to see Ashton alive, and for that he was grateful.

Warren continued through the chatter. "Recently, she returned, this time in an Artificial Existence Being, and impersonated a highly regarded, well thought-of

172

woman by the name of Charlotte Maxwell from Augland 2. Wolfe mentioned that you all met her at the gala a few nights back."

The chatter among the Executives showed the shock around the room. Warren put his hands up to silence them.

"She worked with the Colony and NeuroEnergy and infiltrated Augland to elicit information about all of us here—personal details about our families, private company information—and seduced my son into compliance. He finally came clean to me of her vicious tactics."

The world around Wolfe turned upside down as he listened to his father putting Ashton in such a negative and dramatized light. He looked down, ashamed of his silence.

"While cunning, the plan was poorly executed. Thankfully, she has been caught. Rest assured; she will pay for her crimes."

Ashton shook her head and Wolfe could tell she was seething with anger. The room went silent as each executive eyed Ashton carefully.

"Thank you, Joao, that will be all. It is time for executive business." Joao looked at Warren and then at Wolfe.

Wolfe took one last look at Ashton, and she raised her head to glare intently into his eyes. He softened, but her eyes blazed fire with resentment.

"You're a murderer!" she screamed, tears rolling down her now reddened face, her eyes fixated on Wolfe. Joao pulled her back, but not before she turned her eyes to the rest of the boardroom. "You're all murderers! Selfish pigs!" Ashton's voice cracked as emotion ran deeply within her. Wolfe froze in place. He had no idea why she had targeted him.

"That's enough! Joao, please!" Warren thundered.

Joao picked Ashton up as she fought against him, but she was weak. Her thrashing calmed and she soon stopped fighting. Her breath was heavy. She settled her eyes on Wolfe's again. He could sense her disgust and it was debilitating. What had his father done? What did she think Wolfe had done? She blamed him for whatever agenda his father had. Was this because of the customer service initiative? Or worse?

Ashton didn't know the truth, and Warren had somehow tainted her view of him. Wolfe realized that in her mind, whatever had been done had been done by *him*. The betrayal she felt would be all-consuming. Wolfe swallowed hard. He wanted to scream at her the truth, to tell Ashton everything and beg for her to forgive him for his failure, but he held back. His father would surely kill her if he even hinted anything had happened to the Executives. Wolfe had a feeling there would be no coming back from this, at least between him and Ashton. Joao pulled her out the door and back to wherever his father was holding her captive.

Warren had done what he had said. He let Wolfe know she was still alive but would not let her know the truth. Or even allow him to explain.

"Well, that was eventful." Warren's attempt to lighten the mood did not work, as the board sat in silence. "The next order: Wolfgang's involvement with the young girl."

Warren looked down at his feet and choked on his words for a moment, an act to gain sympathy from the board. Wolfe rolled his eyes.

"It has come to my attention that Wolfgang knowingly let the young worker in here. While I do not blame him for being weak to the persuasion of women, he had a prior relationship with her in Land of Legends and has made it known he helped her escape. He also knew about her ties to the Colony and NeuroEnergy, and instead of reporting immediately, supplied her with AEC property to help aid her ability to come into our home."

"While I love my son, this is disappointing and not what Augland needs as a CEO. Finding out this lie has been hard for me as a father, but Augland is too important not to act against this. To put us, your families, our livelihoods, Augland's success in jeopardy . . . he's misguided and needs time to find himself once again."

"Is this true? You helped her?" Boren leaned in, keeping his eyes on Wolfe. It had come time for Wolfe to admit to Warren's lies.

"Yes," Wolfe whispered after some time, keeping his eyes away from Boren.

"Why? Why would you do that?" Wintefred crossed her arms, creasing her perfectly tailored crimson jacket.

"Wolfgang hasn't been too forthcoming with me on the reasons, but I believe we have all done something we aren't proud of, and he will see the consequences for his actions. If you don't mind, we need to continue with Wolfe's confession for the record before we decide what will happen moving forward." The room nodded in acknowledgment.

"Do you deny aiding the young girl from Land of Legends to escape Augland?"

Wolfe took a deep breath as his father asked a question that rang true. While he didn't aid Ashton with her most recent endeavor, he was guilty of going against his father, and it was about to become known.

"No." Wolfe wanted nothing more than to be out of this room.

"Do you deny helping her escape the cages once she was found?"

"No."

"Do you deny helping her obtain an Artificial Existence Being of her own so she could come in and spy for NeuroEnergy?"

With that last question the room was deathly silent.

"No."

"Very well, we appreciate your honesty. Do you have anything you'd like to say?"

Wolfe thought long and hard. Warren had listed offenses that were somewhat true, but out of context and nothing compared to the indiscretions of his father. He wanted to scream like Ashton, but Warren had scripted something for him to say, and Wolfe couldn't take any chances.

"I've failed this board; I became emotionally involved with a worker that used me to get the most secretive information of Augland, and for that I need to give up my right as your CEO. I've gone against my better judgement, my moral compass, and for that I'm ashamed. I . . . I'm no longer fit to be your Chief Executive Officer, and I believe that my father, Warren, should become interim until another meeting is set to decide on a new acting CEO."

Warren looked almost surprised by his suggestion. In another situation, Wolfe would have laughed. All this was so obviously scripted, but the board seemed to be taken in by Warren's acting like they always did.

"Thank you, Wolfgang, I'm honored. And while I've enjoyed my time away, I can't say I'm not a bit excited at the prospect of returning. Retirement can be boring," Warren chuckled. He scanned the room for a moment before continuing. "Should we vote? I understand the timing is short but I do think it beneficial to have an interim CEO until proper plans can be made to find a replacement."

The room hummed with understanding and acknowledgment. Wolfe's mind went numb as he accepted full defeat. Warren had won. None of the board members spoke up or denied his request.

It didn't take long for the vote to be finished, completing the shift in power. It was that easy. Warren had known all along that this would happen. In a way, Wolfe had known too. Warren rarely did anything without already knowing the outcome.

"Thank you everyone for your agreement. As the new acting CEO, I'd like to propose Wolfgang's punishment." He paused as if saddened by what he needed to say next. "He will be stripped of his Executive title and will be put on indefinite leave. I've suggested he find a home and settle down. As a father, I must forgive my son for his naïve ways, and I hope you can all find it in your hearts to do the same. I'm disappointed, but he's taking accountability and . . . he's family. Let's let him live in peace."

The board fell into the manipulation sinkhole of Warren's compassion for Wolfe, like Warren had been the real victim in all of this. His plan had succeeded, and Wolfe had failed.

CHAPTER 29

Ashton
THURSDAY 1:07 p.m.

Ashton fumed as Joao carried her from the conference room. She kicked and screamed until the door of the Executive boardroom closed and she knew it was no use. Joao put her down and directed her back to the gondola station that would return them to the Apparel entrance just outside of Predator's Biome.

As Ashton trudged behind him, she shook her head and wrapped her arms around her waist. Her earlier exhaustion was gone, replaced by the frantic adrenaline that now ran through her body. All her hurt bundled inside of her like a tornado, waiting to cause destruction where it landed. She knew it was pain. She knew Joao wasn't her target, but at that moment, she wanted someone else to feel her hurt. She began muttering all her frustration, letting all the words spill that she didn't have the time or courage to say to the Executives' faces. She had lashed out, but not to the extent she could have. She wished she had named everyone they hurt and spat in their faces.

". . . they all sit there smug . . . like what you all do here isn't cruel, isn't flat-out murder."

"Enough, I don't want to hear any more, or I'll be forced to report it."

Joao turned hard and Ashton knew she'd hit his limit. He was tolerant of her, but mostly because he felt guilty about Jagatha. He wasn't cruel, but he wouldn't be any help to her either. She turned away in frustration and looked out at the sun shining on the city.

When they reached the entrance to the building on the edge of Predator's Biome, the one that would take them down to the basement, away from the sun and away from hope, Joao stopped.

He turned toward Ashton. "It's time to pull yourself together."

Joao let Ashton have a moment to herself. He seemed awkward, shifting from foot to foot and avoiding her gaze. Ashton didn't care; she didn't have anything to say to him or any intention of doing anything he said. He most likely was embarrassed by her display, but she wasn't. If anything, she was proud of the emotion she felt. Spewing the truth to people who had only heard how great they were their entire lives felt invigorating.

It didn't come without fear though; she danced on a thin line with Augland and might not see tomorrow to talk about it. There were moments Ashton wanted so desperately to feel alive that anger bellowed out of her like a wave crashing on the shore because she couldn't live in her head, in silence, forever. Apparel would not be so understanding.

Two security guards framed the elevator door as Ashton and Joao stepped into Apparel. Their footsteps echoed as they walked down the rows of tables, the *twish twish twish* of the sewing machines repeating in the air. On the other hand, the room was silent with fear and exhaustion.

They passed designers picking up pieces of fabric and draping them across mannequins, their mouths full of pins as they designed clothes for the Suits. Farther on, cutters worked alongside enormous mechanical arms. Finally, they reached the folding tables. Nothing had changed in Ashton's absence. The steamers were spewing hot smoke, and the "pressers," as Ashton named them, were pressing out wrinkles, the workers working in methodical rhythm.

Before Ashton could sit back down at her station, she heard a new sound: a whistle followed by a slap. She looked around the room, desperate to find the source of the sound. The large room was loud and crowded with machines, making it almost impossible to find a specific sound. But then she heard it again.

Ashton walked a few steps down the center aisle; Joao stayed back, too entranced in his interconnect to mind what was happening. Ashton's curiosity took over as she walked along the hallway looking down the long rows of sewing machines. Then, she saw it. A boy who stood only three or four feet high with short black hair and a soft demeanor broken by the monstrosity of Augland.

Mateo. His wide eyes looked up at the man looming in front of him. Pat, Ashton's own Apparel boss, stood in front of the boy with a thin wooden stick in his hand. Ashton realized it must be the same tool he had used to strike her shoulder.

Pat's lengthy fingers twisted around the stick before raising it above his head and bringing it down hard on the fragile body. A piercing crack caused Ashton to tense. He struck Mateo on the hand repeatedly while the boy sucked in his cries.

This is barbaric!

Ashton's eyes went wide, and the fury she had tried to bury resurfaced. She saw red. The ruthlessness of Augland incapacitating the weak—*again*. Her fists balled, ready to defend and release. She moved without thinking. She passed workers who whispered, but Ashton didn't notice. She had a target, Pat, and nothing was going to stop her. She envisioned taking his weapon and striking him over and over again until he fell to the floor.

Suddenly, an arm yanked across Ashton's waist, lifting her off the ground and stopping her from moving any further toward her target. Joao had caught up to her.

"Put me down!" Ashton yelled. The room around them stopped. Workers around them stared.

Pat didn't notice, but he had stopped hitting Mateo and was now stooped in front of the poor boy's face, yelling. The young boy cowered while everyone around them stared, shifting their gaze between Ashton and Joao, and Pat and the young boy.

"Cool it, you're making it increasingly hard for yourself to stay alive, you know that?" Joao whispered his harsh words as Ashton kicked her legs and tried to pry his arm from her body.

"What was your plan, huh? You would just make it worse for him, and you. You know that, right?"

Ashton stopped. Joao sighed in frustration and put her down.

Joao was right. Intervening would only make things worse for her and most likely for Mateo as well. Her fury toward the other workers abated as she began to understand why they did nothing. They stayed silent and let management be as cruel as they wanted. Ashton wanted to scream at them, tell them to go save Mateo. It felt all too familiar, feeling helpless and knowing everyone around her was helpless too.

"You done?" Joao asked.

Ashton exhaled, her eyes swelling with tears she wouldn't let spill.

"Yeah, all done."

Joao backed up.

"I really have to go. Can I trust you to make it back to your station without incident?"

He eyed Ashton carefully. She didn't look at him. She just nodded as she glanced back at the young boy who was crying at his cutting station and tending to his hand. Pat must have stormed off to harass another worker.

Ashton pulled herself up from below the depths of her own emotional rollercoaster. She had shifted from grief only to be met with the demon of undeniable rage, and now she felt anything but defeat.

Bez's words rang in her ears.

They need to know that they have that strength, that they have that power. All I'm asking is that you be that light for them.

Augland wanted Ashton to be defeated, and Ashton had almost fallen into their trap. But that wasn't her. It never had been. She would always fight against Augland because they didn't deserve her, and they didn't deserve any of the hard-working employees who gave their lives to serve the Suits.

Bez's request hovered in the back of Ashton's mind. She wanted Ashton to help bring freedom to the people of Augland. If they were starting a rebellion, Ashton wouldn't stand in their way, not when she knew there was a way to escape. The boat was coming in about four days. She may not be on it, but she would do all she could to make sure it was filled with as many workers as possible. It wouldn't be easy—it would be nearly impossible—but Ashton had to try.

CHAPTER 30

Wolfe
THURSDAY 6:27 p.m.

Wolfe collapsed into his chair in his office. It was done. He had given up his CEO title to his father. He had admitted to insubordination, letting his father slander his name in front of the Executives. He sunk deep into the chair. He was exhausted and glad all this was finally over. Ashton was safe.

But the look of hatred in her eyes burned in Wolfe's mind. Her anger was well-exhibited. He wished he could have exposed the truth to the Executives. Then Ashton wouldn't have looked at Wolfe with more hatred than she had at the rest of the Executives.

This was the first time they locked eyes on each other in months, and there was no familiarity, no love. From Ashton's perspective, she had seen Wolfe countless times and grown to hate him. The worst part was, Wolfe didn't even know why. He didn't know what his father had done while disguised as him or what he had said to Ashton. She was safe now and that was most important, even as his heart broke.

Warren burst into the room, his Suit basically radiating his smug joy. He was holding a rectangular screen as long as his arm span and approached Wolfe with a large smile. Warren double tapped the screen as he laid it across Wolfe's desk, and a 3D model rose above the thin glass.

"Architectural designs for some homes being built across Auglands. Also, a few nice farms just came on the market in Victorian." Warren swiped through the blueprints on Wolfe's desk and leaned over them. "I personally love the high-rise condominium in the Pyramids of the Deserted in Augland 43, but I thought you'd want to look and select your new home yourself!"

Wolfe sighed. His father was just going to pretend they were picking out a vacation home, not sentencing Wolfe to a powerless exile. He wasn't in the mood to play his father's charade.

"Yeah, I'll look at them."

Warren took a seat across the desk, ignoring Wolfe's obvious hints that he wanted to be left alone.

"I thought you did an excellent job in there. Very believable." Warren looked pleased. He had won the battle and come to make a peace offering after Wolfe waved his white flag.

"When will you let Ashton go?"

Wolfe needed to tell Ashton the truth. He couldn't wait another minute, letting her think he had betrayed her.

Warren paused as if searching for words. "I'm sorry, Wolfgang, but you saw how she acted in there. I can't—I can't let her go with you now. Who knows what she is capable of?"

Wolfe was out of his chair and up before Warren could finish his sentence.

"We made a deal! You said if I denounced my title of CEO, you would let her go!"

"What makes you think she would even want to go with you? She clearly hates you."

Wolfe paused, seething with anger but also the grief of knowing his father was right.

"Fine, don't send her with me. Let her go back to the Colony."

"I can't let that happen."

"You lied!" Wolfe's voice was rising. He was beginning to panic.

"Calm down. I won't talk to you when you are having a childish tantrum."

Wolfe eyed his father carefully, but something caught his attention in the corner of his eye.

Warren continued, "Besides, today should be a momentous day! It's your day of freedom. No more locked doors, no more tiny rooms. You're a free man now."

Wolfe looked over at the door and noticed something his father had not. In his haste to show Wolfe the blueprints, Warren had not shut the door behind him completely. In the crack of the open door was a shadow of a figure. He couldn't make out who it was, only that there was someone who could be listening in on their conversation. Even if it were just a sliver of a chance, here was his opportunity for someone to know Warren's secrets, if he could get him to talk. Wolfe didn't think that would be a problem; his father had no trouble talking about himself. No matter who was behind the door, a worker subjected to the customer service initiative or an Executive, it was a chance Wolfe was willing to take.

". . . Wolfe, you're being ungrateful, you need to think of the—"

"Was this your plan all along?" Wolfe interrupted his father. He knew he probably couldn't get Warren to say that he had impersonated Wolfe, but he may not dispute it.

"What? Was what my plan all along?" Warren took the bait.

"You were the one to suggest I become CEO. You imprisoned me after I was voted in, just to create a Suit that looked identical to me so you could prove, what? I was not capable of leading? So, you could do horrible things to the Colony, to the workers, without your name connected to it? I need to know."

"We've been through this, Wolfgang."

His father eyed him carefully, clearly growing suspicious, but Wolfe needed more.

"So why have me confess in front of the board then? Because you wanted to regain power and you saw the opportunity when you caught Ashton? Was that it? Pin it all on me, ruin any future I might have in Augland 54 or anywhere else?" The last part wasn't a question; Wolfe already knew that was exactly what his father had intended.

"What is . . ." Warren suddenly contorted his body around and saw the half-opened door, but whoever had been standing there was already gone.

"What game are you playing?" Warren laughed sardonically. No one cares enough to come knocking on that door. No one even noticed that I was you!" Warren leaned back in his chair. "Even your security friends had no idea!"

Wolfe ignored his father's hurtful words and played dumb. He only hoped that whomever he had seen had stuck around long enough to hear the truth.

"No one will save you Wolfgang: not workers, not your mother, not Reuben! Even if anyone heard the truth. It's over. You know it, I know it."

Warren steamed with frustration, but Wolfe could tell he had hit a nerve with Warren's paranoia. Warren would overthink their conversation, trying to find out who could have listened to their conversation, who could know the truth.

"You know, I thought this could be our resolution, our time to put the past behind us. But you can't let things be. But you know what? You're gone tomorrow. Tomorrow. And about your 'girlfriend,' I hope she loves her new home, because she will die there."

Before Wolfe could even respond, his father rose from his chair and swiftly turned toward the slightly ajar door.

Warren exited, slamming the door behind him hard enough to make the walls shutter. Wolfe heard the familiar beeps of his father locking him in again. It was a bittersweet victory though, even if the person behind the door hadn't heard, or even cared. Wolfe had caused some displeasure for his father. But it was at a cost.

The room fell quiet, and Wolfe was left to his own thoughts and the spread of blueprints on his desk, a reminder of his bleak future.

By the time night fell, Wolfe had packed up most of his belongings. There weren't many things that he needed. His clothes, a few of his favorite pre-war memorabilia passed down from previous generations, and a picture of him and his mother, Anastasia. He had picked a home, a nice small cottage on the outskirts of Predator's Biome, with a small farm where he could raise animals. He thought he should leave Augland 54 but couldn't bring himself to do it. Not now, anyway; he needed to think. There had to be a way out of his dilemma.

He rested on the couch, the light above him turned dim to match his mood. He wished he could sleep, but his mind was too full of anger toward his father and the horrible knowledge that he had failed Ashton.

Suddenly, the lamplight flickered and turned off completely, leaving the room pitch black. Wolfe stood up, feeling his way in the dark of the room to the light. He turned it off and back on again, but nothing happened. Something was wrong; the Executive Suites had never lost power. And even if they had, the generators would have kicked on by now.

A scratching sound, like metal against metal, came from over by the door. Wolfe tiptoed to the drawers of his desk where he kept a flashlight, but his father had taken everything out of his drawers that could be used as a weapon.

With a click, his door unlocked. Wolfe pinned himself against the far-left wall where he had a full view of the shadow that entered his room. He watched the outline of the intruder walk toward his bed and Wolfe saw his opportunity to pounce. He left from the wall and wrapped his arms around the person's neck and pulled. The man grunted and pulled on Wolfe's arm, but Wolfe was too strong. After a moment the man went down to his knees.

"What are you doing here!" Wolfe demanded, but he realized he had limited the man's ability to speak. Wolfe loosened his grip.

The man coughed, taking in oxygen.

183

"It's me," the man gasped. Wolfe recognized the voice. It was strained, but he would have known it anywhere.

"Joao!"

Wolfe released his friend and Joao fell to his hands as he gasped.

"I'm so sorry, are you okay?" Wolfe put his hand on Joao's shoulder, he still couldn't see his face in the darkness.

"Fine," was all Joao could muster as he pulled himself together.

Wolfe waited impatiently for Joao to tell him what he was doing there and how he was able to get in.

Finally, Joao spoke. "I heard you and your father. Is it true? Was he . . . you? This entire time?" The oddity of the statement sounded forced as it left Joao's lips.

A weight lifted from Wolfe's shoulders. His plan had worked. Joao must have been the figure listening at the door.

"Yes! I don't even know where to begin . . ."

"We should go somewhere safe to talk, not here."

Wolfe hugged his once colleague, both because of how proud he was of Joao's resourcefulness, and because he was a faithful friend. He was risking too much to come here and rescue Wolfe.

"We have to go; everything will turn back on soon. I didn't want anyone getting concerned the generators weren't working. I needed some time to talk to you."

Wolfe didn't wait for Joao to finish his sentence before heading out the door, leaving it slightly ajar for his return.

Wolfe brought Joao and slipped into an empty office, one that would surely be less bugged and full of cameras if the electricity came back on.

"I can't believe I didn't see it! I saw you acting strangely, keeping away from me. I thought it was because of your new status as CEO."

"Joao, I need to know what happened. What Warren has done."

Joao shook his head. "Wolfe, it was bad. You, Warren I mean, he started by taking people from the cages. Experimenting on them for hours, even days. He made us take them, starting with some of the old workers, but even some of the young ones. They would test the implants, and some of them worked, but others didn't. When it didn't, it confused them. The workers would act erratic, even crazy. The customer service initiative . . . it transforms them. They aren't who they were. They don't think the same, feel pain. Everything is muted and robotic."

184

Wolfe paused: it *was* worse than he thought. All those people in the cages. Joao sighed, the blood leaving his face as he recounted all that he had seen.

"What about the Colony attack?" Wolfe didn't mean to change the subject so suddenly, especially since he could tell Joao was stressed and needed comfort, but they didn't have much time; he needed to find out all he could.

Joao took a deep breath in. "Warren wanted to see if the implants would work better on children, from infancy to nine or even ten. There aren't many children in Augland." Wolfe nodded, trying to follow what Joao was saying. "By taking kids from the Colony, he could experiment on them: they would be no use to Augland if they spread rumors about the outside world, so they were perfect fodder for the experiments. So, he planned the attack. He knew where they were and gave me the orders to create a subdivision of the security men. The orders were to go in and take them at all costs. Even at the cost of Colony lives."

Wolfe could taste bile in his mouth. His father had given him a version so far from the truth that it didn't resemble it. He had twisted the narrative so much in his own mind that he thought he did good for Augland.

"That's not all of it, Wolfe," Joao almost whispered. "When he found out Ashton came in as a Suit, he was mad. He ordered me to take the girl Ashton helped escape from the Augland cages—the golden-eyed girl was taken in the raid of the Colony as well, you know the one—Warren had me bring her to his quarters where he used the girl to get information from Ashton about the Colony and NeuroEnergy. It worked, but then he—" It was not like Joao to get emotional. He was a caring man, but he had always been logical, a straight shooter. He didn't meet Wolfe's eyes as he continued. "He dropped her from the balcony."

Wolfe's world spun. Jagatha. Dead. His father had done the unimaginable. While Warren had no problem ordering death and experiments, he had never known his father's to be the hand that did the deed.

Things now became clear to Wolfe. Ashton's evident hatred for him was because she thought he had killed Jagatha.

CHAPTER 31

Ashton
FRIDAY 10:01 a.m.

The monotony of folding was made even worse by the knowledge that Ashton had lost almost every hour of sleep allotted to her. The adrenaline of her journey up to the boardroom, where she'd finally had a chance to let out some of her anger, had long worn off and she now felt the exhaustion begin to settle in.

She hadn't experienced rage like she had in the Executive's boardroom since she saw Sheva, standing alone in her armored attire, waiting for the Suit, Chandler, to slice her in two with his barbaric blade. It was the injustice of it that had propelled her feet across the Land of Legends plateau to save an innocent person from being slaughtered. Seeing the Executives sitting smugly in their tower, creating an augmented world for the Suits without regard for the lives of workers, had filled Ashton with the same fervor.

A manager walked by a few tables in front of her and Ashton saw a woman tense up as he passed, almost shaking with fear. This was what Augland wanted, to control by fear. They were all equally subject to the cruel whims of Augland's power; some just had more privilege along the way. The Suit-less managers weren't bad people. But they *were* letting the Suits live in their fantasy parks, and the Executives sit in their board rooms without getting their hands dirty. Their relative comfort came at the expense of fellow workers.

Ashton picked up another thin, black shirt from the endless pile. It was the uniform all workers were required to wear unless they were in costume. She had had many shirts like it. It was a clear identifier of their status within Augland. Ironically, Apparel workers did not wear the black uniform of the workers above, but rather a white, starchy dress that hung off most of their bodies. It was a blatant statement of Augland's disregard for their existence and a demonstration of their low-class status. They weren't going to be seen, so they didn't even deserve a worker uniform. Management was at least given half-decent black shirts to wear with bulky sweaters that helped keep them warm against the basement's cold.

Ashton placed the garment onto the steamer and watched as the smoke bellowed out the sides. She tensed as she waited for it to finish. Flashes of young Mateo's face made her fist ball and she shifted in her seat. Ashton couldn't do this. She couldn't keep watching these poor people suffer, and she wouldn't. She was done suffering, too.

Bez was right; risking life for freedom was worth it. Ashton resolved to risk her life to get out of this prison. This was no life for her anyway; she hadn't even made it five days into the monotony! And she knew she couldn't take much more.

As expected, Bez was in laundry, the towering machines spinning like a vortex behind her. It was the first bathroom break of the day, and just like before, they didn't have much time. Bez's eyes widened at Ashton's sudden appearance in front of management and other workers.

"Can I help you?" Bez asked as she eyed Ashton.

"I'd like to talk to you."

Bez looked dumbfounded by Ashton's up-front request, and she eyed the management that surrounded them. Pat stood nearby, berating a worker. Bez was visibly irritated, and her pause was growing awkward. Ashton didn't care, though; what she needed to say was time sensitive.

"Why aren't you at your station?" Bez hissed.

Ashton shifted her feet, usure what she should say in return.

"I'm busy," Bez whispered again. Please go back to your station."

"But—" Ashton started.

"If you don't leave now, I'll report you."

"Fine."

Ashton sighed. She didn't know what she'd expected, but she had hoped Bez would figure out a way for them to have a word. But Bez wasn't going to say anything that would break her façade of being in support of management. How she'd secured that position was still unknown to Ashton, but she understood why Bez needed to appear dismissive toward her. All she needed was for Bez to know they had to speak, and she had done that.

Ashton turned and found her way back to her folding station. The break wasn't over, but Ashton stood by her station, watching the world around her.

When the break ended, Ashton found it hard to pick up another garment. She was ready to aid in the escape. To release her anxious energy and inch her way to freedom again. The feeling was exhilarating and created an uneasiness as she sat quietly at her station. She focused on what surrounded her. The sewing machines were in the distance, plugged in by a long, tangled cable that hung from the ceiling down to the floor. Her mind raced with ideas. She could tear down the wires and use them as ropes to tie up the management team. Same with the steamers, using the hot water to deter anyone that came near her. Her mind burned with excitement. She didn't want to hurt people, but she knew she would need a defense plan if they were going to make it out of Apparel.

By sheer numbers, the workers had the upper hand. Augland had made a mistake by not arming management with Suits, especially at a time of potential rebellion. And the workers were fortunate that, with so many years of obedience in Augland, management wouldn't be prepared for the unrest.

Ashton narrowed her attention to a design table where two people bent over lengths of fabric, using scissors and small needles to form the loose outline of a garment. All those things could be used as weapons. From what Ashton could tell, the androids that helped around the department were harmless, only doing what they were programmed to do. Ashton smiled. For now, she would focus on a plan and not draw attention to herself. The minutes crawled by as she waited for the moment she could speak to Bez and organize a plan of escape.

Ashton's excitement wore off as the hours continued slowly. The rhapsodies of planning drained her. It was now almost midnight, and her mind went back to the nag of needing rest. Her eyes bobbled in her head, threatening sleep. It had cost her twice today when she had fallen asleep with her fingers too near the hot steam.

When the time finally came for bed, Ashton welcomed it, lining up behind the others as management guided them to their small sleeping cubbies. Tomorrow, she would approach Bez again; until then, she would fall into the sweet release of sleep.

Ashton sunk to the ground into the area that only fit her body when contorted into the fetal position. The soft, crocheted blanket was only half the length of her, and a wadded-up pile of sheets was her pillow. At that moment, she didn't care about the discomfort, only that her head could rest and her eyes could close.

What felt like only moments later, someone shook her awake.

"Ashton."

Bez hunched over her, both hands on Ashton's shoulders. Ashton hummed as she fought the attempt to wake her.

"Ashton." This time Bez shook harder, making it impossible for Ashton not to slowly open her eyes. Her eyes narrowed so she could focus on the woman with sandy brown hair who was crouching in front of her.

"Bez?" Ashton asked groggily, still trying to place herself in the darkness.

"Get up. We can't talk here." Bez pulled Ashton, dragging her out of bed. Ashton slowly rose and followed Bez through the maze of cubbies and snoring bodies. Her mind was now fully alert; she was finally getting to talk to Bez. Still, she envied those who slept around her.

Bez led her to a dimly lit stall of an old bathroom that smelled like it hadn't been cleaned in months. She silently closed the door behind her, then turned to Ashton.

"This better be good," Bez started.

"I—I—I'll help you and the other workers," Ashton blurted before she could explain why her attitude had shifted.

Bez sighed in relief. "That's great news—"

"There's more. I have a way out, but we have to move quickly." Bez furrowed her brow, trying to understand the new information Ashton was throwing at her.

"A way out? Out of Apparel?"

"No, out of Augland."

Bez's eyes went wide. She wrapped her hands around her waist as if keeping herself warm and looked intently at Ashton.

"How? We can't swim. They put a net down beneath the glass after your last escape."

"Not a swim, a boat!" Ashton's excitement was growing. "I came in here to get what Wolfe stole from the Colony. Our way out was the supply chain boat. We know the captain of the ship and he's expecting us with the kids that were taken. It's coming soon though. Very soon."

"Wh—you know the captain? Of the Augland supply boat?" Bez looked stunned. "And you trust this . . . person, who works for Augland?" Bez had a point.

"As much as I can . . . it was going to be my way out. And it was my way in."

"How much time do we have?" Bez paced in the tiny stall.

"Monday. If we aren't on the boat by seven a.m., it's leaving."

"Two days! That's not enough time." The excitement that had begun to grow vanished. Bez continued in a harsh whisper, "I mean, we aren't near that kind of communication yet."

"Communication? And who's we?"

"We've developed a method of communication. Me and this guy, Fox. While we were in the cages, he got sent back to the parks and I got sent here. We use symbols to communicate through the tags on clothes. But it's not efficient just yet; we've only got a few people from each park who know." Bez was going too fast for Ashton to keep up.

"Tags?" Ashton questioned.

"Yes, you know those things on the back of the shirts that say 'Property of Augland 54,' woman's whatever size, with a barcode?"

Ashton knew that every garment in Augland had a tag sewn on with information, but she did not understand how Bez was using the tags to communicate.

"Don't look at me like that. It's the best we've got here. We put symbols on the tags, and we can communicate with workers throughout the park."

Bez pulled out a tag she'd brought and held it up to the small light above them. Ashton studied the small piece of fabric. It had the standard "Property of Augland 54" on it, but below that, Bez pointed out a stick-figure horse on the bottom of the barcode and "BR," "T," and "D," followed by numbers.

"What does that mean?"

Bez smiled. "It means Victorian, then there is this 'BR' that is the brothel and a day and time. It still needs some work, but we've sorted out a system. They let us know what they need; we let them know what we need. It's flawed, doesn't always work, but we are getting better." Bez beamed with pride as she glanced over her work on the tiny fabric. Ashton studied the tag; it seemed too simple, too vague. She wouldn't even call it communication.

Bez continued, pointing out a small mark on the tag Ashton hadn't noticed. "The small bee there, that's my code name with Fox. That way, we know that the person we are talking to is legit. We've got a few people scattered through the parks who we trust. We can't just communicate with anyone, so we've got people who are with us, and they get the word out. Fox helped find them."

"So, is this what you meant about the rebellion? You're working together with people above ground?" Ashton didn't know if it seemed like much of a rebellion. It was a good start, but she didn't know if it would be enough.

"Yes. Wait—where will the boat take us?" Bez backtracked.

"NeuroEnergy."

Bez jolted her head back.

"I know what you are thinking, but they are good people. I mean, I think they are. Hunter believes in them. Either way, we can leave there and go straight to the Colony."

Bez exhaled heavily. "This is crazy, Ashton. Two days. And for what, to go to another company? I've got these people's lives here. You need to be sure if we are going to ask them to do this. Sure that it will happen."

It was a valid question for Bez to ask. Ashton second-guessed herself for a moment. Was she leading them to something that would not happen? This would mean putting all their trust in Georgina back at NeuroEnergy that the boat would come and the captain would let them walk on.

"Bez, I wish I could say it was for certain, but if you're asking me if I'd take the risk to get on that boat. The chance? Yes. One hundred times, yes. I've been there, outside these walls. I had a home, I had choices, no one forced me to do anything I didn't want to do. I worked because I wanted to."

Ashton's heart ached as she remembered her life that had only been weeks ago. Deep in her heart, she wished she had never left, that she had never returned to Augland. But there was no time to think about that now.

"That is freedom. And it's worth everything. This? This place? These rules? It's killing them regardless."

Bez paused for a moment, looking intently at Ashton before finally speaking. "All right. I'll recruit who we can and spread the word. I don't know if this is going to work. But we will try." Bez smiled. "The woman in red leading us to freedom."

Ashton laughed. "Who's the woman in red?"

Bez looked stunned for a minute. "It's you, silly! The woman in red who escaped Augland."

CHAPTER 32

Wolfe
FRIDAY 2:48 a.m.

Wolfe had never become used to the dampness of the underground cages. Cold, steel bars lined either side of the hallway as he and Joao walked down the first floor. The hallway was narrow, and water dripped somewhere in the distance. Wolfe tried to ignore the imprisoned workers. Some yelled as they passed, but most stared back at him with blank, hopeless eyes.

Wolfe knew he should head back to his office in case his father came looking for him. The lights had gone out around one a.m., and now it was almost three; time was not on Wolfe's side. If Warren had taken notice of his absence, he might have notified security. Regardless, the brief power outage in the Executives' suites would have tipped Warren off that something was up.

But Wolfe couldn't worry about Warren right now. He needed to take the chance to meet with Hunter, whom Joao said had been captured when Ashton was exposed and imprisoned down in the cages. Hunter had the answers to why he and Ashton had come back to Augland, and maybe information that could help Wolfe to plan his next moves against his father.

At the end of the hallway were the enclosed rooms used for the interrogation or "rehabilitation" of those workers who were considered especially aggressive. Joao had requested Hunter be placed in an interrogation room so Wolfe, Joao, and Hunter could talk in private. Joao had remote access to the cameras through his interconnect and would make sure they were shut off before Wolfe entered. They didn't want any recordings of their conversation in case someone was watching, which could be used against Hunter or Wolfe in the future. Even Joao was at risk of questions, and consequences, from Warren. Not only that, but with privacy ensured, Hunter was more likely to feel confident telling them everything he knew.

Wolfe tried to suppress his sense of nausea as he followed Joao into the dimly lit interrogation room. The small, cement room smelled of musty sweat and urine. Hunter had a thick mustache, and his long, shaggy brown hair was pulled back into a bun. His clothes were nice but smeared by the muddy ground of the cages.

"Hunter, how are you?"

"I don't know who Hunter is, my name is Alonso." Hunter crossed his arms in a clear attempt of defiance. He was still trying to continue his disguise as Alonso, Charlotte's personal worker. "You know, Charlotte will be truly angry when she hears about my captivity. Do you know who her father is? Charles Maxwell?"

Hunter thought he had a trump card with the name drop of an elite Augland 2 member, but he had no idea how much had happened while he had been captive down in the cages.

"You can drop the act; Ashton's been exposed. Her Suit malfunctioned and she was taken out of her pod. Warren knows. That's why you are here."

Hunter paused as he examined his surroundings, trying to act unfazed by the news. The walls around them were thick and dark, fully enclosed. There was no one who could hear them or witness what went on. Wolfe could see the wheels turn in Hunter's mind as the realization of his situation darkened his mood. Wolfe let Hunter process, being patient as the room grew increasingly quiet. He could see the rising of Hunter's chest as panic set in and he tried to control his breathing.

"Don't worry, I'm here to help you," Wolfe tried to reassure him.

Hunter's eyes shifted to Wolfe as if trying to figure out Wolfe's angle. Hunter could try and continue the façade, but Wolfe knew too much for him to keep pushing the lie.

"You say you're here to help me?" As Hunter regained composure, he tried to negotiate. "Then let me go." Hunter leaned back in his chair casually; he had a point. If Wolfe's intentions were pure, why didn't he just let him leave? Unfortunately, Wolfe needed more information before that could happen—if it even *could* happen, given Wolfe's own predicament.

Wolfe was cognizant of the fact that Hunter, like Ashton, likely believed that he had attacked the Colony and ordered the kidnapping of its children. He would feel just as betrayed as Ashton did.

"I'll need something from you before I even think about letting you go." It wasn't the best start if Wolfe was trying to win back Hunter's trust, but he didn't have time for niceties right now.

Hunter chuckled; he knew it wouldn't be that easy or he wouldn't be locked in the interrogation room with Joao and Wolfe. He retorted, "Then tell me where Ash is. Tell me she's okay."

"Apparel, that's where Warren sent her." Joao spoke up for the first time. "She's fine."

"Then bring her here. You're the CEO . . . you can do anything. And then let us go. If you do that, I'll tell you anything you want to know."

"I—I can't do that . . ."

Hunter scoffed. Wolfe knew the only way to get Hunter to talk was to tell him everything. It wouldn't be easy, but he needed to gain his trust for any plan to work.

Wolfe picked up one of the two chairs that sat across the interrogation table and brought it around to sit next to Hunter. Wolfe looked him straight in the eyes. Hunter sat back defensively, putting space between them.

"I made a mistake . . ." Wolfe looked down at his hands. He exhaled hard as he admitted something he wasn't proud of. "I tried . . . when you and Ash left, I thought I'd be able to win over the Executives. But these people don't play by the rules. They play dirty. Unfair. They have no remorse." Wolfe shook his head. "I called Warren out. I had another Executive's support to take over being CEO. I thought—I thought we won, but Warren didn't let that happen." Wolfe wasn't used to admitting failure and it was difficult for him to tell the truth. It was still painfully raw.

Wolfe continued to explain everything that had happened to him. How Warren had taken him prisoner and impersonated him with a Suit that looked identical to Wolfe. How Warren had pretended to retire and installed "Wolfe" as the new CEO. Once his plan succeeded, Warren had done horrible things in Wolfe's name. He told Hunter that Warren was to blame for the attack on the Colony.

Finally, Wolfe explained the customer service initiative. Vulnerable workers were being experimented on to create a new technology that could be used to augment workers. Sometimes it didn't work, and workers were left with scars, technology-glitched minds, or dead. And when the technology did work, their very bodies, eyes, and minds could be manipulated by Augland. And Hunter, a prisoner in the cages, could be next.

Hunter eyed Wolfe carefully. "Seems convenient."

Wolfe knew that Hunter had never liked him. Their relationship had sustained a certain mutual mistrust since their time at Lands of Legends. Wolfe remembered Hunter's roller-coaster history with Ashton during their training at Legends and had always considered him to be self-serving. Neither of them had fully understood the other's motivations, and Wolfe's perceived betrayal had solidified everything Hunter had always suspected of him.

"Not really. I've got no proof. All I ask is that you believe me. I wouldn't go back on my word to protect the Colony, to protect Ashton."

"It's all true, Hunter," Joao spoke up from the corner of the room. But it didn't help. Hunter had no idea who Joao was, only that he was a friend of Wolfe's.

Hunter inhaled deeply. "Considering I don't have much of a choice here, I'll trust you. Not saying I believe you. If you are telling the truth, then you can help me get the Colony children back and Ashton and I'll get them out of Augland. If not, we're screwed anyway."

Wolfe breathed a sigh of relief. Hunter saw things as they were, and even if he didn't trust Wolfe, he knew there was no benefit in refusing him and going back into the cages.

Wolfe thought for a moment. Even if there was a way to get to the children, they had already been dispersed across all Augland. The chances he would even be able to locate them were next to none.

"How would you do that? Get them out?" Wolfe pressed to gather information before letting Hunter down about the children's unlikely rescue.

Hunter paused, still uncertain how much he should divulge before he lost his leverage completely.

"Look," Wolfe continued, "I can't promise the children; chances are they are already in the system. I'd need every name and even then, they are probably numbers now. But if you have a way out of Augland, take the people here." Wolfe opened his arms to indicate the men, women, and children imprisoned around them. They had already suffered so much and were doomed to a further life of torture through the customer service initiative if they were to remain in the cages of Augland. Wolfe's chance of ending the initiative by becoming CEO was now a fading dream.

Hunter sat quietly, thinking over Wolfe's proposal. Wolfe continued, "Let me do this; let me prove that I'm not the monster here. If you have a way out, have help from outside these walls, tell me so I can make it possible. I know Augland. Joao and I have resources that could help."

Hunter still didn't look like he trusted Wolfe, but his shoulders sagged in resignation. He had been captured, and if he didn't agree, he acknowledged there was no way to get anyone out of Augland, including himself.

"The supply boat, on Monday," Hunter said reluctantly. "NeuroEnergy has some deal with the captain. Ashton and I were meant to grab the children and be on that boat to be dropped off at NeuroEnergy's location. In exchange, Ashton just needed to get enough intel from you or, I suppose, Warren—if you're telling the truth—to help aid in NeuroEnergy's fight to keep—" Hunter stopped, nervous about continuing. Wolfe ignored Hunter's hesitancy.

"Why would NeuroEnergy help you?" Wolfe asked, more for curiosity than a need for knowledge. There was so much to take in, he didn't know where to start.

"They suspect a hostile corporate takeover of their energy plants. We were told to get inside Augland 54 and get information. That was the tradeoff for Ashton's Suit."

Wolfe sat back in his chair, still only feet away from Hunter. The shadows from the overhead light only illuminated half of Wolfe's face. He had long known of NeuroEnergy's insecurities about Augland 54's intentions, and they were right to be suspicious. It was clear Warren hated the power that NeuroEnergy had over them. If NeuroEnergy decided, they could turn off the power to the Suits and the generators. Doing so would eliminate their source of revenue, and it wouldn't be long before their world collapsed. In turn, without the need for electricity, NeuroEnergy would be obsolete.

There was a long history of distrust between the two divisions of the AEC—the Augland parks and NeuroEnergy plants—a never-ending battle to be the AEC's most powerful branch. The AEC was no saint in all this. They stayed neutral and thought it was a healthy competition for the parks that served the Suits and the energy that powered them.

What concerned Wolfe was the fact that NeuroEnergy was using Ashton and Hunter as pawns in its ploy for information. Both were naïve to the inner workings of corporate politics, and because of that, they had risked their lives. Wolfe shook his head in frustration. NeuroEnergy was not as bad as Augland, not nearly, but manipulating Hunter and Ashton into believing they could save the Colony children was a risk-free way for NeuroEnergy to get what it wanted.

Georgina would have known it was impossible to save the children. She had taken advantage of Ashton's compassion for the workers and children and what she was willing to do to protect them. Wolfe now understood why Ashton and Hunter had come to Augland, and the purpose of the Suit, Charlotte. NeuroEnergy had used her empathy to obtain information about Augland without risking one of its own.

"Are you willing to save the people of the cages? Instead of the children? There is no way to find them now, not in my current situation."

Hunter thought for a moment. "If we can't get the children, the least we can do is save the people here. They will be happier outside these walls." Hunter sighed. "Not sure how Georgina will take it."

Wolfe half smiled. "She probably won't like it, and it is not a good political move, but saving these people who need help may appeal to her compassion. If Georgina won't help, Cahya may."

"So, what happens now?" Hunter inquired, his body shifting upright as a new sense of purpose and adventure took hold of him. No doubt, he was itching to get out of Augland and was counting down the hours until that boat arrived.

"Joao and I will need to prepare; there will be a lot to do before we can safely move the caged workers from here to the Maya Bay shores. During that time, I think it's best if you stay here."

Wolfe knew it wasn't an easy ask for Hunter to set aside his pride and leverage in hopes that someone would help. Hunter had grown up a lot since their time together in Land of Legends, more than Wolfe had imagined.

Joao and Wolfe left, ushering Hunter back into his cage with promises of the latest information as soon as things progressed. Hunter hadn't been happy, but unfortunately, it would be too suspicious to do anything else with him. Wolfe and Joao were still operating under the radar, and the longer they could keep it that way, the better.

Joao and Wolfe jogged side by side through the cages until they made it to the supply office where spare security gear was kept. Joao picked up various guns while Wolfe found two hoverbikes. They were an easy mode of transportation and one used often by security around Augland. It would take longer than the train or gondola—it was at least an hour's drive from the cages up through Victorian—but Wolfe could make it back before anyone noticed he had gone.

As they drove the hoverbikes through the emerging light of artificial sunrise, Joao spoke to Wolfe through the helmet interconnect: "If this works, and I mean *if*, how are you going to explain your situation to NeuroEnergy? No doubt they think you were the CEO and led that attack on the Colony. Or they might consider you a spy for your father. They may even torture you for information. Kill you . . ."

Joao was right. Wolfe knew he could be walking into a hostage situation; Georgina could turn on him along with the rest of the escaped workers. Wolfe didn't have much choice, though; his guilt for not seeing through his father's plan, and what had happened as a result, fueled his desire to make things right, even if it meant he was walking into the line of fire.

"Maybe. We will just have to risk it."

Wolfe sped ahead of Joao, twisting and turning through the Victorian landscape toward the small door in the wall between the parks that led to Hollywood Boulevard.

CHAPTER 33

Wolfe

FRIDAY 8:42 p.m.

The plan had begun. Joao had his own tasks to complete, and it was time for Wolfe to return to the Executive Suites. The plan had been made and all things set in motion. Joao had told Warren he had moved Wolfe to his new home, which bought him the day to put things in order.

Wolfe had every confidence that Hunter would do everything he could to get the workers out of the cages to the beach of Maya Bay on time. Wolfe himself could not be involved with the escape right now; his absence would only cause suspicion and put everyone in the cages at risk. Right now, he needed to concentrate on a diversion.

Wolfe rounded the final corner to his office and stopped in his tracks. The door was open, the light was on, and he could see the outline of a Suit against the window. The Suit was tall and broad with dark hair, but it wasn't Warren. Wolfe entered cautiously as he began to recognize the man who stood staring out of his window.

"Reuben. Didn't realize you were going to stop by." Wolfe didn't have time for this. Either Reuben was stopping by for an idle chat, or his father had sent him, and Wolfe's plan had already come to an end.

"What can I do for you?" Wolfe tried to act casually. Reuben turned and stretched out his hands to Wolfe in staged pleasantries.

"Wolfgang, I'm sorry for appearing without notice. I wanted to chat with you before you left for your new home. I thought I might have missed you."

"Depends on the purpose of the meeting." Wolfe needed to get Reuben out of his room quickly so he could continue his plan. "What can I do for you, sir?"

"Oh, nothing, this is a . . . personal visit. Not technically professional."

That took Wolfe by surprise; he didn't know whether to act casual or continue to be suspicious of his unexpected visitor. He went with suspicion.

"I'm a little busy at the moment." Wolfe eyed Reuben cautiously.

"May I?" Rueben pointed to the couch. Executives had a habit of wanting to be comfortable before a serious conversation. Wolfe nodded, slowly entered the room, and sat down behind his desk.

"I—I have connections at Augland 13 and . . . I know they need a security manager there. I'd be willing to put in a recommendation for you. I have a home there where you could stay." Wolfe folded his hands on his desk.

"Why would you do that?" Wolfe knew to be cautious around Reuben, especially now, when he couldn't tell his motives.

"I care for you. Your well-being. I know what your father said in the boardroom was not all true and it cast a light on you that was unflattering. You're a good kid; you've got a big heart and you are good at what you do. I do hate to see your reputation be questioned like that . . ."

Wolfe scoffed.

"You don't believe me, but I would do anything for you. Now, that doesn't mean I'm your ally in this, but I'm not your enemy either."

Reuben was dancing around the subject. He either knew that Wolfe's father had impersonated Wolfe or that he had lied. Either way, Reuben was telling Wolfe he wouldn't fight for justice but would help with the recovery. Wolfe couldn't take the political games anymore, and he didn't have to. By Monday, he'd hopefully be out of Augland forever.

"Reuben, you can't play both sides. Someday, you'll be called to pick. If you aren't my ally, then, unfortunately, you're my enemy."

"Wolfe—"

Wolfe stood. "I think it's best you go. Wouldn't want Warren believing you're a conspirator. You know how paranoid he can get. Especially when it comes to his family members." Wolfe knew Reuben had some kind of relationship with his mother, and he could use that leverage against him.

Reuben sat, his face stoic and unmoving as he glared intently at Wolfe.

"Very well . . . know my offer still stands." He didn't need to be ushered out to realize the conversation was over.

Now, Wolfe needed just a few hours of sleep. The next two days were going to be long.

SATURDAY 3:45 a.m.

It took Wolfe only moments to pack everything he would take with him. Music cards from his favorite artists, black shirts and sweatshirts, a couple pairs of pants, his cuffs, his photon gun, chargers, and the interconnect Joao had given him. It wasn't much, but he didn't need many things.

The ache in his heart was not because of how much he would miss this way of life. It was whom he'd most likely never see again: his mother. He feared her staying in the political world with people like his father and wanted to give her a chance to join him.

It was close to four a.m. as Wolfe walked down the hall. He walked slowly, making sure to pay attention to any noise around him. The last thing he needed was to be found outside of his office by one of the Executives or his father. He rounded the corner past his father's shady oak doors and to his mother's bright and vibrant entrance.

Wolfe paused, experiencing *déjà vu* from his childhood, back when his parents first separated and his mother moved into the adjacent apartment. He had stayed with his father back then, but whenever he had nightmares, he would sneak out in the middle of the night to see his mother. She would console him, stroking his hair as he fell asleep in her arms. Then, she would wake him up early enough that his father had no idea he had left. She had always protected him. Wolfe paused and shook the memory away.

The fact that his father had given him every reason not to trust anyone had jaded Wolfe. He didn't know how much his mother knew about the recent events with Warren. He wanted to ask how she didn't see the lies. Why hadn't she come for him when Warren had him cast away? How his mother had not seen through Warren's mask would always be a mystery to him, but he had never asked her about it. Perhaps he didn't want to know the answer.

Wolfe lightly tapped on the door, enough that his mother would know someone was there. There was no answer. He tapped louder until he heard the stir of light footsteps approaching. The door unlocked, and Anastasia opened the door with half-open eyes and messy mahogany hair wrapped in a braid to the side of her shoulder. She wore matching pajamas but hid behind the entrance door.

"Wolfe? Is that you?" She looked Wolfe up and down, seeing the toll the past few months had taken, ravages that no one else would or could see.

201

"I'm sorry it's so early, but I need to talk to you."

"Of course, darling." She opened the door, allowing him to step inside and out of view from anyone outside of her safe walls.

Anastasia led Wolfe to her dining table. The painting he had last seen her working on was now hung on the wall. His mother's attention to detail made each blade of grass look like it was perfectly swaying in a nonexistent wind. The soft lamb was front and center, a rich white that contrasted with the swaying green.

"I haven't seen you for some time; I was beginning to worry. Why didn't you visit?" Anastasia asked a single question, but Wolfe knew there was much more she wanted to know. He didn't know how much she already knew, or even if he could trust her. But he had already decided he would.

Wolfe sighed. Where should he begin? How much should he tell his mother? And what consequence would that have if he did? If she didn't know the truth and Wolfe revealed it, what would Warren do?

"I haven't been myself. So much has happened, but I don't have time to explain. But . . . I need your help."

Anastasia turned to hand over a cup of freshly brewed coffee from her espresso machine. She typically only drank tea, but she kept coffee around for Wolfe. She knew how he liked his coffee and even had a button specific to his preference: two shots of espresso, a quarter-cup of whole milk, no sugar, and a dash of cinnamon. He only drank it with cinnamon when he was with her. It seemed too pretentious in front of his security men and the other Executives, or to even order from workers. But with his mom, he had always felt safe.

"Reuben said you've been . . . distant. Since you became CEO. Said you had told him you were too busy to visit." Wolfe could tell that was not what Reuben had said verbatim.

Wolfe wasn't sure how much Reuben knew or whose side he was on. He was still confused over their conversation hours earlier.

"I don't have much time. I'm leaving here . . . Augland 54." He couldn't look at his mother; instead, he played with the coffee mug. "I'm going to do something risky, and I need you to help me keep Warren busy. Now, I can't tell you what—"

"What do you need me to do?" Anastasia's brown eyes glistened warmly as she placed her hand on top of Wolfe's. She didn't question him, want to know more, or even reprimand him for anything Reuben had said he had done. Wolfe sighed in relief. It was the sign he needed from his mother.

"I—I don't know. All I need is for Warren, Father, to stay busy long enough so I have time to get out. Out of Augland . . ."

"Where will you go?" Anastasia eyed him carefully.

"Not another Augland."

"The Colony?" Wolfe didn't say anything. There was silence between them as his mother carefully studied his face. He was never good at lying to her.

"No, no not there . . ."

Wolfe's mother looked confused. "But why?" He didn't even have to say where he was going; she already knew. Wolfe couldn't answer as it would only put more people in jeopardy. He couldn't expose the security team, or anyone else for that matter. This had to be only him.

"Please, just, I know this doesn't make sense and I've been away for some time, but I can't stay here. Not in Augland . . . and I've got people with me."

Anastasia looked down and pulled her hand away from Wolfe's. It broke his heart, knowing the pain he was causing her.

"You could come, you know. Leave here and come with me. With us."

His mother half smiled to mask the sadness she felt.

"No, I can't, but you should. I wish you weren't going to NeuroEnergy . . . but I've never wanted the Augland life for you. I've never wanted this life for myself." Anastasia sighed, tears welling up in her eyes as she looked away from him. "But you play an extremely dangerous game going to Georgina. She's been vocal about her theories of Augland 54. And . . ." She paused. "Your father will never forgive you."

Wolfe knew his mother was right; Warren would never forgive him. If he left and brought workers with him, he would make an enemy of his father.

"Because you are more of a man than he will ever be."

Wolfe looked up in surprise. Anastasia never spoke ill of Warren. Especially being Suit-less and vulnerable, she never teetered beyond the middle ground.

She wiped the tears as she pulled herself together. "I'll need to know the distraction at least, and when you need it."

Wolfe put his hand on hers. He saw her age showing through by the light freckles on her tiny hands and long fingers.

For the next hour, they spoke about what Wolfe needed from his mother. He hadn't thought of exactly what it would look like, only that his father's attention would need to be somewhere else for the next forty-eight hours. It couldn't be directed toward Wolfe or what was happening down in the cages. He wouldn't supply details. If Warren asked, Wolfe was in his home in Predator's Biome. That was one thing he'd learned from his father: if you wanted things to be discreet, the less people knew, the less they would be able to thwart the plan. Joao had his part, his mother hers, and he had his.

Wolfe had forgotten how much he enjoyed spending time with his mother. She was a bright and vibrant woman. She was fearless when she needed to be, but compliant when not. It was her curse and her blessing. She had an infectious smile that brought warmth and love during the darkest of times. Wolfe embraced the feeling and didn't want to leave, but there was so much to do before the boat left Monday morning.

"Thank you," Wolfe said, and he began to stand up. His mother, realizing their time together was ending, began to tear up. His heart sank as he feared this was the last time he would see her. "Goodbye, Mom. I love you." He swept her up in an embrace. She felt so small in his arms. He put his arm up around her head and kissed the top, feeling her holding back sobs.

Wolfe stiffened as he left, forcing his face into a mask. He had a job to do, and his emotions would not help him now.

As soon as his mother's door shut behind him, Wolfe had a sinking feeling in the pit of his stomach. He wanted to go back in and give her another hug, but he knew it would only prolong the inevitable. His life here had ended, and he needed to say goodbye to the place he'd called home his entire life.

CHAPTER 34

Ashton

SATURDAY 2:15 a.m.

Ashton left Bez in the bathroom and snuck back to her sleep cubby, past all the other sleeping workers. Despite her exhaustion, she tossed and turned, her mind racing with the anticipation of another Augland escape.

She dreamed she was back home at Hood Canal, sitting out on the rickety dock, watching the stars sprinkled above her. Sparse clouds hung low, hovering above the still water. A warm fire sparked in a steel bowl as smoke twirled up to the sky. Ashton was wrapped in a handmade quilt Versal had made from fabric scraps. She relaxed as she took in a deep breath. The coastal sea smell and frigid air cleansed her. A shadow appeared behind her, but Ashton wasn't frightened.

The shadow enveloped her and wrapped its arms around her. There was a familiarity to its presence. It was Wolfe—as he always had been in her memory. She placed her head against his rough chin and closed her eyes, taking in the bergamot and cedar scent of him. Wolfe breathed in and tightened his arms around her, admiring the sparks of the fire as they both looked onto the serene water.

Abruptly, the shadow dissipated—Wolfe loosened his grip and disappeared, leaving Ashton alone in complete darkness. Fear took over. She called out, but there was nothing. Her home had disappeared. Then, in the silence, Jagatha's deathly screams. In the darkness, the screams came at her from every direction. Ashton called out to Jagatha, but the screams only continued. Ashton recoiled, lowering her body to the rocking planks of the rickety dock. She placed her hands over her ears to stop the loud screams, but it did little good. She sobbed as she relived Jagatha's falling body as if it was her own.

Ashton woke panting, the faint cries from her dream still echoing in her mind. She had only just stopped dreaming of Sheva, who had now been replaced with Jagatha. It was better to be awake in this place than in her savage dreams. Only two more nights of this and maybe she could be back home—maybe.

Ashton dragged her feet across the hard concrete ground and tried to refrain from breathing in the bleach-filled air. It burned her nostrils. In a single-file line, the workers divided across the many rows of laundry, folding, cutting, and finally sewing. She looked down at Mateo's folding station. He swung his feet and concentrated hard on pressing the heavy machine down onto the shirt he was pressing. The buoyancy of his youth still shone through, but Ashton could tell Mateo was exhausted. His tiny palm was still wrapped from Pat's beating and dark blood seeped through the white cloth.

The person behind Ashton accidentally bumped into her, causing her to break her gaze away from Mateo's hand. Ashton apologized but the worker behind her didn't respond. The silent monotony of the workday had started.

As Ashton worked, she planned. They would need to leave the next day to make it to Maya Bay in time for the boat's arrival. But that meant figuring out how to get past the guards, up the elevator, out to Predator's Biome, and onto the train that would lead them to Maya Bay. The plan became more dangerous the more Ashton considered the details. But Bez and Ashton would not be alone.

Bez had taken the risk to send Fox a direct message. She knew it would put them in danger, but at least they would be somewhat protected by their code names.

In the message Bez related to Ashton, she had simply asked, "Would you follow the red path?"

It was a simple message, unclear, but discreet. She hoped Fox understood what she had asked. She hoped he saw through the coded message that she was asking about the woman in red, and her path to freedom.

That day, her answer appeared. A worn tag with the words, "All in," written in red ink. Bez smiled with relief. Fox would rally with her.

Ashton folded slowly and periodically stole glances at the elevator on the other side of the vast auditorium of Apparel. She didn't have a clear view and her short stature didn't help. Two guards always flanked the elevator doors. Management staff didn't have clearance to open them, or else Bez would have access, so that meant security personnel were the only ones who could go up and down the elevator.

Ashton thought about the vents, but she didn't have a mental landscape of where they went, and there were too many people to go that route. She thought there could be an underground tunnel, maybe connecting the cages to Apparel, but again, that was knowledge she did not have and didn't have the time to find out. The only way out would be through the elevator, up two floors to the hallway that divided the outside rim of Augland's walls to Predator's Biome. That would mean overpowering the security guards, who had guns, radios, and the full force of Augland to back them up.

Ashton took her eyes off the guards as Forest, a manager who worked with Bez, came into view and slowly made his way, row by row, to the folding station. Ashton put her head down as she pressed her hand against the lever of her steam machine and began putting the two boards together. All day she had pressed worker attire: black pants and black shirts, over and over.

Forest approached Ashton, his figure casting a shadow over her table. She looked up at his darting eyes, wondering what he wanted. He looked nervous, and for the first time, Ashton noticed his uneasiness, so different from the usual management authority. He coughed and placed a new bag of clothes on her table.

"We will be refolding all these. Mishap with the tags. Begin a new pile and take the old ones to Sewing Section 2." Ashton looked perplexed. "It's going to be a late night tonight." Forest paused awkwardly for a moment, as if unsure of where to go next. "Please hurry; these will need to go out for shipping today."

Ashton was horrified. "How many?"

"At least seventy pallets, more if we can manage. I'll have others on it as well."

Suddenly, Ashton understood. Bez must have figured out a way to send a message through the tags. There would be no other reason to change out old tags for new ones. She looked at the rows of new clothes being brought to folding. It was an impossible amount of work, but Ashton was ready.

"Of course. I'll get working on that now."

"Thank you." Forest hovered for another moment before burying his face in his interconnect and walking away. She looked at him as he left. He walked with a slight hunch, but Ashton now knew that he had courage. He was part of this. Whatever "this" was.

Making sure no one was looking, Ashton opened the enormous bags of clothing and ripped out a shirt to see what the tag said. She spread the cloth across her small desk. She still saw the typical tag, "Property of Augland 54, Men's XL," with a barcode at the bottom. But when Ashton looked closer, she saw that an "X" crossed out the word "Augland" and replaced it with the words: "The UnSuited."

It was a bold statement, not like what Bez had suggested. Ashton looked at the barcode. The two squiggly lines that Bez had said stood for the waves of Maya Bay, then "BF700 – D1212." Ashton read it carefully. It wasn't discreet at all. She stood up, determined now to find Bez.

"This isn't code! This is flat-out telling them what we are doing," Ashton whispered heavily as she showed Bez the tag, following behind her among the spinning bundles of clothing.

"Well, what did you expect?" Bez kept walking but kept her voice low so others couldn't hear. Ashton recognized the instantly defensive tone. "We don't have a stick figure for 'Let's meet at this location to leave Augland because the woman in red from Land of Legends came back and she's helping us escape on a boat.' Haven't quite gotten there in our pictographs."

"This isn't what we talked about. It's supposed to be silent, stealthy." Ashton took another glance around her, but the tumbling of the dryer drowned out their conversation.

Bez sighed. "We don't have a choice, and you know what? Who cares? We want them to know. We want them to feel our pain. What better way than to leave our mark? Let them know who we are."

Bez had a point. Ashton hated to admit it, but chances were they weren't going to go quietly, so why try to be so discreet?

"What if they see this before we even have the chance to escape? We need to be smart, have a plan."

"Is that what you did when you destroyed that Suit? Stopped to plan before running to protect your friend?" Bez narrowed her gaze at Ashton. It took Ashton by surprise. She hadn't thought about it that way; she hadn't planned anything she did in Land of Legends. It had all been on instinct to protect Sheva. Ashton sighed.

"I want you to look around," said Bez. "Look at the people over here."

Ashton cooperated as she slowly reviewed her surroundings, looking around the vast room segregated by departments of laundry, cutting, and sewing. The workers of Augland had more energy today and some even smiled. Ashton hadn't noticed, but the atmosphere in the room had shifted.

"These people look up to you. They see what you went through, what you sacrificed, what you've had. They believe you can help them, and it's given them a lust for life. I can tell you I haven't seen them like this since I got here. The excitement, the . . ." she paused, "desperation for change."

Ashton's eyes widened. What Bez said was true, and Ashton felt it. She hated to admit it, but Bez was right. What the workers of Augland 54 needed was a spark of hope that blazed the way to freedom. They were willing to risk their lives for the chance.

Ashton wasn't a leader, but the woman in red was a sign Bez had used to her advantage. If anything, it gave these people hope. Bez was much better at rallying people and exuding confidence. She would be their natural leader, but Bez needed someone to light the rebellious flame. And igniting the flame was something Ashton thought the woman in red could do.

CHAPTER 35

Ashton
SUNDAY 6:11 a.m.

P at was preoccupied. Things were going wrong in Apparel, requiring his frequent attention. There was a suspicious number of machines breaking down at the same time.

Ashton couldn't help the small smile that formed on her lips. There was an invigorating spirit in the workers around her. The powerless workers had a secret, and it gave them strength. For the first time, they were working together with precision and authority.

A woman "accidentally" spilled bleach on a pile of clothing going to Venus. Pat was enraged. Then a man bumped one of the long-armed sewing machines hanging from the ceiling, knocking it off its track and making it nearly impossible to use. Finally, a red dye was put into a washing machine, causing all the clothes to turn a deep burgundy color. It was going to be a customer service nightmare.

Ashton heard Pat scream from across the room. "What is happening around here?!" He yelled more than once, spiraling out of control as the mayhem of unnoticed mutiny rallied around him. But they were just getting started. A tidal wave of malfunctions and mishaps was planned throughout the entire day.

Everyone had their part, including Ashton. She folded quickly but took the distractions as opportunities to continue figuring out how they were going to get out of Apparel.

The point of all the malfunctions was to find means of protecting themselves. They needed weapons that would protect them and deter the management and security personnel from fighting back. Bez was clear: she didn't want to harm people, only disengage them. Ashton agreed. She wasn't a killer, and neither were any of the people here. The workers in management were Suit-less just like the rest of them. They did what they were told and for that they shouldn't feel the wrath of the UnSuited.

But when they were out of Apparel, they would be fighting security, who had guns, and Suits, who could fight with their robotic strength and suffer no physical harm. They needed anything sharp. Needles. Scissors. Metal machinery.

As soon as Pat was out of her sight, Ashton pretended she had a task to do over by the manufacturing tables. It was a risk, but she couldn't sit still any longer.

The world around her silenced to a hum as she paced in between the rows of workers. She took notice of everything: pencils that drew the shapes of the clothes on a long sheet of cloth, long threads of diverse colors that wrapped around and around tiny plastic tubes, and the steel rods that supported the mannequins. This would have been easier if she had been given a tool like the ax she'd wielded as Freya, but it was time to improvise and be resourceful.

Ashton picked whatever she could. An older woman slipped her an extra pair of scissors and Ashton stole a pair of long, sharp needles from a cushioned pad. She tucked her stolen items into her pockets, and then when those were full, under her shirt. As she walked along the rows, Ashton noticed that workers around her had been watching and they were now making eye contact as they slipped items into their own pockets.

"How are we doing?"

Bez came out of nowhere and made Ashton jump. But Bez didn't look at Ashton, she kept her eyes turned toward laundry where Pat was screaming at a group of workers.

"We need people to grab what they can to protect themselves. Not just to attack, but also to protect their bodies. I don't know, like shields or something," Ashton whispered as she pulled out a pair of scissors she had fashioned into a long knife using the rods of two hangers she had found. She wrapped her contraption in a shirt and handed it to Bez.

"They'll be ready. They just need your signal. When do you think you'll attack the guards?" Bez danced on her heels and Ashton could tell she was nervous.

"At seven p.m., I'll give the signal. Twelve hours before the boat leaves." They had only the day to prepare, but in a way, the workers had been ready their whole lives. Bez had traded with her UnSuited above ground contacts for Augland 54 brochures that outlined the all the parks. She put an "X" where the Predator's Biome train would

211

be and another for the boat in Maya Bay. It would help some of the apparel workers who had never seen the world above them know where they needed to go.

"Perfect." Bez turned and marched back to laundry. Ashton watched as she barked orders to the workers, who had just been reprimanded by Pat. Bez was the perfect double agent.

Ashton sat back down at her station. All around the room, she saw the other workers doing what they had seen Ashton do: taking the used hangers, needles, curved embroidery scissors, and pens.

A young worker came to her side and dropped the next load of worker shirts to fold. He bent down to pick them up and slid something under her table.

"Took the wheels off the laundry carts and wrapped cords from the sewing machine." His grin was wide as he spoke without looking at Ashton. "You can spin it and throw the wheel. I thought it could help; might even be used to tie them up."

"Amazing," Ashton said under her breath. He took a shirt out of the pile and gently placed it on Ashton's lap.

"Made that one for you." Ashton unwrapped the shirt to see the long, gray wires wrapped around the metal casing of a laundry cart wheel.

"Thank you." The young man beamed with pride before turning and making his way back to his laundry cart, placing more piles of clothes down at the various steamer stations.

Ashton felt an overwhelming sense of empowerment from the others around her. This time, it wasn't just her. It was so different from her previous attempt, back in Land of Legends. There had been no plan. She had seen Sheva about to be attacked and Ashton had retaliated against a Suit. But this time, the men, women, and children around her were ready.

Ashton was impressed by the workers, but she didn't know how to lead them. She had no idea what she could do to help mobilize and direct them, but that wasn't what most of them needed. They didn't need someone telling them what to do. All they needed was an opportunity.

As the hours went by, Ashton could see confidence rise within the room. She was deep in her work, allowing the monotony of steaming and folding to calm her mind as she thought about the night ahead.

She jumped as she heard a throat clear next to her. She did not have the time or patience to deal with Pat now. But to her surprise, Bez was standing near with a bag in her hand.

"Take the bag." Bez dropped a plastic bag near Ashton's seat. Ashton looked down and saw a glimpse of tiny red threads. "It's the sign. Put it on when you're ready."

Ashton stuck her hand into the bag and felt the stringy, synthetic hair of a wig. She was confused as she touched the fabric, wondering why. She could only assume they wanted her to be the woman in red, the one Mateo mentioned, the one whom Niall had seen, the one Bez said would be their hope. Then it clicked: they wanted Freya, the warrior with red hair who went against the odds. In all honesty, it felt foolish and Ashton wished she didn't need to wear it, but Bez was insistent.

Freya was an act; a character Ashton had embodied. She hadn't been that woman in a very long time. She didn't know if she had the strength or hope to lead these people to freedom. But there was no going back now. At seven p.m., she would put on the wig and become the woman in red.

SUNDAY 6:57 p.m.

The night came quickly and with every hour that'd sped by, Ashton had become more unsettled. Her palms were damp and cold as she shook with a nervous twitch. She could no longer pretend the beading drops on her brow were from the steamers.

It was 6:58 p.m.

Bez would be telling everyone to wait for her signal, and Ashton could feel the weight of a hundred eyes waiting for her to move. In two minutes, Ashton would disappear and the woman in red would emerge.

It was 6:59 p.m.

Twelve hours until the boat arrived, and they would need to be on it. Ashton took a deep breath in, her heart beating erratically. The workers around her shuffled but remained still, quiet. No one spoke; it was eerily quiet in the open space.

Ashton dug her hand into her pocket and grabbed the scissors she had wrapped with a folded metal clothes hanger, the edges sharp enough. The wig was hidden under a pile of clothes she had been folding for the last two hours. She tore a thin, black strip of cloth from a shirt and wrapped it around her waist, cinching the white Apparel dress. She tucked the scissors into her new belt.

Breathe, Ashton, just breathe, she told herself. Remember what Wolfe taught you. You can catch the security off guard. *Read their body language to know when one of them is going to attack and move with your reaction.*

213

Ashton wiped her hands on her white dress, but she couldn't do anything about the cold sweat on her brow and under her arms. The security guards would have weapons too, photon guns, and they would shoot.

Ashton's breath quickened, and she could feel the blood rush from her face. She unwrapped her wig, the vibrant red of Freya shining back at her. She ran her fingers through its thick, long strands. She wished she could say she'd missed it, but she hadn't. It was a painful reminder of what happened in Land of Legends. The people who died. Sheva. Ashton closed her eyes and took in a deep breath.

She ducked her head down, ran the outer rim of the wig across her head, and stuffed her brown locks inside before pulling her head upright. The long red hair fell down her back. It was now or never.

Seven o'clock.

The world around her slowed and silence wrapped around the room. Apparel workers stopped what they were doing and followed her with their eyes. She could feel the beating of her heart through her chest.

Then, Ashton stood, and the workers around her stood, too. As if on instinct, the workers formed a shield around Ashton as she began to head straight for the security guards. All around the room, others stood up and rallied behind or in front of her.

Ashton took her time so she wouldn't draw attention to herself, but she was quick, too. Her long strides gave force to her mission. The moment had come. The cement walls echoed with the rallying whispers of encouragement.

Finally, the two security men by the elevators stopped their conversation and looked up, boredom and exhaustion on their faces.

"Sit down! Back to your station," one of them said casually. Ashton, her red wig still hidden by the workers encircling her, froze. How would she begin this? How would she strike?

Ashton could feel the stares behind her, the workers wondering why she didn't move. They had garnered the attention of the managers as well. It would be only moments before Pat and the others figured out what was going to happen.

"You deaf? Go back to your station now!" The other guard chuckled, and Ashton turned her attention to him, stepping out from the circle.

"Gi—give me your key card," she demanded, her voice shaking. The two were Suit-less, but still, they doubled her in size.

"Excuse me? Are we going to have a problem?"

The security guard on Ashton's left raised his weapon, but as he did so, Ashton reacted. Grabbing the gun, she pulled herself toward him and propelled her knee up, hitting him between the upper thigh and groin. Ashton breathed sharply as she struck hard and fast. It was a beautiful moment, to see the looks of astonishment and despair—the first stone thrown at the fragile system.

The security guard pushed back, but Ashton held onto the gun. The workers looked on as if they too were astonished that the fight had finally begun.

Ashton pulled back, her energy depleting quickly. The security guard was swift and strong. He shoved her off again like a rag doll. Ashton was out of time. The second security guard threatened her by pulling out his weapon, coming alongside his comrade. Ashton wasn't even able to take on one of them, let alone two. She retreated into a low crouch, ready to strike up; this wasn't going to end well.

Suddenly, out of the corner of her eye, Ashton saw a man barreling toward her. He held a steel pipe in his hands and swung hard at the security guard who was pointing his gun at Ashton. The guard went limp, slouching back onto the wall and sliding down. The left guard, who had only just reached for his gun, glanced at his comrade and then back at Ashton, fear in his eyes as he realized it wasn't just her.

The security guard lunged at Ashton, and she recoiled, grabbing air and stumbling backward. She was a foot away now and his gun was raised. She stared at the man; his eyes were wide with fear and his shaking hands were causing the barrel of the photon gun to vibrate. The moment should have made her back up, should have caused her to surrender. Instead, as she faced her fear, she felt a calmness wash over her. She didn't fear death anymore; didn't feel the need to tighten her grip on life. Augland, and the people caught up in its machine, had taken everything from her. She had nothing more to lose.

Ashton lunged at the guard, a battle cry screaming from her throat. It gave her strength, a release. The pain and suffering needed to end, and it would end now. The man's gun fired.

But a thrust from Ashton's grip had tilted the weapon toward the ceiling. Startled, the guard fumbled backward, and she pushed him hard against the concrete doorway. His head struck the door jamb with a thud.

Ashton pressed down on his chest with her knee, her scissors held tightly against his neck. They locked eyes. She didn't want to hurt him, but she would, if necessary. The guard's shoulders slumped and he dropped the gun. Apparently, he was not will-

215

ing to give his life for Augland, Ashton noted. But then, they had never given him a Suit; why would he give them his life?

The Apparel worker who had knocked out the other guard grabbed both photon guns, pointing them at the guards. They weren't going to take any chances.

Ashton grabbed the key card, jumped up, and swiped it across the access box. The adrenaline in her surged as she maneuvered around the guards slouched in their surrendered position. The elevator doors opened.

A cheer sounded around the room. The stunned management team stayed silent as they looked wide-eyed at the empowered workers. Ashton slowly turned toward the hundreds of faces that now gazed expectantly at her, smiling and hugging one another. It was pure excitement.

Bez screamed and wrapped Ashton in a hug. The man beside them, who Ashton now realized was Forest, handed them the photon guns and picked up his metal rod. Ashton stood still, unsure of what to do next.

"Just . . . say something to them." Bez nudged her. Ashton swallowed; she hadn't realized she'd have to say anything, then again, she hadn't been sure this would work. She cleared her throat.

"We can do this! All of us. There is a world out there that will embrace you, love you, care for you. It's outside these walls, away from the tyrants who have scripted our lives for too long!" Ashton was screaming now, her energy building. "Let's go; be brave and fearless. Show Augland we won't conform any longer! We won't sit back and let them beat us, command us. Degrade us!" Ashton proudly shouted out the words as they came to her. The room erupted in shouts and cheers.

Bez turned toward the workers. "You heard her! This is our day, our time, our lives! We don't know what to expect when we get to the parks. All we know is there is a way out! Get to that train station and to Maya Bay! Get on that supply boat and finally feel freedom. Augland is no longer our home, and we don't serve the Suits. We are the UnSuited!"

All the workers cheered, roaring and pounding on the tables. Bez inspired them. Her words also inspired Ashton; they pulled her in and gave her a sliver of hope that every one of the workers would make it to the boat.

CHAPTER 36

Wolfe

SUNDAY 1:13 p.m.

The objective now was to stay low, create a distraction, and help Hunter lead the caged workers to freedom. It sounded easy when Wolfe spelled it out like that, but he knew it would be much harder.

He had thought of every angle as he spent the day allowing the Augland cameras to follow him to his new home, diverting Warren's suspicions of him. Then, Joao gave him the signal of the camera's continuous footage loop, and he was freed. He had an entire day and night's worth of camera footage that would play repeatedly, allowing him to roam Augland.

Wolfe opened the steel door to the first floor of the cages. Joao stood waiting for him, holding a backpack.

"Did you get what I asked for?" Wolfe walked past Joao and down the long hallway lined with cages. They had less than a day to get everything to work.

"Yes, all set and ready to go." Joao followed Wolfe. "Are you going to fill me in on what we are doing?" Wolfe was sure Joao had pieced together Wolfe's plan from the supplies. It didn't take a rocket scientist. A fusion box. Magnetic strips times five. Spark plugs times three. Photon source batteries times two. If Joao read between the lines, he would know.

Wolfe and Joao walked quickly along the dimly lit hallways. Groans from caged workers echoed in the air but Wolfe tried to ignore them. Other workers stared with blank eyes as they pressed their faces against the cold steel. Wolfe desperately wanted them to know he was doing all he could but giving them hope now might give away the plan. This had to go perfectly.

"Did you get the items from different sources? Have different members check them out of the vault?"

"I'm not an idiot." Joao would have been flagged at once if he had checked out all the items from the security vault, no matter his status. Wolfe gave a half smile at Joao's choice of words. He had taught Joao well; his friend knew how to fly under the Augland radar.

"The intermap—we will need to give it to Hunter. Give him some good faith that we are on his side."

The intermap was a live feed map of Augland 54 that would help Hunter lead the caged workers out of Victorian and into the Maya Bay park. It also registered the whereabouts of all security. Joao and Wolfe would be too busy creating the diversion to help keep Hunter safe; he and the workers would need to make their way through the parks undetected.

"Who have we lined up as his backup?" asked Joao.

"Sirus will—"

"You've briefed him, right?" Wolfe didn't wait for Joao to complete his sentence. He knew Sirus and trusted him. He had been on Wolfe's detail when he led security. "He knows to wait in the supply cargo until the ship's arrival?"

"Yes, sir." Joao was too good to be a right-hand man; he had the instincts of a leader. He knew when to speak up and when to listen to directions. Wolfe knew Joao had handled everything on his list, but he needed a mental check. It was also his way of coping, not just from his month away from his reality, but at the crumbling of his life before his eyes.

When they were three-quarters down the hall, they stopped in front of Hunter's cell. Hunter paced back and forth. The cell wasn't long enough to make two full strides before he had to turn around and walk its length.

"Finally! It took you guys long enough." Hunter came to the bars of his cage, waiting for Wolfe and Joao to set him free. Joao's pocket jingled as he brought up a ring full of hard keys. Each of the cages had an electronic thumbprint pad, but using those would alert security that the cages were being opened and by whom. Right now, they needed secrecy.

Hunter stepped out of his cell, a visible weight off his shoulders.

"Here." Joao handed him the ring full of hundreds of steel keys. "In exactly four hours, you stop, you get out, and you head down the pathway."

"That—that's not enough time." Hunter looked down at the seemingly endless corridor looming in front of them. "Can't we unlock the doors electronically, all at once?"

Hunter was right, but the problem with technology was that it tracked everything. The moment they unlocked the doors it would trigger an alert—and the cameras, which were currently on a loop. Wolfe didn't have time to explain any of this to Hunter.

"That's all the time we have. You want to make it to the boat by seven tomorrow?" Wolfe was direct. It didn't feel good to say they couldn't save everyone, but they could try to take as many people as possible. "We have a few select men to help; they are discreet, and I trust them with my life." Hunter's mouth gaped and he shook his head in sarcastic disapproval.

"Just open all the cages! We have to get everyone out." Hunter disregarded Wolfe's attempt to negotiate.

Now, Wolfe was getting frustrated. Hunter was talking loudly and the workers around them were starting to get rowdy. "If we opened all the doors, hordes of security will be down in the cages within minutes. The chaos will worsen if anyone tries to leave their cage. It will be better to go around the technology, use the physical keys, and keep this escape secret for as long as possible." Wolfe needed time to allow his diversion to work. "Every second you waste here is one less person free."

Hunter closed his mouth and nodded quickly, getting back on board.

Joao became busy in his interconnect, which Wolfe assumed meant that the security men he had rallied during his time with Anastasia had come.

"They're here."

Sirus, Jaq, and Ragen rounded a corner and spotted them in the hallway. Wolfe felt a sudden rush of emotions for the friends he hadn't seen in months. It was yet another goodbye that he didn't want to think about. A trust he was sure was not going to be redeemed. A loss he would need to deal with eventually . . . but today wasn't that day. Maybe he would see them in the world outside Augland if all went to plan. But for now, if they had any animosity toward Wolfe, they didn't show it. They trusted Joao enough to obey orders.

"All right, we move quickly. Hunter, you'll be accompanied by Sirus. He will help you make the way to the supply boats."

"Sirus? I thought I'd be with you." A note of fear pitched in Hunter's voice.

"He can be trusted, don't worry. Again, wasting time as we sit here." Wolfe was growing impatient. "Si will meet you at the end of the hallway and he will begin on the floor above, then you go to the other two. Once you meet back down here, you'll go out the security door into Victorian, follow the wall, then you'll make it to Maya Bay's door. Ragen and Jaq will help delay the security rotation.

"The supply boat is the farthest southwest boat off the long curve that creates the cove of Maya Bay. It's the industrial district, away from Suits, and it houses all the cargo meant for other Auglands. You hide there. Here," Wolfe handed Hunter the intermap which he could use to see all security guards and their locations. "This will show any security personnel. If they come close, you get Sirus."

Hunter nodded and took the intermap from Wolfe's hand. He looked at it, and Wolfe could see that it did exactly what they had hoped. It gave Hunter a sense of security.

"See you on the other side then . . . oh, that is if you're not double-crossing me." Wolfe chuckled as Hunter gave him one last look over. He then turned away, searching for the key to unlock the first cage. He bent down and pulled the old man up to the bars, speaking to him as he unlocked the door.

Wolfe watched for a moment before turning to Joao, taking a deep breath. "You ready?"

Joao nodded. Wolfe wasn't sure if Joao and the other security guards knew what they were ready for, but he appreciated their loyalty to him. Joao was prepared to give up his life and Wolfe understood what he asked of him.

Wolfe wondered what he had done to deserve this power. He wouldn't ask his friend, not yet, but eventually, he wanted to know how Joao really felt about all this. How had he determined Wolfe's innocence with so little information?

Joao and Wolfe were shoulder to shoulder as they ran in the opposite direction of Hunter and Sirus. Wolfe knew the underground world of Augland like the back of his hand. There wasn't much time before someone caught wind that something fishy was going on. Wolfe wanted to make sure the thing that caught his father's eye was far away from the fleeing workers.

"Where to?" Joao said under his breath. They had reached the security vault that housed the photon guns, extra interconnects, and hoverbikes. The irony was not lost on Wolfe that these were the very weapons he had once used to maintain worker control. Now they would be used to free them.

The security vault was a fully enclosed steel room that required identification to check in and out of. Jaq had dismissed the guard on duty, and Wolfe and Joao entered without the typical protocol.

Wolfe threw Joao a bag and instructed him to fill it. Wolfe grabbed everything he needed and even some things that might come in handy in case things didn't go according to plan, which was likely.

Pair of cuffs in case someone needs to be apprehended.
Small baton that spikes out to a disarming weapon.
A first aid kit in case things get out of hand.
Extra electrical batteries and chargers for the hoverbike.
Photon gun and charger.

As they worked, he could tell Joao needed more information to prepare himself for what was to come. It was late enough in Wolfe's diversion scheme that he could give Joao another piece of their plan.

"We need to create a distraction big enough to call for an all-consuming security breach that Warren can't ignore. It needs to be something that will draw attention away from the caged workers and Hunter. We are going to Venus, to the Centauri Club."

Wolfe turned to look at a cautious Joao as he stuffed his bag with another electrical charger for his gun. Joao's brow furrowed before turning back to the photon guns mounted on the wall.

"The floating star on Venus?" Joao chuckled, pulling his gun up and checking the electrical charge. "You're going to blow it up . . ."

Venus was the park farthest away from Maya Bay. It also housed some of the most expensive and well-developed, gravity-defying elements, most notably the giant floating planet that rose above the buildings and hung like a white moon in the sky. The park catered to only the most elite of parties. Blowing it up would leave debris hovering all over the park and cause a big enough scandal that Warren would have to address it.

"Your father is going to kill you . . ." Joao said shaking his head. Wolfe smiled. If Warren found out what he was doing, blowing up a club in Venus would be the least of Wolfe's worries.

It was time. They both had what they needed. The journey to Venus would take some time, much longer on the hoverbikes than by train or gondola, but it was the best way to stay under the radar. Jaq had made sure the tracking was turned off, so neither Joao nor Wolfe would show up on an intermap.

The single-rider bike turned on and hovered just above the ground. Wolfe mounted it and bounced slightly as it calibrated to his weight. Joao did the same before situating his helmet on his head. Wolfe followed. The slight hum of the electric motors meant that they were ready. Wolfe turned on the accelerator and drove out of the vault, Joao a few feet behind him.

CHAPTER 37

Wolfe

SUNDAY 4:51 p.m.

The sun hovered in the sky above the grassy fields of Victorian. Porch-lined mansions with elaborate turrets dotted the landscape, interwoven with grassy knolls topped by gondolas and greenhouses. Wolfe's hoverbike glided a foot above the ground as he sped through the park. He usually loved any opportunity to bike through the parks and he had missed the slight rush of adrenaline. But tonight, the adrenaline was caused not by the bike's speed, but by the ticking clock and uncertainty as he rode toward what could be a nail in his coffin. He was on his way to create a distraction that would free him of this world, only to be cast out into a world that would never trust him again.

After driving through Victorian for a few hours, Wolfe and Joao finally came to the edge of the park. The fastest way to get to Venus would be to pass through the Augland Center, which would also allow Joao to check in with security and continue to play the double agent. Wolfe was reticent to leave the serenity of Victorian to pass through the Center. Not only would there be more security, but the Center always brought back mixed feelings of nostalgia and guilt for him.

While Joao checked in on some security matters, Wolfe parked his bike and waited in a small alley in which he had often hid as a boy.

The Augland Center housed all the young children of Augland. Or at least it used to. These days, the rooms were mostly bare. Due to the infertility caused by radiation from the Suits, and Augland using younger and younger workers, there was less need to house and educate all the children. Wolfe also presumed the successful integration of the "customer service initiative" had contributed to the vacancy. Using chips to control the minds and movement of workers would require less propaganda and education. Still, it was strange how empty the Center was now.

Wolfe had gone to the Augland Center as a child. Anastasia wanted him to learn from the Center and be with the other human kids while they developed skills that would help them in Augland parks. He had learned and played with the other children, but at the end of the day, he went back to Hollywood Boulevard and the Executives' suites while the others stayed in the Center. All of them were now workers dispersed throughout Augland 54. Wolfe saw one of them once in Hollywood Boulevard, working as a janitor. The man didn't remember him, but Wolfe never forgot his face.

Warren pulled Wolfe out of the Augland Center when he turned ten. That was the day he realized how alone in the world he really was. He wasn't a Suit, and he wasn't a worker. At the Center, he was just a kid—that is, before the burden of being the CEO's son became a title that called for division and solitude.

Warren had provided a tutor for Wolfe, a young Suit from another Augland hoping to make his way into an executive position. He had taught Wolfe to fight, to understand technology, and to utilize business fundamentals. At that time, Wolfe wanted to be with the other children, but at twelve years old, he hadn't realized the difference between them. All he knew was that he was different—alone. While he slept in privilege and enjoyed luxuries, the other kids were destined to live a life of servitude.

Joao returned and stopped his hoverbike next to Wolfe. Grateful to keep moving, Wolfe hopped back onto his bike and it rose a foot into the air.

"Go ahead," Joao commanded into the interconnect.

For a moment, Wolfe was jealous that Joao had the communication channel. Wolfe liked to be in control, but he knew Joao had become the Head of Security during his absence and he needed to respect that.

"I've finished my rotation in the cages. Should I head out on patrol?" Sirus asked calmly through a coded message. That meant he had let out all the caged workers he could in the allotted time. Four hours. No more, no less. It would take all night to get everyone out of those cages, and the deal was they would take whomever they could.

"Yes." Joao kept it simple.

"Roger that. I'll check in later with a status update."

Joao nodded toward Wolfe. So far, so good. The repetitive loop of the cameras in the cages hadn't been recognized. Now for the tricky part: to get through Augland with a massive group of caged workers who would stick out like sore thumbs. At least it was a straight shot from the edges of Victorian to Maya Bay's southwest entrance.

"You ready to go?" Joao looked at Wolfe.

"Yeah, ready." It wasn't hard for Wolfe to leave the Augland Center. It was only an unwanted memory and an even more unwanted realization of what had become of Augland.

"Head northeast, toward the door to Venus. Ride slow; we don't want any attention."

It would take an hour, maybe a little more at a safe, slow speed, to reach the security door in the wall between the Center and Venus park. They needed to stay under the radar until the precise time.

CHAPTER 38

Ashton
SUNDAY 7:27 p.m.

Two workers carried a large sewing machine into the elevator behind Ashton. Bez was just finishing tying a long rope of bed sheets together and she threw them in the elevator with the first load of workers.

Ashton looked around the room as she shoved the photon gun into her makeshift belt. She would not stoop to the low of Augland and take lives just because she could. But to her surprise, management had hardly fought back. The androids still worked on garments as if the commotion around them didn't exist. Their programming ensured they focused solely on work. The handful of managers was no match for a few hundred workers fueled by anger, exhaustion, and hope. Pat had fought back, but he was now tied up to one of the large sewing machines. Ashton saw his mouth was gagged and she smiled. She had heard enough from him. Augland had done well, pitting workers against each other by rewarding those who pushed others under the bus for their own advancement. They may have acted selfishly, but even they were not about to risk their own lives for the Suits who lived indestructibly in their little pods.

"See you up there." Ashton grinned and handed Bez the key card. The elevator doors closed on what Ashton hoped was the last view she would ever have of the underground world of Augland. There was a sudden silence as they rose to ground level.

The doors opened onto the white hallway, with one wall made completely of glass overlooking the jungle of Predator's Biome. Ashton pulled out her gun and the workers around her followed her lead, pulling out whatever makeshift weapons they had managed to grab. Ashton glanced out the doors and down the long hallway before stepping out. No one was coming. They hurried out of the elevator and sent it down to pick up the next load of anxiously waiting workers.

Ashton turned toward the glass. *Here we go . . .* She nodded to Forest and the other worker holding the large sewing machine, and they threw it hard against the glass window. The glass shattered, opening a hole between them and the Augland park. Instantly, a siren went off, piercing the air around them.

"Throw another one!" Ashton commanded over the noise. A worker did as he was told and threw another sewing machine, creating another hole. Another worker threw down the improvised rope made of tethered sheets till it spiraled to the bottom of the wall.

"Again!" They smashed the glass until there was enough space for people to start climbing down. The drop down to Predator's Biome was only ten feet, but it was still too far for most of the workers to jump. Forest went down the rope ladder first, still holding the photon gun that Ashton relinquished.

Workers were now pouring through the elevator doors from the depths of Augland's belly faster than they could tear through the glass windows and climb down to the floor of Predator's Biome. The walkway between the wall and the park was only five feet wide. The compact hallway was crowded with workers pushing and pulling to get their way to the small, sharp exits. Bez was likely still down in Apparel, helping usher the remaining workers up the elevator to where Ashton was supposed to be helping them descend into the Biome.

The high-pitched alarm blared loudly, pounding in Ashton's exhausted mind. She knew Augland security would be heading toward them, ready to subdue the rebellion's first, and likely only, attempt at escape. Loud shouting reverberated through the long hallway and the wind from Predator's Biome rushed through the opening. The extra noise only heightened the sound of the alarm and flashing red lights that gave away their position.

Ashton was pushed from side to side as the workers around her panicked. They needed to find order and work together. The fear driving the workers' instincts would only hinder their success. Ashton choked on her helplessness. Every ounce of her wanted to huddle down in the fetal position and scream. It was too much chaos. Too much fear. It engulfed her like she was drowning in it. She shrank beneath it.

Breathe—you can do this. Just breathe. Be confident.

ERIN CARROUGHER

Another sewing machine came crashing into the glass to Ashton's left. Workers barreled through the hole in the glass, jumping toward the ground below.

Bez appeared at Ashton's side, which meant all the workers had come up the ladder. Ashton didn't know how Bez had shoved her way to her, but she felt her courage flood back into her body.

"Stop!" Bez screamed. "We need to create some order!"

Ashton joined in, using her red hair as a symbol in the crowd. "Don't panic! Line up, don't push . . . just line up!" She began shouting orders over the sound of the alarm. She pulled at the thin fabric of one worker's shirt, yanking her to one side before pulling another. She repeated herself until finally, the workers listened and the disorganization slowly subsided.

As order began to form, Ashton felt a sense of calm determination as her words gained momentum and the people around her listened. It was the first time in her life that she'd felt in control, and it was an unfamiliar feeling of power. These people listened to her.

"One at a time or people will get hurt," Ashton yelled.

She spoke and they responded. The lines were becoming more defined as people stood in single file to exit the three holes available to them. Still, some jumped, taking the risk of injury to get a head start to the boat. But even more helped each other climb down the ropes of knotted sheets.

"Get to the train station! Go to Maya Bay! Get to the ship! Hurry!" Bez screamed and the workers followed her directions, scrambling and yelling in fear and excitement as they raced out, scattering into the tall trees.

Soon, it was only Ashton and Bez who remained in the hallway that teetered between the Augland parks and the towering walls. Luck had been on their side up to this point. Now came the unplanned, unimaginable task for the workers to get from Predator's Biome to Maya Bay in the next twelve hours.

Ashton looked out the shattered glass. The sun was going down and the night sky threatened to lower its cloak of darkness and limit their visibility. In another circumstance, Ashton would want to stay and enjoy the scenery. Tall mountains dotted with assorted colors and waterfalls. It was majestic. The wind blew and her red wig whipped around her face. She hoped more than anything that at least some of the workers would make it. She hardly dared hope that all of them would. This wouldn't be easy, nor would it be likely, and that scared Ashton. How many more people would get hurt, or worse, die? Ashton felt burdened by the responsibility for others.

227

"Ash." Bez came to her side. "We should go. I think we should try and catch up with them in case anyone needs help." Ashton nodded and took a deep breath. She pulled herself over the side of the wall, carefully avoiding the sharp glass. The wind blew across her, sending shivers down her spine as she slowly glided down the ropes to the dark, dirty ground below. Ashton could feel her muscles shake as she dangled briefly, then dropped to her feet.

The concentrated jungle made it difficult to see where they were going. Predator's Biome was also the largest park in Augland 54, and the walk to the first train station would take hours. The true trick would be to get on it in time and make it, without interference, to Maya Bay. It was next to impossible.

The alarm faded into the distance as they ran farther away from the wall. All Ashton could hear was Bez's strained breathing next to her. The others were tired too. She could tell as some went from a full sprint to a slight jog, taking in enormous amounts of oxygen. The darkness had fully engulfed them now, but Ashton could see the white of Apparel uniforms spread out around her.

Then, they finally heard it. The sound of engines filled the air. Ashton couldn't tell where they were coming from, only that they were getting closer. Both Bez and Ashton stopped, ducking down under a bush, and waving for the others around them to do the same.

Ashton scanned the area. The tall forest around them and the thick underbrush provided no clear indication of where they were or where the threat was coming from.

Ashton could see the frightened eyes of workers around her as they looked at her for guidance. Some panicked workers continued to run away, scared by the sounds. They had the right idea: Ashton couldn't just sit here, not when whatever was coming their way was gaining on them.

Ashton peered above the bush in which she and Bez had found refuge. Her breath quickened as she risked exposure. She needed to plan the next move. Waiting for the security guards to find them was not an option. Her eyes focused on a small, flashing light between the trees. It was faint, like a firefly, but it didn't move. There was something there, a home, a town, something that shed visibility in the wilderness. Ashton didn't need to think twice. They were sitting ducks waiting around in the darkness.

"Come on." She pulled Bez with her toward the lights. Bez held her photon gun tightly, spinning as she ran to make sure their group of workers was protected. The light twinkled brighter as they drew closer. It was exactly what Ashton had expected, it was some sort of structure—but what she hadn't expected was the faint sound of screams.

Large, luxury bungalows scattered the clearing, both on the ground and high up in the trees. Dirt pathways that swerved through the village were lined with fire torches. Spiral staircases ran down the trees and Ashton saw several rope bridges swinging high above their heads. It was another fake world for the Suits, but it was far from idyllic.

Screams filled the air. Workers ran lawlessly. Ashton saw an Augland worker, dressed in all black, grab a fire torch and light a bungalow on fire. Suits cowered beside their bungalows and others lay sprawled on the ground, motionless.

She suddenly realized these were Predator Biome workers, not Apparel, who were attacking the small village. They had seized the momentum of the Apparel workers' rebellion and turned against the Suits. The Suits didn't fight; they didn't use their own size and indestructible nature to defend themselves. They were afraid of the workers. Before Ashton knew it, she was drawn into the light and down the winding pathway through fires and bungalows.

A few workers in black were tying a Suit to a tree. The Suit, a large man with immaculate long dreads, screamed obscenities. Two other workers moved another Suit into a fire pit; Ashton saw the skin of the Suit melt off, leaving just the robotic remains behind. She could care less about the Suits. Their inhabitants would be fine, simply waking up in their pods whenever they'd had enough.

"Look! It's the woman in red!"

A worker from Predator's Biome spotted Ashton, and she realized why Bez had insisted on the red wig. She turned. Workers all around her began cheering. Cries of "The UnSuited!" and "The Woman in Red!" filled the air.

Ashton stood awkwardly, mesmerized by the disorder. The workers were finally getting the revenge they had waited for all their lives. The looks on their faces were not of pleasure or hatred; it was the fractional feeling of freedom. They felt it and were . . . happy.

"The message. It worked. The rebellion has started!" Bez exclaimed over Ashton's shoulder. They watched as the once-luxurious and pristine wonderland of vegetation was scorched with the fire of passion.

The moment was interrupted by the revving of security engines and the BANG, BANG, BANG of shots being fired. Ashton ducked down, dropping to the dirt and shielding her head. The shift among the workers was instant. Screaming vibrated between Biome's mountains, replacing the laughter and chanting with confusion.

Ashton and Bez moved quickly, staying low to avoid being spotted by security. They darted from bungalow to bungalow, gathering workers as they went.

BANG! BANG! BANG! Birds deserted the trees in chaos. Augland security had arrived and was shooting workers down like decommissioned cattle. Ashton's eyes widened and her breath caught. Three guards to her right dismounted their hover-bikes and began spidering out between the bungalows, firing at will. They shot anyone in their way. The shots weren't a warning; Augland security was shooting to kill.

"UnSuited!" Bez screamed at those who had frozen in fear and the others who were scattered across the bungalow village, running into the dense forest. She shot her photon gun into the air.

"Keep going west! Take the train to Maya Bay! Save yourselves!" Bez screamed, knowing this was the last time she would give any command to them—because now, it wasn't *how* they escaped; it was *if* any of them could.

"Come on, Ash!" Bez pulled Ashton's arm and ran.

CHAPTER 39

Ashton

SUNDAY 9:01 p.m.

B ranches whipped and stung Ashton's skin as she slithered through the narrow gaps between the trees. She gripped Bez's hand, dragging her through the forest and away from the screams still ringing from the bungalow village.

"We should circle back and make sure no one was left behind!" Bez wanted to go back and make sure all the workers had escaped safely. Bez felt bold with the photon gun, but Ashton wasn't sure she'd have the courage to use it. At least, she hadn't yet.

Ashton pulled Bez along, not allowing her to go back. They ran past a bush and saw two Apparel men and one woman huddled together. Ashton and Bez nearly missed them.

"What are you doing? Run!" Ashton stopped in her tracks, but the workers did nothing. The woman sobbed and cowered under their protective greenery. Another round of gunshots fired in the distance.

Ashton let go of Bez to drag the workers from their hiding place. The three individuals in white reluctantly stood up and followed.

BANG! Another shot whistled through the forest. It was close, hitting a nearby tree and creating a spark of blue light. Ashton turned in the other direction, but another shot rang out to her left. Two security guards were gaining on them and targeting her small group. Bez and the woman were gaining ground ahead of Ashton, but she was slowed down by the two men she was pulling with her.

"Bez!" Ashton screamed. "Give me the gun!" Bez slowed her momentum enough to throw Ashton the gun. Ashton shoved the two men left toward Bez and veered right, hopefully drawing the security guards away. They were all in white, easy targets among the dark trees, but Ashton hoped her red hair would make her the target.

She shifted, keeping her feet light and bouncing as the terrain became uneven. The photon gun dragged heavily on her wrist.

"Hey!" Ashton shrilled, even though her mind screamed at her to stay hidden. "Hey!" she screamed again, this time waving her free hand above her. Ashton stopped, trying to hear the security guards over the beating of her chest. She waited, breathing heavily, and looking around in the darkness.

BANG! A single shot landed a few feet from her head. The embers around the hole in the tree glowed blue. Ashton ducked. The plan had worked. Now all she needed to do was keep the attention on her so Bez could get as far away as possible. She pulled out the gun and aimed it high above her. She breathed hard as she placed her finger on the trigger. She felt powerful and terrified. She pulled again. And again. The gun vibrated as shot after shot was forced into the tree line. She pulled her hand away and sucked in air but as she listened, she could hear the faint commands of security coming ever closer.

Ashton was small and stealthy, able to weave quickly between the trees. She had her many years of weaving between people at the train station, back when she was a worker commuting to Maya Bay, to thank. She ducked low between a bush and turned to yell.

"Hey! Hey! Over here!" She shot the photon gun into the night sky. She didn't know how much charge it had, but she would use it until she found out.

Ashton didn't know how much time had passed; time swallowed itself in the darkness. She needed to stop before her lungs gave out, and besides, she hadn't heard any engines or gunshots in a while.

She sunk down below a bush and listened. Nothing, just the beating of her impatient heart. The darkness made it impossible to see anything, but there were no sounds of shuffling feet or tree branches breaking. When she felt it was safe enough, she stood up and again waited for some action. Nothing.

Ashton decided it was time to circle back around and see if she could catch up to Bez and the others. She began running in the direction she knew they were headed. This time, she stayed low and quiet to not gain any unwanted attention. She could run faster than the security could figure out where she was.

Finally, Ashton saw four white specks in the distance. She thanked her good sense of direction under her breath and sped up. She saw Bez look behind her and their eyes locked; a look of relief flooded Bez's face. Ashton smiled, sprinting to them. The bushes were still dense, and she had to rise above them to quicken her pace toward her friends. She weaved left, then right. Close now, only a few feet away.

BANG! A photon gunshot rang blue through the air. She didn't have time to look around to see who had fired before a sharp pain radiated through her leg. Ashton's momentum continued but she fell hard against the ground and began to roll, losing grip on her gun. She could feel the cold dirt smear across her face and arms as she tumbled. Bez screamed in the background, but it fogged as the ringing of pain became all-consuming.

Ashton held her breath until she was forced to exhale. She looked down at her leg. A large black circle was seeping through the white Apparel dress that now clung to her thigh. She could feel the warm blood oozing down across her knee. She wanted to touch it, really look at the damage, but Bez pulled Ashton's body, ripping her back up to her feet as the lights of photon shots zipped through the air.

Ashton rose to her feet and immediately stumbled. Bez was pulling Ashton down a hill and she could feel her leg tumbling beneath her. Searing pain blinded her, and white spots began to blur her vision. They were running down a hill that descended into a valley. With each passing moment, Ashton struggled to deal with the pain. She couldn't move her leg and found herself leaning hard against Bez to take the place of that movement. Moments of complete clarity were followed by blurs of black and white spots.

Bez continued pulling Ashton along, which only made the pain worse. They were barely keeping a steady pace. She felt the continued tear of her muscles as she over-extended herself. She bit down hard in agony, but it was drowned out by the screams and photon gunfire behind them. Her leg oozed and Ashton could feel wet blood gushing down her leg again. Smoke began to rise around them as the photon guns trashed the beautiful greenery.

Ashton knew the predicament Bez faced. Her need to save the one falling behind collided with her mission to support the UnSuited in their escape. One thing was certain: the workers wouldn't be able to do it without Bez. The Augland brochure helped them navigate their way. She was their leader, the face, and the heart of it. Ashton was simply a spark that helped light the flame.

"We need to separate." Ashton breathed hard. "We're falling behind." The three other workers who had sought salvation with the two fearless leaders now had fled, saving themselves. Ashton saw movements of white, black, hoverbikes, and photon gunfire volleying through the trees.

Bez finally stopped and cowered behind a nearby tree for cover. Shots vibrated in the wind around them. Ashton sunk to the ground. It was now a full-on war in Predator's Biome with only one side attacking. The workers had their makeshift weapons, but they would do no good against the Augland guns. The security guards weren't trying to capture the workers to bring them back; this was bloodshed.

"You've got to get up," Bez whispered so as not to draw any attention to them. Her face belied her complete exhaustion and sadness. Tears rolled down her cheeks, painting streaks down her muddied face.

Ashton thought about standing back up, but her body told her no. It was done, finished. She had lost blood and would lose more. The sharp pain began to pulse as adrenaline faded from her veins. Bez wouldn't survive if she had to carry Ashton.

Tears welled in Ashton's eyes as the realization set in. She wouldn't make it. Her body had given up and her mind was close to following. It felt bittersweet. She was sad to not make it out of Augland, not to see what would happen to the workers of Augland, but she hoped she had played her part well. She pulled the red wig from her head and set it on the ground beside her. The trees swayed with the gunfire that closed in on them.

"No, no, I can't keep up . . ." Ashton realized she was echoing the plea Sheva had made during her first escape. "You need to help them; they need you."

Another round of fire disrupted their tender moment and Bez buried her face in Ashton's shoulder, protecting Ashton's body from the onslaught.

There was a lull in the shooting and Bez lifted her head, just far enough to check their surroundings. Without saying a word, Bez gathered branches and began to pile them around her wounded friend. Ashton wasn't sure what the point was of hiding her, but nonetheless, she appreciated the effort to save her.

"I'll never forget what you did for us," Bez whispered through tears. She tightened her grip on Ashton's hand before slowly letting go. Ashton choked back the tears that hung deep in her throat.

"Tell Captain Gerhart that Charlotte sent you, that he has to take you all to NeuroEnergy. It's important you say that Charlotte sent you. And that Georgina knows."

Ashton was concerned that without seeing her, Charlotte, or Hunter, the captain was likely to turn them away. Bez nodded and touched her forehead to Ashton's. She took a deep breath before rising and slowly crouching through the leaves, away from Ashton.

Ashton closed her eyes and heard her friend's footsteps disappear in the chaos. The panic of her solitude finally set in, but her mind was having trouble focusing. The trees began to swim in the wind, and all she could think about was how tired she was. In a way, she was relieved she didn't have to run anymore, that she could rest. Or at least that's what she told herself.

Ashton looked down at her wound. Her hands shook as she pulled herself upright, placing her head against the tree. She knew what she had to do next. She untied her makeshift belt and spun the long cloth around her leg. Ashton pulled, hard. She needed to stop the blood loss.

She bit back a scream, grinding her teeth so hard her jaw throbbed. The pain in her leg didn't lessen; it cursed at her as each thud mimicked her racing heart. Ashton fell against the hard-barked tree. All she could do was wait until Augland found her. The world around her began to close in with a darkness she couldn't blink away. She was done fighting. She closed her eyes and slipped into unconsciousness.

CHAPTER 40

Wolfe
SUNDAY 8:43 p.m.

Centauri was not only the most prestigious club in Augland 54, but it was also one of the most famous clubs in all Auglands worldwide. AEC executives were known to visit for dinner in the floating orb, and it was listed as a must-see Augland attraction for any Suit with the money. Centauri was often rented out for large parties and exclusive Executive meetings. The large star was suspended from the Augland sky and hovered above the city. It could only be accessed by a small electrical bubble that acted as its elevator system.

Joao and Wolfe rode in the opaque elevator above the neon city lights of Venus. The glass doors opened into the main room, where a mirrored black glass covered every wall and glittering stars encased the entire interior of the restaurant, giving the illusion of space.

Workers walked along the empty restaurant floor, preparing for that evening's event. They placed crystal wine glasses on glass tables with glass chairs.

Wolfe checked his watch—8:47 p.m. He needed to set the bomb off soon, but first, they had to evacuate all the workers and make sure no one else was in the star.

"Mr. Wolfgang, may I help you, sir? I believe the Executive-sponsored dinner isn't for another 45 minutes." The front desk worker who approached them looked concerned. Wolfe hated the effect his power had on workers; so many approached him with fear. Joao had called ahead and said the entire club was to be reserved for a leadership meeting with no other customers allowed. Wolfe hadn't thought about how much work would be done for this fake dinner, but he had bigger plans on his mind.

"I understand. I realize we are early but I wanted to conduct a quick search of the building before the Executives arrive. I'll need all the workers to make their way down to Venus. There have been rumors of an uprising and Joao would like to make sure the club is secure."

Loud muffled voices erupted from Joao's interconnect, and he turned and walked away to listen, leaving Wolfe with the petrified worker.

"Oh, um. Well, sir, there is a lot we need to do before the event starts. I'm sure we will be fine. I—I'm afraid we may not be completely ready in time if we leave now." The poor boy shifted in his shoes, terrified of what might happen because he was speaking back to the CEO.

"That's fine. We will start a half hour later, but we need everyone to leave, quickly."

"Wolfe." Joao turned to his leader, interrupting his interaction with the young Centauri restaurant host.

Joao's face was white as he kept the interconnect at arm's length. Something was wrong.

"What?" Wolfe walked over to Joao. He could finally make out what the voice on the other end of the interconnect was saying.

"Joao, where have you been? There's been an escape! The Apparel department has left the basement and is fleeing through Predator's Biome!"

Wolfe understood at once. *Ashton.* He should have known she wouldn't sit idly by. But this was not part of the plan.

"I've been on another line; start from the beginning. What's happened?"

"You idiot!" Warren screamed, furry bellowing across the interconnect. "During your absence, the workers in Apparel made an escape and attacked a Biome village. Since you weren't around," Warren sneered sarcastically, "I ordered your security to shoot at will and disarm the trains. Fix this mess!" Warren's anger boiled over and his voice screeched through the interconnect.

"You—" Joao's voice cracked, and a look of shock painted across his face.

"I can't believe this is happening on *your* watch! And the fact that I had to step in here . . . not what I want from the man leading our security teams!"

Joao turned down the interconnect, not caring to hear the rest of Warren's tantrum. He whispered under his breath before turning his eyes to Wolfe.

"What do we do?" Joao searched for answers. Wolfe needed a moment to think. The Apparel department had never been a cause of concern for an uprising. That was, until Ashton arrived. He should have known she would cause some sort of disturbance. He sighed in frustration. Of course, Ashton would act on her own and thwart any well-thought-out plan. But shooting at will? His father had ordered murder, and that meant if Ashton was found, she would be one of the victims. His mind raced with the worst possibilities.

"We stick to the plan. We evacuate all the workers of Centauri, and once we know they're safe, we execute . . . you execute the plan," Wolfe corrected himself. "Then you make your way to the boat with the others. Make it to NeuroEnergy. Get them there safe."

"What about you?" Joao had noticed the shift from "we" to "you."

There were too many variables now; Hunter and Si leading the caged workers to Maya Bay, the bomb they were about to set off on Centauri, and now a full-on war in Predator's Biome. He had people he trusted in place, and it was time he let them do what they could. Joao was a smart man.

"I'm going to go find Ashton," Wolfe said without hesitation. He needed to make a choice and, unlike last time, he wouldn't wait. He needed to help her before his father reached her, or worse.

Joao was shocked at the change of plans but nodded in understanding.

"You'll need this." Joao picked up his interconnect and brought up the employee directory. "Snatched an extra one." He let a smirk escape his mouth before tossing it over to Wolfe.

Scrolling down the various Apparel department employee ID numbers, he pulled up Ashton's. "She was given a tracked barcode. You'll be able to see exactly where she is in the park." Joao brought up the location. "It looks like they're on foot, heading west toward the train station. And," here Joao paused, a hitch in his voice. "She's with Bez. If they're together, grab her too, would you?"

Wolfe nodded. This night had turned to chaos and now the only goal was to get as many workers as possible to the boat by seven a.m. He would do what he could, but he didn't have time to plan. If Warren had disarmed the trains, that meant Ashton was stuck in Predator's Biome until security found her and killed her. Wolfe couldn't let that happen.

"Everyone evacuates, now!" Wolfe turned to the boy who nodded in acknowledgment, panicked by the sudden shift in Wolfe's mood.

Wolfe turned to Joao, and added, "Make it big enough to draw their attention."

They needed a distraction now more than ever to get the attention of the escaping workers in Predator's Biome. From Ashton.

CHAPTER 41

Ashton
SUNDAY 9:50 p.m.

Ashton was alone.

The once-subtle sounds of the jungle were riddled with the noise of engines, gunfire and screams, and in the midst of it, she was on her own. Ashton could handle being alone, and at times even craved it desperately, but not like this, not this kind of vulnerability.

She wanted to believe she was strong, brave, and fearless. To be the woman in red she had been just hours earlier in Apparel. But that was a mask, just a character she played, and she knew that. Every time Ashton tried to be brave, people around her died. So many people would suffer tonight because she had told them there was a boat. She had decided to be a beacon of hope—yet she still didn't know if she had done the right thing.

This is it, isn't it? This is the memory of my life I will leave behind. Tortured thoughts ripped at her mind. Ashton would be remembered by some as the woman in red who had escaped Augland and came back to get more workers out. Augland would remember her as disobedient, stubborn, emotional, and even rogue. But she wasn't sure how she wanted to be remembered—maybe it would be as the person she was while sitting on her deck on the banks of the Hood Canal.

This is it, Ashton repeated to herself. The makeshift tourniquet on her leg was now soaked in blood. She pulled down the thin material to expose the deep wound on her thigh, just below her hip bone. Blood had clotted around the wound, but running had reopened it several times, leaving blood trailing down the left side of her body.

Ashton took a deep breath, holding it in as the intensifying pain radiated through her body. She held back a moan and placed a trembling hand over the wound, trying to stop the bleeding again.

There were still the sounds of shots in the distance, but she barely noticed them. Nausea threatened and vibrant white specks clouded her vision. She pulled at the cloth, twisting the fabric to tighten the knot. The pain caused her hands to tremble, but she was able to twist enough to lessen the bleeding. *This is it, the last thing you have to do*, Ashton whispered to herself as she fell back against the tree.

She looked up at the moonlight shining through the leaves. She thought of her friends at the Colony: Rico with his grumpy attitude, and Versal with her sweet presence. She thought about Jagatha and Sheva. Finally, she thought about Wolfe, but not the Wolfe she knew today. She thought of the man in her dreams, the one who helped her escape from Augland. She preferred remembering him that way. She put her hand up to her chest where the small, moonstone necklace used to rest. Now gone. She held its emptiness as the black clouded around her eyes.

This is it. Maybe, for once, it will be easier not to resist.

CHAPTER 42

Wolfe
SUNDAY 9:22 p.m.

Wolfe swerved the hoverbike through the Venus Park streets busy with nightlife. Venus was known for its eccentric clubs and the evening was just getting started. Lamps lit the doorways with black light, painted faces and hair glowed in neon yellows, pinks, and greens. The streets were filled with platform heels, neon signs, and pumping music.

Wolfe turned sharply onto a sidewalk to avoid a giant, hovering spaceship meandering down the main street, partiers spilling out the top. He could never understand how the Suits could be so carefree while the shadows were filled with the workers making it all possible. He swerved to avoid colliding with a group of Suits smoking outside a club. The Suit shouted at him, but Wolfe didn't even look back. He knew Ashton could be in trouble, and Predator's Biome was miles away.

Finally, Wolfe was out of Constellation City and into the suburbs where there was significantly less activity. He revved his engine, tightened his grip on the handlebars, and ducked low to increase his speed. It was darker in the suburbs, with the only lights illuminating the bubbled white houses of Venus. Beyond the houses, the paved road ended, leading into the sandy ash dust of the planet's surface. Outside the city, the rest of the park was cratered and bare, like an alien planet.

Dust kicked back behind the bike as Wolfe neared the wall that divided him from the neighboring park. He looked back once across the deserted space desert to the lights of the city and the giant floating moon in the sky—a moon that Joao was about to explode.

There. Right in front of him was the small, dark outline of a door in the wall. Wolfe gave a half smile. It had taken him less time to find the camouflaged door than he expected. He raced toward it.

Using Joao's security code, Wolfe unlocked the door, flung it open, and drove his bike through. The moon in the Biome had a different hue than the blueish tint of Venus.

He looked down at the interconnect that shone brightly in the darkness. He was still over thirty minutes away from the blinking red dot he knew was Ashton. He needed to ride quickly, at a dangerous and reckless speed. Each moment wasted was a second in time they didn't have.

C'mon, faster! Then, he saw it. The two dots he was following had grown increasingly farther apart. Bez and Ashton must have separated. Bez was headed toward the train, but Ashton? She hadn't moved.

Wolfe began to panic. She was either hiding or she had been injured, or worse. He wasn't sure what he would do if he found her dead. Visions of her pale skin and dull eyes, just like she was in his father's office, haunted him. He took a deep breath and pushed the uninvited images out of his mind. He needed to concentrate on driving through the trees.

BANG! BANG! BANG! Wolfe heard photon guns, followed by screams in the distance. He felt like he was driving into a war zone, but he knew it was more like a massacre. It couldn't be a true war if only one side had all the weapons and power.

Smoke blanketed the forest and impaired Wolfe's vision. Several trees were filled with smoking holes, blue embers still burning in the night. There was smoke everywhere, something he was sure his father hadn't thought about before ordering the aggressive pursuit. And now Ashton was somewhere in the middle of it.

Come on, come on! Wolfe screamed internally. He had to slow down to weave between the trees and tried desperately not to pay attention to the bright lights from the photon electricity that swarmed, in the distance and the few that seared in front of him.

Fifteen minutes until destination. Wolfe's hands were aching from twisting the throttle of his bike handle full force. He had seen a couple of security guards searching bushes and up the trees, in case any workers were still hiding. A few gave him quizzical looks, but no one would question the old Head of Security or CEO.

Wolfe was close. His breathing increased, and he kept his eyes peeled for anything in the distance that would give her away.

Three minutes until destination. He slowed the hoverbike. He wasn't sure how accurate the tracking device was on the interconnect. He didn't want to waste time retracing his steps.

"Ashton!" Wolfe yelled as loud as he dared. He didn't want to attract any security, but it seemed like they had already swept this area. He pulled his body up higher on his bike to get a better view.

"Ashton!" He paused, hoping to hear a response. Nothing.

One minute until destination. Ashton had to be somewhere nearby. Under a tree, bush, somewhere.

You've reached your destination. Wolfe was hovering exactly where the interconnect said she would be. He turned off the bike, which lowered itself to the ground, and stepped into the belly of the dark forest. He ripped off his helmet and listened intently for any stirring, but it was silent, other than his quickly beating heart and the distant shots of photon fire.

"Ash!" Wolfe began to panic. What if the interconnect was wrong? Could someone hack it? Or had Ashton figured out a way to get rid of it? The thought made him frantic. Where was she?

Wolfe began ripping through bushes, searching wildly for any evidence of life. This must have been an area of heavy photon fire because the smoke was an impenetrable fog around him. He looked down at his interconnect again. The blinking red dot said she was right here, right where he was standing.

Wolfe knew he couldn't lose control; he needed to go about this methodically. He would circle on the hoverbike, searching every inch of ground and every tree until he found her. He had to find her.

Then he saw it. A vibrant red among the dark green. It was hair, red hair, lying near a tall tree. He darted forward and dropped to his knees. But all he found were the strands of a dark red wig, laced with dirt and leaves. Wolfe yanked at the threads and wanted to scream. He knew he didn't have time to waste.

Out of his peripheral vision, he saw a white dress, its fabric rippling in the wind and partially concealed behind the green leaves and smoke. He then noticed an arching bush with branches piled around it, like a tent.

"Ashton?" Wolfe tore apart the shelter to see her body lying on the ground, her white dress soaked in dark blood. There was a wound on her upper thigh, and she had tried to wrap a cloth around her leg to stop the bleeding. Her eyes were shut and her face ashen.

"Ashton," Wolfe whispered. He pulled the curly brown hair from her face and put his arm around her, scooting her up onto his lap.

"Ashton, wake up," he said, tears swelling in his eyes. "Please, wake up."

He put his fingers next to her neck, applying pressure to find a heartbeat. He closed his eyes as he wished for a pulse. He patiently waited, pushing deeper down into her neck. He held his breath and wished his heart would stop beating so loudly. Then, there it was. A faint heartbeat.

He sighed in relief. He hadn't lost her, at least not yet. He snapped out of his emotion and into action. Keeping her in his grasp, he reached for his backpack, ripping open the bag. He pulled the small, black first aid kit out and tore it open with his teeth, expelling the thin glass aid conductor. He had used a first aid kit a few times on himself and his security team, but those times were rare. There were so few Augland executives or customers outside of a Suit that first aid was hardly needed, and resources weren't often wasted on workers.

He tapped the glass and it glowed red with an options menu. After selecting "severe," Wolfe's hands shook as he scrolled through the options.

Electrical Burn Skin Graph

Poisonous Animal Bite Antidote

Drowning Oxygen Tank

Broken Bone Adhesive

Wound Clotting Bond

Wolfe selected the last choice and the small, thin glass opened, the red lettering reminding him, "Temporary relief; please seek medical attention." He grabbed the package the kit provided.

A voice spoke from the medical box: "Open package. Take out the bottle and carefully unscrew the top." Wolfe did as it said. "Take clotting powder and place it directly into the open wound." He carefully took the powder and poured it over Ashton's leg. He emptied out the entire bottle, just to be safe. Next, he ripped off her makeshift tourniquet and allowed blood to flow back to her leg. The white powder turned red and bubbled, creating a foam around her wound that began to gel.

As he watched, the bubbling slowed and the gel turned into a soft shell. As far as he knew, it had worked. The bleeding had stopped. Wolfe knew she needed medical attention, but at least the wound was clean and protected.

"Wolfe?"

His eyes darted to Ashton.

"Yes! Ashton, yes, it's me." He cupped her face with his hands, leaning in close.

"It's smoky; did I forget to take the tea off?"

"I got it, don't worry. But I need you to stay awake, okay? I need you to try."

Ashton hummed in response as her eyes rolled to the back of her head. Wolfe grabbed his backpack and shoved the first aid kit back into his bag. He put his hands beneath Ashton's legs and around her back, lifting her to him.

"Keep talking to me . . . " Ashton didn't respond. Wolfe carried her through the trees back to his bike. She dangled in his arms.

"Did I fall asleep outside? I always do that. But the stars are so pretty at night."

"You did. You fell asleep but I have you now." Wolfe picked his bike up with his free hand and placed Ashton in the front, so she straddled the seat and faced him. He put the helmet on her head and opened the visor so he could see her face.

"Can you hold onto me? As tightly as you can." Ashton did what she could, barely hugging him as she bobbed in and out of consciousness. Wolfe took off his jacket and wrapped it around her. He started the bike and it hovered for a moment before jolting to speed. Ashton's limp body made it difficult to navigate through the trees and their pace was slow.

Wolfe had to think quickly. Ashton wasn't strong enough to make it to the boat, and there was no way they would get there in time. If his father shut down the train station, it would take at least a few hours to make it to Maya Bay.

BOOM!

An ear-splitting explosion sounded in the distance and almost threw Ashton and Wolfe off their bike. The ground beneath them shook. Wolfe took his hands off the throttle and looked up.

Joao had done it: he had set off the bomb to blow up Centauri. Wolfe imagined the hovering planet exploding above Venus, a blinding white light above Constellation City. Then another sound split the air. Wolfe froze; there was only meant to be one bomb. This sounded like the crackle of lightening. Then another, and another, and another. The sound was getting closer. The piercing noise was right above him.

Suddenly, over the top of the trees in Predator's Biome, Wolfe saw what was happening. A giant crack was splitting the sky above his head. The bomb he had designed, and Joao had set off had cracked the bubble of Augland. The eerie sound of shattering glass reverberated throughout the park. The crack must have been miles long.

Ashton's head stirred against him, and Wolfe was broken out of his trance, tearing his gaze away from the damaged glass of the dome. They needed to leave. And they needed to leave now.

CHAPTER 43

Wolfe
SUNDAY 10:01 p.m.

Augland had cracked. The globe that had encapsulated Wolfe's entire life was coming apart, and it was Wolfe's fault. The bomb was meant to blow up the hovering planet of Centauri, a point of pride and an economic powerhouse in Augland 54. Wolfe had wanted to strike where it would hurt Warren the most. But the energy from the bomb had reverberated off the roof of Augland and taken the façade of the park with it.

The crack made its way from Venus to the neighboring park, which meant the damage was extensive. Predator's Biome still echoed with the cracking of broken glass. The shadowed, sharp edges of the splintered glass were obvious against the dark night and rising smoke. The half-moon was illuminated by the pixels that flickered out from the crack. The glass dome was covered in tiny screens that projected the illusion of sky; the screens around the blast must have short-circuited, leaving blank squares in the portrayed view.

Wolfe's breath quickened. He had wanted to take Augland 54 down, but he hadn't thought of what it would feel like when it happened, when he finally crossed the line from which he could never return. The explosion was one thing, but a crack in the wall was more than just a distraction. It was a message to both himself and Warren that their perfect world would never be the same.

Wolfe pushed full throttle on his hoverbike. He needed to find the quickest way out; all of Augland would be looking for him now, and he needed to get Ashton real medical attention.

There were only two ways out of Augland now. He could head toward the supply boat on the shores of Maya Bay where Joao, Hunter, and the caged workers were headed. It left in nine hours . . . and Ashton wouldn't last half that. Wolfe knew his father would be looking for him, and he didn't want to draw any attention to Maya Bay. The other way out was the cages. The same tunnel Ashton had used the first time she left Augland 54. Neither option sounded good, and medical attention was going to be a problem no matter what.

Wolfe glanced down at Ashton. Her brow furrowed with pain and she was still ashy pale. He didn't have a choice; he had to leave Augland now and find a way to get additional medical aid. The Underground Tunnels of old Seattle were their only way out.

Wolfe had never entered the cages from the Predator's Biome entrance. The door was clearly marked on the interconnect, but it would be well disguised. Suits had free reign of the parks, and no detail had been spared to keep up the illusion of each park. He scanned the rocky terrain ahead until the sound of falling water crashing on rocks caught his attention. The entrance to the cages must be hidden behind the waterfall.

Wolfe steered closer to the raging water, making sure to stay on the outer edge of the rocky bank just beyond the waterfall's hazy mist. The sound of the rushing water became all-consuming as he braced to squeeze through the small sliver of space between the waterfall and cliffside. Once he entered the door to the cages behind the waterfall, Wolfe would have no idea what to expect. All he hoped was that security hadn't picked up on his trail.

The tunnels were empty and quiet. Wolfe assumed all available workers and security detail were dealing with the mess he had caused above ground. Hopefully, their focus was on Venus and not the workers escaping Predator's Biome or heading toward Maya Bay.

He didn't bother getting off the bike. He would need it once they were out of Augland. He sped down the halls, the automatic lights turning on ahead of him, leaving the hallway behind in darkness.

Finally, he reached the cages. This floor was empty. The men, women, and children who had been locked away just hours earlier were somewhere in the parks above. Wolfe silently wished them luck.

He passed cages 510, 512, and finally, 514, beyond which the small hallway ended in a cement door. He pushed the brakes down hard, jolting Ashton half-awake as he veered left and stopped inches away from the door.

Wolfe leaned Ashton against the handlebars and hopped off the bike, leaving it hovering beside him. He opened the door using a key card Joao had helped secure in case things didn't go according to plan.

The light turned green. Wolfe sighed in relief as he pushed the door open. He turned to the bike just in time to see Ashton struggling to get off, catching her stiff leg on the bike, and crashing to the ground.

Ashton's chest rose and fell in fast succession. She was weak and scared. Looking around, her eyes landed on Wolfe.

"Where am I?" She winced as she moved her leg. Wolfe rounded the bike toward her.

"Careful!" Ashton pulled away from him. "Don't touch me!" she yelled and pushed herself across the floor, dragging her motionless leg.

"You move too much and you'll break the wound's seal and lose more blood. Ashton, please, let me help you."

Ashton scoffed. "Help me? You?" Her eyes rolled for a moment before she refocused.

The echo of steel hitting pavement startled Wolfe into action. He grabbed Ashton and put a hand around her mouth to silence her. He listened intently, ignoring her feeble attempt to squirm under him. The patter of boots on concrete told Wolfe that someone was entering the cages from the security elevator. Whoever it was would soon find out the caged workers had escaped.

He pulled Ashton close to the damp, cold, concrete wall in the narrow corridor near the door. She went still. Wolfe had to think fast. If he was found escaping with Ashton, all the doors would be locked down. Not even Joao's override could stop that.

Heavy footsteps echoed across the halls; Wolfe couldn't tell by the resounding noise how close or far away the security guard was, only that with each step they came closer to them. Wolfe breathed heavily. His mind reeled. He could leave, but the bike would give him away. He could wait, and the man could radio that the workers had escaped and spoil Hunter's attempt to make it to the boat. He glanced at his watch. Almost midnight. They needed more time.

"Ashton," Wolfe whispered through strained breath. "I'm going to let you go. I need you to stay very still and not say a word. I'll be right back. Nod if you under-stand." Ashton slowly nodded, Wolfe's hand still around her mouth. He let go, slowly, hoping she wouldn't yell or give away their position. She stayed silent, eyeing him carefully.

"Okay. Stay here. I'll be right back." Wolfe left her on the floor. She winced. He presumed she would faint soon enough. She was too weak from the movement she had made so far, especially after slipping in and out of consciousness on the exhausting ride from Predator's Biome.

Wolfe took a deep breath before rounding the corner. He held his head high in confidence, mimicking the authority of an Executive. His footsteps hastened as he closed in on the security guard who stood opening one of the cage doors in disbelief.

"You, there!" Wolfe yelled, "what are you doing down here? Why aren't you in Biome with the others?" He hoped the guard hadn't gotten word that Wolfe was no longer CEO or that he had been disowned by the Executive office.

"Wh—where are all the prisoners?" The man stood in front of the unoccupied cells. Likely a new guard, Wolfe surmised, not one of Wolfe's men.

"First, we never call them prisoners; they are detained workers." Wolfe was trying to buy time to think of a plausible explanation. "Secondly, we moved them, for cleaning and inspection." It was the first thing he could think of, not that it had ever been done before.

"Inspection for what?" The man replied with more attitude than a man of his status should have. He had risen to the rank of security, but he was still a worker.

"Excuse me?" Wolfe approached the man. The realization of who Wolfe was sunk in, and the young worker's eyes widened.

"Sir, I'm so sorry! I—I didn't see it was you." Wolfe walked right up to the man, his arms crossed in disapproval.

"You can leave, now. Go to Biome. The workers will be back in their cages soon." The guard's eyes shifted.

"Sir, uh, Warren . . . he said to not take orders from you—" Wolfe didn't let the man finish. He grabbed the man's head and squeezed it between his rib cage and arm. The security guard flailed in an attempt to escape and grab his interconnect. He must have been fresh out of training; he didn't notice his surroundings at all. It was too easy for Wolfe to hold him, making oxygen intake increasingly difficult until his body sank, and Wolfe released him. He wasn't dead, just out for a while, long enough for Wolfe and Ashton to escape.

He pulled the guard's body into a cage and took his interconnect, cuffs, and jacket. Wolfe had given his jacket to Ashton and the road ahead in the wet winter would be tough. He shut the barred door behind him, locking it with the cuffs. It would buy enough time for them to escape and hopefully for the others to make it to the boat.

Wolfe rounded the corner toward his bike and Ashton. He slid on the jacket as he walked and was about to call out to her when he noticed only his hoverbike remained. Ashton was gone. Wolfe cursed as he looked behind him. There was no way she could have passed him without him noticing. She must have gone through the open door. Wolfe sighed, glancing at his interconnect, which showed her exact location. She was making her way slowly down the corridor. This was going to be more difficult than he thought.

CHAPTER 44

Ashton
SUNDAY 11:50 p.m.

Wolfe had left her alone, and Ashton wasn't willing to stick around to see why. She swayed in the dampness of the Underground Tunnels. She had been this way before and knew she could find her way out, if only her body would cooperate.

She remembered getting shot with Bez in Biome, but why was she now with Wolfe back in the tunnels? Her only impulse was to get away. She was close to an exit and would die before letting Augland recapture her.

Her mind said go, but her body struggled to comply. The injury and blood loss had taken its toll. She had to hold the slippery side of the tunnel brick walls to keep her balance.

Ashton stopped, catching her breath, and screamed at her body to keep going. She tried desperately to stay awake.

A sharp pain spun up her leg. The shock slowly took over her body. The world around her became dark as her consciousness teetered. *No, please not again.* Then, the darkness consumed her.

CHAPTER 45

Wolfe
SUNDAY 11:56 p.m.

Wolfe pulled the bike upright and turned it on. Ashton couldn't have gone far. He drove the bike into the tunnel and let it hover as he shut the tunnel door behind him, plunging the hallway into darkness. The only light was the headlight of his bike and the interconnect. He looked down at the blinking red dot; Ashton was about a hundred feet down the tunnel and she wasn't moving.

A sliver of pain ran through Wolfe's spine. She had wasted precious energy to get away from him. Ashton's frame came into view, hunched against the side of the dripping, brick wall. Wolfe slowed his vehicle and came to a stop next to her. She had passed out again. New blood crusted over the dried brown-and-white speckled dressing.

Wolfe dismounted his bike and bent down, frustrated that she couldn't see he was trying to help. Ashton's soft breath was slow and shallow. He scooped her up again and mounted her on his bike as he had done in Predator's Biome. This time, he pulled her in tightly and she didn't resist. She didn't sacrifice precious life to rid herself of his presence.

The soft hum of the bike reverberated off the tunnel walls as they drove toward the exit out of Augland. Wolfe opened the door to freedom. Wind and cold rain pelted them as they exited Augland. Wolfe breathed in the brisk air. He thought of the crack in the dome behind him. Out in the exposed air, he wished they had something to shield them from the harsh winds and unrelenting rain. They had lost the helmet in the chaos back in the cages, but just covering her would help.

Wolfe looked behind him to the towering wall of Augland. It was impressive, standing hundreds of feet high, towering above the trees. He was out, but what now? His chest tightened. He looked down at Ashton, taking his hands off the bars and pulling her face from the jacket.

"Ashton, what do I do . . ." Wolfe whispered, knowing she wasn't coherent enough to answer him. He was out, he was with Ashton, but none of this was what he expected or ever planned for. He was most worried about her. She wouldn't make the trip to NeuroEnergy. It was at least another day's drive. He needed to figure out how to tend to her wound. He propped Ashton back up so she draped farther up on his arm.

The ground was saturated and water continuously pelted Wolfe's face. The wildness of winter heightened his senses, and it sent a shiver down his spine. He breathed hard as he surveyed the open reality around him. His eyes settled on Ashton's soft face resting against his chest. The Underground Tunnels had deposited them onto the stretch of land that reached across the southern part of Elliott Bay. Wolfe started across the water to the dark island in front of him. How had he not thought of it before?

A glimmer of hope appeared, and he accelerated forward. He would head toward the abandoned Colony on Bainbridge Island, and the electric boat he hoped still waited for him on the shore. He had used the boat to visit the Colony over the years and had last used it when he brought Ashton back to the Augland cages when she first escaped. He had docked it on what was once known as Alki Beach, and if luck was on his side, it would still be there.

Wolfe could barely see anything, but he knew where he was going. Ashton hadn't woken up from her unconsciousness since he had picked her up in the tunnels. Not that he needed that right now. She would likely hurt herself more if she woke up, but he struggled to keep her upright and drive at the same time. His bicep shook from cold, and from the constant weight of her body hunched over to his left side.

The water glistened in the distance and Wolfe knew he was close. There it was, rocking back and forth against the crashing waves. The boat that would take him to the shores of Bainbridge Island. After that, he hoped luck was still on his side, because if it wasn't, Ashton wouldn't last much longer.

He placed her down carefully on the back cushion of the boat; it was soaked through. He zipped up the oversized security jacket so more than half of her body was cocooned in it. He parked the bike in the boat and shut it down for the ride. He knew the boat's battery would be dead so he pulled out his extra universal battery, hooked it up, and held his breath. The boat started. Sighing in relief, Wolfe quickly spun the boat around and sped to the shores of Bainbridge Island, only miles ahead.

Wolfe rummaged through the bare kitchen cabinets. Pots, pans, a few expired packages of food, nothing that would help Ashton. It felt strange to be tearing apart Cahya's old home, but the Colony had left months earlier and Wolfe did not have time to care about etiquette.

Where would they have kept the medical supplies? He didn't have time to search every house on the cul-de-sac and he was losing patience and valuable time. It was time for a last resort. Wolfe still had the secure channel he and Cahya used to communicate. The problem would be getting Cahya to answer his call. In her mind, Wolfe was a traitor.

"Cahya." Wolfe held the interconnect up to this mouth. There was silence on the other end. It was early, but Cahya would be awake.

"Cahya, please," he spoke again. *Silence.* The minutes were painful as he waited for a response.

"You have some nerve contacting me after what you did." Cahya's firm voice came softly over the interconnect and Wolfe sighed in relief.

"Cahya, it's—thank you. I—I know what you think I've done is terrible, I—I don't know how to explain or even begin, but right now, I just need your help. It's Ashton." He jumbled his words, but he hoped it would be enough to get her help. "Ashton's hurt. I'm at the old Colony cul-de-sac and I need to know where the leftover medical supplies are, if there is anything I could use to treat a photon wound."

Again, silence.

"Please, Cahya. Ashton's not going to make it if I don't help her now."

"You have Ashton?" Cahya finally spoke.

"Yes, I got her out of Augland."

"Let me talk to her. I want to know you aren't lying to me." Wolfe was growing frustrated with the line of questioning. Did she not hear him? He had said Ashton's life was at risk!

"She's out. Unconscious, which is why I need your help! Please!" There was a long pause. Wolfe held his breath. He couldn't do this without her, not with the minutes that remained.

"I'll get the doc, but I am only doing this in case what you say is true."

"Yes! As soon as she's awake, I'll get her on the line."

Another five minutes passed. Wolfe stood on Cahya's porch and looked around the dark cul-de-sac. The rain was coming down harder than ever. It felt unreal being at the Colony without the hustle and bustle of the children or the constant chatter of Colony business.

"This is Rogan." A male voice came over Wolfe's interconnect.

"Hello, sir. I'm at the old Colony and I need medical supplies."

"There isn't much left, only stuff that wouldn't fit . . . but you'll find whatever's left at 1745 45th Street; that was the hospital's address."

Wolfe ran out into the rain, scanning the faded numbers on the homes. He ran with the interconnect in his hand, surveying each home until he reached an olive-green house with white trim, almost hidden behind overgrown grass.

Flinging the door open, Wolfe burst into the empty house. The only things left were cream-colored cabinets lining the room and a surgical rolling table that had only a single blade on it.

"In the surgical room, cabinets behind the table are where all the medical supplies were."

Wolfe targeted the cabinets and threw them open. He grabbed the few packages left on the shelves; they were all stamped with the AEC logo. Augland 54 had traded outdated supplies with the Colony when they had been on good terms.

"Ashton has a photon wound. Where?" The doctor was obviously familiar with Ashton.

"Left upper leg," Wolfe answered, sorting through the packages.

"Blood loss?"

"A lot. She's in and out of consciousness. I gave her a blood-clotting powder, but the cut reopened."

Rogan sighed. "She'll need perfluorocarbon nano-emulsion oxygen carriers. Synthetic hemoglobin should also be in the kit. That should do the trick. Unfortunately, there are no pain medications left there."

Wolfe scoured the cabinets.

"Fever?" Rogan didn't wait for an answer. "Also, look for plasma expander; it should be labeled—white package, clear liquid. You'll need a long thin tube and needle. And a tissue synthesizer, to stop the bleeding, clean the wound, and close the hole. Hopefully no broken bones." Wolfe struggled to keep up with the items the doctor rattled off.

He ripped through package after package, until he held up a rectangular box labeled "Tissue Regen Kit." Wolfe shoved the box under his shirt and kept looking.

"Plasma Expander?" Wolfe asked.

"Yes, take that too and let me know when you are back with her, I'll walk you through what to do."

Wolfe was out of breath when he reached Cahya's upstairs bedroom where Ashton lay. He spilled the variety of medical supplies onto the bed, next to her.

"I'm here, what do I do?" Wolfe shouted through the interconnect, shaking as he awaited his next direction.

"Rogan!" Wolfe screamed.

"Yes, I'm here . . ." Rogan answered calmly.

The doctor began to walk Wolfe through the steps. First, Wolfe removed the remnants of the clotting material and Ashton's blood-crusted tourniquet. It stuck to the wound and her skin, but even as he removed it as carefully as he could, Ashton didn't stir. He cleaned around the wound, being careful not to go directly over it. A gaping hole cratered her thigh and Wolfe went white when he saw exactly how much damage the photon gun had caused. As he cleaned, an alarming amount of fresh blood came out.

Wolfe did as the doctor had told him and put the thick bandage, saturated with the tissue synthesizer, across her wound. He felt instant relief as the color changed from stark white to blue, which the doctor said would show its working technology.

"That should stop the bleeding."

The next part was what worried Wolfe. He was no doctor and had never placed a needle in anyone's body before. Sweat beaded down his forehead and his hands shook as he searched for a vein. The blue lines were faint on Ashton's arm.

"Hold her arm and apply pressure to bring the vein up closer to the skin. You don't go down, go to the side. You want the needle to go into the vein's center lumen, so the liquid can be pumped through it."

Wolfe pierced her skin. His hands shook nervously. It didn't work.

"Take a deep breath. Steady your hands and try again." The doctor's soothing and reassuring words helped. "You'll know you're successful when a small amount of blood travels into the needle." Wolfe entered Ashton's skin slowly. A small dark pool of blood in the IV appeared, and Wolfe smiled.

"I'm in," he exhaled in pure relief.

"Great work; now slide the IV catheter over the needle and into the vein and remove the needle. Then, tape the catheter in place so it doesn't move. You'll want to hang the pouch of synthetic hemoglobin and plasma-expanding fluid above her so it will flow into her body. Don't squeeze the fluid in the bag; just let it flow naturally into her arm." Rogan added, "It will take a few liters of total fluids and treatment to get her to respond, and if she does, she may pull through. The oxygen emulsions and tissue synthesizers will be next but can wait until she responds to the plasma expanders. Those are not hard to apply and the directions are printed on the labels."

"Thank you, thank you so much," Wolfe choked out as much gratitude as he could convey over the interconnect. He sucked back the emotion he had held back ever since he'd seen Ashton on the ground in Predator's Biome.

"I'll check back in about forty-five minutes. Don't leave her. Call if anything happens." The doctor disconnected and Wolfe dropped his head. He pressed his face against Cahya's bed in silence as he tried to compose himself. An overwhelming emotion took hold as he let the tenseness of the moment fade. It was a waiting game now; Wolfe had done what he could. All that was left was Ashton's will to keep going. *She's tough.* He pulled her hand into his, brought it up to his face, and kissed it as tears ran down his face.

The waiting proved to be harder than Wolfe had expected. He propped Ashton up on a few pillows and put her underneath a blanket he found discarded downstairs. He took the extra battery he had used for the boat and turned on the lights of Cahya's home. For a while, he just paced.

He sat back down at Ashton's side, holding her hand as he waited. He thought he felt the heat coming back into her body, but he wasn't sure if that was his own hand warming her.

Wolfe couldn't be still for long. He brought wood upstairs to Cahya's personal fireplace and began building a fire. The blankets could only do so much, and he needed to stay busy. The fire crackled and Ashton sighed heavily. Wolfe turned, rushing to her side.

"Ashton?"

He studied her as the color slowly started to come back to her cheeks. Still, Wolfe wouldn't be satisfied until she was fully awake. He checked her bandage, still glowing blue. He then checked her second bag, now half-empty.

Ashton's eyes began to flutter. He put his hand against her face.

"Wolfe?" Ashton asked as her eyes adjusted.

Wolfe smiled, "Yes, yes it's me."

Ashton frowned and suddenly pulled away from his touch. Her eyes were still tired, but she was coherent.

"What? When—" She began to panic, looking around until she rested her eyes on Wolfe again. "Get away from me!"

Wolfe put up his hands in defense, backing up toward the fireplace. He kept his eyes on her, surrendering and doing as she asked.

"I'm away. Just stay calm."

Ashton's eyes landed on the catheter in her arm with the long, thin tubing that Wolfe had hooked up to the plastic bag lying flat on the windowsill. Her hand went for the catheter.

"No! Don't touch that, please. You still need it," Wolfe begged.

Ashton processed. She looked down at her wound and the patch on top of it.

"Why am I here?" she finally said, calm in her voice as she realized the mechanisms were helping. She must have recognized the room because she didn't ask where she was.

Wolfe plunged his hands into his pockets, unsure where to start. He wanted to embrace her, but her untrusting eyes told him it wouldn't be received well.

"I brought you . . ." Wolfe said, ready and willing to answer anything she asked. But he wasn't sure how much she would believe.

CHAPTER 46

Ashton

Ashton could tell from the hazy blue outside that it was at least seven in the morning. The boat would have left by now. She was reluctant to engage Wolfe, who stood by the fire, but she had gaps in her memory and wanted to know what happened. She remembered Predator's Biome, and the Apparel escape with Bez. She remembered Bez leaving her under the brush and trees to lead the others to the train station. She remembered ripping off her wig and pulling herself into the shrubbery to shield herself from the oncoming bullets. Everything after that was a blur.

A hoverbike. The cages. Wolfe. Catching her breath in a dark tunnel. And waking up in Cahya's bedroom, the same one she'd slept in when she escaped Augland the first time.

Ashton assumed Wolfe had been the one to bring her here and she also assumed he was the one who bandaged her wound and gave her whatever medicine was in the plastic bag dripping into her vein.

But that didn't add up. Why would he risk anything for her? Did he need her as leverage? Why hadn't he left her in Predator's Biome? There were too many unanswered questions.

"How long have I been out?" she asked the ceiling, not looking toward Wolfe. Ashton didn't want to look at him, but she also wanted him in her peripheral just in case he tried to come toward her.

"Eight hours, give or take." Wolfe was direct, but there was softness in his voice.

Don't be tricked, Ashton, she thought. *He's a monster, remember what he did to Jagatha? The Colony?*

She continued to stare up at the ceiling. Eight hours meant the boat had left, with or without the Augland workers. She desperately wanted answers.

"Can I explain?" Wolfe asked, still direct, with no emotion in his voice. Then his voice wavered. "Please, let me explain."

Ashton didn't want to listen to him try to manipulate her, but she propped herself upright on the bed.

"Careful!" Wolfe stepped forward, but Ashton stopped him with a stern glare. She didn't want him anywhere nearby.

Wolfe bent down to one knee, so he was eye level with her.

"Whatever you think I did, it wasn't me, Ash." Ashton scoffed. Wolfe took a deep breath. "Warren created a Suit of me. After the board made me CEO, he imprisoned and drugged me in his closet and then impersonated me for weeks. *He* attacked the Colony, *he* created the customer service initiative, it was all *him.*" His crystal-blue eyes begged for understanding, but Ashton wasn't falling for what she thought were lies.

She scoffed. Even if she wanted to believe him, what had happened was too much to forgive. She had seen Wolfe. She had heard him. A doppelganger "Suit" seemed too convenient an excuse.

"Was it Warren then who promised me once he received the title of CEO he would stop all this? Was it Warren who dropped Jagatha? Why would Warren be you? Answer me that, Wolfe. He already had the power!"

"He would do anything to be CEO. He took—"

"He was already CEO! You think I'm an idiot, Wolfe? If you're going to lie, at least make it believable." Ashton finally faced him, her icy-cold eyes boring into his.

She wanted to believe him, especially when he looked so innocent. She couldn't stare at his pleading eyes any longer. She sat back against the cushions and sighed.

"The workers, in Apparel, did they make it out?"

Wolfe shook his head. "Joao's not answering. I've tried; he hasn't said anything. I messaged him about Bez." Wolfe paused. "I told him I could only find you."

Ashton's eyes began to water, and she took a big deep breath. Maybe she didn't want an update. If anything had happened to Bez, she didn't want to hear it. She wanted to tell Wolfe to leave.

He must have sensed her need to be alone and muttered something about making coffee. The door shut quietly behind him, and Ashton was left to her thoughts.

Why was he keeping up the charade? Did he really think he could convince her with his lies?

She hoped the workers had made it to the train station and ultimately to the boat that would take them to NeuroEnergy, but her hope was dwindling. She sobbed. She cried until the tears stopped coming and she was dazed with sadness. She was still weak, and her anger at Wolfe and sadness over the Apparel workers and Bez just made it worse. She let herself drift off to sleep. If Wolfe wanted her dead, she would have been there by now.

The next time Ashton woke, the sun was setting, and she was alone in Cahya's old bedroom. She slowly pushed herself up and felt her strength returning. The catheter in her arm was gone and so was the bag of medicine that had hung above her head. Beside her was a cup of water and a bowl of something that smelled delicious. Ashton realized she was starving.

She pulled the bowl to her and looked down at the lumpy, brown goop and the rising steam. She sniffed. *Chili.* She hadn't had canned chili since the Colony ran out shortly after making it to Hood Canal. Before she knew it, the bowl was empty.

Ashton pulled off her blanket and put her feet on the ground. A stick, completely shaven of its bark, lay next to her. She didn't want to use the cane and pushed it aside. Even though Wolfe wasn't in the room, she didn't want to show weakness. But by the time she managed the few steps to the fireplace, she regretted her own stubbornness. Hanging above the coals in the fireplace was a pot of simmering water. A towel and a stack of neatly folded clothes were on a chair.

The fire warmed her, and she bent down to test the steaming water. She washed her face first, sighing into the woody smell of the towel. Then she washed the dirt and blood off the rest of her body, carefully wiping around the medical patch on her thigh. It felt good to be clean. Anything to have a semblance of normalcy again.

The crusted blood and dirt on her stained dress crackled as she lifted it over her head. She quickly scrambled into the thick sweatshirt and oversized sweatpants left on the chair for her. She pulled the sweatpants slowly over her wounded leg, the excess material bunching around her ankles. She felt more like herself. But her full stomach and comfortable clothes did not relieve the looming feeling that Wolfe was still there. The uncertainty of his intentions made her uneasy. She needed a plan to get out of the house and away from him. She looked around for anything she could use as a weapon. Her eyes settled on a metal fire poker. Escape was her best option.

Ashton slowly opened the bedroom door. Beyond it, stairs led down to the first floor of Cahya's house. She could hear the clanking of pots and pans in the kitchen. At the last moment, she grabbed the walking stick Wolfe had left by the bed and used it to support half her weight. She did her best to tiptoe down the stairs, but navigating her new injury made it hard. Her heart beat out of her chest. He hadn't noticed her yet, and she was trying to keep it that way. Ashton was in no shape to fight off an opponent, so her best shot was to sneak out undetected. When she was almost at the bottom of the stairs, she saw Wolfe searching through the kitchen cabinets. His back was to her. *Perfect.* As she stepped on the final stair a subtle creak announced her presence.

Wolfe's head whipped around. Ashton caught his eye, then looked directly at the door. It was close enough that she might be able to make it. She jumped at the opportunity and heard Wolfe lunge toward her in reaction. She opened the door and the frigid wind barreled into the room. She didn't even make it a step before Wolfe yanked her backward and slammed the door.

"Let me go!" Ashton screamed as she pulled at the unyielding knob.

Wolfe let go of Ashton and moved from between her and the door. The door swung open; the cold wind blew in around them. There was a long silence.

"All right, I let you go. Happy?" Wolfe finally spoke.

Ashton fumed with anger and took a faltering step toward the door. She cursed her injured leg under her breath.

"Where are you going to go? You're barefoot and it's the middle of winter. NeuroEnergy is about a twenty-four-hour hike. Another thirty or so if you go to the Colony. Might I add you were on the brink of death just yesterday and have only one 'good' leg." Wolfe sounded frustrated. "Trust me, I'd prefer not to babysit you and keep you captive. I'd rather you stay willingly." His frustration was not lost on Ashton.

Of course, she hadn't thought her plan all the way through. She had only thought of getting far enough away from Wolfe so he couldn't hurt her more or try to manipulate her into thinking he was now suddenly good again. He was right though; she wouldn't get far, not with the weather, not without shoes, and not with one working leg.

Wolfe turned and walked back into the living room, leaving Ashton at the front door.

"Come sit down, please?" He motioned to the couch that was in front of a roaring fire. Ashton sighed and slammed the front door shut. Immediately she felt the warmth of the home and her exhaustion. She sat on the couch, stretching out her injured leg. She wasn't about to leave room for Wolfe to join her.

"Tea, right?" Wolfe asked as he walked back into the kitchen, no doubt gloating in his small win.

"Yeah . . ." Ashton said, thinking tea would be nice.

"Wish right now that Cahya was a coffee drinker, I would do just about anything for an espresso." Wolfe tried to make light conversation. Ashton ignored him.

"It's good to see you feeling better."

Wolfe came by, handed Ashton a hot tea, and pulled a chair from the dining room table closer to the fire.

Ashton fiddled with her mug. "What do you want, Wolfe? Why did you take me out of Augland?"

"Would you have rather stayed?" He tried to be funny, but Ashton was in no mood for lighthearted banter. She didn't even look at him. "You would have died if I'd left you . . . and I know you think I did something horrible—it is horrible—unforgivable even, but I'm telling you the truth, and I couldn't let you just die. So, I found you, and brought you here . . ."

So Wolfe knew Ashton hated him, and he still rescued her. She finally met his eyes and, despite her better judgment, she melted. She knew she hated him, but her heart broke at the sight of him. She believed he was no longer the man she had known; he was a monster. And yet here he sat looking, just as sweet and innocent as ever.

"Later today, if you're still feeling better, I'll take you to NeuroEnergy." Wolfe looked away and stretched out a hand toward the fire.

Ashton lit up. "You'll take me there?"

"Of course, if that's what you want, I'll take you there. Better that than let you walk." Wolfe looked down at his cup.

Ashton was dying to know what happened during the escape and if Bez and Hunter were all right, but she didn't trust Wolfe. He was helping her for a reason, but she couldn't figure out what it was.

"Why do you want to go there?"

"I don't. I'm not sure it's even safe for me to go to NeuroEnergy." Wolfe confessed. Ashton didn't disagree; NeuroEnergy might do anything to get the information against Augland that they needed. "But Joao should be there, and I want to make sure the workers made it safely—Hunter too—that they will have a home."

"Hunter?" Ashton regarded Wolfe with caution. "He's safe? He's alive?" Her heart stopped waiting for Wolfe's response.

"Last I saw, yes; he was taking the caged workers to the supply boat."

Ashton sighed in relief and thought she would press her luck. "What about the children?"

Wolfe hung his head. "No, they couldn't be found in time. They were dispersed to several areas in the parks and there was no time to collect them."

Wolfe studied Ashton but she pretended not to notice. She knew he hoped his actions could convince her of his true intentions, but she wouldn't let that happen. Her trust would be hard-earned. The fact that she was in the same room as him or even looking at him would have to be enough for now.

"I'd like to leave now. I'll grab my things." Ashton stood up and placed the undrunk cup of tea on the coffee table between her and Wolfe. "They'll probably lock you up, you know. NeuroEnergy," Ashton said, turning toward the staircase. She wasn't sure why she warned him, but she wasn't heartless.

Wolfe nodded. "I know . . ."

Ashton turned and walked the rest of the way up the stairs. Her heart sank. How could she feel so betrayed and so sorry for the man downstairs? She needed to stop, snap out of it, and get to NeuroEnergy where it was safe . . . well, safer. She would sort the rest out later.

"I hope they do."

She didn't even believe the words as they left her mouth, but she wanted Wolfe to know she wouldn't forgive and she wouldn't forget, even if he had saved her life.

CHAPTER 47

Wolfe

Wolfe slammed his mug of watery tea on the coffee table and slouched down in his chair. He dropped his face between his hands and rubbed his temples. Ashton had disappeared upstairs to Cahya's room to pack, and he was left in the wake of her last words. *I hope they do.*

He steamed with frustration and grief. He wanted her to understand, but she kept putting up barricades between them. If it was up to Wolfe, they'd stay at the Old Colony until he could convince her of his innocence.

He was exhausted. He wasn't just sleep-deprived; he was growing irritated from constantly having to prove himself. All he had done the last two days was to help Ashton and the workers of Augland. How could they not see the truth?

Wolfe stood abruptly. There was no point brooding, and he had work to do to prepare for the journey ahead. He began re-packing his backpack, this time adding extra bandages for Ashton and waterproof ponchos he had found in Cahya's storeroom. He didn't want Ashton to catch cold in the rainy Pacific Northwest weather.

"Wolfgang." Wolfe heard his name and a familiar voice coming through his interconnect. He picked it up, waiting for the voice to speak again.

"Wolfgang, I know you're there." The voice was calm but unforgettable. Wolfe paused, his hand on the interconnect ready to speak, but he hesitated. He wasn't sure if he was ready to face his father.

Wolfe sighed. "I didn't think I'd hear from you this soon. Checking in on me already?" He decided he would play coy; he wasn't sure how much Warren knew.

Warren chuckled. "Your mother told me you left the home I gave you in Biome. I thought it was rude that you didn't stop by and say goodbye. Where is it you decided to skip off to?"

Wolfe didn't bite. The less his father knew the better.

"The most peculiar series of coincidences happened the day you left. You know that?" Warren danced around the accusation he was dying to make. "An Apparel escape, a riot in Predator's Biome, and an explosion in Venus that caused devastating damage. Funny thing is, workers kindly told us you were there right before the explosion; you said an Executive Summit was being held. Oh! And how could I forget? The workers in the cages were released for some sort of inspection."

Warren spoke so evenly, someone else may have thought he was calm. Wolfe knew better. He knew his father. Warren was probably staring out his window overlooking Augland with a glass of expensive whiskey in his hand, seething with anger.

"That does sound like a coincidence," Wolfe played back, smiling. "Do you not have any other friends you want to gossip with? Not sure the other Executives would like you talking to an ex-Executive about company affairs."

"Don't play dumb with me, boy. I know you had everything to do with it. All of it!" Warren sneered.

"I don't know what you are talking about." Wolfe knew his denial would send his father into a tailspin.

"Several workers died in Constellation City, you know . . . countless Apparel workers in Predator's Biome. Millions in wasted resources will be spent repairing the damage to the glass dome." Wolfe noticed his father's priorities.

"That's unfortunate." Wolfe's reply was stoic, but he had to make an effort to not let the revelation of lost lives shake his voice.

"Wolfgang, this was an active rebellion, a mutiny against Augland! The AEC is not going to overlook this! We were able to explain away the explosion by saying it was an overheated system, but if anything happens again there will be suspicion . . . your pride may have just destroyed the reputation—if not the entirety—of Augland 54. Your actions put everyone in the Executive Office at risk. And your precious workers? What do you think will happen to them? This was beyond selfish. And foolish." Warren spat out the last words.

There was a pause as he waited for Wolfe to take the bait and ask about the workers. Wolfe desperately wanted to know if the caged workers and the Apparel employees had made it to the boat—but he wouldn't ask his father. He knew Warren was cunning and would play every card he had to get information. For all he knew, Warren had camera footage for the Underground Seattle tunnel. Or Wolfe may have been exposed by the young man he had left unconscious in the cages.

"I don't know what you want me to say . . . maybe if you treated workers more like humans, you wouldn't have a rebellion on your hands."

Warren let out a sigh. "If you think NeuroEnergy or that Colony will accept you, they won't. I know you think you can convince them it's me who is the bad guy, but they will only see you as either a bargaining chip or a threat. Either way, the moment you are no longer useful to them, they will discard you. You think I've been like this forever? You think I never wanted . . . that I never thought . . ." Warren's voice broke. Wolfe was taken off guard by the sudden show of weakness. "That I never thought I could create a better world? I wanted that. But the world we live in isn't built for ideals, and there must be sacrifices."

For the first time, deep down, Wolfe knew what his father said was true. He had seen it for himself. He didn't know how to respond to this raw admission.

"Son, go somewhere safe. Not for me, for your mother. Don't go to NeuroEnergy."

Wolfe hesitated. He had been programmed to believe that Warren always had some alternative motive, but for once, he couldn't think of one to explain his father's last words. Warren understood his situation; he was cast out. The Colony wouldn't take him, NeuroEnergy would use him, and Augland would suffocate him. He was an outcast.

"Tell Mom I love her." Wolfe choked out the words before turning off the interconnect. He couldn't take it anymore. Even if Warren's words had merit, he wouldn't listen to the voice of reason or manipulation. Yes, what his father had said was correct, but he had promised to take Ashton to NeuroEnergy and he would keep his word.

He looked out Cahya's kitchen window at the muddy rain. He had to admit he was scared. He feared he would never be believed and it would cost him his life.

CHAPTER 48

Ashton

Ashton awkwardly maneuvered down the wooden steps of Cahya's porch. She was breathless by the time she reached Wolfe, who was packing up the hoverbike in the light rain. His backpack was filled with canned food from Cahya's half-empty pantry, extra Rogen patches for Ashton's leg, his interconnect, and the photon gun. He looked up as she approached and studied her face. Ashton knew she looked rough. She was exhausted even after hours of sleep and she felt flushed, but she didn't need Wolfe's pity.

Wolfe approached and put his hand up to Ashton's face. She pulled away at his touch, but he was too quick.

"You okay? Feels like you've got a nasty fever."

"I'm fine!" Ashton retorted with as much conviction as she could muster. She knew she was sick, and a fever meant a potential infection, but she wouldn't wait any longer at Cahya's house. "I'm ready when you are."

"All right then, let's get going." Wolfe walked past and she saw the disappointment in his eyes. Going to NeuroEnergy was a risk for him, but Ashton was not going to comfort him or let him comfort her.

She followed a few steps behind and watched Wolfe straddle the hoverbike. She stood in the cold rain and crossed her arms.

"Where do I sit?"

"In front. I'd rather you sit facing me; that way, if you pass out again, I can at least catch you." Ashton shifted her stance.

"I can just sit behind you."

Wolfe's patience was growing thin. "Then you're not getting on this bike. You're sick and I'm not taking the risk that you pass out and fall off."

Ashton eyed him before giving in. She swung her injured leg over the seat and faced him.

"Happy?" Ashton didn't look at Wolfe and scowled in protest. Wolfe tensed and shifted in the seat. The last time they sat on the bike, Ashton had been unconscious and Wolfe had held her in front of him. But now she was awake, and they were chest to chest.

Wolfe started the engine and the bike rose off the ground. Ashton tightened her grip around him as they were propelled forward, picking up speed. Bainbridge was an island, but there was still an abandoned bridge connecting it to the mainland in the direction of NeuroEnergy. It wouldn't be a long trip, only about an hour and a half.

CHAPTER 49

Wolfe

The cold and damp Northwest wind froze them both to the bone. Their clothes were soaked, and Wolfe's hands were bright red on the bike's handles.

Finally, they rounded a clump of trees and had their first glimpse of NeuroEnergy. The large, concrete walls of the compound came into view surrounding a small city of identical, gray concrete buildings. Even the ocean behind the compound looked gray, as if NeuroEnergy had sucked the saturation out of the world around it. A sense of dread overcame Wolfe as he knew his freedom and time alone with Ashton was coming to an end.

"Could we stop for a second?" Ashton's voice whispered above the wind howling in his ears. Wolfe parked the hoverbike, welcoming the break from the wind.

"Are you okay?" Wolfe was concerned. He thought she would be relieved by the view of NeuroEnergy.

"Yes, just need a moment." Ashton pulled herself off the bike with the aid of Wolfe. He stayed on, the bike still hovering over the ground. The rain pounded down on the road around them. Ashton sat down on the ground and pulled her leg out in front of her, groaning from the stiff pain.

"Just tell me, why Jagatha? Why lie to me? How you could be so cruel?" Ashton's eyes watered. She didn't wait for Wolfe to answer. "You killed her for no reason! None. She meant nothing to you. She meant nothing to Augland. But she meant everything to me . . . everything. She was just a child, Wolfe."

Wolfe didn't know how to respond. He didn't know Jagatha, had never met her before. He only knew what Joao had told him, and he presumed the rest; that she was at the Colony when Warren raided and from Ashton's reaction, a dear friend of hers.

"I don't know what to say, Ashton. I'm not even sure, specifically, what you're referring to. I told you. It wasn't me. It was Warren. I don't know how to prove it to you. I wish I could. . . but how do I prove it? How do I convince you when you saw what you saw, heard what you heard? I—I can't! You should hate the man that did all those things. I do. But whatever you're talking about—this young girl, 'Jagatha'—it wasn't me. I don't know what you're talking about!" His voice broke on his last sentence, his desperation rising.

Ashton shook her head in disbelief. "Is that how you do it? You . . . you make people believe they're insane? You think I should just forget what my own eyes saw? I saw you! I saw you when you didn't know it was me—when you thought I was Charlotte, when you thought I was one of them!" Her eyes were wide with fury as she referred to the Suits. "You're just like Warren. Maybe worse."

Her fury came at him like a tornado. Returning to Augland had changed Ashton, and she was cold and distant. The more he tried to speak the truth, the angrier she became. Unless he admitted to crimes he didn't commit, she wouldn't be satisfied.

"Answer me!" Ashton demanded.

Wolfe only looked down at his feet. He would not admit to something he hadn't done, and he didn't want to anger her further by denying her own truth. The silence was their only exchange and he hated it. This would most likely be their last conversation. The rain poured as they stared unflinchingly at each other.

Ashton needed a moment to calm down before she came back to the bike. Wolfe didn't press her. He just waited.

Wolfe decreased speed as they approached the tall gates of NeuroEnergy. The entrance was barred and lined with security. The guards raised their guns as Wolfe parked the bike and he and Ashton dismounted.

"Names!" the guard yelled, his gun pointed.

"Ashton and . . ." she paused, ". . . and Wolfgang."

The guard shifted and spoke in muted tones into his interconnect. There was an awkward pause as they all waited for the guards to receive instructions.

"Down on the ground! Down on the ground!" The shout came suddenly, and Wolfe's first instinct was to protect Ashton. But as he began to move toward her, he realized the guns were not pointed at her, but at him. The guards had figured out who he was.

Wolfe obliged and lay down on the ground, his hands folded behind his head. Out of the corner of his eye, he could only see Ashton's feet standing close to him, not moving. The gates opened and she was ushered into NeuroEnergy by a guard, leaving him with the other three. Suddenly, he was jerked upright and onto his feet. He strained to look past the gates to make sure Ashton was taken to safety.

"She's got a fever, most likely an infection. She needs medical attention." Wolfe yelled after her, wanting to make sure she was taken to their medical facility immediately.

"Stop talking," one of the guards barked.

Wolfe kept his eyes on Ashton as a guard took her up the NeuroEnergy headquarters stairs and out of sight. He was being led across the campus in the opposite direction.

"Did the workers make it okay? Just tell me if they made it."

There was a pause while they marched, one guard shoving him so hard he tripped forward. The man in front didn't turn around.

"You'll be disappointed to find out that yes, they made it and are being taken care of. Sorry you lost so many of your experimental test subjects."

Wolfe ignored the last comment and instead sighed in relief. The workers had made it and Ashton was safe. No matter what, that was all that mattered now.

CHAPTER 50

Ashton

Beep, beep, beep.

Ashton's eyes blinked open. She looked around her. Cement walls, a charcoal-gray carpet, and a hovering glass screen at the foot of her hospital bed. Her mind was foggy.

She remembered coming to NeuroEnergy and the guards shoving Wolfe to the ground. And then she had walked away without looking back. She wanted Wolfe to know she didn't care about his fate, even if that wasn't true. No matter how hard she tried to fully hate him, some part of her did care. But now his fate was no longer her concern. He was in the hands of NeuroEnergy.

The door to the room opened and a tall man with long, disheveled hair entered. His smile warmed as their eyes met, and Ashton gave a startled cry in recognition. "Hunter!" She exhaled sharply in relief.

Hunter rushed forward and wrapped his arms around her gently. He inhaled deeply and spoke with emotion. "I—I thought you were dead. I was sure of it."

Ashton began to tear up. "I thought I was too," she whispered through the fabric of his shirt, not pulling away from him. She tightened her grip and noticed, as she did so, that her pain was only an annoyance now.

Hunter pulled away only to grasp her face in his hands, wiping away her tears.

"Well, this is really too bad. I thought I had finally found a way to get rid of you," Hunter laughed between sniffs. Ashton shook her head and smiled. She had missed

273

him more than she'd realized.

"Guess it takes more than just wishful thinking and a gaping hole in the leg to knock you down."

Hunter sat down on the sheet beside her, and Ashton made room for him. He took her hand in his. His smile faded as he tightened his grip.

"Doctor says you'll be fine. Dehydration and some infection. They gave you pain meds and antibiotics. You'll recover just fine." There was a long pause. They were finally side by side again, but all that had happened since they parted ways on the Maya Bay beach sat like a chasm between them. Neither knew what to say or where to start.

"We didn't get the Colony children," Hunter confessed. Ashton nodded; her heart sank as he confirmed what Wolfe had already told her. "We got some caged workers—actually, quite a few of them made it. Ashton, you should have seen it," he began, his eyes wide and his voice pitching in excitement. "There were workers lining up by the ship. Workers from across Augland who had come to get on that boat. Gerhart was furious. The Maya Bay beaches were lined with workers, some even swimming toward the boat." He gave a soft chuckle. "They wanted to leave; they were just waiting for the opportunity."

Ashton smiled. Bez and Fox had managed to spread the word about the boat. They had been able to give hope to the workers of Augland. However, the backlash from the Executives would be fierce and she didn't want to think about the fate of the workers left behind.

"Did you see anyone from Apparel? They'd be in all white, coming from the train station?"

Hunter frowned, "Maybe a handful of them. Maybe more. I—I didn't see everyone but that doesn't mean more didn't make it . . . there were hundreds of workers."

"Where are they now? I want to go see for myself." Ashton couldn't wait any longer. She needed to know if anyone from Apparel had made it. She needed to know her escape plan had not simply ended in bloodshed. She pulled the white blanket, brought her good leg around, and pushed herself off the bed.

"Whoa, no you don't. You've been out for days; you'll need the doctor's okay to get out of here." Ashton wasn't going to listen to Hunter; too many days had already passed.

"I don't need anyone to tell me anything."

"Ashton . . ." Hunter was frustrated. "Rest. Please."

"Take me to where they are." She wasn't asking anymore. She was done being told what to do.

Hunter paused, but Ashton was done waiting and climbed out of the bed. She wobbled and used the side of the bed to catch her fall.

"All right, I'll take you. But then will you rest?" Ashton nodded in acknowledgment. She'd do whatever he said after she saw the escapees for herself.

Hunter tucked himself under Ashton's shoulder for support. "You should know, we will need to schedule time with Georgina. She's requested a meeting once you are well enough. Actually, I think the words were 'the minute she's awake.'"

"Did she say why?"

"Let's just say she wasn't happy when a bunch of Augland workers came knocking on her door. I've avoided her as much as I can, and now that you're awake, I've run out of excuses."

Hunter walked Ashton across the courtyard. Her leg, now bound in a hard shell, ached with pain whenever she put weight on it.

The NeuroEnergy compound was the same as Ashton remembered: dark and gray with smatterings of greenery—although she now thought it looked more like a prison than a sanctuary.

Ashton moved slowly, but Hunter was patient as they walked. He told her how he had escaped. One of Wolfe's guards, Si, had helped the caged workers get from the cages down to the Victorian fields, where they walked through the night. Si had opened the door between Maya Bay and Victorian, where they hid in the warehouses that distribute the supplies delivered to Augland by boat. Ashton was only partially paying attention. The pain in her leg was getting worse with every step.

"And we couldn't have done it without Wolfe and Joao."

Ashton's head shot up.

"What did you say?" She stopped. It was beginning to rain, but she didn't care. Hunter tried to walk forward, but Ashton stood her ground.

"Wolfe, and this guy Joao, they helped us escape. It surprised me too. I thought it would be a trap, but I didn't have another choice really. So, they helped us get out."

Ashton's eyes narrowed. She couldn't figure out Wolfe's motives. How did it help him to allow the caged workers to come to NeuroEnergy? Was this the trap? Had he wanted them all to come here? Is that why he had saved her?

Ashton was beginning to panic as she questioned every interaction she'd had with Wolfe since leaving Augland. He hadn't said anything about helping Hunter free workers.

"Why?" she said aloud without meaning to.

"Why what? I thought you'd be happy. Wolfe helped save us, Ash. He saved you."

Hunter didn't have all the facts yet. He didn't know what Wolfe had done, how he had betrayed her beyond repair. Maybe he could forgive Wolfe for the raid at the Colony, his help with the escape somehow overriding the fact that he had caused this whole mess. But Hunter didn't know the truth yet.

"Hunter," Ashton paused, not wanting to watch his heartbreak. "Wolfe, he killed Jagatha."

Hunter's expression froze. The rain grew heavy as they both stared at each other.

"No . . . what? No, that—that didn't happen."

"I saw it Hunter, she's gone." She wouldn't go into specifics. He didn't need to know the details. She'd spare Hunter the visual. She reached out as he collapsed onto her shoulder and sobbed.

When Hunter recovered enough to talk, he looked up at Ashton, tears and rain streaming down his face. "But Ashton no, it wasn't Wolfe who . . . it was Warren." He continued to break down.

This lie again. Ashton couldn't believe Hunter had fallen for it and still believed it after what she just told him. But she didn't have time to have this argument. It was raining and she wanted to see all the people who'd managed to escape Augland.

They walked the rest of the way across the compound toward one of the gray buildings. How Hunter was able to tell the difference between the NeuroEnergy buildings was beyond her. They all looked the same. He helped her up the few steps to the door of the building and then, with mock theatricality, opened the door.

The noise struck Ashton first. After the muffled sound of rain on the pavement, the wave of voices that hit her felt like sunshine. The hall was crowded. There must have been hundreds of people milling around in groups or sitting beside makeshift beds and tents.

The previous year, Ashton had been one of a handful of people who had ever escaped Augland. And now, here were at least a hundred new faces of Augland, free and full of hope.

"Georgina doesn't have enough rooms for all of them, so they were dumped into this building. Not bad though, right?" Hunter smirked.

Ashton was in awe. "There are so many of them."

"The whole building is like this. Hundreds of workers. Caged, from other parks. All of them here."

Ashton kept her eyes on them, desperately searching for familiar faces. Her eyes scanned the room. It wasn't that she didn't care about the others. She was impressed with how many there were. But right now, she wanted to make sure her rebellion hadn't been in vain and someone other than herself had made it out of the woods.

There. Ashton's neck and shoulders were released as she saw Mateo's face look up from the crowd. Around the small boy stood several other Apparel workers whom she recognized. *They made it; they actually made it.* Not all of them, she was sure. But Mateo now had the chance to grow up free, and that meant something.

Ashton smiled at Hunter, who beamed with pride at what they had accomplished.

"Hunter? I want to go home now."

"Sure. If the doctor clears it, I think you can stay with me. But I've only got one room."

"No, I mean my real home. I want to go back to Hood Canal."

Hunter turned toward Ashton and helped guide her to the exit.

"Of course, Ash, after the meeting with Georgina. I'll take you home." He held her close as she closed her eyes and took in a deep breath.

As they walked back through the compound in the rain, one thought echoed in Ashton's mind. Where was Bez?

CHAPTER 51

Wolfe

The door at the top of the stairs opened, letting in a sharp stab of light. Wolfe heard footsteps coming down the long set of hollow steel stairs. Two more sets of footsteps followed behind. Whoever was on their way was bringing security with them. Just as Warren had predicted, Wolfe was viewed as a threat.

Wolfe was in a windowless basement somewhere in NeuroEnergy. His arms were stretched above him, cuffed to an exposed pipe in the ceiling. Without a window, he had no idea what time it was or how long he had been left in there.

"Hello Wolfgang," a soft voice cooed. Wolfe couldn't make out the face backlit against the light from the door, but he saw the silhouette of a petite woman. The voice was intimidating but unfamiliar. "I've heard so much about you. I wish we were meeting under different circumstances, but unfortunately, you have a reputation."

Wolfe held his head high, despite the strain on his arms. "Doesn't seem fair that you know who I am, but I have yet to meet you. Who knows, maybe I've heard of you as well."

The woman came forward a few steps, keeping the two men behind her, but close. She turned on a bare lightbulb and the room came into blinding focus. The woman's face was stern and her elegantly manicured hair didn't move as she walked. Wolfe studied her. She wore a gray pantsuit that matched her hair.

"Georgina, I presume?" Wolfe didn't know if he should be honored or worried that the leader of the Pacific Northwest NeuroEnergy had come to see him in person.

"Well, it's genuinely nice to meet you—even though, I would say your hospitality could use some work." He knew his comment wouldn't be received well, but he hoped his nonchalance would be viewed as a strength.

A swing came out of nowhere, and Wolfe felt its presence before it landed on his face. His world spun and his vision burst purple. He breathed heavily as the pins and needles of the strike lingered.

"Liam, that's enough for now. Let's give him a chance." Georgina spoke softly to the man behind her before turning to Wolfe.

"Why are you here?" She looked him straight in the eyes.

"I brought Ashton."

"You know that's not what she meant," Liam growled. Georgina wanted to know why the CEO of Augland had come to her doorstep on a hoverbike days after hundreds of Augland workers had shown up at her compound. She wanted a reason, but Wolfe had no ulterior motive. He had nothing to gain by coming to NeuroEnergy.

"Warren told me to leave, so I did. Brought Ashton here and . . . well, hadn't made it past that part."

Georgina ignored him, cutting right to what she really wanted to know. "You are only useful to me if you have information about Augland's energy initiatives. If you truly have cut ties with Augland, then you wouldn't mind sharing what you know."

Wolfe would gladly share what he knew, but his father kept everything concealed, even from the other Executives. He could lie, and say he knew what his father had been doing, but he would need to divulge the details eventually and he wouldn't have them.

"I don't have any information." Wolfe braced for another blow to his face, but this time it came to his gut. His breath left and he struggled to suck in the air. Georgina asked the question again. But Wolfe's answer remained the same. After each one came a blow to his face, his stomach, and eventually his legs.

"I don't believe as the son of the CEO, the Head of Security, and then CEO yourself, you never heard or discussed anything . . ."

Wolfe's father never trusted him, but Georgina wouldn't know that. She wouldn't know that most of his life, Warren had seen him as a disgrace. Wolfe was hesitant to respond. No matter what he said, he feared it would result in a blow.

"I'm no longer the CEO; I was really never CEO. And now I'm disowned. I can't go home. There was nowhere else to go." Georgina put her hand up to stop her guard from going in for another hit.

"And how were you never really CEO?" Georgina inquired.

"My father's insanity and need for power. I know it sounds crazy, but I was CEO for a day before my father locked me away and took over in my place. You have to believe me. He made a Suit of me . . ." Wolfe was interrupted by Liam.

"Ma'am, his interconnect. It's for you. It's Warren." Wolfe realized they had gone through his bag and found his interconnect, but he didn't know how his father knew he was at NeuroEnergy or why he wanted to talk to Georgina."

"This is Georgina."

There was silence while she listened. Wolfe could hear the muffled sounds of his father on the other line.

"I see, and why should I trust you?" Wolfe was glad to see that Warren's charm would not work with Georgina. She was smart to be concerned and wary of whatever empty promises he was spewing.

"Don't trust what he says," Wolfe said under his breath. Liam motioned for Wolfe to be quiet but looked to Georgina before fulfilling his threat.

Georgina stiffened and her brows furrowed. Wolfe's heart dropped as he watched his father's words strengthen their hold on her.

"I'm here with your son now. He tells me a different story." She looked over at Wolfe. Silence filled the air. He was sure his father was spinning a creative story to her, and from the looks of it, Georgina was considering believing him. "You've given me a lot to consider. I'll be in touch soon." She hung up the interconnect and placed it in her pocket. She eyed Wolfe carefully. He needed to gain her trust and gain it fast.

"It's not much, but I'll tell you everything I know." He had her attention. "There's a customer service initiative; maybe you've heard of it. They are implanting chips into the workers' brains; these chips take away all agency and can force workers to do just about anything. Also, it was Warren who attacked the Colony and . . ." Wolfe was growing desperate. "He has plans for Augland 54 to become an elite and self-sustaining Augland. Outside of NeuroEnergy . . . and eventually outside the AEC."

Georgina was silent, waiting for him to continue, but Wolfe didn't know more than that. That was all he had to offer her.

"Unfortunately for you, that isn't what your father tells me. It also doesn't answer my question about the specifics of the energy initiatives. Your father doesn't have the reputation of being light with his threats and I have to say, your story seems less likely."

Wolfe felt hopeless. He added, "I won't tell you something I don't know, but I can tell you this; you do a deal with him, and you'll regret it." Georgina straightened and Wolfe realized he had pushed his luck too far.

She turned and left the room, the two guards in her wake. As the door closed, Wolfe was left to his pain in the dark. For the first time, he truly worried about what would happen next. He had thought Joao would have tried to convince NeuroEnergy, even Hunter, but it seemed that to NeuroEnergy, he was the villain, and he was in their custody.

He slumped against the wall. He was alone.

CHAPTER 52

Ashton

The ashen sky loomed above the small coastal city of Port Angeles. Ashton lay on Hunter's bed, which was tucked under the only window in his small apartment. The NeuroEnergy compound outside the window matched the dreary sky. Hunter was on the other side of the room, sleeping on the couch.

Ashton wished she could sleep, but her mind was tormented with uncertainty about Wolfe. She was battling with his duality—the kind man who had brought her here and the man who had deceived her. She cursed her good nature that even allowed her to consider his innocence. She wanted to believe him. She wanted to finally feel the relief that what he said was true, but she couldn't be hurt again like that. She had gone through too much. She replayed Jagatha's death, and Wolfe's face as he dropped her, over and over in her mind. True, he had saved Ashton, and supposedly the caged workers, and for that she would plead with Georgina not to kill him.

She would see Wolfe at eight o'clock in the morning. Georgina had summoned all parties involved with the Augland mission to her office. Georgina wasn't happy, and postponing the meeting for Ashton's recovery hadn't helped. Ashton would be lying to herself if she said she didn't fear what Georgina would say about the workers, about her and Hunter. Nothing had gone according to plan. She hadn't learned any added information for NeuroEnergy. Neither had they saved any of the children taken from the Colony.

The shadow of Ashton's body underneath the blanket slowly moved across the wall as the sun rose through the morning haze. She heard Hunter rustling on the couch. He rose, squinting as the light blurred his vision.

"Morning."

Ashton faked a smile.

"Might want to shower before meeting with Georgina," he muttered through his yawn. "Might make you feel better . . . not even sure you've showered since we left NeuroEnergy for Augland."

That was true; other than wiping herself down with the wet towel in Cahya's old home, she hadn't showered, and considering the boat, the pod, Apparel, and the injury, it was badly needed.

Ashton rose, her leg still stiff, and closed herself into Hunter's small bathroom. She looked at the young woman who stared back at her in the mirror. Her eyes were shallow and bloodshot. Her hair was frizzy, even for Ashton. The freckles on her face were more prominent against her pale, sunken face. She didn't recognize the person staring back at her.

She had lost weight. Her collarbones stuck out and deepened their craters as she breathed. Purple, blue, and green bruises were all that remained of the Predator Biome attack, but she was alive. Ashton sighed and turned toward the showerhead, letting the steam bellow out into the small bathroom. Her leg still made her hobble, but with the cast, it was manageable.

She showered, letting the warm water wash her. She sank down to the tiled floor, wrapping her hands around her good leg, hugging it toward her. Dirt mixed with blood ran down her body and into the drain. She just needed to get through today; then she could go home to her dock on the Hood Canal.

Georgina's office was just as Ashton remembered: tall trees in cement pots perfectly placed around the spacious room with a wooden desk and large monitor. Rye, Hunter's old boss and right hand to Georgina, led them into the empty office. Hunter and Ashton took a seat, waiting awkwardly for Georgina to arrive.

"Let me do most of the talking." Hunter broke the silence, grabbing Ashton's hand. She felt the nervous sweat on his palm.

The door opened, and Ashton heard the clicking of Georgina's heels behind them. The NeuroEnergy executive didn't acknowledge them as she walked across the room and sat down at her desk. Her dark eyes settled between them while her fingers rested, intertwined, on the desk. This was not going to be a pleasant meeting.

"Well . . . not what we had planned." Georgina's perfectly groomed hair didn't move as she leaned back in her chair.

"Georgina, I can explain—" Hunter started. Immediately, Georgina's hand went up to silence him.

"No, we will get to you. We will get to why you decided to bring over hundreds of Augland employees to our compound, positioning NeuroEnergy as an Augland employee sympathizer and furthering Augland's cause to come for us. I want to start at the very beginning. And that starts with Ashton."

Georgina's emerald eyes settled on Ashton, who shrank beneath her gaze.

"You were in his presence for two days and we received no new information. Nothing we recorded was remotely useful. You know, when I first heard he was CEO, I thought this was a better plan. I thought you knew him . . . according to Hunter, Wolfgang was 'smitten' with you. Unless that was a lie?"

"No, we know each other," Ashton spoke softly. How could she admit she had been played by the man she thought she knew?

"Then you call that an attempt to extract valuable and necessary information?"

Ashton frowned at the accusation. "I did the best I could. How about you explain why you gave me a faulty Suit!" She was halfway out of her chair before Hunter placed his hand on her arm, restraining her.

"I would be careful if I were you. I have half a mind to send you back with the rest of the workers. You came here with Wolfgang, the man who was CEO until two days prior. Some might say you conspired to make NeuroEnergy look like the deviants in this plan—that you brought him here to spy on us."

Hearing Georgina's accusations, Ashton knew this didn't look good for either her or Hunter.

"You wouldn't send them back! How could you do that?" Ashton wouldn't let herself be restrained. Georgina narrowed her gaze.

"I told you not to come back without intel. We would not support you. I was very clear on that."

Georgina and Ashton locked eyes, neither backing down. The two women volleyed a silent argument between them. Ashton didn't look away, even when the doors behind them opened and the jingling of chains echoed louder than Georgina's heels. Georgina's eyes broke first.

284

"Wolfgang, thank you for joining us."

It took all of Ashton's willpower not to turn around as Wolfe was led to the chair next to her. He was only inches away.

"I thought it best for all of us to get everything out on the table."

Ashton didn't look at Wolfe, but she could feel his presence. Out of her peripheral vision, she saw what they had done to him, and her heart sank. His right eye was swollen, and she could hear the pain when he breathed.

"I received a call late yesterday from acting CEO Warren. He is willing to set this all behind us and move forward if we are to return all the workers to Augland, as well as his son, whom he believes is going through some sort of mental breakdown."

Ashton was surprised by the accusation about Wolfe's sanity.

"You can't send them back . . ." Hunter shook his head in disappointment. "Not after what they went through to get out of there." Georgina ignored his commentary. Ashton had expected him to explode in anger, but Hunter, like her, must have presumed their good luck couldn't last long.

"He explained to me that it was Wolfgang's plan to attack the Colony and assured me that he took over as CEO again to correct the wrongs." She turned her attention to Wolfe. "Have you anything to say?"

Wolfe looked up. "Everything he says is a lie." Despite his bruised and exhausted face, Wolfe was defiant. "As I told you, he created a Suit of me. It was Warren who did those things to the Colony. It was Warren who imprisoned me, and Warren who plans to eliminate NeuroEnergy. I don't know how, don't know when, but I know him and that is exactly what he plans to do. I had nothing to do with any of it." He paused, his chained hands clenching. "If you send the workers back to Augland, it will be their death. Their death will be on your hands. Not Warren's, not mine. Yours."

"He said you'd say something like that. I'm sorry, but this story of yours is just so unlikely . . ." Ashton could not tell by the tone in Georgina's voice if she was being sarcastic or if she really wanted to believe Wolfe. She continued, "I'm sorry, but you all have left me with no choice. If you stay, I pledge war against a company with no proof of its plans to overtake energy initiatives. If I return you and what you've taken, I safeguard NeuroEnergy. Warren is being gracious enough to allow the insubordination to stay between us and not report me to the AEC. If he were to do so, I'd have to resign my position."

"So, you condemn all of us then for your own position?" Wolfe's voice shook with anger.

"I won't let you misconstrue the narrative to fit your theory. No. I am no good to NeuroEnergy gone. Sometimes tough decisions need to be made . . ." Georgina sensed the cold shift in the room. "Look, if I had anything, anything at all that . . . helped us, I'd reconsider, but you come here with no proof, with unfounded allegations, with stolen property of Augland. My hands are tied!"

For the first time, Ashton saw Georgina's fear. She didn't want to do this anymore than they did. But she would prioritize the people of NeuroEnergy over the Augland workers, over them. Hunter and Ashton had put her in a compromising position.

"Property . . ." Ashton said under her breath, looking into Georgina's eyes. "Is that how you see us? Property?" It was the second time she had heard it. Property of Augland 54. How could anyone consider human lives so frivolously?

"No, I'm saying that is what you are considered in this business. It's unfair and I acknowledge that, but again, what would you have me do?"

Ashton knew Georgina was not looking for an answer to her question. If it were up to Ashton, she would revolt against Augland and back the workers—the "UnSuited".

Georgina continued. Hunter and Wolfe argued back. Ashton stayed silent. They had lost and soon they would all be back where they started.

"That's enough! I won't debate this with you any further. Tomorrow you will go back to Augland. All of you."

Ashton closed her eyes as the words they all dreaded hearing were finally spoken. She couldn't believe, after all she and Hunter had endured, that they were being returned to Augland. She should have never left the Colony, never left her home, and never trusted NeuroEnergy.

So, this is how it ends. . .

CHAPTER 53

Wolfe

A knock on the door interrupted the tense silence in the room. Wolfe seethed with anger. How had he not seen this coming? Warren had already skewed the situation to his corporate advantage. Wolfe had only been thinking one step ahead, but Warren had already planned out his win. Wolfe had risked his life, all their lives, only to lose again.

"Come in," Georgina ordered. She didn't take her eyes off Wolfe. "Hello, Rye, we were just finishing up."

Rye stepped into the room and cleared his throat. "There are two others, from Augland, just arrived. They've requested to see Wolfe and Ashton."

Wolfe racked his brain. He didn't know who would be arriving at NeuroEnergy so many days after the escape. He looked at Ashton. She met his gaze, looking just as confused as he was, but looked away immediately.

"Who is it?" Georgina sounded exasperated. She had obviously had enough of Augland members showing up on her doorstep.

"Uh, the man says his name is Joao, previously a security guard from Augland. And with him . . . a woman."

Wolfe's eyes lit up as he heard Joao's name.

"Enough. I've had enough of this! This ends here. I am sending you all back. And don't you dare tell all your friends they can find refuge in NeuroEnergy. That is over."

Rye shifted, unsure of what Georgina wanted him to do. "They say they have something for you, ma'am."

Georgina eyed Rye carefully. "What is it?"

"I think you should see for yourself."

Georgina paused as she glanced between Hunter, Ashton, and Wolfe. Despite the pain in his ribs, Wolfe strained to see what his friend had brought for Georgina.

Wolfe couldn't handle the wait. Despite the pain in his ribs and shackled hands, he stood up to pace. His handcuffs clinked as he walked around the room, but Georgina didn't seem to mind the nervous tick.

Finally, the door to Georgina's office opened. Wolfe whipped around toward the door, gasping as his ribs wrenched together. Joao walked through the door first, his hair messy and his clothes drenched from the rain. He looked exhausted. Behind him, Bez entered the room. She wore Joao's coat. It was oversized and draped around her. Wolfe heard Ashton gasp beside him.

"Bez!" she screamed, leaping up out of her chair on her one leg.

The Augland woman shoved past Rye and the security guards who had accompanied them into the office. They met near Ashton's chair, colliding in a hug. Ashton didn't seem to notice anything around her except for her friend. Bez cried. Wolfe had never seen her cry before. She had always been sarcastically strong; it was her defense mechanism.

Wolfe turned his attention to the familiar face he had longed to see for three days now.

"Sorry I'm late," Joao said as he smiled and embraced Wolfe. Wolfe couldn't put his hands around his friend but leaned onto his shoulder. He took in a deep breath, the mixed emotions tearing at him. Joao and Bez would soon realize that Georgina was about to send them back to Augland—and find out that all their work had been for nothing.

"Joao. . ." Wolfe leaned into his jacket. "I'm sorry, I'm so sorry I got you mixed up in all this." Joao didn't look at Wolfe, just pulled away and brought his attention to Georgina.

"We can skip the pleasantries—" Georgina started, but Joao didn't let her finish the sentence.

"Excuse the interruption, but you'll want to see what I brought." Joao dug his hand deep into his pocket and pulled out a small chip, no bigger than his thumbnail.

"What is that?" Georgina rose out of her chair, leaning against her desk to get a closer look.

"Blueprints. Schedules. Memos. It's all on here. The information on this chip shows Warren has been trying to create his own energy source. His first attempt was to use the Predator's Biome waterfall to generate backup systems in case you decided to turn off the power to the Suits." Joao grinned and looked at Wolfe. "And it has so much more; I think it will be sufficient." Joao tossed the lime green chip on Georgina's desk. She inhaled deeply as she put her hand on the tiny storage device.

"How did you get this?" Georgina looked astonished.

"Compliments of the CEO's wife. Anastasia." Georgina shoved the chip into her computer. Wolfe watched as menus, blueprints, and information files popped up on the transparent glass screen. Wolfe looked over at Joao, who smirked with pride.

"Oh, and I've got one more thing." Joao pulled his backpack from his back and slowly unzipped the big pocket. Wolfe furrowed his eyebrows. He couldn't think of what the former security guard could have possibly brought with him that would help the situation.

Joao's hand emerged from his leather bag and pulled out a heavy, round object. The room was quiet, all eyes on the deflating bag. The room gasped. The air froze. Joao pulled out a human head.

Wolfe's own decapitated head stared back at him. It was the best Wolfe had ever looked. His jawline was clean-shaven and his eyes bright. The head Joao held in his hand looked healthy and alive, but the illusion ended in a neck with dangling wires coated in dried green plasma. This grotesque and unnatural sight—his own severed head—was Wolfe's salvation.

He suddenly realized that the room around him had erupted into cries of astonishment. Everyone seemed to be talking at once, but all Wolfe could do was stare at the gift Joao had brought him. The crushing fear that he would never be believed, that Ashton would never forgive him, slipped off his shoulders. He hadn't realized he had given up hope until he felt it restored.

"You found it! You found the Suit!" Wolfe laughed and cried as he tried to embrace Joao, forgetting about his cuffed hands.

Joao smiled, "Thanks to your mom, Ana . . . couldn't have done it without her." Joao held the proof of Wolfe's innocence high. Georgina was speechless. She couldn't take her eyes off the doppelganger Suit head. Wolfe knew what this meant. It meant that Warren was a liar.

He turned to Ashton. She was sitting down, clearly stunned. He saw Bez holding her hand, simply letting her process the sight before her eyes. He wanted to give her space to absorb what this all meant, but he needed her to see him. He took a step toward her and bent down toward her chair. He put his chained hands up to her face and lifted it up to meet his gaze.

"Please. Please, Ashton, know it wasn't me. I would never . . ." Wolfe choked out the words. "I'd never do anything to hurt you. I promise. Please, believe me. I—" Ashton didn't let him continue before throwing her arms around him and pulling him close. He buried himself into her and then pulled back. A tear was rolling down Ashton's cheek and he brushed it away.

"I'm—I'm so sorry. I'm so sorry I didn't believe you. I—I didn't see how it was possible."

Wolfe smiled into her hair. He could never stay angry with her. Ashton pulled away and lowered her eyes, but Wolfe pulled her gaze to him and smiled. She now knew the truth and believed him, and that was all that mattered.

The moment was interrupted by Georgina. "Wolfgang, I—" While Wolfe and Ashton were reconnecting, she had been reading through all the documents on the chip. Her glasses glowed blue, then white, then blue again. The information looked overwhelming.

"I need you all to leave. I—I need to process this information."

Hunter said, "I need to know the workers are safe and that you won't send them back." He jammed his finger on Georgina's wooden desk.

Georgina looked around, her face suddenly exhausted. "For now, given . . . given the most recent . . . intelligence, I'll wait to make any decision on the workers. And Wolfgang, the same goes for you." She eyed them all carefully, knowing that it wasn't sufficient, but it would do for now. "I think you all should go; Rye and I have a lot to go through."

Georgina ushered them out of the room, but before they left, Wolfe turned toward her. "It's Wolfe . . .not Wolfgang."

Never again would he use the name his father had given him.

CHAPTER 54

Ashton

Hunter led the silent group down the corridor to his NeuroEnergy apartment. When he reached the door, he fumbled through his pockets until he found the key card to open his tiny room. Ashton stood beside him, balancing on her good leg, and Bez and Joao followed. Wolfe trailed behind.

When Hunter finally opened the door, Ashton beelined to the couch. The short walk across NeuroEnergy and sitting in rigid chairs in Georgina's office had left her leg feeling stiff and sore. She grabbed the blankets Hunter had used the night before and pulled them around her as she watched the others enter the room. The silence between the friends was awkward. While the reunion was sweet, their lives and those of the workers now hinged on Georgina's decision.

Hunter walked straight to the window that looked out at the cloudy sky. He slid a hand through his long hair, pushing it out of his face, and rested the other on the window, his palm against the cold glass. He sighed in exhaustion.

Bez, almost completely swallowed by Joao's jacket, went straight for the small electric heater beside the kitchenette. Joao followed closely behind her. Ashton studied him, trying to connect the dots of their alliance. She'd be lying to herself if she thought their relationship surprised her. Joao had stood by while Warren killed Jagatha, but he had also been the one to look out for Ashton while she was in Apparel. Looking back, she knew she probably hadn't been the easiest to help. She had been so focused on her own despair to notice the kindness

Joao showed her. Ashton watched him adjust the coat on Bez's shoulders. He obviously adored her.

Finally, Wolfe entered the apartment. Ashton couldn't take her eyes off him. She desperately needed to see how she could have missed what was so obvious. She had never even heard of anyone making a Suit to replicate a particular human; the allure of Suits was the ability to live in an ideal body.

The fake Wolfe had been so convincing—his eyes bold and fierce, his brow line prominent and scrunched, even his walk stoic and demanding. She was not embarrassed that she had been fooled by the technical mastery, but that she had so readily assumed he had turned into a monster. When she had seen him during the Colony raid, she hadn't doubted that the man she loved was, and maybe had always been, evil.

Wolfe's eyes met hers and his face softened. His ocean blue eyes stared into her own. Ashton couldn't look away. She finally realized what she had missed. The difference between what Warren had created and the real Wolfe. His eyes were soft and full of love. He targeted the spot next to Ashton on the couch. He sat down, never taking his eyes off hers. He slid his hand toward Ashton, and she accepted it, slowly intertwining her fingers with his.

Bez walked over and hugged Ashton from behind, ignoring the back of the couch between them. She swung around, plopping herself down beside her.

"I can't tell you how happy I am that you made it out," Ashton said, grinning wide. Bez's hazel eyes mirrored Ashton's. "But how? You weren't on the boat."

Bez took a deep breath. On the other side of the couch, Joao was talking with Wolfe. Though they were in separate conversations, Wolfe didn't stop squeezing Ashton's hand.

"Joao, he came and got me. I was cornered with the rest of the Apparel workers. Only some had made it onto the train. Forest was able to manually start one of the engines . . . then security caught up with us." She pulled away from Ashton, her face pained with the memory. "It was madness. They began gunning us down." Her voice trembled. "Joao, I guess, called them off, and started the train again." She looked over at Joao and smiled. "He took me with him, onto the train with the others . . . by the time we made it to Maya Bay though, the boat was already gone."

Bez returned her gaze to Ashton, who was wide-eyed with concern.

"How'd you get out?"

"Fox had workers rallying everywhere on the beach—met him for the first time— he had this black cloth over his eye, very mysterious hero vibe." An eerie familiarity caught Ashton's memory. Could it be possible? Could her old friend Niall be the mysterious 'Fox'? Had he been helping the rebellion this whole time? Before Ashton could ask, Bez continued. Ashton would make sure to ask about him later.

"Fox took control and started dismantling Suits. The UnSuited fought! I think when people realized the boat was gone and they weren't going to get out, they just snapped. The funny thing is, the Suits weren't even trying to get away, I think they were too worried about the financial cost of the Suit to risk fighting the workers."

There was pride in Bez's voice, and awe at the privilege of being a part of the rebellion. Ashton egged her on. Thinking about the workers left behind was too hard to bear and she still didn't know how Bez had made it out.

"Joao wouldn't let me fight, told me we needed to get out of there. I followed him and we went to Hollywood Boulevard and snuck into the Executive Suites to see Wolfe's mom. She helped us . . . then we were taken through the water main system. I had no idea it existed. A Suit took us there. Big tall guy. Wolfe's mom had given us the chip and bag, the one with Wolfe's head in it. Then we walked for days to get here." She paused, taking a moment to smile at Ashton. "When Joao told me Wolfe had gone back for you, I wasn't sure he'd find you alive . . . I'm so happy he did."

"I—I'm just so happy you made it out . . . the others, they were brave."

"Don't do that, Ashton; don't feel bad for the risks they took. What you started here is bigger than you, bigger than us. We've shown Augland that we won't sit back and let them take us willingly. I feel their strength. Your strength. It's around us and we have a fighting chance now."

There was a knock on the door and the room went silent. Hunter made a movement toward the door, but before he could get there, it opened. Georgina walked into the room. Only she would be so presumptuous to walk into Hunter's apartment without even waiting for a reply.

"Hello, I thought it would be easier if I just came here myself instead of summoning you all back to my office." She looked specifically at Ashton's leg, and Ashton was skeptical of the woman's thoughtfulness. Their lives, and the lives of all the escaped workers, hung in her hands. All she had to do was decide to send them back.

Georgina took a deep breath. "The information we received was . . . insightful," she said haltingly, looking at each one of them. "Warren has been misleading, not only to NeuroEnergy but the AEC too. I will not go into specifics, but I wanted you to know that as of today, all workers of Augland 54 have sanctuary within the compounds of the Pacific Northwest NeuroEnergy. We will protect them and . . . and will not return any unwilling victims, including you, Wolfe. You have my word."

The room turned giddy. Astonishment, excitement, and sheer joy radiated around the room. Even Georgina had a smirk on her face. She might not want to take in hundreds of people, but beating Warren at his own game had to feel good.

"We did it!" Hunter dove into Ashton, crashing onto the couch and laughing. Bez, Ashton, and Wolfe caught him and shoved him off. It was impossible not to catch his joy. Bez hugged Joao, and Ashton realized this was her first real taste of freedom. Bez broke away from a reluctant Joao and swept Georgina up in a bear hug, taking the stoic woman by complete surprise.

Then Ashton's eyes settled on Wolfe. He was patting Joao, rather hard, on the back. The friend who had always been like a brother had saved his life. There was so much understanding and love in that embrace.

Finally, Wolfe turned to Ashton. He bent down on his knees, so he was at eye level with her. He took her face in his hands and touched his forehead to hers.

"Congrats, Ash. You did it." He pulled her into his arms and then slightly pulled back and kissed her.

Georgina cleared her throat. She hung in the center of the room like a gray cloud suddenly blocking out the sun.

"All right, I know what this means for all of you, but this is not over. Warren will come after all of us and we need to be ready. We are going to have to work together."

Ashton sighed and leaned her cheek against Wolfe's hand. Georgina was right; this wasn't over.

CHAPTER 55

Ashton

Swoosh shee swoosh. The tide threatened to come closer as Ashton dug deeper. She always could find the perfect place for clam digging along the rocky shores of the Hood Canal. The hole dug, she pulled out handfuls of clams and plopped them into the rusted old bucket beside her. Rico would have been proud. Ashton had promised to visit him at the new Colony once things settled down.

The sun hovered over the mountain range as she grabbed the bucket with one hand and her walking stick with the other. Versal and Hunter, who had since moved away from the Colony, were visiting from their new home at NeuroEnergy. Bez and Joao had gone with several ex-Augland workers to the Colony, taking refuge there. Georgina had offered them all a place to stay, but Ashton and Wolfe declined. She wanted to go home. Ashton hadn't seen Versal since their return but coming home to a pile of handknit scarfs and sweaters had felt like coming home to her embrace. Ashton couldn't wait to thank her with dinner.

One week after returning home, Ashton sat at the end of her dock. She pulled a thick, crocheted blanket over herself while watching the stars begin to reflect on the water.

"Made you tea." She turned to see Wolfe walking down the floating dock toward her. She smiled as he wrapped one arm around her and handed her the scalding hot cup of tea. He knelt behind her, and she turned to give him a kiss of gratitude. Wolfe gasped in mock disappointment that his gift of tea only received one kiss.

Ashton laughed and granted another tiny kiss before leaning back against him. Then, instantly, there it was again, the sinking feeling she had when the warmth of his affection became too much. Wolfe noticed.

"Is it this place?" He asked. Ashton's defense went up. She didn't want her internal struggle to impact him. He had his own trauma to work through. She loved and hated that he knew her so well.

"No, it's great being home." It truly was, but it was different having Wolfe there. Ashton couldn't tell him what it really was that haunted her every time she looked at him. She knew what hate looked like in his eyes and knew what it felt like to be discarded like she meant nothing to him. The experience—even though she now knew it hadn't actually been him—had scarred her in more ways than she cared to admit. She didn't want to tell Wolfe that sometimes she couldn't differentiate the memories. She feared she wouldn't be able to let anyone else in. Ever. Even him.

"We can't hide out here forever . . ." Ashton finally said. It wasn't a lie, but it wasn't the truth either. She hoped he didn't see through it.

Wolfe sighed heavily, hugging her tighter. "No, we can't. We will have to go to the Colony. And back to NeuroEnergy to figure out what happens next and what the rebellion might mean with their backing." Ashton shivered as a cold breeze hit her. "But this time we do it together."

Wolfe turned her face to look at him. He was too smart for his own good and knew she was keeping something from him, but he wouldn't press it. She smiled, truly feeling the warmth of his presence. She did feel safer with him, and less alone.

Wolfe shuffled around to sit next to her on the dock, his thigh touching hers and his legs long enough to touch the water below. Ashton stared at him while he drank his tea. His eyes were soft, and he looked carefree. He breathed in and she knew he saw the beauty and serenity this place brought to her.

It was all so beautiful and so unfair. It wasn't Wolfe who created this feeling of distrust and distance. He too was a victim in all of this—manipulated, tortured, and cast out because of the man he chose to be. He was innocent and didn't deserve this, especially from her.

Ashton cursed Warren for plaguing her mind and tormenting her consciousness at every turn. She knew one thing: she wouldn't feel normal again, not until Warren paid for what he'd done. Only then would she and Wolfe feel true freedom and the UnSuited be vindicated. Ashton smiled. Someday, soon, she would feel whole, and she knew exactly what she needed to do make that happen.

She leaned her head on Wolfe's shoulder, and he pulled the blanket tight around them both. Ashton touched the moonstone that hung again across her neck; she had returned the watch to Wolfe once she received the treasured items back from Georgina. She breathed in the cold Pacific Northwest air and Wolfe's warm scent. Wolfe kissed the top of her head and she melted into the ease she had always restrained herself from feeling. Yes, they would do this together.

But there was one thing Ashton wanted to do alone. The next time she saw Warren, she would kill him.

ABOUT THE AUTHOR

E rin Carrougher is a Pacific Northwest-based author whose novel series, *Augland,* is set in Seattle's not-too-distant future. While her day-to-day work is all business, working sales in the technology industry, she enjoys fantasizing about dystopian worlds in her spare time. When she's not writing on her comfy couch next to her dog, Griffen, Erin loves spending time with her husband, Joe, and their family and friends, and enjoying life outdoors as much as possible. She's the proud auntie of Annabelle, Wyatt, and Teddy. If Erin has any downtime, she fills it with cooking, reading, and binge-watching reality television shows. You can find her at www.erincarrougher.com.